# Summer Hours at the Robbers Library

## A Novel

### Sue Halpern

HARPER LUXE

*An Imprint of* HarperCollins*Publishers*

SUMMER HOURS AT THE ROBBERS LIBRARY. Copyright © 2018 by Sue Halpern. All rights reserved. Printed in the United States of America. No part of this book may be used or reproduced in any manner whatsoever without written permission except in the case of brief quotations embodied in critical articles and reviews. For information address HarperCollins Publishers, 195 Broadway, New York, NY 10007.

HarperCollins books may be purchased for educational, business, or sales promotional use. For information please e-mail the Special Markets Department at SPsales@harpercollins.com.

FIRST HARPERLUXE EDITION

ISBN: 978-0-06-279188-7

HarperLuxe™ is a trademark of HarperCollins Publishers.

Library of Congress Cataloging-in-Publication Data is available upon request.

18 19 20 21 22   ID/LSC   10 9 8 7 6 5 4 3 2 1

For Billy

# The Marriage Story

## — PART I —

What you need to know about him back then is that if the police put seven college students in a lineup looking for the one who played trombone in the marching band, Calvin Sweeney would be picked, ten times out of ten. And the funny thing is he did play trombone in the marching band, which is how we met. He was a freshman and I was a sophomore, and my boyfriend at the time, whose name was John but went by the French Jean, so certain that he was heir to Cocteau (I had to look him up), asked me to find "a nerdy but attractive enough" guy to cast in the experimental art-house film he was making.

I discovered Cal in the second-to-last row of the brass section during a pep rally the third week of school. He was definitely not my type. My type was tall, confident, and athletic, which probably describes everyone's type at nineteen except the girls who went for the punk stoner boys who studiously avoided washing their hair. Cal Sweeney was neither. Not tall, not short; not intense, not laid-back; not handsome, not homely. Cal Sweeney was unremarkable, with an open face and a fringe of sandy-brown hair that hung like drapes above his round metal glasses, the kind of glasses that had been popular in high school. They magnified his eyes (not brown, not green), making him look permanently startled, like he'd just seen something amazing, or awful.

It wasn't hard to convince him to show up for John's casting call—he said he'd been in *Guys and Dolls* in high school and was "jazzed" to do more theater. Using the word "jazzed," and mixing up theater and film, to say nothing of playing trombone in the marching band, seemed perfectly nerdy, and when I presented him to John he kissed me like I'd just handed him a winning lottery ticket, and was still so excited when we got together that night that he convinced me to have unprotected sex. He said that true artists strove for authenticity in every aspect of their lives.

After that there was no going back, which was terrifying. It was Russian roulette every time he entered me—would I get pregnant? Would I get some disgusting, embarrassing disease? John was thrilled. He said that terror was a pure emotion that I needed to embrace. He said it would strip away everything that was false in me and reveal my essence. He said that the paradox of life was that existence preceded essence. He said that someday we should jump off a cliff together and then we would *know*. Of course then we would be dead, but it seemed small-minded to point this out.

The film consumed him. He stayed up all night making shot lists that, by morning, could run fifteen, twenty, twenty-five pages. He stopped sleeping. There were never enough hours in the day to shoot, especially since all the actors were in school. John was supposed to be, too, but that semester he was taking only two courses, which he signed up for after getting the list of easy As from a football player who traded it for an introduction to a shy, amply endowed girl on the Frisbee team, where John had been captain till he let that slide, too. John was getting frantic. He started following Cal to class and hounding him to leave so they could work on the film. By then he was comparing himself with Orson Welles and Stanley Kubrick and accusing me and Cal and the other actors of holding him back. He said we were all jealous, and that we were undermining his genius, and that we were plotting against him. He was paranoid, yes, but there was some truth to this, too. Cal and I had begun meeting surreptitiously in one of the music practice rooms every couple of days to compare notes and try to figure out if John's wild behavior (like the time he asked me to hold a knife to his throat during sex because he'd read that some French director I'd never heard of claimed it heightened his pleasure) was part of his art, or a sign that he was on his way to crazy and that we should get in touch with the dean of students.

Cal made the call. It was November, the week before Thanksgiving, and the first time we held hands. I remember the date because John had started threatening us. He said that if we went home to our families for the holiday we shouldn't bother coming back. We didn't know what that meant, but it sounded ominous. So Cal called the dean from the practice room and told him that John was behaving oddly and crazily and erratically. When that did not get the man's attention, Cal used a bunch of other words that made it sound as if he were reading from the thesaurus entry on "insanity." A few minutes earlier I had reached over and put my hand over his while we waited for the dean to come to the phone, and without thinking we had locked fingers, and now, with each new word, the two of us squeezed our hands together tightly, rhythmically, like it was a pulse, like we were bringing something to life.

The dean laughed and cut Cal off. *He laughed.* He

said that if he called psych services for every oddly behaved, nutty, erratic college student, the dorms would be empty and the infirmary would be overflowing. Cal, to his credit, was not cowed. He held his ground. I was impressed. A little smitten. I moved closer and rested my head against his neck so that the dean was talking into my ear, too.

"Let me ask you something," the dean said, "and I want you to answer very, very carefully."

Cal said something like "Of course, of course I will." He was an actor, at least enough of an actor to square his shoulders and adopt a grave expression so that the dean, though unable to see his demeanor, could hear it.

"Tell me," the dean said. "Is this young man a danger to himself or to others?"

If he had asked me, I would have hedged, said I didn't know for sure. John had never talked about killing himself, not explicitly, though there was that knife incident and his cliff fantasy. And his threat to us was so vague—what did it really mean? But Cal didn't waver.

"Yes," he said straightaway. "I believe so."

He knew he was sealing John's fate—that within the half hour John would be in a campus security van on his way to the county's locked ward, where he'd be sedated until his parents could arrange for him to be transferred to a less plebian facility closer to their home in Connecticut. A year later, when John came back to campus, he had gotten doughy and docile from all the medications he was on, and if he connected Cal or me with the situation he found himself in, he didn't let on. He was still tall, but no longer athletic or confident.

Once John was gone, there was no good reason for Cal and me to spend time together, but the two of us had been through this thing, and we kept on coming up with excuses to hang out. At first we pretended it was because we were concerned about John: Was he okay? Did we do the right thing? What would happen to him? Should we feel guilty, should we send him a card, call his parents? One of us would look forlorn or mournful and the other would offer words of consolation that led to more hand-holding, that led to . . . nothing.

Did I say that Cal was a virgin? He was. He came to college having kissed no one, ever, despite his especially pliant, well-practiced lips. He liked girls, he said, so it wasn't that. Honestly, I wasn't too far ahead of him, numbers-wise, but after my adventures with John in his jury-rigged loft bed, in the video editing room, on the roof of the media arts building, in the handicapped bathroom in the student center, in his pickup, in the unlocked Frisbee team van, in an apple orchard, in every room of the condo of the professor whose cats I was looking after, and on her balcony, too, I was feeling sophisticated and adult and well schooled.

But I was also feeling bereft. Not because John was gone, and gone in such a deep and fundamental way, but because I had been defeated by love. Maybe what John and I had was only an infatuation, but for a time I was convinced that we were madly, soulfully, singularly in love, and that no one in the history of the universe ever had had a love as real as ours. "You only fall in love for the first time once, Kit," John used to say, which seemed fine to me. I needed to fall in love only once. Then my one true love disintegrated and John's words ricocheted with a vengeance, knowing I would never again get back that feeling of absolute, unrestrained, ignorant exhilaration, knowing that love made promises it couldn't keep. It might come back, but it would come back depreciated, like a new car that's returned to the lot. There was a quote by Adrienne Rich that John had liked, which he wrote down on a piece of notebook paper and slid under my door early in our relationship, when he was Jean, the passionate, uncompromising artist, and I was a second-semester English major mining *The Norton Anthology of Poetry* for truth and wisdom: "An honorable human relationship—that is, one in which two people have the right to use the word 'love'—is a process, delicate, violent, often terrifying to both persons involved, a process of refining the truths they can tell each other." I kept that piece of paper for a long time, first because I was certain it was sage and knowing, and later to remind me that beautiful words can be used to justify ugly behavior.

**Cal wanted** me to take him to bed. He didn't say this overtly—he was too polite, or embarrassed, or callow, or all of the above. Instead, he asked me to marry him. Just like that. Out of the blue, and for no good reason.

By then I was twenty-one and he was twenty. It was 1991. The only people our age who got married were the ones from high school who had no choice, or the ones shipping out for Kuwait, or the ones who were bored.

"Asking someone to marry you is not like asking them to prom," I said. I was not amused. This was not how I wanted to be proposed to, if I wanted to be proposed to at all, and I certainly didn't want to be proposed to by Cal Sweeney over a shared bag of Cheez-Its in a window-less room in the basement of the library with vending machines along the walls and a couple of pockmarked tables in the middle. This was the Cave, where the students who never left the library acquired their calories. I had a work-study job upstairs in circulation, and Cal had made it a habit to show up in the Cave when I was on break, which meant that we were seeing each other fairly regularly, but rarely in natural light.

"Of course not," Cal said. I could hear him channeling the soothing baritone of the college chaplain, whose office we had visited together a couple of times after John had been locked up. "I didn't even go to my prom," he added. And then: "You probably went with the quarterback of the football team." This seemed to make him feel pretty good about himself, like he was in that guy's league now and, possibly, had bested him.

"Who do you think I am?" I protested weakly, not bothering to remind him that I went to an all-girls high school. Why not let him think I was that girl?

"So who did you go to prom with?" he asked.

This was how much we didn't know about each other. Should I tell him that Kyle Mook and I double-dated with Kyle's twin sister, Kylie, and her date, a gorgeous abstinence-only kid from the Calvary Christian Academy, and the four of us ended up drunk in a king-sized bed at the Sheraton Four Points, and the boys dared Kylie and me to make out and we did and then got so into it we didn't notice that her date was jerking off as he watched us until he started crying—not joyous "that felt great, what a relief" crying but sad "I'm going to hell" crying—and wouldn't stop until Kyle reached over me and his sister and slapped the guy a couple times, and we all fell asleep in the bed together and didn't wake up until the housekeeper knocked on the door the next day, and then we went to the beach?

"Kyle Mook," I said. "He's a frat boy now at Bucknell. I mean Lehigh. Engineering."

"There is so much more about you to learn, Kit," Cal said, as if I were both fascinating and a subject to be mastered.

"Hmm," I said, because I didn't know what to say. I liked Cal. I had gotten used to him. He was like a favorite sweater. Do you marry your favorite sweater? Do you even consider getting married to your favorite sweater?

"You have to get back to work," he said before I could say it myself. He didn't look disappointed. He didn't look happy. He looked resolute. He was sitting with his hands folded together, resting on the table, his fingers greasy and orange and flecked with cracker bits.

"You look like you're praying," I said, getting up to leave.

"Maybe I am," he said, not moving. "Just think about it," he added as I walked away.

How could I not? Unexpected and unromantic as it was, this was a serious proposal. Cal wanted us to seal our fates together, to vow to plow through the choppy waters of come-what-may conjoined. As far as I could tell, he was a practical, responsible guy. By then he had declared himself premed: he was going to be a doctor. He had six or eight years of school ahead of him, maybe more. Though he didn't know what kind of doctor, or where, once he declared premed, his future was largely settled. He'd be a doctor from a family of doctors, and having checked off the box for career, why not check off the one for wife? I think I remembered Cal telling me once that the literature showed that married medical students scored higher on their board exams than single med students, that they were less likely to abuse drugs, and that they were more empathic. Yes, I remember him telling me that because he used the word "empathic," not "empathetic," which sounded self-consciously preprofessional and pretentious to me. And I also remember explaining to him that the researchers could have saved a lot of time and money if they'd just watched the reruns of *Marcus Welby, M.D.*

That evening I tracked Cal down in the neuroscience lab where he worked raising rats. The rats were being used to study spinal cord and paralytic diseases, and no matter how much affection you didn't feel for rats in general, the protocols here were so brutal it was impossible not to want to free them all. It was a sterile lab, so I had to knock on the window to get Cal's attention. He was on the other side of the glass in a blue paper lab coat, with protective glasses over his round metal frames and a face mask covering his mouth. Even so, I could tell he was happy to see me. He waved with one gloved hand while the other held a limp rat. He put the rat down on a small machine that looked like a miniature guillotine—where it would be decapitated in order to slice, stain, and study its brain—then stepped out into the hall, stripping off his lab slippers and gloves and coat and mask and tossing them into the trash.

"What's up?" he said. He was beaming, like he knew what I was going to say, which was what he wanted me to say, which it wasn't.

"I'm really mad at you," I said.

"What?" He looked confused, like my words were numbers and they did not add up.

"I'm really mad at you," I said again. "Look, I'm sorry if I'm ruining your life plan, but it just doesn't work that way. You don't just ask someone to marry you out of the blue. It's crazy."

Cal ran his hand through his hair, front to back, slowly, until the back of his head was resting in his palm. Crazy, we both knew, was John. This was something else.

"Okay, not *crazy* crazy," I said. "But not viable."

"It's viable if we make it viable," Cal said. Typical Cal: very practical. There was a hint of begging in his voice, but mostly it was neutral, like he was stating a fact.

"We're so young," I said.

"No one said we have to get married tomorrow," he countered. I couldn't believe it. Somehow the argument had shifted and we were actually discussing getting married, not *not* getting married.

"You said yourself that you hardly know me," I tried.

"First of all, I didn't say that, and second of all, we have all the time in the world to get to know each other. That's what marriage is."

As we were talking, Cal was sliding his back slowly down the cement wall of the hallway outside the lab so that now he was squatting on his haunches and I was towering over him.

"You're not listening to me," I said, ready to be angry again if this was his version of getting down on one knee.

"I am listening to you, and so are my lab mates. They are good lip-readers," he said. "I'm just trying to stay out of sight. You could sit down, too." He pointed to the floor. I didn't budge. No capitulation.

"There are things about me that you wouldn't understand. I'm not a Boy Scout like you. I've done stuff," I said. I was taunting him. I wanted to taunt him. He was so earnest and naive. He was asking for it.

"I quit Boy Scouts in tenth grade," Cal said. "Try me."

So I told him that I'd been seeing Kyle when I went

home for vacation, and that we were on again, off again as it suited us, and that sometimes after he and I were done I crawled into bed with his sister, who had sworn off boys completely—even safe evangelical ones—and went by the name Kyle now, too.

"That's different," Cal said, and it wasn't clear if he meant her name change, or what she and I might have been doing on those sleepovers. I had made it a point never to discuss my sex life with Cal. It seemed cruel, like I was flaunting it. Cal, the virgin, had no sex life to discuss, though he did tell me more than once about the oboist in the college orchestra who had a crush on him, which he was determined to make sure I knew was not reciprocal.

A very attractive (as much as I could tell behind the surgical mask) woman was knocking on the window and gesturing.

"I think she's looking for you," I said to Cal. "She's a babe—why don't you marry her?"

"Because I want to marry you. Not her. You. Kit."

"Why?"

"Because we fit together," he said.

I guess I must be, or must have been, literal-minded, because before I could stop myself, I said—and loudly— "But we haven't even slept together!"

Cal stood up. A knowing smile appeared on his

face. This was not the reaction I expected. He reached into his pocket, took out his wallet, and ran a finger through the coin pouch and pulled something out. I shut my eyes for a second. Had he gotten a ring after all? Was this whole thing a setup? Opening them, I saw, on his outstretched palm, a small square foil packet. It took a second to see that it was a "ribbed for her pleasure" Trojan. In my experience, most guys kept a Trojan in their wallet. It was aspirational. For all I knew, Cal had had this thing in his wallet since high school, though I doubted it. It looked too new. "That," he said, "is something we can do something about."

Who was this self-possessed Cal Sweeney, this man who was so easily—no Sturm, no Drang—suggesting we sleep together? It suddenly occurred to me that I was the one who had been afraid to have sex with him, not the other way around. He was a real person. The sex would be real, too, and that was terrifying. I thought about what John said about jumping off a cliff together, about how essence might actually precede existence.

"You have to get back to work," I said. That was it.

**There is** this thing that women do, consciously and unapologetically, when they reach a certain age, which is check out men as potential fathers. I must have reached that age, because after Cal went back into the lab I found myself wandering around campus thinking about Cal's clear skin and straight teeth, and thinking, "Good," as in "That will be good if we have kids." I tried to get myself to stop thinking like this, but it must be some evolutionary, hardwired thing, because just as soon as I redirected my thoughts, this accounting would come skittering back to mind, and even Cal's deficits would turn up on the positive side of the ledger. He wore glasses—bad—but they were magnifiers—good, our children wouldn't be nearsighted. Cal had no siblings (and neither did I)—bad, no cousins—but good, his mother and father would be doting grandparents. Cal was going to be a doctor. Cal was normal. Cal was musical. Cal was solid. Cal was steady. Was there a better recommendation than that? He would be the dad who got up uncomplaining in the middle of the night to change a diaper. He was the parent who would keep meticulous records of shots and vaccines. He would take off the training wheels at precisely the right moment, and make sure our kids could tie a half hitch and would say their prayers at night. I was not a prayers-at-night kind of person, but it was reassuring to know that Cal was. He'd be a great father. Not that I knew "great" firsthand. My own father was a glossy photograph of a young man with wavy brown hair and aviator glasses

dressed in grimy fatigues standing by the Huey heli-
copter in which he was shot down a year or so later
over Laos during Operation Lam Son. I was a year old
when he was killed, and my mother must have been the
least sentimental person on earth, because by the time
I was old enough to realize I had had a father but didn't
anymore, almost every bit of physical evidence of his
existence was gone from our house. When I was older
and asked her about this, my mother said, "You are all I
need of him," and that was that.

So all I was going on was instinct and TV, and Cal
seemed to have all the attributes that great TV dads had.

I showed up at Cal's dorm room that night around
eleven. I told him to put a sock on the door so his roommate would know not to come in. I told him to turn
off the lights and take off his clothes. There was just
enough light coming through the window that I could
see his narrow white shoulders and the small spray of
hair on his chest. He was wearing tighty-whities. He
didn't take them off.

I pulled my shirt over my head and threw it on the
floor. I turned around and instructed him to remove
my bra. As he leaned in, I could feel the effect I was
having on him. He was breathing deeply.

"Did you ask me to marry you in order to fuck me?"

I said quietly, provocatively—a twenty-one-year-old trying to be sexy.

He let out a small groan. My eyes were closed. I imagined his were, too. Which is why we didn't see it, the firecracker that someone had rolled under the door, and the smoke that was beginning to fill the room.

"What's that smell?" Cal said, and then there was a sizzle and then a flash of light and an explosion a few feet away, and we both screamed and fell back on the bed and could hear Cal's suite mates laughing hysterically in the hallway.

"Look at the wrapper," one of them shouted.

We did. It was called THE BANGER.

"Fuck you!" I shouted.

"No," a male voice replied. "Fuck *you!*" and more laughter.

Cal was sitting there with his head in his hands. "I'm so sorry," he whispered.

"Let's get out of here," I said.

This was in the late spring. We put our clothes back on and walked through the gauntlet of leering boys and out into the soft and dewy night. There is a hill near campus, a grassy knoll that looks out over the town and the farmland that rings it, and we climbed up there and sat side by side, listening to the occasional owl search out a mate. It seemed propitious. Cal pointed out Orion in the night sky and Aquarius and Leo and Lyra, the lyre, the favorite, he said, of musicians everywhere. He took off his jacket and we leaned back on it, not to kiss, but to stare up at the stars, making wishes when we saw one falling toward us. I don't know what Cal wished for—wishes shared out loud never come true—but mine were generic and huge: happiness, easiness, love. For a while we both fell asleep, our heads touching, waking when the slightest sliver of light cut through the darkness like a filleting blade. Neither of us spoke. We didn't have to, or we couldn't. The beauty of another day, rising, infused us. We watched the sun come up as if we'd never before seen the sun come up, watched the beads of dew on the grass refract the light, becoming little prisms, and watched them disappear, gifts returned to the universe.

Cal's stomach rumbled. "Let's get breakfast," I said.

"Let's not," he said, and pulled himself up till he was resting on his elbows, his face inches from my face, and kissed me.

"Not here," I said, "not now," which was possibly the least romantic thing I could have said at that moment, and Cal looked crestfallen, but I led him back to my apartment, a half-step ahead, holding his hand like a mother might, and like a mother told him to undress and get in bed. The sheets were cool and smooth, and within seconds we were asleep, our bodies curled around each other. Cal was right: we fit together. It was still early when we woke up to a soothing chatter of rain on the roof. And then Cal Sweeney made love for the first time in his life. And so did I.

# Chapter One
## 6.7.10 – 6.13.10

There is no Frigate like a Book . . .

—EMILY DICKINSON

The girl looked like an orphan. Not that Kit, forty-four and childless, or Kit, ever, knew what a real orphan looked like. This one resembled a movie orphan: wispy blond hair, thin shoulders, a whiff of neglect. The girl, Sunny, was wearing ripped jeans, black high-top sneakers, and a boy's white undershirt with a large question mark, drawn with a black Sharpie, down the front. She said she made the shirt in case people who came into the library had any questions. "I got the idea from those signs on the highway," she said, her eyes cast down at her fingers, which were entwined, the thumbs windmilling around each other like a cat chasing a mouse. Sunny didn't say which signs and nobody gathered at the morning staff meeting, where the head librarian, Barbara Goodspeed, introduced her, asked.

"You'll be shadowing Kit," Barbara said, and when the girl said nothing, Barbara pointed: "That's Kit."

Sunny looked up, nodded quickly at the unassuming woman with curly hair and a pair of glasses sitting lopsided on her nose, looked down again, and said, "Okay," but under her breath, so that only Evelyn Mosher, the permanently grumpy circulation clerk, whose hearing aids were at full volume, picked it up.

"This should be fun," Evelyn said, smirking at Kit, who was trying to think of a way out of it. Kit moved forward in her chair, just about to protest, and then she saw that Chuck, the building and grounds guy, had his hand over his throat, the sign he was about to speak, so she slid back again, defeated.

"How old are you?" Chuck said to Sunny, his words huffing out in a pneumatic monotone from the mechanical voice box embedded under his jaw, the result of a two-pack-a-day habit he still hadn't kicked. That got her attention, and the girl looked at him, her slack expression suddenly taut, reeled in by fear or surprise or both.

"Fifteen," she said.

"Judy's got two fifteen-year-olds," Evelyn said to no one in particular. Judy was one of her daughters, the one on her third marriage. "There's her Tiffany—breach birth, blue baby, pretty much failed those tests they give newborns so everyone thought she'd be slow, which Judy probably wishes she was now—and that one of Chester's they call Beaner. Teenage boy and girl in the same house? Nightmare." But everyone sitting around the table except Sunny already knew this—they had heard the stories.

"Fifteen," Chuck repeated. "A juvenile among the dinosaurs."

"Juvenile delinquent," Evelyn muttered, but if Sunny heard her, she wasn't showing it, and anyway, it was basically true. Sunny had been sentenced to work at the Riverton Public Library for the summer after she was caught trying to steal a dictionary from the bookstore in the mall.

"You'll keep an eye on the girl," Barbara said to Kit as the meeting was breaking up, after Sunny had shuffled out of the room and was flipping aimlessly through a book someone had left at the circulation desk.

"Yeah, she might try to steal our dictionary, too," Evelyn said, and let out a short, unfunny laugh. "You want me to ask the boys to put a tail on her?" The boys,

Evelyn's sons, Jeffrey and Jack, were one-third of the local police force.

"I'm sure Kit will be fine," Barbara said, wrapping up.

So it was settled. Sunny would be Kit's responsibility. For the next twelve weeks, fifteen-year-old Sunny would be hers.

◆　◆　◆

### Sunny | convicted

So in our county they have this thing called kids' court, which is how I ended up at the library for summer vacation, even though I don't have summer vacation since I'm no-schooled. No-schooling is what it sounds like—you don't go to regular school or follow a curriculum. The idea is that the whole world is one big school and you can learn biology from looking at frogs and worms, you can learn fractions from making pies, and you can learn history from talking to old people. But you don't have to. You study only what interests you. "No-schooling is about awakening your passions and following them down whatever path they lead," my mother likes to say. It's also, basically, my parents' philosophy of life. The two of them met at a Rainbow Gathering, and when it was over they hitchhiked for a couple of years, crisscrossing North and South America, stopping to barter or do odd jobs when they needed food or cash.

Kids' court is a real court, with a real judge and a sheriff who yells, "All rise," when the judge walks into the room, though from what I could see, this was less about getting people to stand up and more about the fact that kids' court starts at 6:45 in the morning so parents can get to work afterward, and everyone is really sleepy. It's the place where good kids, or kids who haven't yet gone bad, are sent when they do something wrong, or dumb, or both, like try to slip a book down their jeans at Barnes and Noble when they are sure no one is looking. The book cost $22.95, which was $12.63 more than I had on me at the time.

"Well, Solstice," the judge said, looking down at the papers on his desk before looking at me. He was a black man with a round face and round wire-rimmed glasses, whose head was completely bald and shiny on top, and whose chin was decorated with a woolly gray beard that sprung off his face like coils of steel wool.

"Sunny," I said, my right leg shaking nervously. When I'm nervous I have a tendency to butt in.

"Excuse me?" The judge frowned, making it clear that he was not pleased to have heard from me so soon.

"Solstice is the name on my birth certificate," I

continued, speaking quickly (nerves). "It's my official name. But everyone calls me Sunny." I smiled at the judge. He did not smile back.

"Solstice," the judge began again, "can you tell me why you stole"—he looked down at his papers, squinted, and then cocked his head the way dogs do sometimes when they are confused—"the *Merriam-Webster's Collegiate Dictionary?*"

Okay, easy question.

"Because I didn't have enough money to buy it," I said. People laughed, but I wasn't trying to be funny. I would have bought it if I could.

"Order!" he growled, and threatened to bang his gavel. "I understand that's why you stole. But why did you steal a dictionary of all things? I've had a lot of thieves in my courtroom, but this—this is a first."

The thing is I could afford the paperback, but paperbacks don't last. Their pages fall out, and what good is a dictionary that is missing a page now and then? You go to look up a word and it isn't there and you can't prove it ever was. The hardback was solid and sturdy, and it was beautiful, with gilt edging, which made the book itself look twenty-four-karat-ish. Did I say that my mother makes jewelry that she sells at a kiosk in the mall—the same mall where I sucked in my stomach and tried to cram in a 532-page book between my belly and the waistband of my jeans?

"I'm waiting," the judge said, startling me.

"Okay," I said, inhaling deeply. "I was tired of always having to ask someone when I didn't know the meaning of a word. Like 'sesquipedalian.'"

"Which means?" the judge said.

"That's the thing," I said. "I don't know."

People behind me tittered in their seats. I thought I heard a boy say, "She's crazy," and someone's mother whisper harshly, "Why couldn't you be like that?"

"What about the Internet?" the judge said. "There are dictionaries on the Internet."

"We don't have a computer," I said. "We don't believe in it."

Actually, it's my parents who don't believe in it. I believe in it completely. My father says that screens rot brains and make us stupid and lazy and behave like herd animals. He says it's already happening. Every time there is a school shooting or some crazy story about people parachuting off tall buildings, he says, "See, screens. Those people all spent too much time on screens." I used to argue with him about this—how could he know they did these things because they spent a lot of time playing video games or looking at the web?

how could he know it wasn't because they drank milk when they were five or wore shoes or once had the flu?—but there was no talking him out of it or talking him into a PC or iPad or cell phone. "Read this," he said, the last time I asked, which was more than a year ago because I've learned that asking only makes him launch into a lecture on how the government is using all these electronic devices for mind control and to spy on us. He handed me a copy of *1984*. It's not like I didn't already know all about Winston Smith and Big Brother and doublespeak; *1984* is like our family bible. So no computer, no phone, no discussion.

"Are your parents or legal guardians present?" the judge asked. "If so, I'd like them to stand up."

"My mother is here," I said, pointing to the woman sitting next to me, wearing a sleeveless blue-and-green-striped dress so long it skimmed her sandals. Maybe the judge could see the rainbow tattoo on her left shoulder, maybe not, or the yin-yang symbol on her right one. Unless she spoke or smiled, he probably would not notice her pierced tongue.

As my mom stood up, the judge looked down and shuffled the papers on his desk. "Mrs. . . ." He paused, scanning the pages for a last name—which he wasn't going to find.

"We're not married," my mother said. I was waiting for her to explain how marriage was a construct of the state and how it was false consciousness—words I'd been hearing all my life until I stopped asking my parents why they weren't married or when they were going to get married.

"Of course," the judge said with a sigh, and then turned to me.

"Solstice. Sunny. Young lady." He pulled on his beard. He frowned. He tapped the back of his pen on the top of his desk. "Stealing a dictionary is a very unusual act of petit larceny. I assume you know what 'larceny' means, but for those who do not, I will tell you. It means taking something that does not belong to you. Sneakers, phones, money, cars—pretty common. Books, rarely. Dictionaries, as far as I know, and I've been doing this for over a decade, never. It's admirable to want to expand your vocabulary. It's admirable to want to know the meaning of words. It's a rare thing these days. I know that. But theft is theft. You can't just go around taking things because you want them. What kind of world would that be? This is not a rhetorical question. It has an answer. And the answer is that it would be a world without laws. A lawless world. A scary, lawless world. Do you understand me?"

I nodded. So did my mom, even though I knew for a fact that neither of my parents was a big fan of laws. Or, at least, of laws they didn't like. But he didn't ask them, he asked me.

"Say it out loud," the judge said.

"I understand," I said.

"It's a slippery slope," he said.

"Yes," I said.

"This is kids' court," the judge went on, looking over my head to the rows of other teenage villains whose turns were coming up, and addressing them as much as he was talking to me, "and in kids' court we try to find a punishment that fits the crime. No one who comes before my bench will go to jail unless"—and here he paused for a meaningful half a minute as he scanned the room—"they fail to carry out the sentence handed out by this court. Do you understand that, Solstice?"

"Yes," I said again, and for the first time that morning, I was scared. I had been nervous when I went to bed and nervous when I woke up, but nerves are different from fear, and until that moment I hadn't been scared of what was going to happen to me. The judge was right. He didn't have to say it. I was counting on the fact that I stole a dictionary, not someone's wallet or phone. That day, the day I did it, after the store security team took me from the reference section through fiction to classics and into a back office that smelled like stale coffee had been spilled in a changing room, and after the real police came, a male officer and a female officer, who sneered as they questioned me, and after I was released to my tearstained mother and driven home by my pissed-off father, the idea that I might end up behind bars didn't seem like one of the likely outcomes of, as my father, Steve, put it, my "pointless adventure."

"You don't needlessly invite the police into your life," he lectured me on the way home. This, from a man who has never met a demonstration he didn't like. Other fathers tell their children war stories; Steve tells antiwar stories: how he got penned in and pepper sprayed in New York during the first Iraq war demonstration; how he got shot at with rubber bullets in Seattle during the big antiglobalization demonstration of '99; how he was part of a die-in during the 2003 Republican National Convention; how he sat in a big old tree for three months in Oregon so it wouldn't get cut down—I'm not sure when; and how he went on a hunger strike to protest genetically modified foods and stopped only when he found out Willow was pregnant. And these are the ones I remember. There are more.

"The last thing I want to do is send someone to juvenile hall," the judge was saying, "but sometimes it's necessary. Sometimes it's the only way."

He sounded sad. He looked sad. Then he looked at me.

"Solstice Arkinsky, for the crime of stealing the *Merriam-Webster's Collegiate Dictionary*, I hereby sentence you to forty hours a week of community service at the Riverton Public Library, to be carried out every day during summer vacation until the new school year begins."

He paused, looked down, and started reading some papers on his desk. And kept reading. I didn't know if he was done with me, and I should go, or if I was supposed to keep standing until he told me I could go. Behind me, a boy whispered, "What she supposed to do?" maybe to his mother, maybe to mine. I didn't turn around. I suddenly got worried that the judge had found out something else about me, something bad, something that was making him reconsider. Steve is always going on about how the state knows things about you that you don't even know about yourself and how it will use it against you if you're not careful. The judge looked up, finally, and cleared his throat.

"Any questions?"

I nodded again.

"Yes?" He sounded annoyed.

"I don't go to school," I said.

The judge looked confused, so I reminded him that he had said I was supposed to work at the library during school vacation, but I didn't have school vacation because I didn't go to school.

"Not attending school is a serious offense," he said, shifting his gaze from me to my mother and back to me.

The court reporter stopped typing. The look on her face said, "Whoa!"

"She studies at home," my mother said, the stud in her tongue picking up and reflecting the light from the fixture overhead. I waited for her to explain the whole no-schooling concept, and maybe she would have, but the judge banged his gavel again, not once, but three times, like exclamation points.

"It is the order of this court that Solstice Arkinsky serve June, July, and August of this year at the Riverton Public Library, for no less than forty hours a week. Do you understand?"

"Yes," we said.

"Do you agree?" he asked.

"Yes," we said.

The judge banged his gavel again, and the clerk read out the name of the next kid on the docket, and the sheriff directed us down a long corridor and up a flight of stairs to an office on the next floor where there would be paperwork waiting for our signatures.

My sneakers squelched on the linoleum as we walked,

and my mother's sandals click-clacked, and it was over, and it was just beginning.

◆　◆　◆

One must have a mind of winter . . .

　　　　　　　　　　　　—WALLACE STEVENS

There are 1,687 Carnegie Libraries in the United States. The one in Riverton was built in 1912 when the city was a prosperous industrial hub on the banks of the Connecticut. No more. The mills that made textiles, shoes, and paper had all closed by the sixties and seventies, taking most of the downtown with them. The diner was shuttered, the display windows of Fine's Department Store were covered with plywood, and the pharmacy was relocated to the mall twelve miles away. The library still anchored the town green, and in the evening, when the light was fading and the building's four Doric columns, strung between a run of broad limestone stairs and a frieze that had largely worn away, were in the shadows, you might be forgiven for thinking it was a mausoleum. Still, the library's persistent grandeur was, if nothing else, a sign to anyone passing through and everyone who lived there that Riverton had once been something.

When she moved there, four years earlier, Kit was surprised at how dingy the place was. Most of what she knew about New England came from insurance company calendars, and there were no covered bridges, no tall-steepled white churches to be seen in Riverton, just streets of sagging two- and three-story clapboard houses near the city center and rows of brick mill buildings down near the water. This was in March. There was still snow on the ground. Dirty snow. The library job didn't start till April. She bought a pair of rubber boots so she could walk around, but it turned out that dirty snow was more dirt and crushed rock than snow and ice and the boots were pointless. She was staying at the Travelodge out on the highway, eating cups of yogurt and pastries lifted from the breakfast buffet and watching *Law and Order* reruns when she wasn't looking at real estate ads or talking to real estate agents, who were excited to have a live one on the line.

Rent or buy? That was the question. Prudence said rent. It also said buy. She had some money. Loss was tricky that way—it turned out that a negative balance sheet didn't always leave you in the red. That's what she'd said to the therapist back in Michigan, who believed in positive psychology and was trying to get her to believe in it, too, urging her to find the good in things when and where she could. "See, it's a lose-win situation," she told him, "so it's like semi-positive psychology." He was not amused.

"Come on, Kit," Dr. Bondi, the therapist, said, urging her, she knew—yes, she knew!—to reel off lines from the script he'd been trying to drill into her in an effort to supplant the one that was currently resident. Cognitive behavioral therapy it was called, CBT. Bondi swore by it.

"I've learned that I am much stronger than I thought I was!" And, "I've learned that even if the situation is crazy, it doesn't mean I'm crazy!" And, "I've learned that the past is a story, the future is a story, and the only reality is right now."

She could say these things, but they were just words. Words that didn't mean anything to her.

"You know what's rich?" she said, then paused for effect. "I am. Lucky me. Apparently, I won the life lottery."

"I understand your anger, Kit, I really do," he said, looking at her in a way that she could only describe as meaningful. He wasn't unattractive—she had to give him that. He was lean and fit and in the nearly year they'd been meeting appeared to be permanently sun-kissed, even his hair. Sometimes, thinking about him when they weren't together, she wondered if his presentation wasn't part of his practice—was he try-ing to project healthfulness onto the sad sacks who took up residence every hour on the hour in one of the plush brown easy chairs placed strategically across from where he sat, upright and probing? It seemed possible. She knew enough herself to show up at his office clean, teeth brushed, hair brushed, in laundered clothes, so he would not think she was depressed. She wasn't de-pressed, just exhausted.

"Why shouldn't I be angry? You think things are one way and it turns out that they are another. What's that line? Everything solid melts into air? But the joke is that it was never solid in the first place."

She leaned back in the overstuffed chair defiantly. Dr. Bondi pushed a box of tissues in her direction. Dry-eyed and seething, she pushed them back.

"I admire your resilience, Kit," Dr. Bondi said. "I really do."

"And I admire your persistence," Kit said, stand-ing up. By now she was well trained. The fifty-minute hour was over, and soon, it turned out, they'd be saying good-bye for good.

It had all happened so quickly. Everything was moving in slow motion, the way it does when you're in an accident, and then, as if someone leaned over and pushed fast-forward, everything sped up. She barely remembered applying for the Riverton job. It was through one of those online things. But there was the job offer, in her in-box, and two weeks to give her answer. Two weeks to decide to pack up and leave. No—that was not true. She had to leave. It was just a matter of when she'd go and where she'd go. Inexplicably, out of the whole wide world, she'd chosen Riverton, a declining, flea-bitten city where winter began in November and didn't disappear for a good six months. When she asked herself why, the answer was always the same: Because it was there.

◆　◆　◆

### Sunny | one book

Everyone wanted to know why I stole the dictionary. The people at the store, the police, the judge, my parents, the other kids at kids' court. Each time they asked, I'd say that I didn't steal it and wait until they got the joke. Eventually they'd ask me why I had wanted to steal it, and I'd say I was tired of bothering my parents or I needed it to study for the PSAT, which is what I told the judge. But there was something more, something I hadn't said out loud to anybody, because it was personal and I didn't want to be made fun of. Then Kit, at the library, sort of asked me. We were down in the children's section, just the two of us, shelving books and not talking—not because it's a library, and you have to be quiet, but because Kit doesn't say much and mostly keeps to herself. And then, out of the blue, she said, "So, the dictionary," which sounded like a statement, not a question, which meant I didn't have to answer it if I didn't want to, and maybe I would have, but at that very moment I noticed that someone had left a copy of *The Velveteen Rabbit* on one of the little tables they have down there, and I got excited and said that it was one of my all-time favorites and stopped to thumb through the pages. I asked Kit if she knew it, and she said that she knew of it, but hadn't ever read it, probably because she'd missed lots of children's book by not having kids. I told her she should bring it home and read it, and she said maybe, which I took to mean that she was worried that Evelyn at the circulation desk would make it a point to remind her that she wasn't anyone's mother if she checked it out. So I skimmed through and found my favorite passage and I read it to her.

"Listen," I said before I started reading, "all you really need to know is that there is this stuffed animal who is a rabbit, and another stuffed animal who is an old, worn-out horse, and they are having a conversation about how you stop being a toy animal and become a real one. Okay, here goes:"

"Does it hurt?" asked the Rabbit.

"Sometimes," said the Skin Horse, for he was always truthful. "When you are Real you don't mind being hurt."

"Does it happen all at once, like being wound up," he asked, "or bit by bit?"

"It doesn't happen all at once," said the Skin Horse. "You become. It takes a long time. That's why it doesn't often happen to people who break easily, or have sharp edges, or who have to be carefully kept. Generally, by the time you are Real, most of your hair has been loved off, and your eyes drop out and you get loose in the joints and very shabby. But these things don't matter at all, because once you are Real you can't be ugly, except to people who don't understand."

I closed the book and put it back on the table. I looked over at Kit and saw that behind her glasses her eyes were glistening and her nose was a tiny bit red and she was pinching it at the bridge. It was a little awkward. She was a grown-up. But at that moment she seemed real to me, and I seemed real to me, and it dawned on me that one way to find out if someone is trustworthy is to read her a passage from one of your favorite books and see how she reacts.

"So the dictionary," I said.

And then I stopped. I wanted her to like me. And it was odd, because she was older; her wavy brown hair was on its way to gray, and she had squint lines, like parentheses, on either side of her eyes.

"It's stupid, really," I began again. "But it was this thing I read someplace, and it really got to me. It said that a dictionary is every book ever written and every book that will be written, just in a different order. And it seemed magical. You could own every book just by owning one book. I loved that. And I just had to have it."

◆　◆　◆

What might have been and what has been . . .
—T. S. ELIOT

One thing Kit made sure to do before she left her old life was change her name. Katherine was common enough, so she decided to keep it, but finding a suitable new surname was trickier. She made a list and auditioned each one, saying it over to herself as she lay in bed, or when she was driving, or watching TV. Sullivan? Too Irish—it would attract attention from other Irish people, which didn't include her. Johnson? That was her mother's mother's maiden name. Smith, Brown, Williams, Jones? So generic that when she said them out loud they sounded fake, like names you might choose if you were choosing a new name. It took a while—Clemmons, Shea, Cross, Peters, Roberts, and on and on, every name, it seemed, except Jarvis. That she found on the label of a ninety-five-dollar bottle of Chardonnay locked away in the premium cooler at the liquor store. Jarvis: it was distinguished enough to sound authentic, but not so distinguished that it might wave any flags in her direction. Katherine Jarvis. It sounded good, too.

"I once helped a murderer change his name," the affable, gap-toothed clerk at the county administrative office told her as she was handing over her name-change petition, driver's license, and passport. "I mean I didn't know he was a murderer. A serial killer, actually. Prostitutes and runaways. You would not believe what he changed his name to."

"John Doe," Kit said at exactly the same moment he did.

The clerk looked amazed. "How did you know?"

"It was all over the papers," she said. "Didn't they interview you?"

"They tried," he said, "but I didn't say anything. I could have made some money from that, too. *National Enquirer*, the *Globe*, they were all dangling cash. My wife, bless her soul, said I should take it, but I couldn't risk losing my job. We've got rules about that sort of thing."

He studied her petition, checked her IDs against each other and then against her. Her hair was longer in those pictures and without a hint of gray, and her face was fuller and unlined.

"That's what happens when they let you go a decade between photos," she joked when it seemed to be taking too long.

"You look familiar . . ." he said at last.

Her heart skipped a beat. She must have looked alarmed.

The clerk let out a booming belly laugh. "I say that to all the pretty ladies," he said. "Then I tell them they look like Angelina Jolie. Or that other one who was married to Brad Pitt."

"Jennifer Aniston."

"Right, her," he said, stamping Kit's papers with an official seal and handing everything back to her. "But you don't look like either of them. You look like . . ." He paused, then winked. "Katherine Jarvis."

# Chapter Two
## 6.14.10 – 6.20.10

human voices wake us, and we drown.

—T. S. ELIOT

What do you talk about with a kid who calls her parents Willow and Steve because calling them Mom and Dad "just perpetuates the patriarchy"? This question had been bothering Kit all weekend, and it bothered her now as she studied her face in the mirror, adding a touch of concealer under her eyes and a stab of blush along each cheek before declaring herself done and ready for work. "Three points for the patriarchy," she thought, stashing her makeup bag in the vanity drawer and taking out a brush and pulling it a few times through her mostly untamable hair.

What do you ever talk to other people about, she wondered, especially when you didn't want to talk about yourself, since you knew if you asked them about themselves they would inevitably turn it back to you. Ask about their kids, they'll ask about yours—unless they knew you didn't have any, and then, without fail, they'd ask about your parents, or your dog, or some other relationship, as if a conversation was like tennis: you hit to me, I hit to you, you hit to me, quid pro quo. So what did that leave? The weather? (It was summer. It was nice out. It was . . . sunny. How many times had the girl heard that joke?) Sports? (Not Sunny's style, or Kit's either, for that matter, so they had that in common. Not that you could talk about something that was nothing.) Food? That should be easy—everyone eats—but no. Food was out. Food went out days ago, even before it had the chance to be in.

"Is that what I think it is?" Sunny asked on Thursday, pointing at Kit's ham sandwich. "Eww."

They were in the staff room, just the two of them, which is how it was going to be for the rest of the summer. Sunny and Kit. Kit and Sunny. Or, as Evelyn had taken to saying each time they passed her desk, "Kit and her little bundle of sunshine."

Kit examined her sandwich, turning it over in her hand. It looked all right. A little mustard had leaked through one of the holes in the bread, but other than that, it looked fine, like a ham sandwich was supposed to look.

"What?" she said, waiting for an answer before putting it in her mouth.

"It's a pig," Sunny said. "You are about to eat a pig."

"Well, technically, yes," Kit said. "Ham does come from a pig. So do pork chops and spare ribs." Sometimes, Kit was learning, it seemed best to pretend Sunny was a visitor from another country who was unfamiliar with local customs.

"Pigs have a face," she said.

Kit was confused. "Yes," she said, still poised to take a bite. "So do you. So do I."

"Right," Sunny said. "I wouldn't eat you, and you wouldn't eat me."

"That's why we don't eat each other?" Kit said. Was this fifteen-year-old logic? We didn't eat each other because we had faces? More likely it was thirtysomething-year-old logic that Sunny had picked up from her vegan, nonpatriarchal parents. Say what you will about parents called "Mom" or "Dad," she thought, in her experience they never made you feel guilty for eating a ham sandwich.

"It's one reason," Sunny said. "And anyway, who are we to have power over other animals? Why do humans get to do that?"

Kit felt a shiver of recognition quickly snake up her spine. She knew that Sunny was making a statement, not asking a question, but even so, there was, in fact, an answer: "And God said, Let us make man in our image, after our likeness: and let them have dominion over the fish of the sea, and over the fowl of the air, and over the cattle, and over all the earth, and over every creeping thing that creepeth upon the earth."

The words slid off Kit's tongue like orange Jell-O at a church supper, though she hadn't learned them in church, but in her "Bible As Literature" class, sophomore spring, many years before.

"It's from the Bible. The book of Genesis. Some people take it as the word of God," she said as Sunny grimaced and let out a short groan. "I'm not saying it's right. I'm saying that that's where they got the idea."

"Well, it's a bad one," Sunny said. "Like a lot of other things in the Bible."

So that's what they could talk about if they had to talk, Kit decided, grabbing her keys and bag and heading out the door. Theology.

◆ ◆ ◆

The door may open, but the room is altered.

—ADRIENNE RICH

Monday mornings were so reliably slow at the library that Evelyn used the time to do that day's crossword puzzle, calling from the foyer to the reading room when she was stuck on a clue. "Who said 'I pity the fool'?" she'd call out, and when no one answered, she'd say, "Three letters"—silence—"come on, people." And if Kit, or Chuck, or Barbara, or one of the handful of patrons didn't yell out, "Try Mr. T," she'd dial up the station house and ask Jeffrey or Jack. When they didn't know, she'd say, "Well, tell me something you do know," and ask them who had been hauled in for DUI over the weekend, and who was sleeping it off in the drunk tank and did their mother know.

"Aren't there laws about that?" Kit asked Chuck the first time she heard this, and the handyman rolled his eyes, covered his throat, and let out a metallic "Ha!"

When she first started at the library, Kit would arrive on Monday morning freshly showered and ready to do something—anything—only to be greeted by her own footsteps echoing off the worn linoleum floor.

Bored and worried that she'd be out of a job as soon as someone realized Riverton didn't need a reference librarian after all, Kit busied herself by roaming the stacks looking for books that were out of order.

The bookcases were tall and made from the trees that used to fill the forests outside town, forests that were now given over to the tract homes just outside of town. Maple and oak, planed by hand and bleached by time and the sun, they stood in long rows, one after the other, like sentinels. Kit would run her fingers over the wood, tracing the path of all the fingers that had come before hers, more than a hundred years of fingers, whose cumulative touch had worn the varnish bare in spots. She thought of the people whose fingers those were—mill workers and mill owners, shopkeepers, teachers, students, immigrants—not bothering to wonder where she fit in, knowing that she didn't.

Fiction, nonfiction. Biography, memoir. Science, psychology. History. Everything had its place. That was the beauty of libraries. No surprises except when someone screwed up, or was lazy, or was a thief. On those first Monday mornings, when Kit would patrol the stacks on the lookout for disorder and not find the third volume of a six-volume set, or notice that there was a second copy of a book that didn't have a first one, she'd fill out a missing book form and put it in an expanding accordion file, until Barbara Goodspeed took her aside one day and told her to stop. "Our funding depends on the size of our collection," she said, meaning that none of those books was going to be replaced—there was no money for that and there would be even less if this fiction wasn't maintained.

Kit retreated to her desk in the reading room, content to peruse the Sunday papers from cities she'd never visited and, if it was an especially slow morning, comb through the copy of *The Norton Anthology of Poetry* that she'd found on the giveaway rack. It was the same edition she'd had in college, only this one's spine was not cracked in so many places the binding was flaking off. She'd open the book randomly, looking for something she couldn't quite describe, some combination of wisdom, solace, companionship, and voice, as if it were a Magic 8 Ball, or a prayer.

Then Sunny showed up, and the poetry book was left in the desk drawer, and it was back to busywork, anything to keep the girl occupied and at arm's length, even though Kit could recognize something in Sunny that, while mirroring her own reticence, was fighting it, too. She was an odd duck, that girl, but so was she, as if one were a merganser and the other a bufflehead, alike enough in their differences to know they were related. What did it matter? Sunny would be gone in twelve weeks, then eleven, then ten, and the quiet of Monday morning would settle over Kit again like the falling motes of dust illuminated by the windows ringing the perimeter wall.

◆　◆　◆

## Sunny | co-sleeping

Willow says that one of the great disappointments of her life is that I did not nurse past when I was out of diapers. When you're part of the homeschooling/no-schooling movement you run into kids like that, big kids who stick their heads under their mothers' shirts and come out a few minutes later with milk on their chin and burp really loudly. My teeth came in early and sharp, and I guess I used them enough that Willow gave up and switched me to solid food before I turned one. "That's when I knew you'd be different," she likes to tell me, and what I am pretty sure she means is that's when she knew I'd be different from her.

Everyone who meets her loves Willow. She's that kind of person. When she meets you for the first time she gives you a big hug and looks you in the eye and tells you how happy she is to know you. The thing is it's not for show. She really is happy to know you. She's that kind of person, too. I'm more like my father: act first, ask questions second, which is why I don't think he should have been as angry as he was about the dictionary. Willow calmed him down. She usually does. Her voice is soothing. Steve calls it "snake charming," as in "Are you going to snake charm me into giving you my cinnamon toast?" Well, yes.

Willow's snake charming couldn't keep me in the family bed, though. The family bed is when the whole family sleeps together. It's very popular among the homeschool/no-school contingent. Maybe we have more time to spend in bed than families that have to get up to go to school. Co-sleeping, which is also what they call it, is supposed to encourage bonding between parents and children, but in our family it was just the opposite. When my parents rustled the sheets I'd sit up and want to know what was going on, and when I heard them whispering I'd want to know what they were saying and then I'd get angry if they said "grown-up stuff." Then Steve would get angry, and Willow would be caught in between us, literally, since I was on one side of her and Steve was on the other. She would talk in her snake charmer's voice and try to get us to do her special breathing, and most of the time I would fall back to sleep but Steve wouldn't, and then he'd be grumpy the next day and yawn a lot so we would know how tired he was. For my fourth birthday, they got me my own bed. They made like it was a big deal—"a big kid's bed," they kept calling it—and Willow had tears in her eyes when she said it.

"It's not like she's moving away," Steve said.

"No," Willow said, "but I can see it now. This is the beginning. My duckling is fledging."

She buried me in a big hug. Then Steve hugged her, which meant hugging me, too.

"Family sandwich," he said. "Tastier than a family bed because Sunny's the cheese!"

He and Willow squeezed tighter. Somewhere above me, I could hear them kissing.

◆　◆　◆

the river / Is a strong brown god . . .

—T. S. ELIOT

Kit bought a house. How could she not—they were giving it away.

"It's the economic downturn," Daisy, the anxious, perfectly coiffed real estate agent told her each time they went to a showing. "Their loss is your gain."

And Kit could see it in the abandoned swing sets and hot tubs and tree forts and gardens, evidence that whoever lived there before had left in a hurry, pursued, she figured, by loan officers and collection agents. People who planted hostas and daylilies and echinacea—perennials—assumed they were not going anywhere. People who attached guy wires to a Little Tikes playhouse were planning on staying put.

"Their loss is your gain," Daisy said for the four hundredth time.

"I get that," Kit said, surveying the neighborhood.

"It's a buyer's market," Daisy said.

"So you say," Kit said.

The house in question was a four-bedroom town house in a formerly gated community about twenty minutes outside of Riverton. It had granite counter-tops in the kitchen, cherry vanities in the bathrooms, wall-to-wall carpeting everywhere but the foyer (which was terra-cotta tile), skylights and energy-efficient win-dows, and a two-bay garage, and resembled every other town house on the street and on the streets that snaked behind and around it, many of which had FOR SALE or FORECLOSED signs displayed on their still-trimmed lawns.

"It seems a little lonely here," Kit said.

"Maybe," said Daisy, "but this house is a steal, and as soon as the economy turns around this place is going to be hot again. You know what they say, 'buy low, sell high.' Also," she added, "the unit comes with a key to the clubhouse." She pointed to a low-slung white brick building down the street.

"What happens at the clubhouse?" Kit asked.

"That's the thing," Daisy said. "Anything you want."

Kit could feel Daisy's desperation. It was making her tired. "I don't need four bedrooms," she said, and before Daisy could explain how she could turn one of them into an exercise room and another into a sewing studio, Kit was walking toward her car.

**And then** she went and bought a house that had more than four bedrooms. It had five, though three were tiny, no bigger than monks' cells, built for the serving girls who worked for the mill owner whose palatial residence stood a few acres back until it burned down decades ago. 1635 Coolidge was a two-story carriage house with rotting window sashes and plank floors that doubled as the ceiling upstairs. No one had lived there in years. One bathroom reeked of mildew, and the toilet in the other was filled with brown rusty water; there were spiderwebs hanging off spiderwebs and random piles of mouse droppings, little cairns in a forest of decay. The street itself was in similar disrepair, potholed and lined with cars and houses that had seen better days. But there was a park, now, where the mansion had been, and she could see the river from the upstairs bedroom, and Kit could imagine lying there in the morning watching the rising sun reflected on the water, or, even better, climbing to the belvedere up top and watching it go down.

"I like it," Kit said as Daisy tried to talk her out of it. But she already knew it was nutty: the wiring was old, the plumbing was older, the one tree out front, an ancient elm, was threatening to take the whole place down. But it felt like where she was supposed to live. Inexplicably, this shell of a house felt like home.

◆　◆　◆

**Sunny | notebook**

There are mysteries everywhere. Willow says you have to be open to them because that's what makes life precious. She is often pointing them out to me, but I've gotten good at seeing them myself. The mystery of the morning: Kit. I don't mean only this morning. I mean every morning. Every morning I get to work and she's there first. That's no mystery—she walks to work and I have to get a ride because we live nine miles away. It's been the same each morning when I walk in the door: Evelyn is counting the petty cash she'll use for fines, Chuck is making sure that the trash cans he emptied the night before are still empty, Barbara is in her office with the door closed, talking on the phone to her husband Larry's caretakers—he has Alzheimer's and lives in a "home"—and Kit is at the reference desk, reading the newspapers and jotting things down in a small spiral notebook.

Like today, when I said hi to Kit and she looked up, startled, and said, "Oh, wow, I didn't know you'd be here so early." And I said, "The judge says I have to work nine to five, and it's nine o'clock." Actually, it was 9:13. Technically, I was late. There is something wrong with the starter on our Subaru, according to my father, who has been trying to fix it himself because he thinks you shouldn't own things if you don't know how they work, though in this case he does know how it works and can't seem to fix it anyway.

"What are you doing, exactly?" I asked. I'd been wondering before but was too chicken to bring it up.

Kit closed the notebook and dropped it in her bag. "Reading the paper," she said. "The papers. That's what I do before I put them out on the racks."

"And you take notes?" I asked. This was the mystery. Who takes notes when they read the newspaper?

"You might say that," Kit said in a way that made it clear she was not going to say anything more about it. "Here," she said, pushing a copy of the *New York Times* in my direction. "Read it."

"What am I reading it for?" I wanted to know.

"What do you mean, what are you reading it *for*? You're reading to know what's going on in the world."

Was she angry? She seemed a little angry. I hoped she wasn't angry. At home Steve was already calling Kit the "boss lady." "She's not like that," I told him, but how could I really know? It was just a feeling I was getting. Kit was cool. Cool like a little distant, and cool like the kind of person who just seemed to know things, things she could just pull out of the air, like knowing why there were steps leading up to the front door of the library, or that Bible verse. Even though her hair was a little wild and she wore Birkenstocks, she wasn't like any of my parents' friends. I couldn't imagine Kit at one of their potlucks or scavenging fallen apples to make cider. Don't call them hippies, though. "Hippie" is a historical term from the sixties, according to Steve, who was born just over the line, in 1973. "We are not hippies," he likes to say. "We're alternatives. We live an alternative lifestyle." In other words, we don't eat meat. We oppose factory farming. We reuse, reduce, recycle. Willow says that hippies basically wrecked the world. According to her, once hippies turned thirty, they cut their hair and started wars and developed GMOs and industrial agriculture, and that's how we got to the mess we are in now, even if we do have a black president.

And yet, people often call us hippies, especially at the

mall. "Go see what the hippie family is selling today," they say. It's embarrassing. I know they don't mean anything. I've done it myself. When I was little I called an Amish family selling wood-peg clothes racks on the side of the road hippies because they looked a little like us. (Men with beards. Women in long dresses.) I probably said, "Let's see what the hippie family is selling today," since I'd heard it so many times myself. Which was not half as bad as when I was seven and there was a very short woman at the playground who was somebody's mother and I asked Willow why her little kids were taller than she was and I didn't use my indoor voice. Willow, being Willow, said, "Well, Sunny, that is one of life's mysteries."

And now Kit was one of life's mysteries, too. Was she angry? Did she like me? What about that notebook?

"I just thought, since you were taking notes, there was some other reason we were reading the paper," I said. "Sorry."

"Nope," says Kit, hardly looking up from the *Wall Street Journal* she had spread out on the desk. "Just read."

So I sat down at the table opposite her and skimmed the front page. Oil was spilling into the Gulf of Mexico because an oil rig had exploded, Germany beat Australia in the first round of the World Cup, and Afghanistan was rich in minerals but that might not turn out to be a good thing. An article called "Do Kids Still Matter to Marriage?" was on page C3 and I read it all the way through. The gist was that fewer and fewer people think children are necessary to have a happy marriage, and that children are "less central" to our lives. Ha! Not in our house. In our house, I'm the cheese. In our house, I'm the sun around which my planetary parents revolve, as they have told me all my life. If it weren't for me, they might not still be together. This they've never said, not to me, but you hear things when your bedroom shares a wall with your mother's workshop. You hear things that you'd like to ask someone about, but the only people you can ask are the people who will get mad (Steve) or weepy (Willow).

◆　◆　◆

There was an old, old house renewed with paint . . .

—ROBERT FROST

The house needed a lot of work. In her old life Kit hadn't been a homeowner, so this was all new. Daisy found her a contractor, an older man named Ray Wagonner who walked with a limp—"occupational hazard"—and who had grown up in one of the other run-down houses in the neighborhood before, he said, "the Americans moved out and all those strangers moved in." Coolidge and the streets around it were where the government had been resettling refugees for the past few decades—"It's like the United Nations over here" is how Daisy put it. "Almost no one speaks English," which suited Kit just fine.

When she confessed to Ray that she was in over her head owning such a derelict property, he told her that there were only three things she needed to know: "Benjamins. Benjamins. Benjamins." Money she had, thank God. For the first time ever, she had an overflowing bank account and nothing but this house to sop it up.

The old windows were replaced first, taking with them the draft that had sent her burrowing under three quilts most nights, and after that a new boiler, insulation, and radiators. Every other week Ray would hand her a bill and she would write a check, on the spot, without looking it over. For all she knew he was ripping her off, and for all she knew, he'd figured out she didn't care. Three months in and Kit came home from work to a new bathroom; the original claw-footed tub had been refinished and now sat gleaming against a matte black slate floor. "This is too nice," she complained to Ray, who took it as a compliment.

In December a pipe froze under the sink, swamping the new floor, which Ray said shouldn't have happened, which was small consolation since it did. "Mice," he said. "Mice ate through the insulation," and since the pipes were on an outside wall, they didn't stand a chance. An exterminator came, a large man wheeling a canister with a hazard sticker on it. CREATIVE PESTS, his shirt said. The exterminator told her that in addition to the mice there were flying squirrels in the attic and that he'd set some traps. He also mentioned carpenter ants, termites, spiders, and cluster flies and urged her to sign up for a monthly service that included unlimited follow-up visits and a free Creative Pests T-shirt, so she did. He also mentioned that she should probably be in the market for a new roof—he'd found a few places where the vermin had eaten through to the other side. It occurred to her that he was in cahoots with Ray and that each would get a kickback from the other, but she just couldn't care. Ray liked her attitude but found it strange. Most of his clients were all over him to cut costs and speed things up. Kit was content to let things unfold. It wasn't normal, but who was he to complain?

The new roof went up in May. It had been a rainy April, but the sun came out on the second and stayed there for most of the month, and by the third week rows of gray utilitarian asphalt shingles had replaced 1635's weathered cedar shakes. Though Ray, especially, was sorry to see them go, he promised Kit that she now had herself a "fifty-year roof," which was like saying she had a roof for life. "Till death or a category five hurricane do you part," he said, handing her a bill.

◆ ◆ ◆

### Sunny | moving

"Wake up! Wake up!" This was Willow, whispering in my ear. I was seven and curled around my stuffed panda in a corner of my big kid's bed, sleeping soundly. Willow's hand was on my neck. It was cold, like she'd been outside. The shades were drawn, but when I cracked open my eyes I could see that it was still dark out.

"Are we getting a puppy?" I asked. Willow sometimes told me the story of how her parents woke her up in the middle of the night and dropped a little dog into her sleepy arms and said, "This is Joseph, he's a Weimaraner."

"What? No," she said.

"Ten minutes," Steve called from the other side of the apartment.

Willow pulled back the covers and lifted me out of bed and walked us into the living room. The bookshelves had been stripped bare, the futon was gone, and there were boxes on the floor. I burst out crying.

"We don't have time for this, Willow," Steve said. He was wearing an old army jacket and a black wool hat that, when it was pulled down, doubled as a face mask, the kind with holes for the eyes, nose, and mouth. Steve liked to wear it that way on Halloween, when kids came to the door.

"I know," she said, then planted quiet, tickly raspberries on my neck till I giggled and squirmed to get down. I was fully awake now, and she handed me a granola bar and told me I didn't have to change out of my pajamas and could go back to sleep on the drive. I didn't ask where we were going, or why. It was like a dream. I just followed her down the stairs, then let her carry me the rest of the way to the station wagon, which was full of our stuff and attached to a trailer that Steve, who was right behind us on the stairs, was also loading. Willow tucked me and the stuffed panda into my car seat, covered us with a blanket, put the car radio on, said she'd be back soon, and disappeared into the house. Steve clomped down and up the stairs, down and up. I couldn't see him, but I heard him and felt him, since every time he put something into the trailer, the whole car bounced. The music on the radio soon turned to news, just a lot of voices talking about things I didn't understand until they mentioned the circus (I had just been to the circus), and I must have fallen asleep because the next thing I knew my parents were in the front seat, the motor was running, and we were driving away from home, and it was still completely dark out. I followed the path of the high beams down the street as we drove, but everything on either side had vanished, as if it wasn't us who were leaving the neighborhood, but the neighborhood itself that had moved on.

"Don't forget my bike," I said to the backs of my parents' heads. I loved my bike, a banged-up blue Trek I'd inherited from another homeschooled kid who probably got it from another homeschooler who probably got it from another homeschooler. It was my first two-wheeler. I am not sure they heard me, because neither turned around right away. Instead, Willow was looking at Steve, and Steve kept his eyes on the road.

"Right," he said after a moment. "No worries," and I was too young to know that this is what he says when, in fact, there are worries.

"Sunny," Willow said suddenly, "can you count to one thousand?"

Willow knew I could. We'd been working on this. But I took it as a challenge and launched right in and Willow did, too: "Forty-seven, forty-eight, forty-nine, fifty. Fifty-one, fifty-two . . ." I heard Willow's voice. And then I didn't.

◆ ◆ ◆

Silence is a gleaming sword.
—ROBERT WILLIAM SERVICE

"Can I ask you something . . . personal?" Sunny said when they were culling the periodicals, tossing old magazines and newspapers, holding some for the free bin that greeted patrons just inside the library door and putting the rest into recycling. It was an overcast, humid Thursday morning, threatening a thunderstorm that was edging ever closer, as towering cumulonimbus clouds drifted in from the south. Kit had an umbrella in her bag, but if it poured she was sure to get soaked on the five-block walk home. Riverton weather was unpredictable in the summer, but when it rained, the streets reliably flooded. Somewhere in the city's decline, the decision had been made to pretend its infrastructure had been built to last indefinitely; as long as its sewers, bridges, and roads were still there, that was enough. Kit looked down at her feet and vowed to go barefoot rather than ruin another pair of shoes. These were just a beat-up pair of sandals, but broken in and comfortable, with an impression of her feet cast into the bottoms. Riverton was once the shoe manufacturing capital of the United States. Now it didn't even have a shoe store. People shopped at the Walmart out on Route 5 or at the mall or online, or they picked up flip-flops and knockoff Crocs at the Dollar Tree across the town green from the library where, like many things, they cost more than a dollar. If she wrecked her sandals she'd have to get a new pair, which would mean a trip to the store, and she hated to shop, hated the whole ritual of it, hated the whole trying to care if the blouse was blue or green and made her look busty, if the shoes showed off her calves, if cowl-necks were out or in. But what she hated most was seeing herself in the three-way mirror. Straight on, confronting her puffy eyes and the gray creeping through her hair, was bad enough, but catching sight of her unsprung rear end and the cellulite that had attached itself to her thighs like barnacles was more than she needed to know about herself. And then, invariably, that line from Milton, or what she thought she remembered was that line from Milton, would pop into her head: "I myself am hell." Such were the joys of having studied literature once upon a time.

And then she looked up and noticed Sunny staring at her.

"Did you say something?" Kit said, still surprised

to see that sometime between yesterday at five in the evening and this morning at nine, Sunny had dipped the ends of her bangs into some kind of vermillion dye or paint that made the hair covering her forehead look like matchsticks.

"I was just wondering . . ." Sunny began, then stopped, took a deep breath, and, as she exhaled, inflated then deflated her cheeks. "I was just wondering if I could ask you something kind of personal." Sunny was focusing on her feet when she said this, but looked up long enough to see Kit recoil, her head bouncing slightly backward and her eyes narrowing, as her gaze shifted from distraction to high alert.

So this was it, Kit thought. This was the moment when Sunny tried to breach the barrier. This was it. Usually people didn't ask for permission, they just barreled ahead: "Are you married?" "Don't you wish you'd had children?" "Do you mind living alone?" She felt every muscle in her body contract, as if she were a turtle, tucking into its carapace, only there was no shell and she was going to be asked to account for herself, and by this peculiar girl with her severe opinions.

"What I was wondering is," Sunny said in a rush, pretending that the temperature in the room hadn't just dropped precipitously, "why do you do this? I mean not what we're doing right now. I get why we have to recycle old magazines. I mean why did you become a librarian?"

The girl was wearing a dark green oversized T-shirt that said QUESTION AUTHORITY, which, Kit decided, if you wanted to be literal about it, Sunny was doing now. Kit found herself smiling, despite herself.

"What's so funny?" Sunny demanded. "Was that a stupid question?"

"No, no, not at all," Kit said. She hadn't thought of Sunny as fragile, but she could see it now: this was hard for her. "I guess, to answer your question, it's because I'm a big fan of silence."

Kit was turning back to sort a pile of *National Geographics* when she caught sight of the smallest trace of disappointment on Sunny's face.

"No, I'm serious," Kit said. "I like the silence. There aren't many public places where you can get paid to tell people to be quiet."

Sunny considered this for a moment. "Before I was born, my parents used to go on these ten-day silent meditation retreats where they had to sit all day and practice their breathing. They said it was cleansing."

"I'd like the silent part, just not the sitting part," Kit said. "I don't think I could do that."

"Me, either," Sunny said. "Willow says that if you don't have the right mind, mindfulness is impossible.

She says it's something you have to cultivate, and she's sure I'll get there someday."

"Not me," Kit said, smiling. "I'm cultivating mind-lessness. And the way I'm doing it this morning is by separating out the old magazines from the new."

She pushed a stack of *Sports Illustrated*s over to Sunny, and for the next twenty minutes or so they worked side by side easily, without saying anything.

"The other thing is," Kit said, picking up the conversation later, "it's a job, and jobs are hard to come by in this economy, especially for people who love books."

She wasn't actually looking at Sunny when she said this. She wasn't looking anywhere except backward: the résumé writing, the job search, the need to be someone with a relevant and cherry-picked past. The last time she'd gone job-hunting no one was connecting through LinkedIn or searching through Monster.com. She wasn't opposed—the system worked the way it was supposed to and she got a job halfway across the country with only a CV and the briefest Skype interview—she just thought that calling it social media made no sense.

"It's doublespeak. It's the opposite of social," she told Dr. Bondi, who had been encouraging her to "go digital."

"Is that a complaint or an endorsement?" he asked. Was he teasing her?

"Very funny," Kit said.

"No," he said, "I'm serious."

"Right," Kit said. "I forgot that every single thing I say in here can and will be used against me."

"Well?" he said.

"Okay, yes, I like that it's impersonal," she said. "I don't think it's good for humanity, but I do think it's good for me."

Dr. Bondi wrote something on the pad he always had resting on his knee, on which he sometimes drew little pictures and diagrams to explain things to her, like Maslow's hierarchy of needs, or Kübler-Ross's five stages of grief and also, for reasons she could no longer remember, how the catalytic converter in her car worked. He drew and she sat there thinking how nice it was he cared, and how expensive.

Kit hesitated, then asked, "What are you writing down?" She nodded in the direction of the legal pad.

"I'm making a note to tell my supervisor how difficult I sometimes find your humor. Not because it isn't funny. It is. You are. But it's a defense, and it's challenging, and I probably shouldn't be telling you I feel this way, but I want this space, and our relationship, to be one of transparency and truth."

"Your supervisor?" Kit said.

"Yes," he said. "The therapist who helps me process my work."

"You see a shrink?" she said.

"I do," Dr. Bondi said. "I find it very helpful. What about you?"

He had her there. "Nicely played, Doctor," Kit said, and didn't answer.

Dr. Bondi didn't push her. Instead, he said nothing. Kit knew this was strategic. His silence was a squeeze. She felt it tightening around her torso, just under the ribs, a Heimlich maneuver to get her to dislodge her feelings—or at least answer the question.

"Yes," she said finally, "I do find it helpful."

"And why do you find it helpful?"

"Is this 'make Dr. Bondi feel good about his work' day?" she said.

"Would that be so bad?"

She ignored this.

"You know, Kit, you and I have spent a lot of time teasing out a lot of negative stuff. Maybe it would be helpful to flip it around and look for positives."

Kit felt herself color and get instantly angry. "So I'm supposed to find something positive in the mess that's been made of my life?"

She was incredulous, furious, full of venom for this

clueless man who didn't understand anything but his happy platitudes. Her life was in shambles, her husband was dead to her, her marriage might have been the greatest story ever told, and where was the plus side in all of that? But then, just as quickly as her anger had risen, it receded and she laughed. Her husband was dead to her and her life was in shambles. Kit laughed so hard that tears rolled down her cheeks.

"At least I don't have to pretend to like sailing anymore," she said.

"There you go," Dr. Bondi said. "A positive. What you've got to believe, Kit, is that there are very few situations in life that are one hundred percent bad. Did you know that two years after becoming paralyzed, most paraplegics say that their life is better off than when they could walk? We are an adaptive species. Try to embrace that."

# Chapter Three
## 6.21.10 – 6.27.10

Remorse—is Memory—Awake . . .

—EMILY DICKINSON

This Monday, when Kit got to work, Evelyn was at the front desk counting the day's petty cash as usual, but seeing Kit, she started waving her hands wildly, as if she were trying to stop traffic, or at least slow it down.

"Don't say anything about it," she hissed.

"Don't say anything about what?" Kit didn't bother to lower her voice. Evelyn was prone to inventing conspiracies and controversies, and Kit was not prone to humoring her.

Evelyn gestured toward Barbara's shut door, which at that moment began to open, and before Evelyn could pretend to be separating nickels from quarters, and before Kit could turn to make her way toward the reference desk, the library director stepped over the transom and stood there, arms crossed, eyes frightened. Though they had worked together for years, Kit couldn't really say they knew each other. To her, Barbara was a particular type of woman: sturdy, with angular features and a white pageboy, handsome, not pretty—a sensible shoes kind of woman with proper manners, manners proper enough to keep her from prying into the lives of the people she worked with or trading gossip, a woman who was standoffish by breeding, not intention. But here was that woman, just standing there—no, not even standing, leaning against the doorjamb, and this Barbara was stoop-shouldered and her hair was unwashed and lank and her face was swollen and bruised, especially around her nose, which had a length of white tape stretched cheekbone to cheekbone over the bridge.

"What happened?" Kit blurted out, keeping her gaze on Barbara since Evelyn, she knew, would be shooting full-bore dirty looks at her.

Barbara opened her mouth to speak, but instead of words, short high-pitched bleats came out, little stuttering burps of sound, as if she'd forgotten everything she knew about vowels and consonants and how they fit together. She took a step forward, or pitched forward, because before Kit knew it, Barbara's head was on her shoulder, and Kit was holding her up.

"Husband. Larry," Evelyn said by way of interpretation, as Kit, knees bent and core engaged like she'd seen on a TV strength-training fitness show, supported their boss. "Came home for the weekend from the memory care unit at Rose O'Sharon—the nursing home—for their forty-fifth wedding anniversary. Their kids were flying in, too, even the one that's in the Philippines. Husband's in the army. Or maybe navy. Friday night, Barbara hears something in the house and goes to check and sees that Larry is out of his bed, roaming around downstairs. She goes to find him, and when she does he goes ballistic, starts shouting for her to get out of his house, and starts beating her up. And he's not a small guy, especially now, eating that starchy crap they serve at that place."

"He didn't know it was me." This was Barbara, mumbling into Kit's shoulder. She had found her words again, but barely.

"Of course," Kit said as she mechanically patted Barbara's back the way she remembered being consoled as a child when something didn't go right. This, she knew, was a different order of magnitude of not going right, but it was the best she could do under the circumstances: it had been years since another person's body was in such close proximity to hers, and years since the tears on her neck were not her own.

"You don't understand," Barbara said clearly and forcefully, abruptly disengaging from Kit. "He was surprised. I surprised him. He got agitated. It's a real thing that happens to Alzheimer's patients. It's called sundowning. His doctor says that when I surprised him it triggered his fight-or-flight response and he just reacted the way his brain told him to react. It was not his fault." She looked at them defiantly and, with two black eyes and a broken nose, like a boxer challenging them to take a swing.

"So," Kit said slowly, not wanting to antagonize, "what are you going to do?"

"Hey, what's going on?" Sunny said, stepping into the main building from the vestibule before Barbara could answer. Kit turned at the sound of her voice, not sure what to say. Barbara turned, too, but in the opposite direction, walked into her office and shut the door.

"Loose lips sink ships," Evelyn said to Kit, nodding in Sunny's direction.

"I'm pretty sure that ship is on its way to the bottom of the sea," Kit said.

"What are you guys talking about?" Sunny said, ping-ponging her head from one woman to the other and back again.

"Later," Kit said, which was either a good-bye to Evelyn or a promise to Sunny, but in either case, it was her signal for Sunny to follow her to the reference section. The library wasn't open yet, so the reading carrels along the perimeter were empty, and Chuck's polish job on the long oak tables in the main reading room hadn't yet been erased, and quiet filled the room like weather. Sunny wanted to ask Kit what was going on, but she knew better, so she just walked alongside, hoping her patience would be rewarded.

"You know what I can't stand?" Kit said as they passed five carts of books that needed to be reshelved. "I can't stand the words 'reading for pleasure.' All these parents—most of whom haven't read a single book since high school, unless maybe they picked up *The Da Vinci Code*—drag their kids in here every summer and say, 'Find something to read for pleasure,' which just means that most of the time the message these kids are getting is that reading is not pleasurable. Do you see how that works? It's like reading is a punishment. I hate that."

Sunny looked at her curiously. "Wow," she said.

"Wow what?"

"Wow—I guess you really care about that."

"I guess I do," Kit said, though her little outburst surprised even herself. She had spent a long time being angry, and though, over time, her anger had receded like water after a flood, like water after a flood it had left channels that could backfill and overflow quickly, without warning.

"Anger is good," Dr. Bondi told her. "Anger lets you know what you're feeling."

"Yes," Kit told him. "It lets you know you're feeling angry."

"True enough, Kit," he said. "It does. But it's more than that. You know when you're on the highway and you stop at a rest area and there's a big map of the region and a big red dot that says YOU ARE HERE?" Dr. Bondi said. "That's anger. That's what anger can tell you. It can tell you where you are."

Kit thought about this as she handed the day's *New York Times* to Sunny and took the *Financial Times* for herself, holding the closed end of its slippery plastic wrapper and watching it slide out and drop with a satisfying thud on her desk.

"No," she decided, Bondi was wrong. The metaphor was wrong. Anger could be like pain: you think it's your ankle that hurts when it's actually your knee. Anger could be referred. She pulled out her notebook, opened it to a blank page, wrote down the date, then watched as her pen stayed suspended above the otherwise blank page.

◆ ◆ ◆

## Sunny | wilderness

That night, the night we left our apartment, I think we drove a long way, because when I woke up it was raining, and Steve said that even though we couldn't see them, there were mountains all around us and did I want a cookie. This was big: Steve and Willow had different ideas about sugar, and because Willow was certain it would turn me into a hyperactive monster child, I almost never had it. Offering me a cookie meant that Steve had won whatever argument they'd had when I was asleep, which was very unusual, given Willow's way with words. Either that, or this cookie was Willow's idea, but she didn't want me to know that because it would open the door to more cookies and maybe cupcakes that weren't baked with stevia. I grabbed the cookie quickly, before someone changed their mind. It was chocolate chip, but in place of the chocolate chips there were M&M's, and picking them out and eating them one by one kept me occupied for a long time. Every once in a while, though,

I'd asked where we were going and when we would get there, and either Steve or Willow would say, "All will be revealed in good time, Sunny. All in good time."

At some point I realized we weren't pulling the trailer anymore, and then I wondered if I'd imagined the trailer, and this time when I asked, one of my parents, I don't remember which, said that we'd dropped it off back in Pennsylvania, but when I asked where in Pennsylvania, all that they said was "Somewhere safe."

I remember stopping once to pee on the side of the road when the rain let up, which is when we all realized I wasn't wearing shoes and that my shoes might be back in a box in the trailer, which made Willow groan and Steve swear under his breath. He carried me outside and had me stand on the tops of his shoes and hold both of his hands with both of mine and lean back so I wouldn't pee on him. Willow said it looked like we were contra dancing, which we do sometimes, or he was teaching me how to do a backward dive, which he never has.

A couple of hours later we stopped again and Steve took the map from Willow, traced a route with his fingers, and declared that we were almost there. I asked again where "there" was and got the same answer as before, so went back to looking out the window, counting the few cars that passed. I could read well enough to know we were in New York somewhere and, with the

fog lifting, could see the mountains Steve had been talking about. We turned off the main road onto a bumpy
dirt road, then turned off that road onto an even nar-
rower one that was so rutted every few seconds I almost hit my head on the ceiling of the car. And then we
slowed and came to a stop because the road stopped. It
just ended. There were a couple of other cars there, and
Steve pulled up behind one of them, turned off the engine, let out a big sigh, and said, "Honey, we're home."
Willow laughed, but I couldn't see what was so funny
or how we could be home. We were in the middle of
the forest in the middle of nowhere with nothing around
except big, tall spruce trees. I thought they were pine
trees, but they turned out to be spruce.

There was a path, and a sign, and a book you were
supposed to write your name in to say you were there
and how long you expected to stay, and I wanted to put
down our names but my parents both said no at the
same time and kept walking. Because it had been raining, the ground was squishy and covered in soft brown
and yellow pine needles that stuck to the bottoms of my
feet. In a couple of minutes we came to a pond where
the trail split, and we went to the right. Steve said he
was going to run ahead and scout it out before we made
a final decision. What this decision was, he didn't say.
Willow and I kept walking. We heard a loon on the pond

and some squirrels in the branches overhead, but aside from those, nothing until we heard Steve jogging back toward us. "Found it!" he said, and had us turn around and walk back to the car to get our stuff: bedrolls, a tent, a camping stove, a bag of food from our house, and some clothes. Then we walked back along the path, past the place where we'd turned around, until we came to a tree with a sign marked #3 and a fire pit with a bunch of old burned-out beer cans in it and some split logs stacked nearby.

"Look, we've got our own beach," Steve said after we'd dropped all our junk in a heap on the ground, and led us between the trees to where the water lapped at a small patch of sand. There was nothing around—nothing but water surrounded by tall green mountains. It felt like we were the first, and the only, people who had ever been there.

"Go ahead and yell," Steve told me.

"Why?" I said.

"Just do it." He was smiling. "Shout your name."

So I did, and within seconds, my own name, in my own voice, came booming right back at me.

All those books—another world—just waiting . . .

—NIKKI GIOVANNI

In the four years that Kit had been working at the Riverton library, she noticed that most patrons fell into one of four categories. There were the retirees, all older men, who treated the place like a clubhouse. They came first thing in the morning with their refill mugs of coffee, went straight for the newspapers and magazines, grabbed a few and set up shop in the easy chairs not far from the reference desk. They'd read and sip, read and slurp, blow their noses, clear their throats, shuffle pages, trade publications, quietly discuss the merits of Randy Moss and Tedy Bruschi, Barack Obama versus John McCain, each guy having his say until they weren't quiet anymore and Kit had to tell them to turn down the dial, which gave them the opportunity to flirt with her, which they did competitively and with panache. Kit protested and shooed them away, which only emboldened them, since they all knew her protest was a feint, Kit most of all. She had grown accustomed to them showing up every morning like the newspapers tossed at dawn onto the library's front steps. The Four Quartet, she called them, first to herself, later out loud, and they loved it, not that they got the nod to T. S. Eliot, but because it meant she liked them even more than she let on. Over time they shortened it to the Four, as in "The Four would like to take you out," to which she'd routinely reply, "Shh." There was Patrick, the widowed general practitioner who was always absent on Wednesdays when he took the bus down to the casino on the Indian reservation to, as he liked to say, "enhance the kids' inheritance—or not"; Carl, the group's cutup, which everyone said was appropriate since he was a barber; Rich, who started as a stock boy at Derry Paper and rose to vice president; and the other Rich, who drove Riverton's only taxi, back when Riverton had a taxi, which was back before the other Rich's company sat idle. Like clockwork, the Four were in at 10:00 and gone by 11:30, 11:30 being the time that the cafeteria at the Riverton Mercy Hospital—the only establishment left in town that cooked food for the public and took money for it—began serving lunch.

Then there were the unemployed. They came in, used the computers, flipped impatiently through *What Color Is Your Parachute?*, paid ten cents a page to print their résumés, studied the autobiographies of billionaires, and combed through every "help wanted" section in every newspaper that still had one. They were a transient, ever-changing bunch, so absorbed by their quest they rarely acknowledged they were all traveling in the same swamped boat. Someone would be there day after day for weeks, and then disappear, or come in once, or just a few times, and Kit never knew if they had gotten a job or given up or moved away. They were not all men, either. Downsizing turned out to be an equal opportunity unemployer.

Toddlers and their caretakers were the third and fourth groups. Kit had learned not to call the adults "parents." "Caretaker" was neutral. It didn't imply status. If it was judgmental, it was judgmental in the right way. When she started at Riverton, Kit was amazed at how many children in this relatively poor city were brought to the library by nannies. But when she realized she was seeing those same women on the streets around her house strolling arm in arm with the fathers of the children they were bringing to story hour, it dawned on her that these were not nannies at all, they were mothers. Her neighbors. Refugees from Burundi and Somalia and Nepal and Ecuador. So much for not making assumptions.

This cohort—"cohort" being another word, Kit had learned, from Evelyn of all people, that could not be construed as culturally insensitive—arrived just after lunchtime, for story hour. The children sat on the floor around the reader, while the adults stood behind them in concentric circles that reminded Kit of ripples in water after a rock was tossed in.

Story hour was once a week, on Wednesdays, and now that Sunny was around, it fell to her to choose the storybooks, read the storybooks, and pick up the detritus after the tide of little children receded. "This is going to be your domain," Barbara told her early on. "I'm sure you'll be great." And she was. She let the children sit in her lap. She let them play with her hair and pull on her shoelaces. And she read, as Kit's third grade teacher liked to say, "with expression," giving elephants deep nasally voices, or having mules stutter and frogs say "ribbit ribbit," and when, in the story, Clifford the Big Red Dog played dead, she'd fall out of her chair onto her back and stick her arms and legs straight up in the air, as her audience howled with laughter.

"You are quite the actor," Kit said. "They love you."

"Goes with the territory," Sunny said as patches of red bloomed on her cheeks.

"Which territory? You're blushing."

"The whole homeschool/no-school territory. Older kids and younger kids are always tossed together. No one really makes a distinction. When you're little, you idolize the older kids, and when you're older, the little kids idolize you, and you get used to entertaining them."

"Well, it's nice," Kit said. "You should do this more than once a week."

And so she did. At first it was Monday and Wednesday, then it was Monday, Wednesday, and Friday, and then it was daily, because contrary to the law of supply and demand, the more she did it, the more popular it became. For an hour every afternoon, the basement of the library was packed with happy future readers sitting knee-to-knee, and for another hour after that, Evelyn was busy checking out *The Very Hungry Caterpillar* and *Mrs. Piggle-Wiggle* and other books Sunny was putting in the small, clammy, eager hands of her biggest fans.

Their parents, though, no matter how flimsy their command of English, Kit refused to call "future readers." Kit called them "readers," called it to their faces because many of them were just becoming literate, and calling them readers gave them a boost. "How much does it cost?" people would ask when she guided them to books she thought they might like or find helpful, and then be confused when she said the words "nothing" and "free." "Nothing" and "free" were words they knew by definition only. The idea that they could come to this place and take whatever they wanted was crazy and fantastical and proof that America was great. Once they understood that Kit was serious, that the books on the shelves were theirs for the taking, they came to the library with plastic grocery bags balled up in their pockets and walked around the place filling them indiscriminately, like participants in a shopping spree contest with fifteen minutes to race through the store tossing king crab legs and T-bone steaks and lamb chops and whatever else they could fit into their carts. For the first time in a long time, books were flying out the door of the Riverton Public Library.

"And we've got Sunny Arkinsky to thank," Barbara said at the end-of-the-month staff meeting.

"What kind of name is Arkinsky, anyway?" Evelyn wanted to know. "I'm thinking it could be Polish. One of my girls went out with a Polack once. He had a '-ski' at the end of his name. But Jews have that, too, don't they?"

No one responded, not Sunny, and not even Kit, who knew that Arkinsky had been invented by Sunny's parents, apostles of the Rainbow Gathering, to infuse their baby with its spirit. Arkinsky, from *arc en ciel*: French for "rainbow."

"Moving on," Barbara said. "People are taking out lots of books, which is good, but not bringing them back, which is bad. Or when they do bring them back, they're coming back late, and when we tell them they have to pay a fine, they tell us that you"—she pointed at Kit—"told them it didn't cost anything to borrow books, which is technically true, but . . ." Her voice trailed off. She still had raccoon eyes, but the bandage was off her nose and the swelling had gone down and she was back to being all business. If she wasn't going to say any more about what happened that night, and what would happen in the future, no one else would, either.

"But our numbers are up, right?" Kit said. "Thanks to Sunny."

"Yes," Barbara said. "Thanks to Sunny. But boots on the ground, as our generals like to say, are not to our advantage if we're losing our collection and losing revenue and don't have the funds to replace missing books let alone buy new ones."

"Why don't we limit the number of books people can take out when they first get their library card," Kit suggested. "A probation period until they prove they'll bring them back."

"Good idea," Barbara said.

"Good idea if you're not the one who has to be the bad guy," Evelyn said.

"Actually, Evelyn," Barbara said as a sly smile infiltrated her usual poker face, "I think this plays to your strengths."

Kit laughed. Chuck's voice box rattled. Evelyn, who didn't know if this was a compliment or an insult, said, "If you say so," and got up to pour herself a cup of coffee.

"Thank you for reminding me," Barbara said. "About the coffee: from now on, we each have to put in five dollars a month. The library can't afford to subsidize it anymore."

"We're that poor?" Kit said.

"We've got some serious budget deficits," Barbara said. "Every little bit counts."

"You can say 'little bit' again," Evelyn said.

Barbara sighed. "I'm all ears if you—if any of you—have suggestions for how we can trim costs. We've already cut back the acquisitions budget."

"And no one's gotten a raise in two years," Evelyn said.

"Let's charge," Chuck said.

Barbara frowned. "It's a public library, Chuck. Public. We don't charge."

But Kit, who had a hunch about what he was getting at, said, "That's not what he meant."

Chuck gave her a grateful, friendly nod, then turned up the volume of his voice synthesizer so they could hear him more clearly. "It's like when you get a burger," he began, and even Kit looked at him skeptically. "The burger costs $6.95, but if you want cheese it costs more, and if you want cheese and bacon it's even more than that." He paused for a moment, caught his breath, continued. "Or pizza. Plain is $12, but add pepperoni and it's $14 and $16 if you add pineapple and ham."

"I never understood why people like Hawaiian pizza," Evelyn said. "I don't think anyone does. Not even the Italian people in Hawaii."

"Are there Italian people in Hawaii?" Chuck asked.

"Okay, okay," Barbara said, "thank you, Chuck. I think I see where you are going with this."

"To dinner, obviously," Sunny said.

Everyone laughed. It was after six. There used to be snacks at the staff meeting, but not anymore.

"Seriously," Barbara said. "What are—as Chuck says—our toppings? What can we charge for and still keep to our mission as a public institution?"

"Computer," Chuck said.

"I don't think so," Barbara said. "The library is the only place a lot of people have access to the Internet. And it's the other thing that keeps our numbers up, which is important when we go to the city council for funding."

"Using the computer, fine," said Chuck. "But all day?"

Everyone knew what he meant. For the past three days they'd watched as a man none of them had ever seen before showed up around 11:30, just as the retirees were leaving, and parked himself in front of one of the library's four computers and stayed there until right before closing. He was polite enough, making sure to say "good morning" to Evelyn as he walked in, and nodding to Kit and Sunny or Chuck if he was around, asking for nothing. He seemed to be on a mission. He was in his mid- to late thirties, carried what Kit knew to be an expensive messenger bag, and wore a charcoal pin-striped suit with a blue spread-collar dress shirt, like he was coming from a business meeting. His auburn hair was long in the back for a businessman, though, overhanging his collar by half an inch, and pushed back from his tanned, unreadable face by a pair of black Ray-Bans planted on the top of his head. James Bond, Evelyn started calling him. She was sure he was a spy.

"Who would send a spy to Riverton?" Sunny asked her.

"You never know," Evelyn said. "Don't forget, there's been all that weird stuff going on at Culvert Medical over in Sandown."

"Yeah, I heard my parents talking about that. The animal testing and the people who want to shut it down."

"Precisely," said Evelyn. "Precisely. Remember, spies don't usually look like spies. They look like you and me."

"Maybe you're a spy, Evelyn," Kit said.

"Maybe I am," she replied.

"I don't think so," Sunny said. "But maybe because I don't think so, you are. This is really confusing."

That was a few days ago, and the man—who had what was either the start of a beard or a well-tended five o'clock shadow—kept coming back and using the computer for much of the day, and none of them was any clearer about what he was doing or why he was doing it in their library.

"The thirty-minute rule only holds if someone else wants to use the machine," Barbara said. "Otherwise it can be used indefinitely, so I don't think that could be a source of revenue."

"Then change the rule," Chuck said. "Easy-peasey. Thirty minutes free, ten bucks an hour after that. Or twenty. That place at the corner of Phelps and Spruce that has Wi-Fi in the back of the store charges a dollar a minute."

"That's because guys go there to look at porn," Evelyn said. "They can charge whatever they want."

"How do you know?" This was Sunny. They all turned to her, waiting for one of the others to respond.

"You know what I don't understand?" Kit said, causing everyone to look away from Sunny and at her. "I don't understand how a city that has so little money for its public library can afford such a big Fourth of July celebration."

Everyone said, "Yeah," or nodded their head. And it was true. Riverton's fireworks were famous. They drew people from all over, who lined the waterfront, squeezing shoulder-to-shoulder to get what they thought was the best view. The mayor defended the expense, said it brought people to town who ordinarily would avoid it, and those people brought money—which, as the Four pointed out, would have been a reasonable argument if those people had anywhere in Riverton other than the Dollar Tree to spend it. Or if the city had enough police to issue enough fines for public intoxication and disorderly conduct and parking violations to raise sufficient revenue to pay, at least, for the street cleaning the next day.

**"So are** you going to watch the fireworks?" Kit asked Sunny as the meeting broke up.

"I don't think so," Sunny said. "Steve says fireworks are a display of military might in disguise. We don't believe in them."

"I'm pretty sure it's not a matter of belief," Kit said. "How can you not believe in them when they are so loud they make your brain shake?"

"You have to know Steve," Sunny said. "His father was in the army all his life and Steve grew up on military bases, and now he doesn't like anything that reminds him of all that. He says that fireworks are all about bombs bursting in midair and are a way that the government tricks people into supporting unjust wars."

"Well, if he says so, but seems a little extreme to me,"

Kit said. "I think most people think they are kind of magical—all those designs that just appear out of nowhere. From the top of my house you can see the fireworks in the sky at the same time you see them mirrored in the river. It's spectacular."

"Can I come?" Sunny asked.

◆  ◆  ◆

## Sunny | #3

Steve said that even though the days were long, we should set up camp before it got much later, but Willow said we should eat something first so our blood sugar didn't drop and we didn't get grumpy. She pulled out peanut butter and jelly sandwiches wrapped in wax paper that she must have made sometime the day before and dealt them out like cards, one for Steve, one for me, one for her, one more for Steve, a half for her, and a half for me. Steve paced while he ate his, looking for the perfect spot to pitch the tent, but Willow and I sat on a big rock that she said was a glacial erratic—a rock that had been left behind when the glaciers retreated—and watched a red-tailed hawk making wide circles overhead. I patted the rock, which was warm, and Willow said it was warm because it was a thermal sink, which at the time I thought was hysterical, because it was a rock, not something you'd find in a kitchen or a bath-room. She said if I was interested, we could do a unit on rocks, but only if I was interested, which I said I was.

"Why don't you start a rock collection?" she said, and told me to look around and see if I could find ten different kinds of rocks while she and Steve were set-ting up camp. She gave me a bag, and I set off to the pond, where there were so many rocks it was hard to decide which to choose, especially because when rocks are wet they are so shiny and colorful, and I kept on thinking I was going to find something rare and valu-able that had been hidden from view under the water. By the time I was done, my bag weighed a ton and I could barely lug it down the path.

Back at #3, the tent was up and Willow and Steve were trying to stake it to the ground, but the ground was barely budging. "It's like cement," Steve said to me over his shoulder, and went back to pounding the tent stake with a rock. Nothing. Steve gave the cable attached to the stake a little slack and poked around in the dirt to find a softer spot. He pushed on the stake and it went in maybe the distance between his fin-gernail and his knuckle. Then he started pounding again.

"You don't want it to break," Willow cautioned. She was using her soothingest voice.

"No kidding," he said.

"Maybe it's time to take a break," Willow said, which was a very Willowy thing to say. "Let's see what Sunny has found."

It worked. Steve put down his rock to come look at my collection, which I pulled, one at a time, from the bag. By then the wet rocks had become dry rocks, and there was no way to tell them apart and no way for me to say why I thought most of them, which had become dull gray, were special. But parents can be surprising. I'd show them a rock, and they'd take it from me and turn it over and over, and then say something like, "Very cool, check out all the mica in this one," or "This one has lots of feldspar in it," and before I could ask what feldspar was, one of them said, "Did you know feldspar is the most abundant mineral on earth?" which caused the other of them to dig through a duffel bag filled with books and come back with an old field guide that confirmed it. Then we had a discussion about the difference between rocks and minerals, which had something to do with rocks coming from the earth's crust, which made me think of bread and pie and pizza, and then Willow handed me the book and told me to use it to try to identify the rest of my collection while she and Steve went back to work.

This time the tent stakes stayed in the ground, and

they had no trouble attaching the rainfly or zipping on the very cool vestibule with plastic windows on both sides. When that was done, Willow disappeared inside, bedrolls hung around her neck and balled up in her arms, and when she came out she started taking clothes from our suitcases and bringing them into the tent, one armful at a time. Steve, meanwhile, was a few yards away from #3, throwing a rope into a tree. He'd toss it up and it would come back down, then he'd toss it up and it would come back down. It looked like he was playing catch with it, but from the expression on his face, I was pretty sure he was not.

"What are you doing?" I said, leaving the rocks and the book on the ground and going over to him.

"We need to hang our food," he said. "Because of the bears."

"Bears?"

"They're only black bears. The only thing they're interested in is food."

"Bears?" I said again. I had read *Blueberries for Sal* and knew that you didn't want to get between a bear cub and its mother.

"Once the bears figure out that there is no food here for them, they will move on," Steve said, as the rope flew from his hands and caught in the branch of an old birch tree. Big sigh. He gave a tug and the rope came down and so did the tree branch, which crashed and bounced and landed a few feet from us.

"Step back, Sunny," he told me, kicking the branch to the side.

He stood there, not moving, staring at it. I would have asked him what he was doing but knew he'd say, "Thinking," so I stood there and thought about that. All of a sudden he reached down and broke off a small piece of the branch and tied it to the end of the rope. He said it was like putting a weight on your fishing line so it would sink to the bottom.

He tossed it up; it came down. Tossed it up; it came down. Tossed it up, and it curled around a high branch and dropped over on the other side.

"Bingo!" he said. And, "Persistence, Sunny."

He told me to go over to our pile of stuff, get a sack and pack food in it, and bring it back to him when it was full. When I got back, he took the bag from me, clipped it on to the end of the rope, and hoisted it into the air till it was hanging there like a piñata. Then Steve took the end he was holding and tied it to one of the lower branches. He looked very pleased.

"No PB and J for you, bears," he said.

"But what if they are hungry?" I asked.

"Bears need to eat bear food, not human food," he said. "It may not seem like it, but giving them human food is just plain cruel. It upsets the natural order of things."

**Back at** the campsite, Willow had arranged everything so that it was very (unnaturally) orderly. She had put puddle boots and rain jackets on one side of the vestibule, and books on the other, and the doormat from the apartment where we'd been living less than twenty-four hours before in the middle so we didn't track dirt into the tent itself. It was a big tent that Steve said was supposed to fit six people, though four was more like it if they weren't planning on living in it—really living in it—like, I was starting to realize, we were. My underwear and socks were stacked next to my jeans and shorts, which were stacked next to my tops. Same for Willow's and Steve's, on the other side of the tent. Willow had piled a mess of quilts and pillows in the middle, and hung lanterns through loops in the ceiling. She asked if I thought it looked cozy, and I said it did and, to prove it, dove into the blankets and rolled around and promptly fell asleep. The next thing I knew, rain was pattering overhead, and it was getting dark outside, and I couldn't see either of my parents and was just about to shout for them when I heard Willow's voice and Steve's laugh and went out to see that they were just a few feet away, sitting under a tarp, on the folding chairs we got at Walgreens that summer to take to the beach in case we went to the beach, which we never did, drinking beers.

"Have a seat, Sunny," Steve said, patting the ground.

◆　◆　◆

The grave my little cottage is . . .
                                                    —EMILY DICKINSON

Kit jumped. At least it felt like she'd jumped when Sunny asked to come over. The last person besides herself to walk into her house was the exterminator, and he came when she was at work. Children sometimes knocked on the door selling raffle tickets and chocolate bars for school trips, and campaign workers showed up around election time, but none of them ever crossed the transom. On Halloween she retreated upstairs and drew the curtains and sat in the glow of her computer screen as trick-or-treaters bypassed the darkened house. In her old life there was plenty of socializing. In her new life, blessedly, there was almost none.

"I thought you didn't believe in fireworks," Kit said when Sunny asked. This, she realized later, was a mistake, an opening.

"Maybe I should make up my mind for myself," Sunny said, smiling slyly.

"What about your parents?"

"They have plans that night, and they wouldn't even have to know."

"No," Kit said firmly, but if Sunny heard her, she didn't let on.

"I could just say I'm going to your house for supper. Or to spend the night."

"No," Kit said again. And then: "You cannot spend the night." It was another mistake, another opening.

"So I can come over for supper?" Sunny said. "And then we can watch?"

She was looking at the older woman eagerly, like a puppy anticipating a walk. Despite her best efforts, Kit was not immune. She found the girl strange, but oddly appealing.

"I don't know," Kit said. "Let me think about it."

Kit thought about it. That night, pacing her kitchen, she thought about how strange it would feel to have another person sitting with her at the table and how unsettling it would be to have to consider what she might like to eat. Since Kit had moved to Riverton, she had lost her taste for food. No—that happened before she got there. Food was fuel. That's what Dr. Bondi kept telling her, not that she didn't know this. She knew it and stopped eating for a while anyway, waiting for the thrum in her head to slow down and shut off, the way her car did when it ran out of gas. When, sevens pounds lighter, she explained this—rationally, she thought—Dr. Bondi said, "No, it doesn't work that way, not eating makes it worse, the engine revs up and your thoughts spin out of control." He also might have said, "It's dangerous. You can crash and burn," but her head was spinning like a top and she'd stopped listening to anything but the sound of her pulse in her ears, as if she'd been running. She had been running.

"It's a metaphor," Kit said, out of the blue.

"What's a metaphor?" the doctor asked.

He had kind eyes, Kit decided. She wondered what it would be like to look into the mirror and have eyes like that looking back at you.

"Running," she said.

Kit left his office and went to the drive-through and ordered a chocolate milk shake and sat in her car working the cold, viscous sweetness up the straw into her warm mouth, where she held it awhile before releasing it down her throat. After that she started to eat again. People she didn't know said she looked good. People she did said she looked better. But she was neither good nor better, just less withered, less like a plant someone forgot to water. Dr. Bondi suggested she read the cooking section in the *New York Times* every day to jump-start her appetite, so for a while she read about the right way to braise pork chops and considered the benefits of brining a turkey and learned the difference between Belon and bluepoint oysters, and it all made her tired. Soup from a can, grilled cheese, tortellini, anything else she could throw into boiling water for a few minutes—food was fuel. She would say no to the girl.

◆　◆　◆

**Sunny | broken**

Even though Steve didn't like the family bed, he had no choice when we were living at #3. That's what we called it, then and now, when we talk about old times. Steve says nostalgia is a waste of energy, that it's bogus because people are always fashioning the past to fit whatever reality they want to believe, but even he likes to reminisce about our time at #3, when the three of us slept like puppies, burrowed among the blankets and quilts, me in the middle since I was the only one who never had to get up in the middle of the night to pee. Willow said that living at #3 suited me because children were meant to live close to the land, in nature. "Shoes deform the foot, and houses deform the spirit," she would tell me sometimes when I asked when we were going to move back to our apartment. Until the first snow, none of us wore shoes.

The story we never retell is the one I remember best, about the afternoon I was scrambling up a boulder and dislodged a piece of rock—schist, Willow told me later—that slammed into my left foot and pinned it so I couldn't move. I must have yelled louder than I'd ever yelled before because both my parents came rushing up the trail within seconds.

"It's okay, baby," Willow said in her most soothing voice.

From what I could tell, she thought I'd climbed too high and was too scared to come down, which really pissed me off.

"My foot!" I yelled down to her.

Steve was already climbing up the boulder, and when he was eye-level with my foot, he picked up the rock that was crushing it, called out to Willow to watch out, and tossed it aside. Then he carried me down and hustled us to the lake, setting me down in damp sand at the shore edge, so my foot could rest in the water.

It was almost fall by then. The nights were colder and there would be a frost most mornings. We didn't have a calendar, so I don't know how long we had been at #3. When I'd ask what day it was, either Willow or Steve or both of them, in unison, would say, "It's today!" which they seemed to think was hysterically funny, so I stopped asking.

The lake water was freezing. Not literally freezing— that happened later—but so cold my foot went numb. That was the idea, Steve said. "Cold water is Mother Nature's anesthetic," and he held my foot down when all I wanted to do was pull it out. I was crying, and my cries were ricocheting off the mountains, and the sound must have gotten to Willow, because she told Steve they needed to take me to the emergency room.

"That is exactly what we don't need," he said, cautioning me to keep my foot, which I could no longer feel, underwater.

"Someone should look at that foot," Willow tried again.

"I'm looking at it," Steve shot back.

To him, bodies are like cars, and he'd never take his car to a mechanic. I, after all, his only child, was born in a hot spring in California, no doctor, no midwife, just Steve coaching Willow, who was floating on her back as he held on to her shoulders till I came out and he tied off my umbilical cord with a piece of dental floss. Steve is opposed to doctors. He says they are part of the medical-industrial complex, that they are owned by the drug companies, and that the drug companies put profits before people. Don't get him started. But Willow did, and he ignored her, even after he lifted my foot out of the water and the top of it was purple and puffy and Willow swore it was broken.

"The foot has twenty-six bones," Steve said.

"What's that supposed to mean?" Willow said. She sounded angry. "That there are spares?"

Meanwhile, I was just sitting there, shivering and crying, with a broken foot, Willow said so, and there was no way that I was going to the hospital and Steve was pissed and Willow was angry, and Steve scooped me up without saying anything and took me back to #3 and told me to crawl in, take off my damp clothes, and get under the covers.

It was my fault my parents were mad at each other. It's always my fault. I could hear them arguing on the other side of the nylon tent. I even yelled, "I can hear you!" to get them to stop, but they couldn't hear me over their own voices and they didn't. After a while Willow came into the tent and got under the covers with me and told me it would be fine. I didn't know if she meant my foot or my family, but with her hand stroking my forehead and her fingers running through my hair, I believed her. Later she rubbed some arnica on my foot and gave me a cup of valerian root tea that made me gag but also put me to sleep. I didn't notice when my parents came to bed, or if they came to bed.

Steve and Willow were both out of the tent when I woke up. I listened to the sound of their voices: Were they still angry? Had that storm passed? Was Steve grumpy, was Willow sad? When you're an only child living in a tent with your parents, you get good at knowing what's going on even when you can't hear a word of what your parents are saying. It's all about tone. I wasn't hearing anything, though. Not voices, not the sound of a stick prodding the coals. Maybe they were being quiet because they didn't want to wake me. Or maybe they had stopped talking to each other. My foot was killing me. It was twice the size of the other one, scabbed where the rock broke the skin, and black and blue everywhere else. As I was inspecting it, Steve opened the tent flap.

"Rise and shine!" he said enthusiastically, practically shouting it. He had a big grin on his face, like it was Christmas morning and he had a surprise for me. And he did: a pair of crutches he'd made with tree branches and twine.

"Don't put any weight on your foot and you'll be fine," he said.

A couple of days later, when I was sick and tired of

hobbling around #3 on Steve's crutches, which were hard to use on the uneven ground around our campsite, I gave them up.

"See? What did I tell you," he said to Willow when he saw me limping and hopping without them.

And I wondered: What did he tell her?

# Chapter Four
## 6.28.10 – 7.4.10

She staked her Feathers—Gained an Arc . . .

—EMILY DICKINSON

S o I hear that the little ray of sunshine is spending
July Fourth at your house," Evelyn greeted Kit
when she got to work.

"That's news to me," Kit said. She made her way
to the reference section, where Sunny, who had gotten
there early, was unfolding the day's newspapers.

"How do you like this?" Sunny sang out as Kit ap-
proached. Attached to the sign that said REFERENCE
DESK was one written with colored pencils that said
ANSWERS!

"I made it myself," Sunny said proudly.

That, Kit reflected, was clear. "But why?"

"Because some people don't know what 'reference' means, but pretty much everyone knows what 'answer' means. My parents say it's fine, by the way."

"What's fine?"

"You know, for me to come over."

"But you can't," Kit said.

"No, really, it's fine with Steve and Willow."

"That's not what I meant," Kit said, but Sunny didn't seem to hear her.

"Steve says he can drop me off at four. The thing is, the babysitting job I was supposed to be at in the afternoon fell through—both kids have whooping cough, and since I'm not vaccinated my parents didn't think it would be a good idea for me to go over there, but they already had plans to go out, so they didn't even seem to mind. About the fireworks."

Kit looked dubious, though she knew she shouldn't be surprised. "You're not vaccinated?" she said.

"Nope."

"Aren't you worried?"

"I'm worried about the government controlling my body. Why should the government get to tell you what you can and can't do?" Sunny said.

"Do you wear a seat belt?" Kit asked.

"That's different," Sunny said.

"How?"

"It just is. No one is poking holes in your skin when you put on a seat belt."

Kit groaned. She pulled her hand through her hair and looked at Sunny with renewed sympathy. This kid was being raised by people who probably thought jet contrails caused cancer and fluoride in the water was a government plot to create docile, submissive citizens.

"Fine," she said. "Come over and we'll make hot dogs, like real Americans on the Fourth of July."

"No," Sunny said.

"No?"

"No hot dogs. I'm a vegetarian, remember?"

"All right, I'll have a hot dog. You can have a tofu dog."

"Tofu pup," Sunny corrected her.

"Okay, fine."

"I'll bring a sleeping bag."

"I'm sure you will," Kit said.

Later, looking back on their conversation, Kit wondered why she hadn't put up more resistance. She knew what Dr. Bondi would say—that, despite herself, she wanted Sunny to come over and intrude on her solitude—but she wasn't convinced. Solitude suited her. She was looking forward to climbing up to the roof,

Chardonnay in hand, to watch the fireworks and listen to the crowd and feel the warm summer air wrap around her. No—it wasn't that she didn't not want to be alone; it was that she didn't want to feel responsible for Sunny being alone. Not alone in her house while her parents were out that night, but alone in the future when she would be lost in a world that was so alien to her. Why not expose her to something normal?

"How rich is that?" she could imagine herself saying to the doctor. "I am someone's conduit to regular old life." What she couldn't imagine is what he'd say back to her.

◆ ◆ ◆

### Sunny | fireworks

Steve and Willow dropped me off on the corner of Coolidge because the street was blocked off for the fireworks. When I got to 1635, Kit was sitting on her porch reading *The New Yorker*, and I guess I was quiet as I approached because she jumped when I said hi and then was embarrassed that I'd startled her. I didn't care. I mean I cared that I had startled her, which was not cool, but it wasn't a big deal.

"Did you bring a book?" she asked, and when I said no, she brought me inside to a room, full of them, and told me to pick one.

"I can't pick just one," I said.

"They are not potato chips, Sunny," Kit said. "Take a couple. Maybe you'll find one you like."

I know I shouldn't have been surprised. She's a librarian. She has this conversation dozens of times a day. I've heard her.

The house was dark, though it was still light out: it didn't have many windows, and the ceilings were so low they made me want to duck. I'm about five-eight, which is a guess, but Steve says he's five-ten and I'm about two inches shorter, which puts me on the tall side for girls, and Steve about average for men. Kit's ceilings sagged, and the doors were framed with thick old beams that made the place feel like a hidey-hole. There wasn't much furniture in there, either. A couch and a coffee table in the living room, a table and a single chair in the kitchen. A desk in the room off the kitchen that probably used to be the dining room. There was a cot in there, too, and that's where Kit told me to leave my stuff. There were extra bedrooms upstairs, she said, but she had never gotten around to getting beds for them. I started to tell her about the kind of blow-up bed we eventually got when we were living in the tent and it was getting cold out and the cold was seeping up from the ground—which I've always thought was odd since heat, not cold, is supposed to rise—but Kit said she didn't need any more beds.

"What about Jane Austen?" she said. "I liked Jane Austen when I was your age," and pointed to a copy of *Pride and Prejudice* on the coffee table that she must have put there earlier, on purpose; it was like she was waiting to have this conversation, and waiting to give me the book and set me up on the couch, just like she did to people at work.

"I read it already," I told her.

"Oh," she said.

She seemed nervous and like she didn't know what to say, so I told her it was a long time ago—it wasn't—and sat down on the couch and turned the pages while Kit sat opposite me and seemed to be doing the same with her magazine. After what seemed like forever but was probably about fifteen minutes, Kit stood up abruptly and asked me if I wanted to go for a walk, so we put down what we were "reading" and emerged from the dimness of the house into the early-evening glow. There was a steady stream of people making their way down Coolidge, and we joined in, stepping behind a family of four holding hands in one long, impassable line and in front of a man with a little girl on his shoulders. People were walking in the opposite direction, too, and some of them recognized us and called out, "Library, library!" or shouted my name, and a few little kids actually broke away from their families to give me a hug or a high five.

It was fun. About four streets from Kit's, the crowd broke up to grab seats on the metal bleachers that had been set up there. There was an ice-cream truck and a man selling frozen lemonade from a cart and people grilling meat on hibachis and a reggae band that we listened to for a long time. Kit had a smile on her face. She seemed relaxed. But not so relaxed that when I tried to get her to dance around with me, she said, "We should go soon."

The sun was starting to descend, and the sky was getting dark, and it took some weaving in and out to skirt the crush of people heading to the waterfront. Back at Kit's, she turned on the lights and pointed to the sofa and to my book, making sure I was sitting down before she retreated to the kitchen to make dinner. I asked if I could help her, but she said she was fine doing it herself. She did say that it felt odd, having someone else in the house, and that she hadn't made dinner for someone else in a long time. She shouted this from the kitchen, and I could hear her just fine, but when I shouted back to ask her how long it had been, she didn't respond. After a while she summoned me to the kitchen, which was bigger than I imagined it would be, and had one of those old-fashioned Franklin woodstoves next to something more modern and electric, a smallish refrigerator, and a table with a one-caned chair. There was nothing hanging on the walls except an oven mitt near the stove and a calendar from an exterminating company with pictures of waterfalls and snowy mountains over the table.

"Here," Kit said, and handed me a plate with two tofu pups and a bunch of potato chips, then looked stricken for a moment and asked me if I was allowed to eat potato chips. "Or," Kit said, "don't you believe in them."

I think she was trying to be funny, but it seemed a little mean, and she must have seen something in my face because she said, "Sorry," but I pretended it was fine and told her that Steve's biggest vice was barbecue potato chips, really greasy ones that turn your fingers orange, and that he tried to get me and Willow hooked, too, but we thought they were disgusting.

I was telling her this as we carried our food up a narrow set of stairs to a tiny room at the top of the house that had a wooden bench built in along three walls. It was amazing up there—we could see the park behind us, dotted with people picnicking on blankets and little kids and dogs, and the tops of trees, and the river, and on the river a wrinkled image of the sky, so that the lazy, usually brown water was a deep blue with golden highlights and, eventually, the sun lowering like a flag till we were sitting in darkness.

And then, out of nowhere, there was a huge American flag, stars and stripes, hanging in the sky that preceded a huge boom and then morphed into bits of smoke that left an impression, like warm breath on a cold window, before disappearing altogether behind a steady stream of starbursts that bloomed red and silver and green and gold, then rushed like rain toward the river, which carried them away.

"This is awesome," I said to Kit, who was sitting catercorner to me with our knees almost touching so I could feel her jump a little each time a new rocket exploded.

"I had forgotten how loud this was," she said, pouring herself another glass of wine. "Every year, I forget."

She didn't seem to mind, though. I could see her smiling sometimes in the glow of a rocket, not a big, toothy smile, but something quieter, what Willow calls a *Mona Lisa* smile, though I doubt Kit would have admitted it. I don't think she's being mysterious on purpose. It's like she can't help it. She's not shy—she'll talk to anyone—and she's not exactly distant, but even so, she's unreachable, as if there's an invisible fence around her, or a force field that repels whatever gets too close.

When the fireworks were over, people began cheering and whistling and then booing when it was clear there would be no more. Kit and I climbed back down the narrow stairs, carrying all our stuff to the kitchen, and I helped Kit clean up, her washing, me drying.

I know she knew I was there—she kept handing me things after she'd rinsed them—but it also seemed as if she'd forgotten I was. She was quiet, preoccupied.

"Penny for your thoughts?" I tried, which is something Willow sometimes says to me when she wants to know what I'm thinking.

"What? Oh," she said, and then paused. It was a long pause. The kind of pause where you're pretty sure after waiting and waiting that nothing is coming after it. But then she said, "Maybe Steve is right. About fireworks."

"Not you, too," I said. This was truly disappointing. Why can't adults just enjoy things without having to—as Willow also sometimes says—bring along their baggage?

"It's late," Kit said, handing me the last plates to dry. "You know where your room is. There's a little bathroom opposite it. If you want to stay up reading, there's a light on the desk. There are lots of books in there. Some of my favorites. Feel free to browse."

That was it. Another library speech. I followed her into the hall, and she was about to go up the stairs and I didn't want her to. Willow says that the best way to make friends is to ask them something personal but not too personal about something or someone they care about that will have more than a one-word answer. Bad example: "Can I pet your dog?" because they will say yes or no. Good example: "How did you train your dog to walk without a leash?" because then they have to go into a long explanation and you can ask more questions and then you're having a conversation.

"Can I ask you a question?" I said. I saw her grip the banister as if she were catching herself from falling, though there was no chance of that since she was standing flat-footed on the landing. I guess I spooked her, but I went ahead and asked anyway: "When you read a book, do you skip to the last page first so you know what's going to happen before you even start?"

Kit let go of the banister and folded her arms across her chest and seemed to be thinking what to say. My plan seemed to be working.

"Let me sleep on it," she said after a long pause. And then, from the top of the stairs, "Don't stay up too late," which just seemed like a throwaway line after a night of saying very little. Does she even like me? Hard to tell.

◆   ◆   ◆

In my beginning is my end.

—T. S. ELIOT

Kit reached her bedroom, slid one foot and then the other over the threshold as if crossing home base, shut the door, and landed on the bed. She was panting slightly, as much from the exertion of climbing the narrow staircase as from being with, and getting away from, the girl. Kit leaned back and let her sandals dangle at the end of her toes before dropping to the hardwood floor, one after the other, with a *thunk*, remembering too late that there was someone below her who could hear and who would know precisely what she was doing right then: lying on her bed, looking up at the ceiling (which, despite Ray Wagonner's best efforts, needed another layer of spackle, she noticed). It had gone pretty well, Kit decided. Not that it was over, since Sunny was still in the house and they would meet again in the morning. But overall, it hadn't been too bad. The girl was an odd one for sure, mostly untouched by the world around her. Not going to school suited her, Kit decided. But being schooled by her parents? Kit was not sure.

It was an interesting question Sunny asked, too: Did Kit read the ending first? She thought about this for a while, remembering all those Nancy Drew and Agatha Christie mysteries when, yes, she'd skipped ahead so she knew which clues to look for as the story unfolded. But later on, no. There was no peeking. It seemed wrong. She didn't know why.

"If you know how a book is going to end, would you read it in the first place?" Kit asked herself later, as she stood in the bathroom, an electric toothbrush winding its way around her mouth. "Do you stop reading a book because you don't want to watch the characters you like turn out to be unlikable, or the ones with which you identify denied the happy ending you believe they deserve?"

**"I want** you to write down the story of your marriage," Dr. Bondi told her not long after they began meeting. "The beginning, the romance, the whole thing, as much as you remember."

Kit pushed back: the assignment seemed pointless.

"Why do I have to spend more energy putting this story on paper when I tell it to myself all the time?" she complained.

"Because that's not the story I mean. You are telling the story from the point of view of its ending. I want you to tell it from the beginning, when everything was possible."

Kit protested. It was early enough in their time together that she didn't realize this was what he wanted: he wanted to know her soft spots, the places he could press on and get a reaction.

"How about this," Dr. Bondi proposed. "Just write the very beginning. Let's call it the prologue. If you want to keep going after that, do. If not, stop."

Kit winced.

"You know what I mean, Kit. The origin story. How you two met and fell in love."

"I don't remember," she said flatly.

"Meaning?"

"Meaning, like I said, I no longer know that story. The narrator is unreliable."

"Go on," he said, in the neutral, slightly disinterested way she would soon come to think of as his radio voice. Did he talk this way at home? Did he have a home? Of course he had a home—he had to live somewhere—but did he have a wife and kids, a boyfriend, a girlfriend? Did they, too, find his practiced compassion annoying?

Kit sighed. "The narrator is unreliable because she no longer believes the story she used to tell."

"How is it different from the one you tell yourself now?" he asked.

"One is made up and one is real," she said. "You know how when your house burns down, the insurance company asks you to list everything you lost? Well, one of the things I lost is the story I would tell about my life. Whatever story I tell now will be told by someone—me—who knows that that story was a lie."

"It wasn't a lie, Kit," he said, "it was your reality."

"And my reality was a lie, plain and simple," she

countered. Is this what therapy would be like—one long, frustrating running argument? She sighed again. What was the point? Wasn't she already having these arguments with herself? A sudden rage came over her, sparking like a mountain thunderstorm.

"This is stupid," she said.

"What's stupid?"

"This," she said angrily. "This whole thing. This conversation. Of course my reality was a lie. If anyone should know that, it's me."

"Your reality at the time was your reality," he said firmly, and with such conviction it made her laugh.

"I'm sorry, but that is pure, unadulterated crap that sounds like something they tell you to say in psychology school."

"That doesn't make it wrong, Kit," he said gently.

"There was an end, and it colors everything, even the beginning," she said. "Why can't you see that?" Was he being dense on purpose? Was it some sort of ploy?

"I know you're not liking me very much right now," he said, "which is fine. You don't have to like me. But try to hear what I'm saying."

"What are you saying?"

"I'm saying don't assume that what happens in our

future invalidates what happened in our past. Isn't that a big assumption?"

"Maybe," she said. "But say you voted for Nixon because you thought he was a man of integrity and then Watergate happens. Don't you reassess how you feel about Nixon?"

"Yes, of course. But does what he did affect who you are? Is his lack of integrity your lack of integrity?"

"His lack of integrity may not be my lack of integrity, but it makes me a chump," she said flatly. "I should have been a better judge of character."

"Characters change," he said.

"No, they don't."

"From where I sit, they do," he said.

"From where you sit, you need to think they do," she said, not bothering to hide her contempt. From where he sat, everything was fixable. Or, at least, everything could be made better. It was an attitude she just didn't share, though when she replayed the conversation in her mind—how many times?—she realized that if she didn't think so, too, she wouldn't have kept seeing him, week after week, month after month.

"I can't make you," he said, uncrossing his legs and leaning in her direction, "but I would urge you to write down the story you told yourself. Call it fiction if you like. Whatever it is, it will be true to you."

❖ ❖ ❖

**Sunny | notebooks**

Kit was right: the light on the desk was bright enough to read by because the room itself was so small. Besides the cot, the only other piece of furniture was a bookshelf crammed with magazines she probably got out of the library recycling bin, and worn paperbacks that looked like they had been read by more than one or two or three people, and, on the bottom shelf, a couple of cardboard boxes. I am not going to lie—I pulled out the box nearest to me and opened it up. Inside were bank statements, pay stubs, tax returns—boring. So I put it back and pulled out another box, folded back the flaps, and knew I was onto something—something big. Well, something big to me. Inside were fourteen small spiral notebooks, the same kind that Kit wrote in every morning. My hands were shaking. I made sure the door was closed and locked, and pushed the cot across to block it from opening. I knew I shouldn't look through them, but I knew I had to. Kit was a puzzle and here, maybe, were the pieces.

Were they in some sort of order? I couldn't tell. If they were, and I messed it up, Kit would know. I could hear her walking around upstairs. I took out the notebook on the top left pile. It had a yellow cover on which Kit wrote:

*3.22.08–10.15.08.*

For a second or two I thought about putting it back, but my curiosity got the better of me. I flipped open the cover. On the next page, Kit had written the same thing, only less abbreviated. *March 22, 2008, to* was in blue ink and *October 15, 2008* was in black ink. The house had gotten super quiet. Kit had stopped moving around. I was holding my breath so she couldn't hear me, even though I knew she couldn't hear me. I think kids who have siblings are much better at sneaking around than kids who don't. That has been my experience, anyway. I turned the page carefully. The date was written again at the top—*March 22, 2008*—this time in block letters. And then, this:

NOT THAT GIRL

NOT IN KADHIMIYA PRISON, IRAQ ("THE CRIMINAL INVESTIGATORS RAPED US.")

NOT IN LHASA, TIBET ("TIBETANS USUALLY ARE SO CALM AND FRIENDLY, BUT SUDDENLY THEY WERE INSANE," SAID BALSIGER, 25, A TEACHER.

"THEY WERE HOWLING LIKE WOLVES. . . . IT WAS SO BRUTAL, SO VIOLENT.")

NOT EDNA PHILLIPS (THROTTLED WITH HER DOG'S LEASH AND STABBED 86 TIMES. BY TWO 17-YEAR-OLD GIRLS.)

NOT SILDA SPITZER (AGAIN. STILL. SIGH.)

NOT WITH BEAR STEARNS

That was it. It made no sense. I turned at random to another page. June 18, 2008:

NOT IN IOWA, MISSOURI, WISCONSIN (NOT A FARMER)

NOT ON HEPARIN (EXTREMELY LOW BLOOD PRESSURE, SWELLING OF THE SKIN AND MUCUS MEMBRANES, SHORTNESS OF BREATH, AND ABDOMINAL PAIN)

NOT THAT GIRL

NOT AT THAT BUS STATION IN BAGHDAD ("IN THE BOMBING, SOME VICTIMS BURNED TO DEATH OR

DIED FROM SMOKE INHALATION IN THE APARTMENT BUILDING, ACCORDING TO AN INTERIOR MINISTRY OFFICIAL. BYSTANDERS CLIMBED ONTO ROOFTOPS 20 TO 30 YARDS AWAY TO GATHER FLESH STREWN BY THE FORCE OF THE BLAST. IRAQI POLICEMEN STACKED BODIES SEVERAL FEET HIGH IN A PICKUP TRUCK, BUT SOME FELL OUT OF THE TRUCKBED WHEN THEY DROVE AWAY.")

NOT AT THAT CAFÉ IN BAGHDAD ("LET THE WORLD SEE WHAT'S HAPPENING TO US," SAID ALI AHMED, WHO WAS WOUNDED IN THE EXPLOSION. "WE CANNOT EVEN SIT IN A SIMPLE CAFE," HE SAID FROM HIS HOSPITAL BED. "I HATE MY LIFE!")

I had a hunch, so I turned to another page—I don't remember the date—and there, among the other "nots" was the one about "that girl." I did it again and again, and it was like flipping a trick coin where both sides are heads. "Not that girl" was on every page. Often she was at the top, like Kit had her on her mind right then, and sometimes at the bottom, like it was necessary to write those words before she turned the page. Just to confirm, I took out a different notebook, a blue one that covered about eight months in 2007, and there she was again, that girl, among the tornados, the car bombings, the car crashes, the rapes, the plane crashes, the food shortages and drought.

◆ ◆ ◆

You are not the same people who left that station.

—T. S. ELIOT

"Sorry, I guess I stayed up kind of late reading," Sunny said when she wandered into the kitchen the next morning.

She was barefoot, in a faded Hello Kitty nightshirt that would have made her look like a little girl but for the dark smudges under both eyes that instead made her appear ragged, like a shabby doll.

"*Pride and Prejudice.* I love that book," she said. It wasn't untrue. She did love that book. But it was a lie. It was a big fat lie. "Don't make eye contact," she coached herself. "Don't do that nervous foot-shaking thing. Say something innocuous. Keep talking."

"You look . . ." Kit hesitated.

Sunny took a deep, quick, panicked breath.

". . . very tired." Kit laughed. "I've always read that teenagers stay up late and get up late, so I guess it's true."

Sunny looked around for a clock. "What time is it?" she asked.

"After eleven," Kit said. "There's cereal. Raisin Bran.

The milk is in the fridge. Or you could have some toast. Or both." She had been practicing these words silently all morning so they would come out easily, as if she weren't speaking a mostly forgotten language.

"Raisin Bran is good," Sunny said, pushing off from the counter at the same moment Kit stood up from the table so the two of them nearly collided. Kit put out her arms to steady herself, and Sunny did, too, and for a moment they were locked in a strange embrace.

"Sorry," they said at the same moment, releasing each other and taking a step back.

"That was awkward," Sunny said. Her clammy palms left a faint residue on Kit's forearms, like a temporary tattoo that said Sunny had been there and was leaving.

Kit looked down, expecting to see something, but her bare arms were unmarked. "The milk is in the fridge," she said again. "Take the chair." There was only one.

Sunny opened the refrigerator. She had recently read (in an old *Woman's Day*, at the library) that you could learn a lot about a person from the contents of her refrigerator, like if she was obsessed about her weight (a trifecta of Diet Coke, pickles, and jars of Better Than Broth), if she had a drinking problem (wine in a box, tonic water, limes, vodka in the freezer compartment, spicy V8), if she was lonely (half-eaten containers of takeout). There was an infographic laying it all out. She wondered what the author would make of Kit's fridge. The egg tray cradled four eggs, the cheese drawer was empty, the crisper was empty, a pint of milk sat next to two sticks of butter, there was a container of coffee yogurt on the second shelf, a bottle of white wine lying on its side, and the packages of hot dogs and tofu pups from the day before. Not a lot to go on, Sunny thought. If she was going to find out about "that girl," it wasn't here.

"I guess I should go to the supermarket," Kit said, realizing Sunny was taking stock and probably judging her. That's what people did. They looked inside your refrigerator and passed judgment. Even hippie vegetarian girls. Maybe especially hippie vegetarian girls.

"I'll go with you," Sunny volunteered.

◆　◆　◆

## Sunny | shopping

She could have said no, but Kit let me tag along with her to the store. Her car, a Volvo, is newer than ours, which isn't saying much, and the radio works, and she turned it on as soon as we left the curb. The news came on and we both listened as if we cared that the Minnesota state government had been shut down, though it's possible that Kit really was interested. Not me. Politics

is just a bunch of adults talking. I was interested when
Barack Obama ran for president, even if Steve kept explaining to me and Willow, who was excited, too, that
it didn't matter anymore who was president, because
the American system was so corrupt. "Everyone is a
tool of Wall Street," he'd say, and tell Willow to make
sure I read *A People's History of the United States*, even
though no-schooling is all about "letting young learn-
ers forge their own path without outside intervention,"
and even though that book is, like, eight hundred pages
long. And then Obama won, and every time he did
something that favored corporations over people, Steve
would say "I told you so," and Willow would tell him
he was going to trample my youthful idealism before it
could take root, and I guess she was right. It's good, I
guess, that we have an African American president, but
politics seems pointless to me.

It was a quick trip. Kit bought the usual things—milk,
eggs, bread, butter, bananas, deli meat, more coffee yogurt, the newspaper, a cooked chicken—but also some
pita and hummus in case I was still going to be around
for lunch. The phone was ringing when we got back
to Kit's, and it was Willow, who said she'd been trying
to reach us for almost an hour, and I considered using
this as an opportunity to point out that she would have
had no trouble calling me if I had a cell phone, but she

sounded rushed and out of sorts and told me to sit tight, they were running late and would be there eventually.

"I think the Subaru might have finally died," I said to Kit, when I explained that my parents would not be picking me up any time soon. She said she'd drive me home, but there was no way to get back in touch with my (cell phone–less) parents to tell them this, and I didn't really want to leave, so I told her that it was better if I just stayed there until they showed up. She looked annoyed for a second, long enough for me to notice, but then suggested we make lunch and take it and our books onto the front porch, so we did. I brought *Pride and Prejudice* and Kit brought the newspaper and her little notebook. I tried to come up with a way to ask about "that girl" without letting on that I had peeked inside her notebooks, but all I could think to say was "You're taking notes again," like I didn't see her do this every morning at the library.

Kit didn't say anything, and I couldn't help myself and I asked her why. She still didn't look up or talk, though she lifted the pen from the paper and was shaking it back and forth like it had run out of ink, even though it was one of those Bic pens where you can see how much ink is left and there was a lot. I couldn't tell if she was thinking what to say or ignoring me. Finally, and with great effort, it seemed, she said, "To keep track."

"To keep track of what?" I said. "All the horrible things that are happening in the world?"

I wondered if I'd gone too far, if she'd know, now, that I'd been snooping, but she said, "Something like that," and went back to scanning the front page.

"But why?" I said after a while. That got her attention. I think she thought she had put this conversation to rest and may have felt cornered. We were only a few feet away from each other.

"You are a very curious girl, Sunny," she said, and it was clear that this was not a compliment. I thought it was her way of telling me to back off and shut up, but then she said, quietly, more to herself than to me, "To remind me."

Did she really expect me not to ask "Remind you of what?" Well, if she did, she was wrong. "Remind you of what?" I said.

I should set the scene here. Kit was sitting on a porch rocker, I was on the porch swing, and there was a small table tucked into the corner between us. Lunch was on the table, though by then I was the only one eating it. Kit was rocking back and forth slowly, the newspaper in both hands, her notebook and pen underneath, on her lap. She had a distant look on her face, not dreamy, more like removed. Every so often a car would come down Coolidge and each time I'd expect it to be the Subaru, and so did Kit I think, but none of them slowed. It was a warm day, and parents were out pushing strollers and little kids were riding bikes along the sidewalk, which is a lot different from where I live. Every so often someone would call out a greeting to Kit, and she'd wave and they'd move on.

"Is that your daughter?" some guy with a foreign accent shouted, and this time Kit was forced to respond.

"No," she said. "A friend."

So I was a friend. Good. I was happy to hear it. And then, before she raised the newspaper in front of her face like a shield, she turned to me and said, "To remind me that Wallace Stevens was right."

"What are you talking about?" I said.

I was exasperated. And she was exasperated right back. She let the newspaper drop to her lap.

"Wallace Stevens, Sunny," she said, as if repeating his name a second time would jog my memory, though you can't shake loose a memory you don't have.

"'The Emperor of Ice-Cream'?" she said.

"I like ice cream," I said eagerly.

"Wallace Stevens was a poet." Kit sounded like Willow sounds when she asks me to recall something I am supposed to know and she has to tell me the answer. "One of his most famous poems is called 'The Emperor of Ice-Cream.'"

I'm not sure how or why I was supposed to know that, but from her tone (irritated), it sounded like she thought I was.

"Okay," I said, "but what was he right about?"

Kit closed her eyes and slowly pumped her foot a few times so her chair began to rock back and forth again. "'The wind shifts like this: / Like a human without illusions, / Who still feels irrational things within her,'" she said softly. She opened her eyes. "That's from a poem of his," she added, as if I was such a dunce, I couldn't even figure that out. "You should memorize some poems, Sunny. You never know when they'll come in handy."

Let the lamp affix its beam.

—WALLACE STEVENS

The afternoon unspooled slowly. Sunny lay on the porch swing, her head leaning uncomfortably against one arm, her knees bent, and her feet poking over the edge. It was a less than ideal vantage point from which to observe Kit, since Kit was mostly obscured by the *Boston Globe*, but it wasn't bad, either. Kit knew she was hiding, but what was she supposed to do with a teenager all day? What did parents do? she wondered. Probably nothing, she decided. The last thing teenagers wanted to do was hang out with their parents. The neighbor, Jorge, who asked if Sunny was her daughter would have known that. He was probably just being nosy, she guessed. She had never thought about it before, but a woman living alone in an old house like this with only workmen for visitors must be a curiosity. "Without meaning to, I've become the neighborhood weirdo," she thought, which struck her to be so absurd that she laughed out loud.

"What?" Sunny asked.

"Nothing," Kit said. "Just something I read."

"Are you going to write it down?" Sunny asked.

"Maybe I will," Kit said, but made no move to pick up her pen.

**Sunny's parents** showed up a few minutes past five, when Kit was already wondering if she was going to have the girl there for dinner again. Willow and Steve came walking slowly up the sidewalk, heads close together, talking so intently they went past 1635. Kit was surprised at how normal they looked, Willow in a sundress, Steve in jeans and a T-shirt, his long braid coiled under a trucker's cap, the two of them indistinguishable from any other couple on the street.

"Hey," Sunny called out. She had been watching them, expecting that they would look up and see her when they approached the house, and when they didn't stop, called out, "Hey, guys!" to reel them back.

"What were you guys talking about?" she said when they got closer, and saw Willow gently nudge Steve, who said, "The car. I don't know if you've noticed this, Sunny, but we spend an awful amount of time talking about the car."

Sunny knew he was lying. She wondered if Kit, who was reading an old issue of *The New Yorker*—another gift from the recycling bin—did, too.

"Where were you?" Sunny asked.

"With Beth and Sam," Willow and Steve said at the same time, as if they'd practiced.

"I said 'where,' not 'who with,'" Sunny said. She was being ornery, she knew, but she was tired of the way adults shut her out. It was like there was a whole world out there, a parallel universe, where real things were happening, that was unavailable to her, and it was pissing her off. First Kit and her notebooks, now this.

"We were celebrating Independence Day," Steve said, and he and Willow smiled at each other coyly, and Willow told Sunny to get her things, and Sunny held up her knapsack, which was under the swing, and said she was ready to go. There were a lot of thank-yous to Kit, who said it was no problem having Sunny around and seemed most animated, Sunny noticed, when she was expecting them all to leave.

And then, finally, they departed, and the house was returned to its steady state. Kit took deep breaths and listened to herself breathe, but the quiet that descended did not bring the relief she expected. Or maybe, she thought, mindlessly turning on the TV, it wasn't the quiet that wasn't soothing, it was that she was aware of being by herself, aware of the starkness of it. This was a surprise. She had lived alone for so long now. That was the way she liked it.

"I'm a misanthrope," she told Dr. Bondi. "Being alone suits me."

He was skeptical. "Maybe," he said. "Maybe now, but I don't think it's your nature."

Kit laughed. "If it's nature versus nurture, in this case nurture wins."

"Like I said, I don't think it's a permanent feature."

But it was. That's what it had become. And Kit had come to think of herself as a loner, at home in her solitude, like one of those self-reliant spinster women from literature. By the end of the workday she craved nothing more than to hear the creak of the floorboards underfoot and the hum of the refrigerator that suffused her house. By the end of the week she was content to putter, to speak only the occasional greeting to passersby if she happened to be on the porch, to ask little of others and be asked little in return. Did it make her happy? "Happiness is overrated," she complained to Dr. Bondi whenever he asked her this, but years afterward, years in which she'd gone to bed alone, risen alone, sat in her single kitchen chair sipping coffee brewed exactly as she liked it, eaten on no fixed schedule, and been accountable to no one but her boss at work and once a year to the Internal Revenue Service, she could say yes, being alone made her happy. Or, at least, it was what she liked. And now this: a sense of unease in her own house. And that displeased her.

Kit went into the kitchen, put a tofu dog in the microwave, and, as the timer counted down, listened to the TV news floating in from the other room. The usual stuff: people who had blown off limbs setting off fireworks, tall ships in Boston Harbor, a break-in at a pharmaceutical company where some research animals were released from their cages, which made her think of Cal's rat guillotine, which made her think of Cal, and when the microwave dinged she didn't hear it because she had walked away and turned off the TV, which didn't hush the voices in her head and the random cascade of images crowding out the present with words and thoughts and scenes from the past.

"Trauma is not just one thing," Dr. Bondi had to remind her. The news was full of stories about soldiers returning from the Middle East with post-traumatic stress disorder. They'd be driving to some mall in suburban Phoenix and a stray piece of trash, blowing across the road, could make them feel an overpowering need to jump out of the car. They were hypervigilant. What seemed like the most innocuous thing could bring them right back into battle, to the smell of burning hair and flesh. A washing machine on its spin cycle could reduce a grown man to a scared, inconsolable, and furious little boy.

"You've got it, too, Kit," he said. "That's what trauma does. It lodges in our reptilian brain. It's insidious that way."

"Tell me about it."

"Sarcasm helps, believe it or not," he said.

"Well, at least I've got that going for me," Kit said.

"You've got a lot going for you, Kit. You're stronger and more resilient than you know. What the literature shows, by the way, is that the most effective way to neutralize trauma is to relive the event until it loses its power."

"That makes no sense," she said. "And what if there is more than one event? What if the event is your whole life—or, at least, a lot of it?"

"It's harder, obviously. But the treatment is the same."

"Well, if that's the treatment, I'm in luck," she said, "since reliving the trauma is basically what I do, over and over."

"Time will help," he said. "Give it time."

Did time help? She supposed so. The demands of the present had a way of crowding out memories of the past. But then something would happen—a word would be spoken, or a story would come on the radio, or someone would ask for a particular book, or she'd hear a song, or bite into a sandwich, or note the time of day, or hear the siren of an ambulance, or think she heard the siren of an ambulance—anything, everything, nothing—and she'd be right back there, in the thick of it, or in a slice of it, stray bits of conversation coalescing into a string of words that she had heard before but understood differently, because history is always rewriting itself.

"The mind is pliable," Dr. Bondi said. "But it can bend in many directions, not all of them healthy. One thing I can suggest is that when you start to go to a dark place, for you to consciously redirect your thoughts. Mind over mind. Make yourself think of something completely different. An image of something joyful or silly, and focus on that. Go watch some cat videos on the Internet."

"So your prescription for dealing with trauma is to watch cat videos?"

"It can't hurt," he said.

"Unless you were traumatized by a cat."

"In which case I'd recommend bunnies. Or puppies," he said. "Just give it a try."

Kit did. She felt ridiculous, but he was right—the videos gave her something else to think about when she started to get into what Dr. Bondi called a "ruminative loop." It was as if her mind were a theater where bad actors could be run off the stage by a pack of adorable, yelping dogs. All she had to do was remember to let the dogs out of their pen. It didn't work every time, but it worked enough of the time that Kit lost a certain amount of respect for the mind—hers and everyone else's. It could be so submissive.

But it could also be willful and unrelenting, pushing memories to the forefront of her brain, like rude people cutting in line. And not just rude, but people who were noisy and smelly and daring you to challenge them.

Kit walked back into the kitchen, took the tofu pup out of the machine, took a bite, spit it out in the sink, and tossed the rest in the trash.

"I don't see how anyone can eat this," she said out loud, to no one, though she could imagine Sunny's objection.

"I guess it's what you know," she said, carrying on the conversation, and remembered Cal's face the first time he ate sushi. She had tricked him, didn't tell him it was raw mackerel until he had chewed and swallowed it, and he was angry and she was laughing, so there was that.

Kit poured herself a glass of wine and climbed up the stairs to the roof. A nearly imperceptible breath of wind carried the aroma of meat grilling in the park behind her house and the sound of children pushed to the top of the swing set, first the grind of metal, then the squeals of delight. She wondered about Sunny: what she was doing right then, what Sunny would say about her, if it would be awkward between them at work, and if—and this surprised her, too—Sunny liked her.

# The Marriage Story

## — PART II —

We didn't get married right away. We were both still in college, and the best rationale for tying the knot was to get better housing in the dorm lottery, but I was living off-campus anyway, and when my roommate graduated, Cal moved in and we stopped talking about getting married, though Cal would always introduce me as "my fiancée." I hated it. It wasn't that I felt uneasy about being married. At that point marriage seemed as far away as Pluto, which had just been demoted from our solar system, a controversy that obsessed Cal for a while. And it wasn't that I was uncomfortable with the word "fiancée." It was the word "my." The possessive. Like he was claiming me, the way houses under contract have a SOLD sign on their front lawn before anyone has moved in. And it made me think sometimes that I hadn't been wrong, that he had asked me to marry him because he wanted to get that part of his future lined up and settled and out of the way. Marriage, check.

Our life was uncomplicated. We'd go to class, we'd come home, we'd study, write papers, cook pasta or omelets or have breakfast for dinner, watch a little TV, go to bed together. Not "go to bed" as in sex. That happened some of the time, but more often it was "go to bed" as in lie next to each other with our feet entwined under the covers. We were companionable. We fit together. It was easy, pleasant.

And my mother liked him. This was a surprise. I had known my mother only as a woman who felt misled by marriage. The vows said "in sickness and in health"—they didn't say anything about "in death in an undeclared and unpopular war, leaving you a widow at twenty-six with an infant, a mortgage you couldn't possibly afford on your elementary school teacher's salary, car payments, and credit card debt." After my father was killed, she and I moved back to her childhood home and lived with her bridge-playing, gin-sipping, perpetually upbeat mother, three generations of Oliver women under one roof. It took me years before I could see how hard this was for my mother, who, from what I could tell from the photos, seemed to have grown old and puffy overnight. When my grandmother urged her to find another man, she'd say she didn't have time or didn't have any interest, but I think that as lonely as she probably was—and she never said she was—the real reason was that she was scared to cast her lot in with someone else again. It was safer to be alone, even if being alone meant living with her mother as a single mother to a girl who would grow up without a steady masculine presence in her life. Someone my mother had known in high school came around for a while, and I remember her going to the movies with him, but after he stopped calling I heard my grandmother scolding her for sending him away.

Then there was Greg. Greg was the music teacher at the school where my mother worked. I don't know when he started to be a feature in our lives, but my mother had known him for years before he materialized in our house, sitting between my mom and her mom, passing the popcorn bowl back and forth while they watched *The Mary Tyler Moore Show* and *Cheers* and any musical that had made it to film, and helping my grandmother roll out pie dough—she was getting arthritic; he was big—and calling my mother "girlfriend," not in a possessive way, but in a friendly, intimate way. "Hey, girlfriend, let's do the dirty," he'd say, which I learned only later was a joke, since in their case it meant "let's do the dishes." My grandmother thought he was wonderful: kind, attentive, funny, and, in a pinch, willing to sit in on a hand of bridge. She was certain he was the solution to my mother's problem. My mother said she didn't have a problem, or that her only problem was that my grandmother thought she had a problem. I could hear them talking; their voices carried through the heating vents.

One night, after years of this, my mother explained that Greg was gay, a homosexual, that he didn't like women. My grandmother said this was hogwash, the proof was in the pudding (she actually said these things), and the pudding was that he spent so much time in our house, where there were only women. "You want proof, you want proof?" my mother said, and ran up to her room, pulled open a few drawers, went downstairs and showed her a photo of Greg on a trip to Chicago wearing leather chaps, a sleeveless leather shirt, and a spiked dog collar and with his arm around another man, dressed similarly, standing in front of a bar called Boize Town. (I had seen this picture myself, rifling through my mother's bureau, which I did every once in a while, looking for I don't know what, maybe the secret of life, and knew immediately what it meant. I was probably twelve.) My grandmother pushed it away and said it didn't matter what he was, that Greg was a good man and obviously loved my mother and me, and that was all that counted.

A few days later, Greg came over when my mother was out, and he and my grandmother holed themselves up in the kitchen not eating the éclairs he'd brought, and I don't know what they said to each other, but after he left I could tell she'd been crying, and it wasn't long after that that we started hearing more about the gay cancer. He lived longer than she did, but not by much.

So my mother, I'd say, had been unlucky in love, though I suppose you could also say she was lucky in love—two men had loved her dearly—but either way, I didn't expect her to approve of my engagement to Cal, whom she'd never met before I unveiled our plans. Cal was there when I told her, standing next to me in the kitchen of the house where she and I had both grown up and where, for all I knew, she had told her parents she was going to marry my dad. Cal's arm was around my shoulders; my arm was around his waist. I was nervous. He wasn't. The three of us chatted aimlessly about the weather, about Cal's work in the lab, about our four-hour drive and the red-tailed hawk we seemed to be following for part of it. Mother mentioned that the basement sump pump had stopped working again, and Cal offered to take a look. He was solicitous and polite. I suppose that after Kyle and Kylie-Kyle and crazy John, he seemed blessedly less "interesting"—the good provider type—which is why I assumed that as soon as

I told her we were engaged she'd demur, take me aside, warn me off of this marriage ship on which Cal and I were embarking. She had not raised me to be someone's wife; it certainly wasn't the example she'd set all her life. So my knees were bent, my stance defensive, waiting for the inevitable pushback.

And then, nothing. Or, rather, nothing like that. Upon hearing our news, my willfully single mother jumped up from the table, went to the sideboard in the dining room, and retrieved a bottle of Jameson and three small cut-crystal glasses. Then she toasted us to a long and happy life together. Cal extended his arm and raised his glass high, said cheers, and threw back the whisky as if he was doing shots. Mother said cheers, too, and swallowed hers in a single slug. They seemed to realize at the same moment that they'd left me out of their salute and simultaneously held their empty glasses in my direction so we could clink them in unison, and then watched with apparent approval as I downed the alcohol, which scorched the back of my throat. I realized, looking at the two of them—he beaming, she dewy-eyed—that I'd been unconsciously counting on my mother to shut this whole thing down. I also realized that that wasn't going to happen. Mother was happy. She was passing the baton to the not short, not tall, not boy, not man standing in her kitchen, and the baton was me. The project that she'd had little choice but to take on at the age of twenty-six and pursue for the next twenty-one years was coming to an end. She was almost fifty years old. For the first time in her adult life, I would be someone else's responsibility. She could relax. When I thought about it that way, I was happy, too—happy for her.

One parent down, two to go. We drove to Grosse Pointe the next weekend.

The Sweeneys' house, at the end of a winding, poplar-lined driveway, might not have officially qualified as a mansion, but it was bigger than any house I'd ever been in and surrounded by a placid, well-tended ocean of Kentucky bluegrass. Think of a southern plantation and you'll get an idea of its sprawling, portico'd grandeur. It wasn't old, just built to look old, but I wouldn't have been surprised if servants stepped out to attend to us as we approached.

"You didn't tell me you were to the manor born," I said to Cal as the place came fully into view, wondering for a minute what he must have thought when he saw the Oliver homestead, a one-thousand-square-foot Sears kit house sold under the name "the Puritan" back in the 1920s, which could use a new coat of paint and had a chimney that was disengaging from the roof.

But servants didn't emerge from the etched glass double doors, Cal's mother, Lydia, did, a compact woman with a damp handshake and a breathy voice that did not carry. She gave Cal a quick, distracted hug; looked me over, up and down, as if I were a dress in a store window; smiled wanly; and directed us to drop our bags and go into the kitchen, where there were sandwiches, cut into triangles, on the table. I had heard about finger sandwiches, which is to say that I knew they were not made from chopped-up fingers, but I didn't know anyone who actually called them that, or made them, or served them, or ate them. They were liverwurst, liverwurst and mayonnaise, which Lydia claimed were Cal's favorite, which was news to me and possibly to him. As soon as her back was turned, I dumped mine onto Cal's plate, and he made a face but quickly stuffed them in his mouth.

"You're a good eater," Lydia said to me when she saw my empty plate, but it didn't sound like a compliment. Like Cal, I was neither fat nor skinny, though to some people, if you're not skinny, you're fat. It seemed like she could be one of those people.

The Doctor—also named Calvin—showed up not long afterward in his golfing clothes, a little wobbly on his feet. He had seen patients in the morning and then gone to the club on whose board he sat—a fact he mentioned more than once—and on whose board my Cal might someday sit if he so chose—a fact he also mentioned more than once—deciding who got in and who didn't, even though this was obvious. (The first black member was elected in 1928, by accident, and the next one was elected sixty years later, and in between, members applauded themselves for being affiliated with the first integrated country club in the state.) Side by side, I could see a vague family resemblance between the two Cals, but the Doctor was shorter and appeared to be carrying half a watermelon under the front of his tight maroon-and-gray argyle vest. He spoke deliberately, in what were mostly declarative sentences: "You will join us for dinner." "You will have the Cointreau." "You will sit next to me." "You will let me put my hand on your thigh." Obviously, he didn't say this, he just did it, resting his hand on the top of my leg during dinner, as if it were part of the furniture. Was I wrong to think it was weird? Could it be the custom here? Could it be a welcoming gesture? No one could see. His hand and my thigh were behind the curtain of tablecloth. He had patted the chair, told me to sit next to him, and I'd obeyed. He was a chubby old guy. It was probably nothing. His hand wasn't moving. It was just parked on my flesh. He removed it, though, when Cal announced that we were engaged.

"That's lovely," his mother said in her quiet, uninflected way.

The Doctor was more effusive. He said, "Here, here!" which I took to mean he approved, and made a long-winded speech about palaeogenesis and ontogeny recapitulating phylogeny, which made no sense to me. When he was done he said "Here, here" again and declared that Cal would help his mother in the kitchen so "our special guest" could join him in his study for a "digestif."

"Let me help, Mrs. Sweeney," I said when dinner was over. "Cal can tell you—I'm an excellent dishwasher."

"We have a Miele," Lydia said, and whatever that was, it was obvious that there was no getting out of it. I was going with the Doctor to his study. Even Cal was resigned to it, which did not endear him to me right then.

The digestif turned out to be a "finger"—that word again—of "extremely cleansing" and "extremely expensive" and "extremely rare" Islay single malt that burned my lips before it ever got into my mouth, which amused the Doctor.

"Puts hair on your chest," he said, appraising mine. He swallowed his in one smooth motion, poured himself another, and turned suddenly serious, his brow slightly furrowed and his face wiped clean of merriment.

"Katherine," he began.

"Kit," I said.

He ignored me. "Katherine," he said again, and

didn't wait for me to correct him but instead launched into another oratory, lubricated by generous dips into the extremely cleansing, extremely expensive, and extremely rare well by his side.

"As you know, I am a physician," he said. "My father was a physician. His father was a physician, a small-town doctor. And now my son will become a physician, and you"—here he paused for emphasis and looked at me hard—"you can help or hinder that course. Are you with me so far?"

I nodded meekly. It's here where I should have gotten up, thanked him, and walked out of the room. I didn't, of course. Who does?

He cleared his throat. The Doctor was a showman. I had to give him that. Plus, he had to be more than a little inebriated. I wouldn't say drunk, but definitely getting there.

"As I find myself explaining to my dear wife more often than I'd wish, sex is important for men. The male sex drive is a man's life force."

He wanted me to nod, so I nodded. I really wanted to leave, but he held me down with the power of his stare—his eyes were red and blue—and the punch of his words.

"I understand that I should be grateful to you for, let us say, giving yourself over to my son in this way."

Before I could protest, before I could say anything, he held up his hand and splayed his fingers, like a traffic cop in an intersection. This was a lecture, not a conversation. "The process of becoming a doctor is an arduous one, a long one, and sexual release is as crucial as sleep and food, maybe more so.

"But," the Doctor continued. "But," he said again for emphasis, "we wouldn't want anything to get in the way. Am I making myself clear?"

I said, "I think so," which was an outright lie. I had no idea what he was talking about or why he was saying it.

The Doctor, who had been standing over me, walked over to his massive inlaid mahogany desk and sat down.

"Let me be as clear and as frank as possible," he said, knitting his fingers together and leaning his chin on his steepled hands. "Are you using rubbers?"

"Rubbers?" I echoed, confused for a moment. "Oh," I said, deeply embarrassed. "That."

He looked at me, waiting for an answer.

I nodded my head. Barely.

"All of the time, or some of the time?" he asked.

"Most," I said. "Most of the time." I was mumbling, but even so, I couldn't believe I was having a conversation with my future father-in-law about my sex life with his son.

"I am a doctor," he said, which I suppose was meant to make this less weird, but didn't. "You need to use rubbers all the time. Every time. You can't take chances."

And then, as if he were reading my mind, he said, "I'm telling you this, not Calvin, because in my experience it is the woman who is more responsible in these matters." I was thinking that he meant this as a backhanded compliment, not just to me, but to all women, but then he said, under his breath, "And it is unseemly for a man to discuss his emissions with another man."

The Doctor reached into a drawer and removed an amber-colored medicine vial. "No method is one hundred percent foolproof," he said, standing up and coming over to where I had crammed myself into a corner of his enormous leather couch. He held out the vial, which didn't have a label, and waited for me to take it, and when I didn't right away, he took my hand, unfolded my fingers and wrapped them around the bottle and gave them a squeeze. The pills inside rattled. "Take these in that case."

"You want me to take these pills?" I asked.

"Not at once," he said, and laughed. (*He laughed.* I was terrified. This was not funny.) "Read the instructions inside the bottle. You'll start bleeding. You may experience a little discomfort from the cramping. It's perfectly safe. Trust me."

This was my future father-in-law, telling me to trust him, handing me an illegal abortion drug in order to eliminate his future progeny so it wouldn't get in the way of his son carrying out some master plan, clearly hatched before I came on the scene, but that I was now a part of. And this was me, paralyzed, unable to say what I was thinking ("This is so fucked up!"), unable, even, to move.

The Doctor pulled me to my feet and drew me into a hug.

"You feel tense," he said. "Let me know if you need something for that."

He stepped back, keeping his hands on my shoulders, like a dance move, like one of us was supposed to step to the left or bow, though it couldn't be me. I was frozen in place.

"Look," he said, his voice softening. "I don't like it, either." He let go and went back to his desk, pulled out a pad and pen, and wrote something down and signed it with a flourish. "Here," he said, handing the paper to me. "Bring this to your physician. It's a scrip. He'll know what to do."

"She," I said.

The Doctor looked at me blankly, like I'd just told a joke he didn't understand.

"My doctor is a she."

He snorted and opened the door, and I wandered back to the kitchen. The whole encounter couldn't have taken more than ten minutes because Cal was still cleaning up from dinner.

"We have to talk," I said, and when I told him what had just happened he took the vial from me and put it in his toiletries bag, where I'd see it from time to time when I was looking for dental floss or mouthwash, when I couldn't find mine. The scrip stayed with me.

"I'll take care of it," Cal said, which at the time I found comforting.

# Chapter Five
## 7.5.10 – 7.11.10

Welcome strangers, but study daily things . . .

—DELMORE SCHWARTZ

As soon as Evelyn saw her, she wanted to know how it went, and if Sunny was more normal outside of work, and what Kit fed her, and what they did together. Kit didn't mention the vegan hot dogs or the fact that Sunny's parents didn't show for nearly an entire day. She said as little as possible, but enough for Evelyn to tell her about the boy on her grandson Jayden's T-ball team who found a package of sparklers and tossed them on the barbecue when no one was looking and the fire department had to come.

"As if they didn't have enough to do," Evelyn said, and was about to launch into the stories that had been all over the news about the man who went to investigate why his string of M-80s wasn't exploding and managed to blow off his nose, and the crazy Iraq vet who shot up his neighborhood with a SIG Sauer during the fireworks display because he thought it was under attack, and the idiots who broke into that company in Sandown again and pulled the fire alarms and triggered the sprinkler system, which basically trashed the place. She did tell these stories, but not to Kit, who could hear Evelyn chatting with Carl as she made her way over to reference.

Sunny wasn't in yet, and Kit felt a little apprehensive—what would they say to each other?—but then the girl arrived, and instead of seeming chipper, like she usually did, she seemed downcast and tired. She was also wearing the same clothes she'd been wearing when she left Kit's house. But maybe that was what teenagers did, wear the same outfit till it had to be peeled from their bodies. Wasn't that in that story Sunny liked to read to the preschoolers, *Mrs. Piggle-Wiggle*, where the boy never washed and never changed his clothes and was so dirty that Mrs. Piggle-Wiggle was able to grow a crop of carrots on his skin? But Sunny didn't look dirty, she looked washed out.

"You okay?" Kit asked. The girl was just standing

by Kit's desk, hands in the back pockets of her cutoff cargo pants, her right leg moving rhythmically, as if it were pumping up a tire, eyes fixed on the floor, saying nothing.

"I think I know where that guy is living," she said. "Don't ask me how I know. I just know."

"Okay," Kit said. "But which guy?"

"The guy who comes in here and hogs the computer."

"You can't hog it if no one else wants to use it," Kit said.

Sunny rolled her eyes. "You know who I mean." And then, under her breath, "Adults are ridiculous."

Kit heard, and felt stung, but pretended she hadn't. "Where?" she said. Did she care? Why would she care? But she was curious.

"The Tip-Top Motor Inn."

"Where's that?"

"Not sure. Off Exit 38 I think. We saw his car there."

"We?" Kit said, but Sunny was walking away.

The Four had come in by then and were assembled in their usual places, and when Carl (the former barber) saw Sunny wander away from Kit's desk, he called her over and asked if she wanted a doughnut hole. "It's the chocolate glazed kind," he added.

"You know there's no eating in the library, Carl," Sunny said. This was a common refrain. One of the

Four would stop at the Dunkin' Donuts on his drive in and pick up the morning's coffee—three sugars for Rich (the driver); milk, no sugar for Rich (the former executive); two sugars, no milk for Carl; straight up for Patrick—and doughnuts, though now that Carl was on a diet, imposed by his doctor, doughnut holes, lots of them.

"There's also ones with powdered sugar," he said, holding out the box to her. "Whatever you like."

"You know she's a Veg-etarian," Patrick said.

"What's that got to do with anything?" Carl said, smiling.

Kit, watching this scene unfold, was smiling, too. In his day, Carl must have been quite the ladies' man. Now he was just cute, though she knew better than to tell him that.

Suddenly, like a squirrel that had just spied a nut, Sunny reached out, grabbed a doughnut hole and popped it in her mouth, and started chewing.

"Attagirl!" Carl said. "Have another."

And she did. Kit was amazed. Sunny seemed to be, too.

"These are really good," she said between bites. There was powdered sugar on her cheeks and fingers and a dusting on her shirt.

"That's what I'm saying!" Carl said, and everyone but Sunny laughed. She was too busy chewing.

**Whatever bad** mood, or sad mood, or dark mood, or moody mood Sunny was in when she got to work, she was out of it by the time the Four had moved on to lunch at the hospital. Maybe it was the sugar, Kit thought, but more likely it was the harmony and counterpoint of the Four themselves. Smart and salty, droll and sharp—when they told a joke at someone else's expense, it was never to be mean, only amusing. They were the kids who sat in the back of the class and cracked everyone up, even, despite herself, the teacher. They were the neighbors who shoveled the widow's driveway and made sure she had enough wood stacked before it turned cold. They were the masters of gag gifts. They were the ones who sent boxes of paperbacks and bags of Chips Ahoy! to the soldier kids from Riverton sidelined in Afghanistan and Iraq. They were everyone's favorite uncles. They were the friends who valued loyalty above all else, and without having to say so, Sunny, though she had only recently come into their orbit, was their friend.

"Oh my goodness, oh my goodness," Sunny said, rushing over to Kit's desk shortly after escorting the Four out the front door. She was excited, talking fast, eyes alive with mischief. "That guy? I think he's a spy!" She was whispering, but loudly. "He works for the CIA."

"And you know that how?" Kit said.

"It's on his briefcase. The letters. *CIA*."

Kit had noticed the man's briefcase, too. It was a messenger bag, made of supple leather, Italian, possibly handmade, definitely expensive.

"*C-I-A*," Sunny said. "You know. As in CIA."

"So you're saying that the CIA gives its undercover agents briefcases that say where they work?"

"I've seen people come in here with backpacks that say SIERRA CLUB. Patrick has a duffel bag that says SMITHSONIAN."

"Patrick never worked for the Smithsonian. He was a doctor. Those bags are premiums, Sunny. You donate enough money and the organization sends you one. I don't think that's how Rusty got the bag."

"Rusty? That's his name? How do you know that?" Sunny's arms were crossed, her face petulant. She looked like she wanted to accuse Kit of something but couldn't think what.

"Because he put in an interlibrary loan request the last time he was here. You were downstairs. His name is Cyrus Allen. C.A. I'm guessing his middle name starts with an *I*. But he goes by Rusty."

"What book?" Sunny asked.

"What book what?"

"What book did he request?"

"No book, actually. After he filled out the form I told him he needed a library card, which he didn't have, and that was that."

"What book didn't he request?" Sunny tried again.

"I don't know."

"You didn't ask?"

"We're not part of the FBI, Sunny," Kit said. "As much as the FBI might want us to be."

"Ugh," Sunny said, walking away. "You sound just like my parents."

◆　◆　◆

**Sunny | the Tip-Top**

I didn't tell Kit how I knew about the Tip-Top Motor Inn because, as Steve says, I didn't want her in our business, but it happened right after we left her house. We weren't even off Coolidge Street when Willow announced that we wouldn't be going home for a couple of days. When I asked why we weren't, my parents gave each other "the look." When you sit in the backseat you often see "the look" pass between the people in the front seat, who are almost always your parents.

"We need to—" Steve started to say, only to be cut off by Willow, who said in her most Willowy voice, "We thought it would be fun to visit Rocco and Amelia."

Rocco and Amelia are old friends of my parents from the Rainbow Gathering. Old, in that they've all known one another for a long time, and old in that they are older and have grown children. They're the reason we live where we live. They knew the people who used to live in our house and even helped them build it. It's small, more like a cabin, and it's off the grid and down a long road with fields on either side, and you'd never know there was a city twenty minutes away. Willow likes to say it's secluded, which is a Willowy way of not saying it's isolated. It's beautiful where we live, but there is no one else around, and being no-schooled, it can get pretty lonely. Homeschoolers and no-schoolers have activities together, but they are always planned in advance, usually by adults. That's why, when the judge at kids' court said I had to spend the summer working at the Riverton library, I was even less sorry for what I had done.

Rocco and Amelia used to live nearby, but a couple of years ago they moved to Heart Village, a cohousing community about three hours south. Cohousing is where people own their own place but share things like a kitchen and gardens and toys. They get together every day for meals and to watch movies, if they can agree which movie to watch. One time when we were there they had to have a "Heart-to-Heart," which is what they call it when they ring a huge bell and everyone has to come to a meeting. Some parents were okay with showing *Harry Potter and the Prisoner of Azkaban,* and other parents thought it was too violent, and the people who wanted the movie were telling the people who didn't that their kids could stay home when it was showing, and the people who didn't said that even if they did stay home, the film's violence would poison the air, and in the middle of the discussion all the kids, every single one of them, marched into the meeting room carrying signs that said they'd go on strike and not do their chores if they didn't get to vote, too. Even the parents who had been opposed to showing the movie were so impressed with the way the kids organized themselves that they gave in.

Going to Heart Village for a couple of days was definitely more exciting than going home, but apparently neither Willow nor Steve had checked in with Rocco and Amelia about this plan, so they had to find a pay phone to call them, which they finally found on the highway at a convenience store, and Willow volunteered to give them a call. When she came back, she was shaking her head. "BB answered the phone," she said through the open window. BB is what everyone calls Rocco and Amelia's son, whose real name is Bluebird. "He said that he's there with Chandra and Chandra's two kids, and that this would not be a good time." Once again, my parents gave each other "the look." Chandra is Bluebird's girlfriend. She's older and nobody except BB likes her.

"Now what?" Willow said.

Steve was quiet. "I'm thinking," he said.

"We could just go home," I volunteered. We were only forty minutes away. Sometimes I feel like the only sensible person in my family.

"True," Willow said, but in such a way that I knew it wasn't.

That seemed weird to me, but I didn't know why or what to say about it, so I shut up. Kit had let me take her copy of *Pride and Prejudice*, so I pulled it out of my bag, thinking maybe I would actually reread it, which is when I saw that there was a name written in blue ink on the inside front cover, actually what looked like three names—first, middle, and last. The middle one, Oliver, was crossed out with just a line through it, like it had been a simple mistake, but the other two were scratched out in black ink, the way you scratch out an answer you don't want anyone to see. Even so, because it was felt tip over ballpoint, I could just make out that the first name was Kit. The last one was harder. Maybe something ending in *Y.*

Meanwhile, Steve was saying that he thought he remembered that there was a motel on a hill off the highway that was visible only when the leaves fell off the trees, so Willow went back into the store to ask for directions, and when she came back she was waving a card back and forth. Amazingly, the people who ran the store were related to the people who owned the motel. So Steve turned the car around and we drove off in search of it. That's how we ended up at the Tip-Top Motor Inn. And that is where I saw the car that I was pretty sure was the same car I'd seen the guy from the library driving when I was waiting for Steve to pick me up from work.

◆　◆　◆

The ladder is always there . . .

　　　　　　　　　　　　　　—ADRIENNE RICH

His name was Cyrus, which was old-fashioned, maybe a family name or a place name, though Kit didn't know where he came from or where he lived, because once she told him he needed a library card, he didn't fill out the paperwork that would have had that information. Instead he went back to the computer to try out different sequences of key words, as if they were numbers on a combination lock that would, with luck and the right twist, suddenly open and reveal what he was looking for.

"We've got a lot of resources for job hunters," Kit offered, looking over his shoulder when she was walking by his carrel later that afternoon. The words on the screen were "Riverton National Bank," "Riverton National Bank and Trust," and "unclaimed property."

"So I look like a job hunter?" he said, turning away from the screen. "That's . . ." He paused. ". . . interesting."

He was scowling. Was he scowling? Kit couldn't tell. His eyes—chocolate brown, she noticed—had a distinct glower, but it could have been a fake, like he was trying to make her think he was angry. People did that. He was drumming his fingers on the desk, like he was impatient, like he had something more pressing to be doing than waiting for Kit to explain herself. Definitely a fake.

"Sorry. I was assuming," Kit said. "But that's what most people your age do when they come to the library to use the computer." *Obsessively.* That's what she wanted to say—she wanted to acknowledge he had been using the computer obsessively—but Kit held herself back, knowing it would sound judgmental. It wasn't. It was a fact. It was true. Kit could hear Dr. Bondi, who seemed to have taken up residence in a corner of her head, explaining that the truth was not, despite popular opinion, objective. "Your truth and my truth are not necessarily the same thing, and yet neither is false. How's that for one of life's conundrums?" Even so, she knew she was right. "Obsessive" was the correct adjective, and she couldn't use it.

"And what age would that be?" Rusty asked.

"No idea," Kit said. Not true. He was wearing a polo shirt, khaki shorts, and loafers, no socks. She knew this look. It was all over the catalogs. It was the official look of the Grey Goose ads in the back of *The New Yorker*: stubble-faced male, luminous teeth, dressed in faux casual, chatting up an alluring, windswept woman as they leaned against an oceanfront bar (Hawaii? the Seychelles?), a bottle of vodka between them.

He smelled of something vaguely familiar. She took a deep breath. Couldn't place it.

"Guess," he said. Now he was smiling, egging her on.

"That's a dangerous game," she said. Was he flirting? As much as Kit could remember, it felt like flirting.

"I won't be offended. Give it a try." He had turned all the way in his chair now and was looking up at her and tapping his foot as well as his fingers. "I'm waiting."

"Twelve," Kit said. Now it came to her: he smelled of turmeric. Did turmeric smell? Maybe it was cumin. Yes, that's what it was. Cumin.

"Very funny."

He started tapping more quickly. Ring finger, middle finger, index finger. No wedding band. A player.

"Forty-five," she guessed. Forty-five, divorced, two children who lived with their mother, big alimony check every month.

He touched his hand to his forehead. "Oh God, have I aged that much?"

"Forty-five isn't so old," Kit said. "Or so they say. It's the new twenty-five, right?" Was she flirting? She checked herself. It felt so weird. Like her mouth was moving independently, saying whatever it wanted to say, ignoring her brain, which was waving a big red flag.

"So you're forty-five," he said.

"Not quite," she said. This, she figured, would put an end to it. Telling a man you were closer to fifty than to thirty was like putting on an invisibility cloak.

"Well, you look great for almost forty-five," he said—judiciously, she thought. A throwaway line: "You look great!" What men tended to say, though she never understood why that was okay. And now he'd be waiting for her to thank him.

When she didn't, when the silence between them extended a beat past comfortable, he tried again. "Better, apparently, than I do," he said, and laughed.

"Nice recovery," she said, running a hand through her hair, conscious for the first time in a long time of the coarse strands of gray that had begun to run riot. When she was younger, in college, and a single gray hair would appear out of nowhere, Cal would reach over and pull it out by the root and call her "my old lady," and they would both laugh, as if being old was an impossibility, like being black if you were white, or short if you were tall. And now she was old, or older certainly, and the gray was advancing like a sly and wily enemy, as time, and the scree it carried—down her face, along her neck—were advancing, too.

"Thirty-nine," he said as she made her way back to her desk. And: "You can call me Rusty."

Sunny was downstairs with the toddlers, a few people were browsing the stacks, and a few others had taken the chairs vacated by the Four and seemed to be napping. It was a scorching-hot day, and the library, built largely of granite, was one of the coolest places in town—and it had a public bathroom. Chuck wanted to charge people for the privilege—it was one of his moneymaking schemes—but all the women were opposed, even when he argued that they could put in a machine that would wrap the toilet seat in plastic, and a sanitizing hand dryer, and a chaise or daybed. Evelyn objected—everyone would be asking her to make change—and Barbara objected—"This is a library, not a homeless shelter"—but Kit was unsure. The library might not be a homeless shelter, but some days it felt to her like adult day care. She didn't mind. Everyone needed a place to go. Barbara would come back from Library Association meetings fired up about the "modern" library, but Kit sometimes wondered if the modern library wasn't one that was filled with machines and gadgets, but simply a place with comfortable chairs and a place to pee, especially in a city where the last diner had closed and the Dollar Tree had a big NO LOITERING sign in its window. "We should have a LOITERING ENCOURAGED sign out front," Kit proposed at a staff meeting, only to be met with groans from Evelyn and Chuck, and a "let's be serious" look tossed in her direction over the top of Barbara Goodspeed's reading glasses.

From Kit's desk she had a clear line of sight to Rusty's back, which was again hunched forward toward the computer screen, and the back of his head and his well-developed triceps, which escaped the banded cuff of his shirt. He had been flirting with her, she was sure of that. Some men couldn't help themselves. She could hear Bondi again: "Did you want him to flirt with you? Were you flirting with him?" Was she? He was the type who wore loafers without socks. In other words, someone she couldn't possibly like.

"You are wearing sandals without socks." Dr. Bondi's voice again.

"But sandals are supposed to be worn without socks," she said.

Bondi: "'Supposed to'? Is there a rule? What are you really saying?" Not "What are you saying?" but "What are you really saying? What's the not-so-hidden message?"

Kit thought about this. Was she really saying that by looking at a man's feet she could tell that he was a poseur, or arrogant, or disingenuous, or all of the above? She was.

"People make judgments like that all the time," she could hear herself saying to Dr. Bondi. "It's probably hardwired or something, so our ancestors could quickly assess if someone was friend or foe. Flight or fight. It was probably wise to err on the side of caution."

Dr. Bondi's voice: "And you're fine with this?" She could hear his skepticism and knew it was really her own skepticism. Kit smiled to herself. The good doctor had trained her well. And then, again, Bondi: "No, Kit, you trained yourself. This is you."

◆　◆　◆

### Sunny | spies

Cyrus is definitely in the unique name category, like Solstice. There's a book in the library called *One Thousand Names for Your Baby*, and if Solstice and Cyrus are in it, they've got to be at the bottom of the list. So we have that in common. Also, he's not from here. His car has New Jersey license plates. No one from here drives a convertible. It's too cold, though it's got to be cold in New Jersey, too. Like Willow says, people are mysterious. I still think he may be some kind of detective or private eye, but Kit says that's impossible, because what detective or private eye would have his bag monogrammed? She's got a point, though that could be a decoy. Maybe his name isn't Cyrus. Maybe he's carrying that bag to throw people off. Maybe he wants people to think that's his real name. Maybe he figured that if someone saw those initials on such an expensive bag they'd never question his pseudonym, because who would spend that much money if C.I.A. weren't his real initials? Kit did tell me that L.L.Bean sells lots of monogrammed items that people have returned, and if you don't mind wearing a shirt or a bathrobe with someone else's initials, you can get them really cheap. Steve, for once, thinks I may be onto something. He says I need to steer clear of the guy.

◆　◆　◆

Between the worker and the millionaire / Number provides all distances . . .

—DELMORE SCHWARTZ

Cyrus Ingram Allen arrived in Riverton on June 24 at 4:38 in the afternoon after a five-and-a-half-hour drive from Hoboken. It was a sweltering day, and he drove with the top of his Mercedes CLK350 down and the wind wrestling with the sun to keep him temperate and in a better mood than he should have been in. It had been a rough nineteen months as all the pieces of his well-constructed life had fallen over in quick succession like a stack of dominoes: the financial crisis knocking over the job at the boutique investment firm; knocking over the expense account; knocking over the weekends in Cabo, the nights-to-days at Tenjune, the bottle service at the Marquee, the gorgeous women who seemed to materialize by his side and disappear when he tired of them; knocking over the Hamptons summer share; knocking over the retirement account (uninsured; insurance was for pussies who didn't understand the relationship between risk and yield); knocking over the Jersey condo with its unadulterated view of the Manhattan skyline. Gone, all of it gone, but not the car. At least he had paid cash. Walked into the showroom on Eleventh Avenue, pointed to the steel-gray cabriolet with the pillarless rear windows and AMG wheels, and said, "I'll take one of those," as if he were ordering a hamburger at McDonald's. An hour later he was on the West Side Highway, driving up to Westchester on the Saw Mill, playing with the acceleration.

"What's with you guys?" the state trooper said when he pulled him over. But the officer got it, he was a guy, too, and let him off with a warning—not that Rusty heeded it. The car was just too fast and too responsive to treat like some elderly relative with a faulty ticker. So the car survived, even after he had to give up the spot in the parking garage that cost as much as a family in Newark spent on rent, which was either a lot or a little, depending on how you looked at it, but either way was, eventually, moot. And worry as he did at first that the car would be a target out on the street, it turned out to be just one in a line of Audis, BMWs, a Jaguar, a Porsche, and other Mercedes hugging the curb. All these cars like his, no longer under protective cover, which was as clear a sign of the times as the FOR RENT sign on the Gentlemen's Barber Club, where guys had been happy to leave a fifty-dollar tip for a fifty-dollar shave and shiatsu.

He had his car, and in the trunk were the last remnants of the life he had been leading—two suitcases and a duffel (Fendi, matching)—and that was that. He was thirty-nine and shedding everything that had made him feel successful, which were the same things that made him feel, more recently, like a failure. He was on the road. The car radio no longer worked, and he could never hear it anyway with the top down, but he had his iPhone (reduced to iPod status now that he had canceled his data contract) and a pair of headphones, and why not listen to the Red Hot Chili Peppers and Nicki Minaj full bore, drilling into his brain and filling it with voices other than his own?

He still had some money, what a few years ago he might have blown on a quick trip from the L.A. office to the Beverly Hills Hotel to play poker. Rich people, potential clients, trusted you more if you were willing to lose large sums playing games with them, so wagering mid-five figures wasn't gambling, it was business. But what had been Monopoly money before was real to him now. He had taken accounting, knew all about cash flow to assets, but when money was pouring down like a Niagara, the balance sheet was beside the point. You could drown in money, and that would be a stupid way to die. That's what they told one another, sitting in the steam room, sitting in the sauna, sitting at the bar. The operative equation was simple: money in, money out. That was the measure of success. Was he happy? Was that even a real question?

And he had done it: He had left Duluth, gone to the university, done the internships, skipped the MBA, gotten the job with Morris, Maines on adrenaline and sheer determination, the same adrenaline and determination that put him in line for partner. He was successful. Didn't his mother drum into him that happiness and success were the same thing? Lucky she was gone (six years already) before that rush of money ran dry and the only things accumulating around him were rejections from firms where he'd hoped to make a lateral move and past due notices from a lifestyle that seemed increasingly out of reach, as if it were a kite that had been enormous and pretty on the ground, but was only a speck in the sky now, its string unspooled, and soon would be out of sight. The guys he had worked with had disappeared, too. One to teach math at a private boys' school—"Brutal," he called it, but it was a job—a couple to the Dubai International Financial Centre where money, apparently, was still flowing, though in dirhams, and a bunch to AA and NA and sometimes both. They no longer kept in touch. What was the point?

In the beginning, and for months after that, Rusty approached unemployment the way he'd approached employment, throwing himself at it with the same will to win that had powered Lance Armstrong up the Alpes d'Huez all those years, despite the cancer, despite the crashes. That's how he saw himself: like Lance, a winner against all odds. He'd get up early, go to the gym, and work out hard with his trainer when he still had a trainer, then approach his day as if it were a mountain he had to attack. Squats, dead lifts, footwork drills, again and again, until the sweat would overrun his headband and drip onto his cheeks and puddle on the floor. "Bring it!" he'd say to the punching bag as it sprang back at him. And: "Motherfucker!" It felt good. No, it felt great. Other people meditated or visualized success. He had seen success. He knew what it looked like. It looked like the guy at the top of the podium. He'd finish his workout, shower, put on a suit, and step into the river of commuters heading into Manhattan. He could tell, now, the ones with multiple copies of their CVs in their briefcases: the ones who didn't have jobs. He could smell their defeat. The train car reeked of it. He started to drive instead, so that the odor was not clinging to his clothes when he sat in those windowless interview rooms, upbeat, confident, praying.

When he wasn't getting any more callbacks, Rusty

rewrote his résumé, pretending to have less experience than he had, as if HR departments all over the city hadn't seen that trick before. If they were hiring at all, they were looking for young guys and he, Rusty was surprised to find out, was no longer considered one of the young guys.

It occurred to him that maybe Lance really was doping and that the system was rigged. That was a low day. He'd already given up the trainer, and given up cold calling firms angling for an interview, and given up, most days, driving the four miles into Manhattan, where everything cost more than it did in Jersey. He'd always known that, but now it mattered. He started living off his closet, getting sixty cents to the dollar for his Hugo Boss and Tom Ford suits, selling his custom Serotta road bike (not that he ever rode it), parting with his prized Mizuno golf clubs.

And then, one morning, digging around in his underwear drawer, thinking he might discover a stray fifty buried under the mountain of dress socks he had little use for, he found instead an old bankbook in his mother's name that he vaguely remembered tossing in there after she died, because its single $5,000 deposit, made into a bank he'd never heard of, was too inconsequential to deal with when dollars were raining down from a cloudless sky. But now—*now*, actually looking at it and seeing that that single deposit was made in 1950—it was like finding a winning lottery ticket that he hadn't remembered buying: $5,000 compounded over sixty years! He did the math, over and over, in the shower, eating breakfast, pacing his apartment. It was astonishing! $5,000 over sixty years at 5 percent was $93,395.93, and that was if it was compounded only once a year. Compounded quarterly, the amount was closer to $100,000, which was brilliant. At 8 percent, compounded annually, that $5,000 would have grown to half a million dollars—$506,285.32 to be precise. He wrote that number down, checked his calculator, ran it again, and that number appeared once more: $506,285.32. In theory he was supposed to split all assets with his sister, but she had disappeared long ago, following a yogi to India, where she renounced all worldly possessions by handing them over to him. This money, potential as it was, was his. All he had to do was retrieve it.

◆ ◆ ◆

History has to live with what was here . . .
—ROBERT LOWELL

Unclaimed money was typically turned over to the state, Rusty knew, but which state? There were Rivertons in Missouri, New York, New Jersey, Connecticut,

Utah, Pennsylvania, and Wyoming. Rusty sat in front of his laptop for days, waiting impatiently for Google to lead him down and through and out one rabbit hole and into another. It felt good to be working again, to be sitting in the glow of the computer screen long after the sun had gone down, drinking cowboy coffee—the Keurig and the espresso machines were long gone—reading about places that might exist to bring him good fortune. After five days he narrowed the list down to four states, and after seven days, he'd whittled it down to two: Kansas and New Hampshire. Kansas because Rusty could find so little about the Riverton there, and New Hampshire because its Riverton had once been a big-deal industrial hub, a big enough deal, he figured, to boast a national bank. Yes, he decided, that had to be it. Riverton, New Hampshire. His Riverton.

How his mother had come into possession of a bankbook from there, Rusty had no idea. As far as he knew, his mother had never set foot in the Granite State. Still, his mother was inscrutable, as many parents are, but she possibly more than most. Rusty was in his teens when she mentioned she'd been adopted, news that meant little to him at the time. He asked the basic questions and got the basic answers: it had been a country-club adoption—a girl got "in trouble," was sent away, and a deal was made through a lawyer or a judge to hand over the baby to the adoptive parents as soon as it was born. Easy. No traceable records. The girl would return home before a year was out and resume whatever life she'd been living. There was a birth certificate, his mother said, issued by a hospital in upstate New York, but that wasn't much of a clue: there were homes for unwed mothers tucked in out-of-the-way places all over the country, and once the adoption had gone through, the birth mother's name would be expunged. Someone with more imagination than his mother might have made some inquiries, but Ruth Allen, née Ingram, chose to let it be. She had two perfectly acceptable parents who would have been stung if she stirred up that hornet's nest.

Rusty took a beer from the fridge, popped it open, and put his feet on the dining room table (cherry, Thos. Moser; the new tenants were buying it at cost), satisfied with his detective work. Riverton, New Hampshire. He leaned back in his chair, and because there was no one there to high-five, slapped the table once, hard, so hard his hand stung, and that felt good, too. He was smiling—he hadn't smiled this broadly in he couldn't remember how long. It was a little kid on Christmas morning kind of smile, a dizzy drunk kind of smile, only he wasn't drunk, not on alcohol. Rusty lowered his computer into his lap and began typing, navigating to the abandoned property website, eager to file for the jackpot he was imagining on the other side of the screen. Free money—what could be better? Two lines in, though, he was brought up short. To make the claim he'd need a permanent address and soon he wouldn't have one.

"Damn," he said, and decided, right then, that the only sensible thing to do would be to get in his car and go to Riverton. It had to be cheaper there than New York or New Jersey—what wasn't?—and he could file from there. That was his plan: No plan.

**Did Riverton** have a high season? Rusty wondered as he made his way through the worst of Connecticut: Bridgeport, then New Haven. From what he could tell, Riverton was like these, a worn-out industrial city that had shown so much promise a century ago, and then, almost without warning, became a has-been. "Like me," Rusty thought, but not unhappily. It was a gorgeous day, he was driving in a car that fit him like a bespoke suit, and he was free in the way Janis Joplin had wailed about freedom. Back when he carried the American Express black card and the suit guys at Barneys knew his name, the idea that freedom meant nothing left to lose struck him as complete hippie crap. He liked his life. He liked his stuff. Freedom was not having to worry about any of it since it was all fungible. Freedom was being able to put an Aeron Task chair out on the street because an Eames Executive was more comfortable. But today, going 82 in a 65 mph zone up Interstate 95, he got it. His closet was empty and it wasn't even his closet anymore. He was unencumbered. He was free.

**At 4:38** when Rusty Allen pulled into Riverton, the streets were largely empty and the river was giving off an unappealing brownish glow, and the only building that suggested a more prosperous past was the library anchoring the town green. Rusty drove by, making note to go there once he was more settled—settled meaning finding an inexpensive place to rest his head and figure out his next move. He knew there were a couple of bed-and-breakfasts outside of the city, but the last thing he wanted was having to chat with retirees who were crossing New England off their bucket list as their host shoveled pancakes and homemade jam onto their plates. No thank you to that.

Eventually, after driving around for the better part of an hour, rounding the city in ever-wider circles, he came upon the Tip-Top Motor Inn, a mom-and-pop motel up on a hill with a sign outside advertising COLOR TV and only two cars in the parking lot. The mom and pop in question were a youngish Indian couple who had left an older relative in charge while they ran a string of convenience stores not far from the highway. The older relative, a man named Mr. Patel, was heating curry on a hot plate in the office, and the smell permeated the small reception area where Rusty was trying to negotiate a good rate.

"You have a Mercedes, I can see," Mr. Patel said, pushing back. Rusty tried a few more entreaties but Mr. Patel was having none of it. "Two-fifty for the week, two hundred for four days, one hundred a night otherwise."

"I'm here," Rusty began, making sure to lower his eyes and his voice, "because my mother died."

"Ah, I see," Mr. Patel said, and gave him the room for $50 a night or $200 for the week.

"Thank you so much," Rusty said. "And tell me, is there somewhere nearby where I can get such a good-smelling curry?"

"I will ask my wife," Mr. Patel said, handing over a key attached to a wooden block with the number 7 written on it in blue ballpoint, mostly faded.

Room 7, inexplicably two doors down from reception, was clean enough but musty. It might have been months since someone occupied it. Rusty was just opening a window when there was a knock at the door and a small Indian woman stood there holding a plate of curry and some silverware.

"Wow!" Rusty said. "Room service! This is amazing. Unexpected. I meant was there an Indian restaurant in town."

The woman—Mrs. Patel—walked past him and into the room and set the plate on the dresser. "Not in bed," she said, and gave him an imposing look.

"Of course," he said, though just that second he'd been imagining sitting up in bed, eating curry and watching baseball on the color TV. "How much do I owe you?"

"Mr. Patel," she said, which he took to mean he'd have to settle with her husband.

"It is very good, yes," Mr. Patel said, when Rusty saw him the next morning. It was a statement, not a question.

"Very good," Rusty said, and was about to describe the vindaloo he'd had at Veeraswamy in London but then thought better of it—the man might raise his rates. "How much do I owe you?"

"Five dollars," Mr. Patel said, "but not last night. Last night you were our guest. Tonight, five dollars."

And so it was settled that as long as Rusty was staying at the Tip-Top, he'd be eating what the Patels were eating.

Riverton, he decided—though he wasn't sure he was actually in Riverton anymore—wasn't half bad.

◆　◆　◆

## Sunny | steering clear

It's hard to steer clear of someone when the library is basically empty and he's the only one who needs help and you find him intriguing because he's not like anyone you've ever met before. The help he needed was a simple computer reboot—we've got old Dell Dimensions that are constantly running into trouble—and also for me to put more paper in the printer. Theoretically we're supposed to charge ten cents a page, but no one ever remembers to collect it, which may be why the library is running out of money. Barbara says that if the printer money went straight into the employee coffee machine, everyone would remember. It doesn't, and I still wouldn't, since I don't drink coffee.

Because I was helping Rusty with the printer, I got to see what he was printing, and it didn't make much sense. It was stuff about the history of Riverton, even though we have a whole shelf of books about the city. I like the books of photographs best, especially the pictures of mill workers, who are mostly girls my age sitting at weaving machines, row after row of them. When I told Rusty he could take the books out instead of copying them, he said that he'd need a library card to do that and that he'd been staying at the Tip-Top Motor Inn (which of course I knew), and he didn't think a motel would qualify as a permanent address like the library required and he wasn't sure if the Tip-Top was even in Riverton anyway.

"I don't think my post office box qualifies, either," he said. And I said something like, "Not unless you can sleep in it," and he laughed and said that his room at the Tip-Top wasn't much bigger.

He seemed a little lonely, like he just need to talk to someone, about something, about anything. That's the only reason I could think of why he'd want to talk to me, and ask questions about my job, which I had to tell him wasn't a real job, it was what I was doing because I'd stolen a book from the bookstore, and when I told him which book, he laughed so loudly that Evelyn shushed him from the other room. He asked me about my school, so I told him about no-schooling, and he asked me what my passion was, and when I said stories and writing, he said, "That's good, too small to fail," and laughed again and it hurt my feelings, and I decided that Steve was right and I should've steered clear of Rusty and I started to walk away. "Hey! It was an inside joke and the joke is on me. Really." And he started to say something about the financial industry, and about how everyone said the banks were too big to fail, and about how there was all this human collateral and wasn't that failure, and then he apologized again, calling out, "Sorry!" as I was going down the stairs, so loudly that Evelyn shushed him again.

◆　◆　◆

Everybody has roots.
　　　　　　　　　　—WILLIAM CARLOS WILLIAMS

When you work in a library, you see all sorts of people; Kit had never seen anyone like Rusty Allen. He made no sense. He wore expensive clothes, but could use a decent haircut. He should have been at work or looking for work—"should" being a judgmental word, she knew, but what thirty-nine-year-old hung out at the library for much of the day?—but instead seemed to be researching Riverton history, but taking no notes. He had started out keeping to himself, but now he was friendly, almost overly so. He appeared to belong to no one—a stray dog, just like her.

It was hard not to think about him when he seemed always to be in her line of sight. She found herself watching Rusty, observing him surreptitiously as if he were a deer in the forest she was tracking from her tree stand—and didn't know why. And then she'd get up from her desk and he'd nod as she went by; she'd walk back and he'd stop her with a question about anything and she would linger for a minute and then claim she had to get back to work, even when he was the only patron in the room.

"What happened to the Riverton National Bank?" he asked one day, explaining that it showed up in old telephone books and in old photographs, but seemed to have dematerialized.

"I use TD Bank North," she said, and then wondered why she'd told him something both personal and beside the point, and rushed back to her desk.

"You need to talk to the Four," Kit told him later, and explained that if he came in the morning he'd find Patrick, the Richards, and Carl. "Patrick delivered all the babies of Riverton for the better part of fifty years, Carl cut their hair, and one of the Richards drove them around when they couldn't drive themselves. The other Rich is a business guy. The two Riches are cousins but they look like brothers. I think they had the same grandfather. You can tell them apart because Rich the taxi driver only wears Hawaiian shirts. He says that Hawaii is a state of mind. You'll like them."

Whether they would like Rusty, she thought, was

another matter altogether. She imagined they'd be put off by his trendy clothes and city manners, but the next morning, there he was, in khaki pants and a sky-blue polo shirt, sitting among them, chatting away.

"Your parents named you Rusty? Did you have red hair or were you the squeaky wheel?" Carl asked, and then laughed at his own joke.

"No. Rusty's what they called me. My given name is Cyrus. Cyrus Allen. Cyrus Ingram Allen. Ingram was my mother's maiden name." And then, for clarity: "She was adopted."

"Where are your people from?" This was Patrick. Tall and bony, with a full head of waxy white hair and milky blue eyes, he liked to start at the beginning.

"Minnesota. I guess. If you don't count my mother's biological parents."

The Four considered this for a minute or two.

"You used to do that, too, didn't you, Paddy?" Hawaiian shirt Rich said to Patrick.

"Do what?" he said.

"You know, help girls who had gotten into trouble."

"Doctor-patient confidentiality," Patrick said. "But between us, yes. More times than you'd imagine."

"I think it worked out okay for my mother," Rusty said.

"Maybe so," the doctor said. "Maybe so. But tell us, young squire, why have you come to our fair city?"

Rusty cleared his throat. "Long version or short version?" And before anyone could answer, he said, "Actually, they are the same: I lost my job. My firm went out of business and I lost my job."

"Two and a half million people lost their jobs," Rich the former executive said, "but they didn't come to Riverton."

"True enough," Rusty said.

Kit was leaning forward toward her desk, pretending to read the paper, but listening carefully to what Rusty was saying and, more than that, how he was saying it. He was a charmer, that's for sure—able to sit with a bunch of crusty old-timers he'd never met before and fit right in. It probably helped in his business, Kit thought, being able to insinuate himself among strangers until they no longer thought of him as anything other than a buddy. Better to invest with a buddy than someone you didn't know. Your buddy will take care of you. He was genial, likable, and appropriately deferential. He was also, Kit noticed, wearing socks.

"Where did you say you were born?" Patrick was saying. His memory was beginning to dull, and he sometimes asked the same question more than once or failed to make connections that were obvious to everyone else.

"Paddy was our town baby doc," Carl explained. "The next thing you know, he'll want to know who pulled you out of your mommy."

Rusty laughed. (Genuinely, Kit noted.) "Near Duluth," he said.

"Why?" This was Rich the executive. "It's so cold there. Makes Riverton seem like Florida."

"Or at least, you know, Rhode Island," Carl said.

"My father was a steelworker," Rusty said. "He worked for U.S. Steel until U.S. Steel pulled out of Duluth, and then he worked at the port unloading ships. Duluth is right on Lake Superior, that's why it can get so bitter. The wind coming off the lake." He nodded at Rich the executive. "Good hockey, though."

"That's hard work. Steelworker. Dockworker," Carl said, as if he knew this from experience. The others nodded in agreement.

"It was," Rusty said, and stopped and rubbed his hands together as if he were cold. He lowered his gaze, stared at his feet. "He was crushed in a crane accident."

"Sheesh," Carl said.

The others looked away. Even Kit, who had been acting as if she wasn't in on the conversation, bowed her head. It was a reflex, like tapping a knee and watching the leg kick up: say someone had died, but especially say that he had been killed, and people turned away. She should know. So they shared that: a dead father, his life extinguished, and with it the simple assumptions of family life.

"How old?" one of the Riches asked after a while. Kit didn't know which. She wasn't looking. They often sounded alike.

"He was thirty-eight. Younger than I am now," Rusty said. "I was eleven. Sixth grade."

"That's rough," that same Rich said.

"It was bad," Rusty said, "but the company gave my mother some money, I guess so she wouldn't sue, and set up a college fund for us, and the longshoremen had a fund, and the weird thing was that we had more money after he died than we had when my dad was alive—so that when all my friends started working off the books at fourteen, I didn't have to. My mother wanted my life to be easier than my father's. She told me that if I didn't go to college—my father didn't go to college—and get a desk job she would consider herself, and me, a failure. The happiest day of her life was when I got offered the job at Morris, Maines. It didn't matter what I was doing there, just that I carried a briefcase, wore a suit, and sat at a desk. People who sit at desks don't get crushed by cranes."

Rusty stopped to catch his breath. The Four were all looking at him now. Kit was looking at him. He was rubbing his hands on his knees as if he were trying to erase a stain.

"But then a different kind of crane fell out of the sky and landed on me and a lot of other people sitting at their desks. And here I am."

# Chapter Six
## 7.12.10 – 7.18.10

**Sunny | winter**

We stayed at #3 till after the first couple of snowfalls. My foot had healed, though it would ache when rain clouds, and then snow clouds, settled over us. The first snow came early, at the beginning of September. I wouldn't have known it was early—I'd never lived there before—but I heard Willow talking to Steve about it, and she said that if it was already snowing in September we might be able to stay there only another month. And then where would we go? That question was on my mind, but I knew better than to ask. Steve said that the September snow was a freak thing and that it would get warm again soon—Indian summer, he called it—and it turned out he was right. The snow was gone within hours, and by the next week we were back to wearing shorts and Willow didn't bring up leaving again, at least not when I could hear. (I'd sometimes pretend to be asleep so I could listen to my parents talking, since it was the only way I'd find out what was really going on.)

When I think about it now, I realize that I had no idea then what was really going on, and I still don't really know. The whole thing was like a dream. At night Willow would read *The Swiss Family Robinson*, about another family on a wilderness adventure, and sometimes as I was falling asleep I'd imagine we were shipwrecked, too, and chased by pirates, and then feel relieved when I woke up and there were no pirates and we weren't on an island, even if it often felt like we were, and our car wasn't too far away. Steve would drive it sometimes and come back with food, only we didn't call it food, we called what he'd bring back "provisions." We must not have been vegans then because he'd usually return with chocolate, graham crackers, and marshmallows so we could make s'mores. Willow was not thrilled with me getting so much sugar, but Steve (I heard him talking one night) said it was important that I have good associations with our time in the woods. And I do when I think of searching for green sticks, being trusted to use a camp knife to peel back the bark, and standing over glowing coals roasting marshmallows, waiting for the inside to melt and the skin to separate and turn the perfect shade of brown. And not to catch on fire, and not to fall into the fire.

The second snow was a bigger deal. It started before we woke up, and by the time Steve went out to put more wood on the fire so he and Willow could have their coffee, the fire pit was blanketed. Steve came back into the tent and told us that the best thing to do would be to go back to sleep, but none of us could do that because the wind had started to howl—we could hear it coming down the lake—and the walls of the tent were shaking.

"This is fun," Willow kept saying. "Isn't it fun?"

I thought it was fun, but then I got hungry, and since there was a "no eating in the tent" rule, was pretty certain I was going to starve to death, which got me crying. Willow said I was crying because my blood sugar had dropped so much and that Steve needed to get our provisions down from the tree, which made him grumpy, which Willow said was also because of his blood sugar dropping, but Steve said it was because his boots were back in the car and he only had sandals. He went out anyway, and we could hear him swearing in the distance.

Willow was afraid to leave me alone in the tent, and she was afraid to leave Steve out by himself in the blizzard, and she kept saying "I don't know what to do" over and over, which is not the best thing to say when you're with a child who is scared out of her wits. Eventually she went into the vestibule and unzipped the door and stuck her head out just in time to see Steve running back, clutching the bear bag.

"I was worried about—" Willow said, and before she could finish the sentence Steve told her that the wind had knocked down the branch supporting the bag and carried it into the underbrush and it took him a while to find it. He was shivering. His toes were white. He stripped down and got under the covers and Willow stripped down, too, and covered her body with his.

"This is what you do, Sunny, if someone gets really cold," Willow said.

"Yeah," Steve said after a while. I could tell his hands were gripping Willow's rear end. "First aid."

"I'm hungry," I said, and before they could stop me I'd opened the bag and taken out a jar of peanut butter and buried my first two fingers past the knuckle. "Peanut butter lollipop," I said, pulling them out and jamming them in my mouth.

"Let me have some of that," Steve said, and plunged his hand into the jar. But instead of putting the peanut butter into his mouth, he put his fingers into Willow's and said, "Lick," and laughed.

"That's disgusting," I said, and he laughed some more.

"Someday, my peanut butter lollipop, you will not think so."

I can say for sure that that day has not arrived.

◆ ◆ ◆

**Sunny | out of the wilderness**

I don't know what month we left #3, only that Steve didn't want to go and Willow did, and they talked about it a lot, especially when they thought I wasn't listening or couldn't hear. Steve said that things would get more complicated when we were "back on the grid," which to my ears sounded like "back on the griddle," but when I asked what a griddle was, Willow said it was a kind of pan to cook with, which made no sense. Willow said staying in the woods was no longer sustainable, which sounded like "stainable," which also made no sense. It was a confusing time for me, and both of my parents were preoccupied and didn't notice when I went down to the lake one morning, saw that it had skimmed over with ice, and decided to go skating. I didn't have skates, of course—I was wearing my puddle boots. I tested the edge with my toe and the ice seemed strong enough, so I stepped out and took two, then three, then four steps, and without warning I had fallen through. The water wasn't deep yet, but it was cold and my boots were filling with water and I couldn't move more than an inch, even though I was flapping my arms, trying to swim. Luckily, my parents had stopped talking (which is to say arguing) long enough to hear me call for help and they were there in a minute, Steve fishing me out and running us up to the tent with Willow shouting "You're okay!" between taking deep, noisy, theoretically relaxing breaths that sounded like she was pumping up a tire. They stripped off my soaking wet clothes, wrapped me in a blanket, and sat me downwind from the fire pit, where the morning coffee was heating.

"Here, drink this," Steve said, pouring me my first taste of coffee. Disgusting. If my teeth weren't chattering, I would have spit it out.

Not long afterward, we left #3. Steve pulled our food down from the tree where he'd re-roped it after the second storm, Willow folded our bedding and set it on the picnic table, we gathered our clothes and put them on the table, too, and before long the tent was empty and I got to go around the perimeter and pull up the stakes. Then Steve and Willow removed the tent poles and the whole thing started to deflate and then collapse like a balloon that had lost its air, and it was my job to roll it up and stuff it into its sack. I don't know how many trips we made to the Subaru, but eventually the campsite was empty and Steve was raking it over with his feet because he said that the first rule of the woods was "to leave no trace." I asked him if that's why we didn't sign in when we first got to #3 and if that's why we weren't signing out, and he said, "Sort of."

We spent that night in a motel. In a real bed. And got to take a real bath. And the bathwater was filthy, because ever since it had turned cold Willow had been heating up water and giving me sponge baths, which I hated because even though the water was warm, I was always freezing, standing there as she wiped me down. It felt delicious to be clean—"delicious" was the word that Willow used, and once she did I knew exactly what she meant—and delicious to slide between the clean sheets and put my head on a real pillow. Steve slept on the floor. He said that after months at #3, the bed was "too plush." Willow said, "Suit yourself," and got into bed with me.

❖　❖　❖

Fortune and men's eyes . . .
　　　　　　　　—WILLIAM SHAKESPEARE

The Four had a lot of questions for Rusty, and he had a lot of questions for them, so he started to come to the library in the morning with his own refill mug, springing for doughnuts now and then. The guys wanted to know about Wall Street—was it as crazy as they said on the news?—and Rusty told them stories that made their eyes open wide and their jaws drop, stories where the protagonist, always, was money.

"How much did you say again you spent on a tie?" Carl wanted to know. He had already asked this question about Rusty's shirts, his shoes, even his underwear. "Two hundred dollars for a piece of fabric that hangs around your collar like a leash? Jeez. You make me feel rich," Carl said. "I never wore a tie to work in fifty years I had the shop. That's like a thousand dollars a year. That's fifty thousand bucks in my pocket."

"You could've spent it on scratch tickets and gotten some of it back," said Rich the driver.

"That's rich, Rich," said Rich the former executive. "That's wacky math."

"It's better than a noose around your neck," Carl said.

For his part, Rusty wanted to know about Riverton: what it had been like before all the industrial buildings along the water's edge were vacant and boarded up, but none of them could really say.

"We're old, but we're not that old," Patrick said. "My grandfather, when he was fourteen, was pulled off the boat coming in from Cork and sent up here with a ticket for a room at a boardinghouse and guaranteed mill job, and you can bet he took it. The place was thriving then. There weren't enough workers for all the jobs. But it didn't last. It's like your thing, down in New York. These things never do."

"And yet your families stayed and then you stayed," Rusty said.

"Yup," said Rich the driver. "We stayed to fight another day. We're like the last remaining soldiers."

"Yeah," Carl said. "We're like that Japanese officer they found defending his post years after the war was over. No one's convinced us that the war is really over. But you still haven't told us why you've come into our bunker."

"That's easy," Rusty said. "To seek my fortune."

Heard melodies are sweet, but those unheard /
Are sweeter . . .

—JOHN KEATS

Three weeks into his new life, Rusty woke up one morning as the sun was dribbling through the drapes at the Tip-Top and was startled to realize something: he was happy. This was unexpected, and it made him laugh out loud as he stood under the weak stream of tepid water in the permanently rust-stained shower of room 7. It seemed impossible: here he was, out of work, living in a run-down motel room that looked over a run-down city where, until recently, he didn't know a soul. The old Rusty, looking at the new Rusty, would have seen a loser, but the new Rusty didn't care. That was the beauty of it. He didn't care. He just didn't care. On the other hand, if someone waved a magic wand and he could go back to where he was and what he'd had, he was pretty sure he would not resist. He hadn't completely lost it.

He still had a bunch of résumés circulating out there, and sometimes, when he thought about them, the image that came to mind was flotsam floating on the vast ocean, like those islands of discarded plastic out in the Pacific he'd been hearing about, though other times he imagined they were like the satellites he saw overhead at night, orbiting the globe in perfect, endless, oblique circles. It had been a long time since he asked himself what he wanted to do with his life, and when he thought about it now—which he did as little as possible—he realized that there wasn't a whole lot that he could do. Experience—fifteen years in the trenches—was his only credential, but fifteen years doing what? He could hardly remember. And the industry was shot to hell anyway.

He loved that—the way they congratulated themselves by calling it an industry, as if they were actually producing something and not just moving numbers from one column on a spreadsheet to another and calling it a day.

What should he do? Rusty no longer knew. What was that book everyone on the train seemed to be reading a few years ago—*Don't Sweat the Small Stuff*? Why not take it a step further, he thought, and not sweat the big stuff, either? He was happy now when he wasn't supposed to be, and wasn't sure he'd been happy before, when he was. He liked where he was—nowhere. He liked the old guys at the library. He liked the librarian Kit, and he liked her sidekick Sunny, too. Kit was cool, like there was a breeze coming off her, and after his brief torrid affairs of the last few years, if they could even be called affairs, it was refreshing to meet a woman who was indifferent to his charms. It occurred to him that this might have something to do with his reduced circumstances, but the more he observed her, the more he was certain that his reduced circumstances would have been the thing she found attractive about him, if she found anything attractive about him, which apparently she did not. In a way, it was a relief. In his experience, romance was always a transaction, you had to pay to play, and his wallet was too thin for that.

———————

**"You must** be the first person to come to Riverton to seek his fortune!" the old-timer, Carl, said when Rusty admitted why he'd come there.

"Not true," said Rich the former executive, who was the group's unofficial historian. "Albert Robers came here a hundred and sixty years ago, down from Montreal, and built the first mill, and then the second mill, and then the third mill, and then he got people coming off the boats in Boston and New York and lured them up here with all sorts of promises of a better life. Soon enough those mills were jam-packed with eager workers, and then he built the denim mill and the calico mill, and the girls came, and within thirty years the whole town was filled to the brim with people seeking their fortune. That's what this place was, a city built on promises."

"True enough," said Patrick. "Of course, we all know what happened next. What the Lord giveth, the Lord taketh away."

"He means that the mills all closed and the jobs disappeared," Carl explained. "And it wasn't like the streets of Riverton were paved with gold anyway," he added.

"And now they're barely paved at all," Rich the former taxi driver said. "And I should know."

They all laughed, even Kit, sitting at her desk, pretending not to be listening.

"But you know," Carl said, "you've got to hand it to Robers. He's the guy who negotiated the deal with Carnegie and put up the rest of the money for this library. Look it up. When it was first built it was the Robers Library, but everyone called it the Robbers Library. Which tells you something about how people felt about him. The Robbers Library. Took his name off the building about three seconds after he died."

"The Robbers Library," Rusty said. "I like it. Makes this place sound so dangerous."

"We are dangerous men, Rusty," Carl said. "Best that you know that now. And women," he added, nodding in Kit's direction, and they all laughed.

"Last time I checked, this was still a library," Kit said, mostly to herself. The place was largely deserted. The Matz Brothers Circus had set up its big tent for two days on the edge of town and everyone who wasn't in the library seemed to be there.

"Why are you all laughing? I can hear you," Evelyn called out.

"Carl's telling Rusty we are dangerous men," Rich the driver yelled back.

"Now that is good for a laugh," Evelyn said, her voice carrying through the building. "You want to see dangerous men, Rusty, spend some time down at the station house with Jeffrey and Jack."

"Yeah, do that and you'll want to get in that fancy car of yours and hightail it back to New York City," Carl said, but softly enough that Evelyn didn't hear.

◆　◆　◆

### Sunny | circus

The first and only time I got to go to the circus was right before that night we left our apartment in Pennsylvania and moved to campsite #3, back when Steve was still in touch with his parents, before he cut off all communication with them and with all the other members of what he likes to call his "incidental family," as opposed to our "intentional family," which includes me and Willow, of course, and Rocco and Amelia and Bluebird (but probably not his girlfriend, Chandra, or her kids), and some other people we know from homeschooling/no-schooling and the Rainbow Gathering. Back then, my grandparents were visiting from Virginia, which they did two or three times a year, which was always fun because they would take me to Toys "R" Us and let me pick out something, which was nothing Steve or Willow would ever let me do because . . . plastic. They'd never take me to a circus, either, they explained, loudly, to Steve's parents when we got back from our adventure and my fingers and face were sticky from cotton candy. Willow thinks sugar is poison for children, but that's not why she and Steve were angry. The Cole Brothers' big top was in the Toys "R" Us parking lot, so it was inevitable that I'd beg my grandparents to take me inside, but Steve said they should have known he and Willow wouldn't approve. I remember Grandpa Joe saying something about how they were depriving me of a normal childhood, and Steve went ballistic and Willow was trying to calm him down, and Nana was crying and Grandpa Joe was completely silent. That's what I remember most: Grandpa Joe's silence. That must be how memory works: things that stand out get remembered even if they weren't the most important thing, and when you remember those things, other things get remembered, too, though I picked up a book at the library called *False Memory*, about people being tricked into remembering things that didn't happen. But this did happen for sure: my grandparents took me to the circus, and I saw elephants that could balance on their front legs doing handstands, and I thought it was the best thing ever, and my parents thought it was the worst. "Think about those animals, Sunny," they said to me after my grandparents had packed their things and left. "Elephants are supposed to walk on all fours and live in the jungle, not in some cage. Think about that elephant and how sad her life must be," and I went to bed in tears, and it was right after that that we moved.

Steve and Willow must not have told anyone where we were—though it's not like at #3 we had a real address—because I didn't get a birthday card from anyone that year, even my grandparents, and we didn't see Grandpa Joe again until his funeral, when I was eleven. Steve didn't want to go, but Willow said it would bring him closure, so we drove down for the service, and Steve's sisters were there, my aunts who are older and live in Germany because they are married to army officers. It was a military funeral, with an official twenty-one-gun salute and horses pulling the casket, and when they were ready to lower it into the ground, one of the soldiers gave a folded-up flag to Nana. The flag was too heavy for Nana to hold, and it got passed to Steve, who had to cradle it in his arms like a baby throughout the rest of the service, which Steve said was Grandpa Joe's final "F you" to him and our alternative lifestyle. This was when we were in the car, driving away. "It's all in the rearview mirror now," Willow said, and Steve said, "Yeah," and I said, "What about Nana?" She was my last remaining grandparent. Willow's parents had disowned her when she quit school for the Rainbow Gathering, and now Grandpa Joe was gone, and Nana, whose eyes everyone used to say I had, was it.

"It's a values thing," Willow said. "You'll understand when you're older."

"I am older," I said.

"Even older," Willow said, which pissed me off. I could feel my ears getting hot and my jaw clenching.

"What if I grow up and decide that I don't like your values?" I said.

"Why wouldn't you like our values?" Willow said. "We value the earth and all living things." She sounded hurt, like I had just said she wasn't a good mother.

"That's not the point," I said. "Maybe when I grow up I won't want to value the earth and all living things."

"Then you'd be a psychopath," Steve said.

"That's not funny," Willow said.

"What's a psychopath?" I said.

"People who don't honor the earth and all living things," Willow said, cutting off Steve, who might have been saying "Grandpa," but I couldn't tell for sure.

"Stop making fun of me!" I said.

"We're not making fun of you," Willow said in a very Willowy way.

"So what would you do if I grew up and wouldn't see you anymore because I didn't like your values?" I said. Again.

"I'd be incredibly sad," Willow said. "It would be tragic."

"I'd be okay with it," Steve said. "It would be fine."

Willow and I both said, "What?" at the same time. And then Willow said, "Really?"

"Sure," Steve said. "If Sunny rejected our values, I really wouldn't want to have anything to do with her. That's the whole point of values—to live them."

Maybe my parents are right. Maybe this will make more sense to me when I'm older, but at the time it seemed really mean and stupid and it still does.

"You'd better stop the car and let me out," I said. (I didn't mean it. It was a dare.)

"Why?" Willow said, as Steve eased the Subaru onto the shoulder of the highway and turned off the engine.

"I know what she's saying," Steve said, and popped the locks.

"Stay in the car, Sunny," Willow said. She sounded a little panicky. "Start the car, Steve." She also sounded mad. He started the car.

"What was that all about?" she wanted to know when we were back on the road.

"Do you want to tell her, or should I?" Steve said, looking at me in the rearview mirror.

"I think what Steve said is stupid," I said.

"And?" Steve said.

"And since I think it's stupid, and he thinks it's smart, we don't share the same values, so we shouldn't have anything to do with each other anymore. Like with Nana and Grandpa Joe," I added.

"You should be a lawyer," Willow said.

Steve laughed. "Don't become a lawyer, Sunny. Then we really won't share the same values," he said. "It's like that Willie Nelson song, 'Mamas, don't let your daughters grow up to be lawyers.'"

"It's cowboys," Willow told him.

"And babies," I added.

# Chapter Seven
## 7.19.10 – 7.25.10

Who never lost, are unprepared / A Coronet to find!

—EMILY DICKINSON

The first time Rusty drove through Riverton, back in June, he was on the lookout for the building that drew him up north in the first place, the Riverton National Bank. His mother's old passbook didn't have an address, a feature that Rusty was certain spoke to the bank's prominence in the city: Why waste ink when everyone knew where it was? And where it was, he figured, was smack in the middle of town. Just as malls had a Sears anchoring one end and a JCPenney anchoring the other, in Rusty's experience towns were

230 · SUE HALPERN

moored by the library, the church, and the bank. All he needed to do was find one and he'd find the others.

And there was the library, straight ahead when he made the turn onto Main Street—so far, so good. And there was the church, a white clapboard rectangle of modest size topped by a stubby bell tower, with a light box sign out front that reminded Rusty of the *Wheel of Fortune* puzzle: ATH _ I _ T: A PERS _ N WITH _ O INVISIBLE M _ ANS OF SUP _ ORT.

"That's me!" Rusty said out loud on his second pass when he had solved it: "Atheist: a person with no invisible means of support."

Rusty parked the Mercedes near the library and began walking counterclockwise along the mostly empty sidewalk, looking for the bank. He passed Carl's Barbershop, closed and for rent, its red, white, and blue barber pole still intact, and the old diner, also closed and for rent, and a pawnshop that used to be an appliance store, its window displaying a drum kit and a case of mismatched high school class rings. Fine's Department Store, on the opposite side of the green from the library, was now a Dollar Tree, the newer store's plastic green sign unable to mask the original, which had been hammered into the limestone facade and looked to Rusty like a grave marker. Someone had won $500 from a scratch ticket purchased here, and American Spirit cigarettes were on sale, and on a lark, Rusty pushed through the heavy beveled glass doors, surprising the cashier, who jumped a little, took a step back, and narrowed her eyes, which were ringed with bright blue eye shadow.

"Hi," Rusty said brightly, letting her know he was no threat.

The girl—though she might not have been a girl; her age was indeterminate (the extensions in her hair ended in silver tips that reminded Rusty of shoelaces)—nodded.

Rusty surveyed the candy rack, fingered a KitKat and put it back, and took a package of Polo mints and laid it on the counter. "How much?" he asked.

"You know this is the Dollar Tree, right?" she said.

"What about tax?"

"What about it?"

"Is it still a dollar?"

"Like I said," she said.

Rusty counted out three quarters, two dimes, and a nickel and slid them toward her. "So where's the bank?" he asked.

"What bank?"

"The Riverton bank. The national bank. Riverton National."

"The only bank I know is People's out on Route 5."

"Route 5."

"Yeah."

"There's no Riverton National Bank?"

"Nope. Just People's."

"You've lived here all your life and there's never been a Riverton National Bank?" Was he sounding desperate? He was feeling desperate. Had he made a mistake? Was he supposed to be in Kansas? Or Utah? Or Wyoming? Or back in Jersey?

"No," she said.

"No, there was no Riverton bank, or no, you haven't lived here all your life?"

"No, I haven't lived here all my life. We moved when I was two."

Rusty did a series of quick calculations. If she was twenty-five, which her clothes suggested she was, then she'd been here for twenty-three years, but she probably wouldn't have been aware for a couple of years after that, so say twenty years back and no Riverton National Bank. But that was still forty years after that money had been deposited. Of course, if she was forty herself, which the lines on her face and the foundation she'd applied to hide them also suggested she could be, she would have been coming to consciousness around 1975, which was a gap of only twenty-five years. His head was spinning.

"Okay, thanks," he said, pocketing the mints and

walking out the way he'd walked in, and as he did, an alarm sounded and the doors locked with a decisive click.

"You can't do that," she said, nonplussed.

"I can't leave?" Rusty said.

"Not that way. You have to go out the exit."

"Geez," he said. "This is worse than New York."

"Whatever," she said.

Outside again, Rusty resumed his circumnavigation, passing the church, which could do with a fresh coat of paint, and nearly missing the two small bronze plaques affixed to lower corners of the squat, unassuming Riverton Municipal Services building: 1919, one of them said; RIVERTON BANK AND TRUST, said the other. He read it again, and then another time, tracing the letters with his finger. RIVERTON BANK AND TRUST, it said. Not Riverton National.

He had gambled, and he had gambled wrong.

"Fuck," he said to the air.

The still point of the turning world.

—T. S. ELIOT

Even after he began to pick the hive mind of the Four, Rusty spent his days at the Riverton library, reading old newspapers and poring over old copies of the Yellow Pages on a hunch, hoping to prove to himself that Riverton National Bank was in fact Riverton Bank and Trust and he had picked the right Riverton after all.

"It's not exactly the hero's journey," Kit said to him when he described his quest, but she was compliant and helpful, retrieving cardboard boxes from the basement when he couldn't find what he was looking for on the shelves.

"Behold our archives!" Kit said to him, dropping slightly damp, slightly moldy boxes on the table opposite her desk. Inside were newspaper clippings in file folders organized by year. He skimmed them diligently, reading about Riverton's support during World War II of men and materials, and how, postwar, the shoe factory was losing out to cheaper manufacturers in Brazil. He read about union fights, contract disputes, high school wrestling, and a protracted debate over a municipal bond to fund the hospital. In the file folder from 1952, Rusty read a story about a cow that had wandered onto the field during a football game and blocked the wide receiver, and another about the death of King George VI in England, and one about Richard Nixon's dog Checkers.

"Nothing here," Rusty told Kit, "but this clip is pretty funny."

He handed her the story about the football-playing cow, and when he did, he saw, on the other side, an ad for the bank, only now it was called the Riverton National Bank and Trust Company, RNBTC. "Wait," he said before she could finish reading, and took the paper out of her hand, turned it over, and placed it on the table. "Look!" He pointed to the ad.

"It's got a different name," Kit said, stating the obvious.

"Yes, but it's got to be the same bank."

"Yes and no," Kit said. "The national bank could have bought the trust company. Or the trust company could have bought the bank."

"Okay, fine," Rusty said impatiently. "But the point is that at least in 1952, we know there is a bank in Riverton with the word 'national' in the title."

Kit nodded her head. "We." He said "we." That's all she heard.

# The Marriage Story

## — PART III —

Meeting Cal's parents made me grateful for the cramped, estrogen-positive household I'd grown up in, with my eccentric grandma and overworked mother who had enough time, even so, to put funny notes in my lunch box when I was little and take me to Planned Parenthood in high school when I told her about Kyle and me—because of course I would tell her about my first. We had our differences, the three of us; with three generations of females living in tight quarters, that was inevitable. But I don't think that anyone who stepped over the threshold into our house would have come away with any other impression than that we loved one another and also that the notion that women are the weaker sex is completely wrongheaded.

Cal's parents gave me the creeps. I pretended they

didn't and it worked, because Cal was so used to them and their idiosyncrasies he couldn't see them. (The idiosyncrasies or, for that matter, his parents.) He thought our visit had gone well, and he was happy for it, and it felt cruel to try to disabuse him of that. Meeting the Sweeneys, though, convinced me that I didn't want a fancy wedding at their country club, where his father could take the microphone and make inappropriate comments masked as a toast, and dance with my friends as he inched his hand slowly down the small of their backs, and I didn't want a wedding where the Sweeneys' money, and my family's lack of it, would mean the Doctor and his wife would pay, and they would run the show, with my mother and me reduced to stock characters: the raggedy Joads moving up in the world.

You might think that all this would have given me pause—that it would have encouraged me to step back and survey the situation and at least wonder how growing up with parents like his "influenced" Cal—and cause me to pull the emergency brake on our plans. Instead, I became protective. I wanted to shield Cal from his mom and dad. I wanted to throw a bag over his head and hustle him out of that family and bring him to a safe house where there was only warmth and love. And so, on a nondescript day in March, not sunny and not cloudy, not cold and not hot, we got up at seven as usual, ate our usual cereal breakfast, and skimmed the *New York Times*, each of us sequestered behind a curtain of newsprint. Then we washed the breakfast dishes, showered (separately), and at 9:30 went over to the county clerk's office to get married. I had tipped off my mother, who drove through the dark to be there, and Cal asked the chipper, stuttering, unmarried head of his lab to be his best man, and for a few minutes that morning as the four of us stood before the justice of the peace, Cal in his navy-blue interview suit and me in a maroon, cowl-necked sweater dress I'd bought a few days before, with each of us flanked by an adult who wore their dress-up clothes with more authority than we wore ours, I harbored the fantasy that when Cal and I stepped up to what passed for an altar, the other two would look into each other's eyes and fall madly in love. It was nutty, and the consequence of watching too many romantic comedies, but also an expression of my guilt: If I could find happiness with a man, why couldn't my mother? I wasn't discounting my father. I know she had been in love with him, but that was a long time ago. Yet happiness was not my dominant emotion. What I remember most from that morning was a deep feeling of contentment and the sense that now my life as it was supposed to be lived would really begin.

Back at the apartment, our friends had gathered for

a party, and there was knockoff champagne and an off-kilter chocolate layer cake with a plastic bride and groom on top who looked like they were about to be swept away in an avalanche of buttercream. A mixtape Cal's lab mates made seemed to be on an infinite loop all afternoon, and people rolled up our throw rug and pushed the furniture toward the walls and danced until someone noticed it had been snowing, and we all went outside and threw snowballs at each other, forgetting, or maybe not caring, that we were wearing our good shoes. Our friends, who were twenty and twenty-one and twenty-two like us, had seen the future—Cal and I were the future—and their response was to behave like the children they still wanted to be and that they were.

After everyone cleared out and my mother went back home, we called Cal's parents and told them what we'd done. His mom said she was sorry we didn't get married in a church, and the Doctor sounded pleased that we'd just gone out and "taken care of it," like we were puppies doing what was necessary and getting spayed. A week or so later we got a card in the mail from them and a check for $1,000 made out to Mr. and Mrs. Calvin Fortune Sweeney (the Fortune, meant to suggest a family name, was completely made up and a way to distinguish young Cal from his father, Calvin Masters Sweeney). It was the first time our names were joined like that. Mr. and Mrs. That's what we were. We were a Mr. and a Mrs. It was . . . jarring.

But it wasn't, really. Our wedding butted up against midterms, and Cal's senior thesis was due soon, and within a day our "after" lives were the same as our "before" lives. I was out of school by then, working toward getting my teaching certificate and subbing whenever I got the call. When Cal wasn't studying or working in the lab, he was flying around the country for medical school interviews, even though his first choice was staying right where we were and going to medical school at the university. I was alone a lot, which suited me, but it also gave me a lot of time to think about what I was doing. My mother was a teacher, so maybe it was natural that I gravitated toward the classroom, though how she could get up every morning and corral thirty nine-year-olds all day and not go crazy, or get mean or bored, seemed remarkable to me after spending a day or two here and there sitting at the teacher's desk and trying to assert what little authority I had. And this was high school. High school, according to the other subs I met in my travels, was easier than elementary school—and forget middle school or junior high. Getting called for a middle school or a junior high was worthwhile only because it paid more. Jailer's wages, they called it.

The other thing I learned, sitting in those teachers' lounges, was that high school English was a magnet for aspiring actors, published poets, screenwriters, and would-be novelists, who jockeyed to be assigned to all-day detention, where they could be paid to knock out a chapter or two. Most, like me, had studied literature of some sort in college. And most, like me, were drawn to the miracle of the blank page and how, when seeded with letters, it blossomed into words and sentences and paragraphs and stories. We understood that Genesis wasn't the first story but, rather, that the creation of Genesis was. I'd go into the classroom prepared to discuss whatever book or poem or passage was on that day's agenda, and sometimes, against all odds, those discussions were spirited and engaging, and they told me everything I needed to know about my future as a teacher: I had none. It was books I was drawn to—the smell of them, the feel of them, the way they invaded and captured me—not talking about books. I enrolled in library school and got a part-time job at a used-book store, taking orders over the phone.

Cal, meanwhile, was into medical school. His father wanted him to go to Rush, in Chicago, his alma mater, and then accused his son of blowing the interview when Rush was one of the few places that didn't accept him. Our university did, and with a substantial scholarship, which insulated us a bit from Cal's parents, though we still needed their help. The first two years of medical school are in the classroom or studying, so our lives, Cal's and mine, while largely parallel, would intersect in the library or at our dining room table, where Cal would have his biochemistry charts laid out at one end, and I'd be doing the reading for my "Organization of Information" class at the other. This was our life together, and despite the typical stresses and strains, it was calm and unremarkable.

In June, Cal took his second-year board exams and I received my master's, and to celebrate we decided to take the honeymoon we'd never had and go to San Francisco. We both had always wanted to go out west, so we took the $1,000 Cal's parents had given us for our wedding and booked flights and found a room in what the travel books said was a funky hotel, even though no one would have described either of us as funky. In our three years of marriage, Cal had grown into his body without me noticing. It wasn't that he was taller or more muscular or wore smart, rimless glasses, though all these were true. It was that he walked with confidence, and spoke with confidence, and projected confidence—all good things if you are going to listen to people's hearts and tell them they need coronary bypass surgery, or cut into their brains, or tell parents that everything that could have been done for their child had been done. Cal was handsome now in an unassuming way. His wardrobe was as limited as ever, but clothes no longer hung off his body; instead, his body inhabited them. It had taken up residence. The doctor was in and he was attractive.

No one had told us about the fog at that time of the year, or that it was shaping up to be one of the coldest summers in San Francisco history. The first morning when we opened the curtains, all we could see was a reflection of ourselves against a dull gray background. We fell back into the bed, and one thing led to another and we were taking turns looking at the other's naked backside in the overhead mirror. (That turned out to be the funky part of our funky hotel.) At some point it came to our attention that the room was bathed in bright sunlight, and we stood at the window again and this time saw the ups and downs of the city, and the Bay Bridge off in the distance. So that became our routine: sex in the morning till the fog burned off, then the typical tourist stuff, including a trip out to the old prison on Alcatraz Island and a hike across the Golden Gate Bridge. We were just another out-of-town couple on vacation, walking hand in hand.

The trouble didn't start until we were home for a few weeks. Cal had begun his first clinical rotation, in internal medicine, at the university hospital, and was spending nights and days there. I had taken my first real job, back at the library where Cal and I used to hang out when we were undergraduates, and where he'd come to see me during my work-study shifts. They put me in special collections, where my job was cataloging new acquisitions and making sure the scholars or students or whoever was in there poring over the letters of some World War I general or World War II POW or troop carrier manifest—because we specialized in military documents—was wearing the special white gloves we made them put on to keep the oils from their fingers from rubbing off on the originals. It was nice and cool down there, which is how I knew, on my eighth day of work, that there was something wrong with me. I was sweating like I was in the tropics, and when I wasn't sweating I was shivering. My teeth were chattering so loudly that I had to stuff one of those gloves between them to dampen the noise.

"Summer flu is the worst," my kind and elderly boss said, when he told me to go home and get into bed. I could barely nod my head in agreement. And that's where Cal found me, asleep, or maybe unconscious, in our bed. He was making one of his rare appearances there after a thirty-hour shift, and was so exhausted himself it hardly registered that there was something unusual that his wife was fully clothed and unmoving under the covers in the middle of the day. Cal crawled in beside me and snuggled up to my back, throwing his arm around my torso and pulling me tight. And then, in what must have been a nightmare for a sleep-deprived medical student coming off an endless day at the hospital, it was like he was right back at work, because as soon as he felt my damp clothes and heard my ragged breathing, his clinical brain kicked in and he pulled off the covers and saw that I was not only sweating profusely, I was bleeding, too. A bright red bloom was spreading beneath my thighs.

"Oh no, oh no, oh crap!"

I could actually hear Cal through my haze. "It's okay," I said, not opening my eyes.

"It is not okay. It is not okay," he said, reaching over me for the phone to call 911.

I remember the words "my wife" and "I'm a doctor," and how I said, "No, no," and Cal said, "What? What's the matter?" and though he sounded far away and underwater, he also sounded panicky and scared, and I said, "You're not a doctor; you told them you were a doctor," and the next thing I knew it was five days later and I was in the hospital, and a man in a white coat with a name stitched into the chest pocket that I could barely see (because I wasn't wearing glasses and my eyes were not working well anyway) came into my room and congratulated me for having the foresight to end up in the same hospital where my husband was on rotation.

"He's got the best bed of anyone in his class," this jerk said, pointing to the cot in the far corner of the room. Mulligatawny. That was his name. Like the soup.

Cal arrived sometime later, I don't know when, since time was a viscous liquid. He was wearing a white coat, too, and the brand-new bright blue stethoscope I'd given him as a present three weeks before was slung around the back of his neck. Someone must have told him I was awake because he was carrying flowers. Daisies. He stood there, two steps into the room, and stopped, arm outstretched, as if he'd been tapped in a game of freeze tag. A nurse came in then and he had to step away from the door, and she said, "Hello, Doctor," to his back before she turned and saw he was a medical student and said "Oh."

"My wife," he said, and she said "oh" again and came over to the bed and checked my chart, adjusted my lines, and switched out one IV bag with another.

"Antibiotics," Cal said, though I hadn't asked. I hadn't asked what was wrong with me, either. This may have been the drugs, or it may have been the fact that not knowing was the same in my mind as not happening.

My mother, who had retired and was on a cruise

along the Danube when all this was going on, arrived two days later and started asking questions, and that's when I learned that one result of all those mornings watching ourselves go at it in that mirrored San Francisco hotel room was that we had made a baby. I was pregnant. I was still out of it enough not to note the tense being used: it was "was," not "is." Or, as my mother, ever the grammarian, said to my husband, who was having trouble saying what needed to be said, "For the sake of clarity, Cal, use the pluperfect. 'Had been.' You had been pregnant, Kit," and that's when the three of us began to cry.

Cal pulled himself together first. And although I was inconsolable, he reminded me that I wasn't supposed to get pregnant, by which he meant that I wasn't supposed to be able to get pregnant, which was not just a verbal sleight of hand. What he meant, he said, slipping into physician mode, was that I wasn't supposed to be able to get pregnant because for the past four years there was a sentry, locked and loaded, at the entrance to my cervix: the IUD his father had prescribed. "Every so often they get dislodged," he was explaining, and I was wondering if it was the time I was on my knees and he was pounding me from behind, or if it was when we were trying out this crazy acrobatic move we saw on the pay-per-view.

"Every so often they get dislodged and they migrate up into the uterus, or perforate the colon and—"

"Enough!" my mother shouted. They must have heard her at the nurses' station because, without being summoned, a woman in lavender scrubs poked her head in and the three of us waved her away.

"No," I said. "Tell me. Tell me what happened."

And Cal recounted, in clinical detail, the whole bloody mess, ending with finding me in our bed, febrile and hemorrhaging, and calling the ambulance and ending up in University Hospital.

"And then what happened?" I asked, as if he were telling me a bedtime story.

Cal exchanged looks with my mother.

"What?" I said, alarmed.

"Well, baby," said my mother, who until that moment had always been so precise in her diction. "Sorry," she said, coloring. "Bad choice of words," and said no more.

"The upshot is . . ." Cal started. "The basic thing is . . ." he said. "The upshot is—"

"You said that already," I said.

And then in a rush of words I might have missed if I wasn't listening very carefully: "We're not going to be able to have kids."

There were tears running down my mother's face, but all I felt was shock, which silenced me, and then doubt—was I really hearing this? was it really true?—and then more shock, and then an emotion that felt like fire and consumed me.

"We're not?" I said, the words flaming out of my throat.

"Yes," Cal said flatly. I knew, then, how he'd be with his patients: clear but careful, using as few words as possible so there would be as little confusion as possible.

"No!" I said.

"I'm afraid, hon, that it's true," he said, steady despite my anger. "We're not." He really was going to be a good doctor, but as for being a good husband, I was no longer sure.

"No," I said, seething. "Not we. Me. Not you. Me. I can't have children. I. I can't. My body. I. Me. My body." As mantras go, it was remarkably focusing.

The deepest feeling always shows itself in silence . . .

—MARIANNE MOORE

Rusty took the library steps two at a time, pushed open the heavy oak door, and bid a cheerful "good morning" to Evelyn, who had taken to calling him "our best customer," even though he never took anything out. He made a beeline for the local history section and pulled a few books off the shelf and piled them on one of the long reading room tables, just as he did the day before and the day before that. This was his job now, reading about the rise and fall of Riverton, *The City That Could*, as one of the book titles declared, until it couldn't.

"It's a fascinating story, a real American tragedy," Kit heard Rusty say to the Four one day, who found it less fascinating, having lived it.

"It's not that interesting, trust me," Carl said. And: "Let me bring in my shears, you're starting to look like Meat Loaf."

"Eww. Disgusting," Sunny chimed in. She had been standing off to the side, listening.

"Meat Loaf is a musician, dear," Carl explained. "Look him up."

And the next morning Carl took Rusty out in the alley behind the library, had him lean against a trash can, and cut his hair.

"In New York, that would be one-fifty," Rusty told him.

"In Riverton, you pay for the view," Carl said, tucking his comb and scissors into a black zippered case and spreading his arms wide to take in the row of trash cans and an overflowing Dumpster. "We call it atmosphere."

"The thing I don't understand," Rusty was saying as they walked back inside, as the other members of the Four whistled and catcalled, and Sunny said, "Good job, Carl," and Evelyn blushed and so, to her chagrin, did Kit. "The thing I don't understand," Rusty said, ignoring them all, "is how a person from Duluth, my mother, ends up with a bankbook from here. It makes no sense."

"However it happened," Carl said, "I doubt you're going to find the answer in those books you've been reading."

"That's for sure," Rich the driver said.

Still, Rusty kept pulling books off the shelf and turning the pages, and watching him, bent over an oversized volume of black-and-white photographs, his brown hair no longer spilling over his collar, it occurred to Kit that he liked it there in the Riverton Public Library, shabby as it was. He liked the routine. He liked the people. And the person he seemed to like best, to Kit's surprise, was Sunny.

They made an odd pair, Rusty in his Brooks Brothers khakis and Ralph Lauren polos, and the girl in her baggy T-shirts and high-top sneakers, but most days, when she wasn't busy, Sunny would sit next to Rusty and they'd pass books back and forth, urging each other to read a particular passage or look at a particular image. Heads together, they'd giggle, or exclaim, or speak quietly, and sometimes, when she couldn't hear what they were saying, Kit would feel a pang of jealousy and have to remind herself that it was better this way. As long as Rusty was going to come around, and as long as Sunny had to be there, it was better that they had each other, better that they left her alone.

"Can Rusty have lunch with us in the staff room?" Sunny asked Kit on a rainy Wednesday when what had become their usual spot on the library steps wasn't feasible.

"He's not a member of the staff," Kit said, surprised at how sharp her voice sounded.

Sunny looked hurt for a moment, then rebounded with a smile.

"Neither am I," she said.

"Special circumstances," Kit said. "It's for staff and people serving out their court-mandated community service." She couldn't believe how mean she sounded. Mean and small.

"Are you saying Rusty has to steal a book to be able to have lunch in the staff room?" Sunny shot back. She had her hands on her hips. She was rolling her eyes.

"No, Sunny," Kit said. "I'm saying no."

The girl turned and walked back to the table where Rusty sat reading with earphones plugged in his ears. Her hands were shoved in her pockets and her shoulders sagged, and Kit told herself she didn't care. She left the room.

When she returned, Sunny and Rusty were huddled together and Rusty was showing something to Sunny—Kit couldn't tell what. And then, as if she had popped up from a rabbit hole, there was Sunny again, standing in front of Kit's desk, and before Kit could say no again, Sunny started talking, fast and telegraphically, the way she did when she was excited.

"You've got to see this," Sunny said. "It's amazing. Scan the archives. Put them on a disk or on the computer."

Kit frowned. The sourness she had been feeling intensified. "We don't have a scanner, Sunny," she said, "and we don't have money for a scanner. You know that."

"That's the thing," Sunny said. "That's what's so amazing. We don't need one. Rusty has one." And here she paused for effect. "On his phone!"

Kit had to admit, she didn't see this coming. She knew that there were phones with cameras, but such things came late to Riverton.

"We take a picture of each newspaper clipping and

upload it to a file on the computer, or put it on a disk," Sunny was saying. "No more cardboard boxes—I mean you could keep them if you want, but you wouldn't have to. Rusty says we could even make it searchable."

There was that word, "we," again. Only this time Kit knew it didn't include her, and she was a little sorry.

◆　◆　◆

### Sunny | hat trick

We've always been a threesome, my parents and me. Willow likes to call us a trio or a triplicity or a hat trick; I knew the meaning of "troika" when I was eight. We're a unit: one of us is always the cheese. I guess I knew I'd grow up—people are always asking you what you want to be when you grow up, so of course you think about that, but when I did, it was always short on details, including where I was going to live and who I was going to live with, since I guess I just assumed I'd be a writer and live at home, and that home was wherever Willow and Steve were. Even if it was at the Tip-Top Motor Inn.

Not that it was going to be. We were just there for two nights, unlike Rusty, who has been there for weeks. When we got back from the Tip-Top, Willow had a lot of orders to fill, so she holed up in her workshop, hammering and soldering late into the night. I went to sleep to the muffled banging coming through the wall and the scratch of her chair when she stood up to stretch. Maybe that's what woke me, and then I heard Steve's voice, and the two of them talking in what they must have thought were hushed tones but weren't.

Hammer, hammer, hammer, hammer, and then Steve's voice: "Sunny is going to—" hammer, hammer, so I missed some words, "—part from us."

"Maybe it's for the best," Willow said, before hammering some more. This was Willow. Willow! The one who cried when I got my own bed. She didn't even sound particularly sad.

There was more banging, and then Steve said, "It's the natural order of things," and if Willow said something back, I didn't hear it.

I wanted to walk in there and ask them what they were talking about, but I knew it was useless. Like when we were at the Tip-Top and I asked Willow why we were there, and she said that it was all part of our life plan, and I asked her what she meant by "it was all," except I didn't say it that way, I said, "What is?" and she said, "It's good to be curious, Sunny, but sometimes it's not good to be too curious."

The more I thought about it—because I wasn't going to go back to sleep—the more what Willow said reminded me of the Mr. Men book *Mr. Topsy-Turvy* the kids always want me to read at story hour, but what Steve said made a certain amount of sense.

Steve has always believed that biology is destiny. He's told me that a billion times. When I was little I thought he meant that that's why frogs did the frog kick when they swam and ducks flew in a V. But lately I've been arguing with him about this. "This is the argument people used to keep slaves!" I told him, and he disagreed and said that those people were misguided.

"It's the same argument men have used to keep women out of the workplace!" I said, trying again.

"Again, Sunny," Steve said in that condescending way he sometimes uses when he wants to make you feel like he's smarter than you'll ever be, "those people are misguided. My point is that we don't mess with Mother Nature."

"Fine," I said, but to his back, as he walked out of the room.

So it occurred to me that maybe he was right. Maybe separating from your parents is the natural order of things.

◆　◆　◆

I'm Nobody! Who are you?

—EMILY DICKINSON

Sunny was acting strangely. She came in on time and read to the children and did what she always did, but did it all in a trance, as if her body were a marionette and its strings were being pulled from somewhere far away. Her skin was sallow, her eyes heavy-lidded, and she couldn't stand still, bouncing on the balls of her feet instead, until Evelyn finally told her to cut it out, that Sunny was making her dizzy, and suggested maybe she needed "one of those herbal things you people like to take," but the girl seemed not to hear her and just floated away in the direction of the reference section and Kit.

"I think you might have a fever," Kit tried, and Sunny looked up at her with her tired eyes and said she didn't think so. "You look"—Kit searched for a diplomatic way to say it—"washed out."

Sunny gave her a half smile, said, "Sorry," and backed away as if she'd been cornered.

Kit found her in the children's section, sitting in one of the kiddie chairs at a kiddie table, reading *The Velveteen Rabbit*.

"This is the book you showed me your first day, about the stuffed animal that becomes real, right?" Kit said brightly.

Truthfully, she hated when people did this to her, which for a while they did all the time: pretend they could reverse the darkness by spreading their pretend sunshine all over you. What did Dr. Bondi say? That it was a basic human reflex? That it came from the most basic part of the brain, not the neocortex or the limbic part, and was an expression of fear, not empathy. "You can't take it personally, Kit," he said when she told him how much she despised people who did to her what she was now doing to Sunny, but of course she did.

Sunny didn't look up, and Kit, whose first instinct was to retreat, found herself unable to move. It could have been a photograph or a still life, a teenager looking down at a book, her blond hair falling forward, a white bra strap cutting into the skin along her bony clavicle, watched over by a middle-aged woman whose glasses were partway down her nose, whose arms were crossed over her chest, whose left hand was holding on to her right biceps, her right hand holding on to her left biceps, her skin—because she was wearing a short-sleeved shirt, beige, made from an airy linen fabric—extruded from the pressure, which was the only clue to her emotions since her face was implacable—not angry, just blank.

And then Kit moved. She pushed her glasses back to the bridge of her nose and raked her fingers through her hair, parking some of it behind her ear, and changed her stance, so she was leaning left, toward Sunny in the chair. She wanted to say the right thing, but knew there

was no such thing, and that sometimes—most times—
it was better not to try. She found herself wishing Rusty
was around, but he was up at the Tip-Top, helping the
owners move some boxes, and then had a lunch date. He
called in to Evelyn to tell her. Like he worked there.

"It's lunchtime," Kit said. "Let's go."

And much to her surprise, the girl got up and followed her to the staff room.

"Are you hungry?" Kit asked, sitting down and
taking a sandwich from her bag and holding it out to
Sunny, who remained standing.

"Not really," Sunny said.

"Not really?" Kit echoed. The girl was acting like a
zombie. "Sit down," she said.

Sunny pulled back the vinyl stack chair opposite Kit's
and dropped into it. She balled her fists and leaned into
them and squeezed her eyes shut. Unsure what to do,
Kit continued her interrogation.

"Did you have breakfast?" she asked.

"I don't remember."

"You don't remember? It was only a few hours ago."

Silence. Kit fingered the wax paper around her
sandwich, hoping that the sound might trigger Sunny's
appetite. "Pavlov's bell," she said to no one in particular, and especially not to Sunny, whose entire body
seemed to have contracted.

"Have half my sandwich," Kit said, taking half and sliding the rest across the table. Even if Sunny wasn't hungry, Kit was, and she took a bite. Busy chewing, she almost missed Sunny's words.

"I don't think Steve is my father," she mumbled.

"What?" Kit said.

"Steve. I don't think he's my father."

For the first time since they'd been in the break room, Sunny looked straight at Kit, her eyes open and unblinking. Still, Kit thought, she looked absent.

"Why do you think that?" Kit was surprised to see Sunny reach over, take the sandwich half and eat the whole thing in two bites. Kit pushed the four mint Milanos she'd dropped into her lunch sack before leaving home in the morning in the girl's direction, and Sunny took these, too, and fed them into her mouth, one after the other, like pieces of paper going into a shredder. Kit knew this kind of eating. It was what happened after you said something you'd been holding in. Once it was uncorked, all you wanted to do was fill the gap you'd just opened up.

"I saw his passport," Sunny said, as if that was an explanation.

"I'm confused," Kit said. "What does his passport have to do with it?" In her own case, an old passport would have revealed a crucial piece of information: that her name, now, was not her name before. But people expected that with women, not with men. It was how the world worked. With men it was suspicious.

"The name on the passport wasn't his name. The birth date wasn't his birth date. But the picture was his picture. I mean it was him from around the time I was born. It was an old passport."

"Sunny," Kit began, "I really don't think that proves he's not your dad." She tried to say this without sounding patronizing. The girl was being dramatic, but Kit didn't want her to think she thought so.

"You don't understand," Sunny said, not bothering to hide her contempt. Sometimes she thought Kit was different. Sometimes she thought Kit was just like the other adults she knew, presumptuous and complacent, like they knew everything and you knew nothing, like they were always right because they were always right. This was one of those times. She turned her gaze up to the ceiling.

"What don't I understand?" Kit said, sighing, understanding she was failing here and failing badly.

"I googled the name on the passport," Sunny said, as if talking to an idiot. "Two days ago. Here."

"And?"

"He's wanted by the police. Angus Parker is. In Pennsylvania."

"The police. In Pennsylvania," Kit echoed. (When she recalled this conversation later, she was struck by the strange, staccato way they were talking, but right then it seemed natural, as if both their voices were telegraph machines, dispatching messages with speed and efficiency.)

"Yes," Sunny said.

"Are you sure?"

Sunny took out a piece of paper from her backpack and handed it over to Kit. It was a copy of an article from the *Morning Call*, a newspaper published in Allentown, Pennsylvania.

"That's near where we used to live," Sunny explained, "when I was really little. The only thing I really remember is that I lost my bike. I mean my bike was lost when we moved. The training wheels had just come off. It's funny what you remember."

Kit was barely listening. She was focused on the article, which was about the search for a twentysomething-year-old named Angus Parker, an ecoterrorist, the paper called him, wanted for acts of vandalism at research labs. The only picture authorities had was a grainy black-and-white photo from a security camera at a pharmaceutical company, where he'd allegedly flipped a breaker that shut off power to the company's incubators, where it was growing bacteria to implant in test animals. "He's set back our research by at least three years," the company CEO told the *Morning Call.* "We're estimating that it will cost us twelve million dollars. Our business is to develop medicines for sick people. This man is a terrorist."

"Jeez," Kit said, carefully folding the article into quarters and handing it back to Sunny. "And you're sure that Steve is Angus Parker? I mean, couldn't he be a friend of Angus Parker's and have an old passport of his?"

"Why would they look alike?" Sunny said.

"Maybe they don't look alike," Kit tried. "Maybe that's your brain playing tricks on you. It's an old photo. You don't really know how the young man in the picture is going to look ten or fifteen years later."

"I know," Sunny said. "I've seen pictures of Steve and Willow from before they got together. You know they're not married, right? The Steve in those pictures is the same person as Angus Parker. Angus Parker is Steve."

As Kit was considering this, Evelyn breezed into the room, followed by Chuck, chattering about Jack and Jeffrey, her policemen sons, who were hot on the trail of—but they didn't learn who, because she said, "Feeling better, kiddo?" to Sunny, and plopped herself down on the couch they kept there that was so old no one, not even Evelyn, could remember when it got there or how it fit through the door. Before Sunny could answer,

Evelyn began to explain how one of her grandchildren had a summer cold and how her son wanted her to baby-sit him and how she told him it was elder abuse, which triggered a raspy laughing fit from Chuck and a "Very clever" from Kit, who was already halfway out of the room, with Sunny on her heels.

"You may be getting one, too, hon," Evelyn called out to Sunny, who turned, said, "I don't think so," and didn't stay to hear the woman's recitation of her granddaughter's last few temperature readings.

"What am I going to do?" Sunny said when they had made their escape. Kit was subbing for Evelyn at circulation as she often did when Evelyn was on break, and Sunny was standing right beside her because she was suddenly afraid to be alone. She had confessed. Her secret was out. She thought she'd feel relieved but didn't. She just felt scared. Something was going to happen now. Something was going to happen and she had no idea what it would be. She was bouncing on the balls of her feet again. Her hands were shaking. Kit noticed and, without thinking, covered them with both of her own.

"I don't know yet," Kit said.

The girl's hands were cold, and Kit could feel her pulse looping through at breakneck speed.

"Breathe," she said reflexively. She hated when people said that, but it's what came out of her mouth.

Sunny was close to hyperventilating. Kit wished she'd saved her paper sandwich bag.

"It's all right, Sunny. It'll be okay."

More words she detested. But Sunny's breathing slowed, and the warmth seemed to be coming back to her fingers. Her face was still grayish, and a throbbing artery on the side of her neck looked like a river about to overspill its banks. Kit let go of Sunny's hands and patted the chair next to her. "Sit," she said.

A patron came by then, returning two books—an older woman into genealogy. She was with a boy about eleven, who raced off down the stairs and reappeared within minutes with a copy of *The Hobbit.*

"I really like that book," Sunny said, smiling for the first time.

The boy smiled back. "I know," he said. "You read it to us a couple of weeks ago."

Sunny sat up straighter in her chair. She and the boy chatted about the book while Kit processed it. Sunny was animated and engaged. For a moment it seemed to Kit that Sunny would be okay, but as soon as they left, the girl slumped down in the chair again, shoulders rounded, head hanging and resting on balled fists that looked ready to slug someone.

Kit waited a minute, trying to gather her thoughts, but it was hard. If Steve was not Steve, and if Steve was

Angus Parker, then Steve was, potentially, a fugitive. For a second she wondered if, knowing this, she had a legal obligation to turn him in, then decided no, it was none of her business what happened to Steve. But Sunny was another matter. She was just a kid, and if what she thought was true was true, Sunny was in jeopardy of being a kid without a family.

"I think we have to do more research before we jump to any conclusions. We need to know more," Kit said after a while.

There was that word again, Kit thought, that "we." It was the royal "we," she told herself. A turn of phrase. But she knew that was a lie. She had chosen the "we." It was an unsettling revelation. How strange if Dr. Bondi was right—that over time one's true nature reasserted itself. What did he call it? A "regression to the mean"—as if personality were some sort of math problem.

"Your anger, your fury, your detachment, your—"

"Hatred," Kit inserted.

"Yes," he said. "All those are real and overwhelming feelings, but they are external to you. They are not who you are."

"How do you know?" she asked him, and without letting him answer said: "And what about scar tissue? Adhesions? Things that attach themselves and become part of you?"

"I'm not going to say it hasn't happened, and I'm not going to say it won't happen. If I could predict the future I'd be in a different profession. But I am going to venture a guess that the person you were before"—he paused—"before all this, is the person you still are, and that person will reemerge. I don't know how, or when, but something, somewhere, will pull it out of dormancy."

"Sounds like magic," Kit said. "Like a rabbit coming out of a hat."

"It's not magic, Kit. It's life. You were a loving, generous, trusting person before, and I'm betting that with enough time you'll be comfortable being those things again."

"Stupid," Kit said.

"Excuse me?" Dr. Bondi responded.

Kit laughed. "Oh, not you. Me. I was stupid then, so I'll be stupid again," she said bitterly.

"Maybe," Dr. Bondi said. "But sometimes we have to be stupid and throw caution to the wind to really be alive."

A teacher says, *Take out your pencils. Begin.*

—ELIZABETH ALEXANDER

"Afternoon, ladies," Rusty said, seeing both Kit and Sunny at the circulation desk, as he sauntered into the library. He was wearing blue pin-striped suit pants, a bright red-and-white-striped tie, and a no-iron dress shirt that had lost a good deal of its starching, its sleeves casually rolled above his wrists.

"This," he said, wagging his tie in Kit and Sunny's direction, "is what is known, farther south from here, as a power tie. Do you know why it's called a power tie?"

Sunny said no. Kit just stared at him.

"I don't, either," Rusty said, ignoring Kit and addressing Sunny directly. "Do you know why I'm wearing it?"

Sunny said no again.

"I am wearing it," Rusty said with a flourish, "because today I went to lunch at that spectacular culinary establishment, the Riverton Mercy Hospital. With the Four," he added, as if that weren't obvious.

He was being jolly, oblivious to the tension behind the desk, but then Sunny perked up and asked what he'd had for lunch, and he made her laugh—"Chicken noodle soup à la Campbell's," he said, "and oyster crackers. Green Jell-O parfait."

"How can green Jell-O be a parfait?" Sunny asked.

"A parfait is like—it's like your tie. Striped."

"Then this was a power parfait. Anything is a parfait when you add Cool Whip," Rusty said.

Kit couldn't tell if he was making fun of it, and by extension making fun of the Four, and by further extension making fun of Sunny and herself and everyone else in Riverton. She imagined that if she were an outsider like Rusty, that's exactly what she'd be doing, yet here she was, only four years past being an outsider herself, feeling protective and defensive.

"You know what's weird?" Rusty said, addressing Kit now. "I used to go to all these fancy, expensive restaurants in New York, you know, like the Palm and Gallaghers, and the meat would be dripping over the sides of the plate and the oysters tasted like they'd been hauled from the ocean a minute before, and I don't think I enjoyed any of those meals as much as I enjoyed this one."

"Seriously?" Kit said. This seemed unlikely. A good story. The kind of story a guy like Rusty would be telling his Armani-wearing pals back in New York so they could all get a good laugh. Chicken noodle soup à la Campbell's and the rubes he'd met.

"Seriously. I love those guys. They're the best."

"They are lovable, I'll grant you that," Kit said, standing up abruptly as Evelyn approached to take back her domain.

"To be continued," Rusty said.

Kit rolled her eyes.

"When?" Sunny said, and they both turned to look at her. For a minute or two, they had both forgotten she was there.

"How about we go for ice cream after the library closes?" Rusty said. He was looking at Sunny but addressing Kit.

Sunny brightened, then stuck her hands in her pockets and frowned. "I can't," she said. "Steve's coming to get me at five."

"Call him," Rusty said. "Tell him I'll give you a ride home."

"I can't call him. He doesn't have a phone. We don't believe in—" and then she stopped and corrected herself. "He doesn't believe in them. So I can't." She turned to go downstairs, but Kit called her back.

"When he gets here," she said, "why don't you tell him you're going to spend the night at my house. You can say we have an early meeting."

"But that's not true," Sunny said.

Kit shrugged. "It's not *not* true if we have an early meeting. Over breakfast," Kit said.

**"Very impressive** back there," Rusty said when Kit was back at her desk and Sunny was downstairs. "I didn't take you for fast company."

"Sunny's been having a hard day. I'm just trying to help," she said, annoyed, feeling exposed and found out—but for what? Being unguarded and openhanded?

"Where I come from, that's a compliment," he said.

"Where I come from, I have to get back to work."

◆   ◆   ◆

Meanwhile in other realms big tears were shed . . .
—JOHN KEATS

At five, like clockwork, the Subaru, sorely in need of a new muffler and crankshaft, shifted audibly in front of the NO PARKING, LOADING ZONE sign in front of the library, and Sunny skipped down the steep stone stairs toward it. Kit, who had come out to make sure all was okay, stood on the landing and waved to Steve before Sunny reached him. She watched the girl open the passenger side door and lean in to talk to her father. It was hard, Kit knew, pretending that everything today was the same as everything yesterday, but soon enough Sunny was shutting the door and the Subaru was clambering away and Sunny was taking the steps two at a time.

"He said he was cool with it," Sunny reported, a sloppy grin spreading over her face, as she and Kit walked back inside to tell Rusty, who was sitting in one of the easy chairs that might as well have had the name Patrick or Rich or Carl embroidered into it, paging through a *Sports Illustrated* with a picture of a basketball player on the cover and the words "What Next?" in jumbo type.

And then they were in his car, with Sunny squeezed in the back, sitting sideways so her knees weren't grinding against Kit's shoulders, and the top was down, and Kit's hair, which was never ruly in the best of circumstances, was dancing around her head, and Sunny was shouting things from the backseat that neither Kit nor Rusty could hear, but the tone was unmistakable: she was having the ride of her life. They were on the interstate, the speedometer said 75 and then 80, and then Kit asked him to slow down, which reminded her of how many times she'd been driving with Cal and she'd say the same thing, and then he'd say, "I'm not reckless, you know," and she'd say, "I know," and they'd go on.

"Where are we going, anyway?" Kit said, and Rusty laughed and said, "I thought you knew," and by then they were six towns away, though the river still coursed alongside them, sluggish and brown.

"Let's get off here," Rusty said, and sped up to exit. Sunny yelped with delight, and Kit gripped the armrest, relaxing her fingers only when she saw the stop sign in front of them. Then they were on Route 5 again, but it had turned into a wide thoroughfare lined with the familiar interchangeable mix of big-box and chain stores, a Home Depot followed by a Bed Bath & Beyond followed by a Walmart on one side, and a Lowe's, a Staples, and a Dick's Sporting Goods on the other.

"What do you think the 'Beyond' stands for?" Rusty said when they were stopped at a red light and could hear one another again. But then the light turned, and they couldn't.

"We're getting out of here," Rusty shouted, and made a sharp right turn onto a smaller road, and then a left onto a two-lane macadam that whirred under the car's tires. The busyness they'd found themselves in receded, and they were in the midst of rolling farmland, picture-perfect, with red barns and blue silos, and Holsteins and sheep and horses grazing in green pastures, and cornstalks beginning to bend from the weight of their cobs.

"Turn on the radio," Sunny said from the back.

"Doesn't work," Rusty said, and Kit was glad. The sound of the rushing wind hummed peacefully in her ears.

They rode in silence for a while, until Sunny said, "Maybe it means Mars. Or Venus," and the two in the front seat said, "What?" in unison, and Sunny said,

"The 'Beyond' in Bed Bath & Beyond," and Rusty said something about Martians needing Egyptian cotton pillowcases, and Sunny laughed, and Kit was relieved to hear it.

"This is nice," Kit said quietly, though Rusty heard her and said, "You sound surprised," and she didn't say anything back. She was surprised.

"I'm afraid the only way we're going to get ice cream out here is if we milk one of these cows," Rusty said, talking into the rearview mirror.

"It's okay," Sunny said.

"No, it's not," Kit said, startling them all, even herself.

"Okay, then," Rusty said, and took the next right turn and then another and another, not because he knew where he was or where he was going, but because he wanted to appear decisive and in control.

"There!" Sunny said, and sure enough, straight ahead about fifty yards, like an oasis in the desert, was a parking lot full of cars ringing a three-window drive-in with a big plastic two-scoop ice-cream cone on top.

"Who wants onion rings?" Rusty asked like an excited little kid.

"I thought we were getting ice cream," Sunny said like a disappointed one.

"Of course we are," Kit said.

"Who said we weren't?" Rusty said. "But places like this have the best onion rings."

"I've never had an onion ring," Sunny said.

"What?" Rusty said. "Really? Wow."

Kit wished he'd stop, but he couldn't.

"Okay. Wait here. This is going to be great. No, don't wait here. Go find a table. I'll be right back. This is going to be great," he said again, over his shoulder.

"This is fun," Sunny said, loping ahead of Kit to find an empty picnic table. There was only one available, in a cluster of five, labyrinthine to get to. Kit weaved and dodged her way over, conscious that everywhere she looked, she saw children and parents enjoying an untroubled summer evening out. At least that's what it looked like, though she was no longer so naive as to believe it.

"Got 'em!" Rusty said, waving a white paper bag soaked through with grease. He sat down and held the bag out to Sunny. "Be prepared to have your socks knocked off."

"Says the man who rarely wears socks," Kit said.

"And now you know why," Rusty said.

He waited anxiously while Sunny pulled an onion ring out of the bag and took a bite.

"You see how the batter separates from the onion?" he said. "That's how you know it's good."

"But they all do that," Kit said.

"I rest my case."

"Do you love it?" he said to Sunny, whose mouth was full.

She nodded her head enthusiastically. "Amazing," she said through bites before taking another one.

"Ask that family if they're going to be using their mustard," Kit heard a woman at a nearby table say, and a second later a lanky boy in a Red Sox T-shirt was standing by her side, asking shyly if he could take the jar of Gulden's someone before them had left on their table.

"Yes. Of course. Take it," she said, and waved him away before he learned the truth: that they were not a family.

"I wish you guys were my parents," Sunny said when he was out of range. The words went through Kit like electricity.

"Everybody, at some point in their life, wishes they had different parents," she said carefully.

"Did you?" Sunny asked.

"Sure," Kit said, and gave a short, small laugh. "Until I met Cal's parents."

"Cal?" Rusty asked, suddenly alert.

Kit was flustered. She hadn't meant to say this. It violated the "reveal as little personal information as possible" policy that she usually was so vigilant in enforcing. She could hear Dr. Bondi's skepticism—"Really? Then why did you?"—and she couldn't answer. So how to identify Cal? Not as an old friend—the word "friend" felt like a lie, or at least like the blade of a knife. Old boyfriend? It was true at one time. But so was fiancé, and fiancé would lead to the inevitable question. Kit took a deep breath and automatically shut her eyes. She had been in a car wreck once, back in college, a little fender bender, turning left into traffic, and just before the other car hit hers, she closed her eyes, instinctively shutting herself off from the moment of impact, which of course was impossible. This felt like that. "Husband," she said simply. "Was."

"Sorry," Rusty said. "I didn't know."

Sunny, who had greasy fingers and batter crumbs around her mouth, said, "I did!" like she'd just gotten the winning number in bingo. "I mean I figured," she clarified. "From the book you lent me. Remember? *Pride and Prejudice*? Your name was on the inside cover. Your old name. It was crossed out. So I figured."

"Nice work, Sherlock," Rusty said to be funny, but it caused Sunny to shift moods instantly, reminding her of the troubles ahead at home, now that she'd found Angus

Parker's passport hidden in one of Willow's homeschool teaching binders—the one marked HIST for, appropriately, history. It was as if a massive rain cloud had just settled over their table, bringing with it a chill wind. Rusty picked up on it and took out a twenty from his wallet—his only bill, Kit could see—and handed it to Sunny. "I thought we came here for ice cream," he said lightly, and it was enough to nudge the cloud away.

"Sorry," he said again, when Sunny was out of earshot. "I didn't know."

"Of course," Kit said. "No one here does."

And then Sunny was coming back, saying she needed another pair of hands, and Kit stood up to help her. "It's a long story," she said to Rusty, and followed behind the girl who was moving swiftly and deftly between the tables.

**They were** quiet on the ride back to town. The menacing clouds had disappeared altogether, and it had turned into a soft night, and Rusty drove slowly, almost gingerly, along back roads, trying to extend the evening. Sunny leaned her head against the headrest and watched the stars appear in the sky like distant votive candles, wondering if elsewhere in the world other people were making wishes, too. Kit's eyes were closed, not because she was tired, but to shut out Rusty, who was sure to want to know more. At one point he reached over and gave her arm a light pat. It was a friendly gesture—she knew that—but she recoiled anyway, and he said, "Sorry," so faintly it could have been the breeze.

"I don't know where you live," he said when the lights of the city guided them in, and Sunny piped up and said, "I do," and gave him expert directions that relieved Kit from speaking.

"Thanks," she said when they turned onto Coolidge, and "Good night," when he stopped in front of 1635.

"This was great," Sunny said to Rusty. "I love your car. I love onion rings."

"Let's do it again," Rusty said, looking past her to Kit, who had taken a few steps away from the car and was standing in the shadows on the grass.

"That would be amazing," Sunny said, and it was impossible to tell if Kit thought so, too.

◆　◆　◆

### Sunny | curiosity

I can't say why it was that I decided to look through my parents' things the day I found Angus Parker's passport, or why I hadn't ever done that before. I guess because, why should I? We were a team. And then I heard Willow and Steve talking the night we came back from the Tip-Top, and what were we doing at that place anyway, since it's not far from our house, where we didn't have to pay anyone to stay? So it was strange that we were there, and the first time I asked why, Willow said something vague—something about it being a change of scenery—and Steve didn't say anything and seemed really tired but didn't sleep, just lay on the bed with the TV on, which was a very un-Steve thing to do. Willow and I took a walk, just to get out of the room, and when I told her I thought she and Steve were acting oddly, she made some lame joke about the weather and the effects of global weirding that even she didn't seem to think was very funny. That's when I asked her what was going on and when she said that thing about our life plan and about not being too curious, at which point I got mad and walked away because she was being so ridiculous, and she didn't call me back. The Tip-Top is up on a hill above the highway, but there really isn't anywhere to go up there, so I walked down the long driveway and then back up the hill, which is when I saw Rusty's car. I hung around in the parking lot, hoping he'd come out so at least there would be someone to talk to besides my parents, but he didn't, and I had to pee, so I went back to our room, where both Willow and Steve were asleep, lying next to each other, Steve with his T-shirt pulled over his head, and Willow with her face pressed into his back. They must have been exhausted, because they didn't wake when I slipped the key into the lock and opened the door, which squeaked on its hinges. So much for worrying about your adolescent daughter wandering outside alone in a strange place.

All of a sudden it felt like we were a duplex plus one. Or a duo plus one. Or a duplicity plus the one who was confused about what was going on. All of a sudden it felt like we were a them and a me. So on a Saturday, when Willow was at the mall selling her jewelry and Steve was I don't know where after he dropped her off there, I started my "investigation." Honestly, that's what I called it. If Willow and Steve were not going to tell me what was going on, I was going to find out myself.

This turned out to be harder than I thought it would be. They're not like Kit, who has boxes of notebooks sitting on her bookshelf, even if what's inside the notebooks makes no sense. They've always had this philosophy of "leaving no trace." It's how we managed to live at a campsite for months and no one could tell we'd been there when we left. And it's why we have almost no stuff—no TV, no computer, not even a blender. And it's why we live off the grid. You'd think this would have made my search easier since there wouldn't be a lot to look through, but it actually made it really hard. Neither of my parents has a lot of clothes, so rifling through their underwear drawer or poking around their sweaters was quick and fruitless. I checked all the cupboards in the kitchen and stood on a chair to scan the tops of the bookshelves. We don't even have a lot of books, not because we don't read, but because Willow and Steve believe in recycling: when we buy books, we buy them used and then sell them back to the store or bring them to the Goodwill.

But standing on that chair, looking over our small living room and kitchen, I had two thoughts that merged into one thought. The first was that the only books we buy and don't sell are the ones in my room that we use for no-schooling. The second had to do with kids' court. When it was all over, Willow and I had to sign some papers saying that we agreed to my sentence and that if I failed to complete my community service I'd have to be resentenced by the judge. And it occurred to me that those papers had to be somewhere in the house, and if I could find them, they might lead me to whatever it was that would tell me what was going on. I had no idea what I was looking for: this wasn't like Rusty looking for a bank that had disappeared. So I got off the chair and went into my room and sat on the bed with my legs crossed Indian style and my hands on my thighs as if I were meditating and then very slowly, starting in the left-hand corner, turned my head 180 degrees, trying to take in everything I was seeing.

And then I knew: whatever I was looking for had to be in the books I used when I was really little, because why would anyone bother looking at them now? And those books are out of the way, on the top shelf, which made it more likely. I dragged in a chair from the kitchen and stood looking at the phonics textbook Willow used to teach me to read and the math workbooks I'd hated so much. But I was also looking at what must have been years of dust, dust so thick I could poke my finger through it. If this was a hiding spot, no one had been putting anything up here in a very long time. I looked through all the books anyway. Nothing.

When you're searching for something but you don't know what you're searching for, it helps to know the person or people who have hidden the thing or things you're searching for. It's something I learned at the library. When a book goes missing, the first thing you have to consider is who was probably the last person to be reading it. If it's a picture book, chances are some kid was sitting on the floor looking at it for a while and then slid it back in among the other picture books, not realizing that the books go in a particular order. (I tell them to leave them on the tables or on the cart, but they don't always remember.) If it's an older kid, forget it. They leave books all over the place. Adults do, too, but at least they usually leave them in the same section where they found them.

I was thinking about this when I heard our Subaru chugging up the driveway. It's a long way from the road to the house, and the Subaru just gets noisier and noisier, so it's the perfect early-warning system. I quickly dragged the chair back to the kitchen and positioned myself in front of the open refrigerator so it would look like I was doing something when Steve came in. Only he didn't come in, not right away, so I shut the door and went outside to see what he was doing. And what he was doing was, as usual, trying to fix, as he said, "our damn car."

Eventually he came in and I made peanut butter sandwiches while he rubbed the grease off his hands, and we ate lunch and played Risk, a game Steve is really good at and likes, because he says it will teach me all about world domination and evil empire building. I was in a great mood—not because I crushed him, as Steve assumed—but because I knew that whatever I was looking for was in my room, and as soon as my parents went to bed, I was going to find it.

We all have flashlights hanging above our pillows because the power sometimes runs out and you still want to read or don't want to go to the bathroom in the dark, so it was going to be easy to search once Willow and Steve went to sleep, as long as I was quiet. Risk was helpful: I had been thinking about my strategy all afternoon, knowing that whatever I was after, it was hiding in plain sight in my room. Willow sometimes talks about chi, which has to do with energy, and Steve says that some animals actually have magnets in their bodies to navigate using the magnetism of the North and South Poles, so I sat on my bed, in the dark, trying to "feel" the pull of what I was looking for. The only problem was that I didn't know what I was looking for. I switched on the flashlight, which cast a dim yellow light along the wall. It was running out of batteries—not good. I shut it off and thought some more. And then I knew. It just came to me. Whatever I was looking for was in one of the binders on the bottom shelf where Willow keeps our homeschool/no-school notes and materials. It's actually been a point of conflict between Willow and Steve. He thinks true no-schooling has no curriculum and no materials, but Willow says that no-schooling is about digging deep into subjects, so of course you're going to want to have shovels and picks and hoes, which is her metaphor for what's in those binders.

I turned on the flashlight again and ran the beam down the row. Willow is a very organized person, and the binders have labels on their spines: GEOL for geology, GEOM for geometry, GEOG for geography, LIT for literature (there are four of these), HIST for history. There are five history binders, and suddenly it was so obvious that whatever I was looking for was in one of them that I almost gave myself away by laughing out loud. Like I said, Willow is super organized. I got down on the floor and starting with the first HIST binder, went through them, one by one, feeling less certain as I went down the line and the first, second, third, and fourth had nothing but worksheets about the emperors of Rome and others about the Age of Imperialism, a unit on "Ancient Egypt and Her Neighbors" and another on the civil rights movement. "Last chance," I said to myself, sliding HIST binder #5 off the shelf and opening it. Bingo! Tucked between a booklet called *How to Teach Slavery to Your Children*, which has to be one of the dumbest titles of anything, and a bibliography of books about the Russian Revolution, there was my birth certificate, the stuff from kids' court, the title to our car, and that passport. I didn't know what it meant, only that it had to have something to do with Steve and Willow's strange behavior.

# Chapter Eight
## 7.26.10 – 8.1.10

A blind attendance on a brief ambition . . .

—EDWIN ARLINGTON ROBINSON

Just when Kit had gotten used to Rusty coming in first thing in the morning, meeting her at the top of the stairs before she could get her key in the lock, he stopped. He still came in, but later, slightly disheveled, wearing a faded Vikings T-shirt, not his usual business casual. Kit didn't want to pry, but then she didn't have to.

"Hello, stranger," Evelyn said when he walked through the door after noon for the third day in a row. The way she said it—more editorial comment, less greeting—put Rusty on the spot, and he stopped in his tracks and looked a little abashed, like a boy who had been caught stealing cookies.

"I've been helping out at the motel," he said. He felt embarrassed. She—they—whoever could hear him—were going to think he was a handyman now. What a fall from grace, if you could put "Morris, Maines" and "grace" in the same sentence.

"You're not letting those people take advantage of you?" Evelyn said, not bothering to hide her contempt for "those people," by which she meant foreigners, who she was convinced were taking over the country. "My grandbabies and their babies are going to be minorities. White people are going to be the minority in their own country. Even here in Riverton," she was fond of saying, though when she said this to Sunny, the girl pointed out that if her children had babies with people of color they'd prevent this, which shut her right up.

"No, nothing like that," Rusty said. "Mr. Patel needs someone who is tall to snake out the gutters and swap out the overhead lights. He's taking it off my rent." And then, more to himself than to Evelyn, "I guess it's rent since I've been there more than a month."

"Well, I think it's nice of you," Sunny said, appearing magically in the room, as she so often did.

"Me, too," Kit thought, but said nothing, though

when Rusty entered the reading room she made sure to look up and smile at him. It was a small gesture, she knew, but small gestures were all she had.

Kit was still smiling when Rusty came over to her desk to retrieve the box of newspaper clippings he was working through. He'd photograph them, and Kit and Sunny would suggest captions and he'd type them in with his thumbs.

"What?" Rusty said.

"What what?"

"Why are you smiling?"

"I'm not smiling."

"Then grinning. You are grinning."

Kit paused and shook her head. "You're not going to like it," she said.

"Try me."

"I was thinking that you're actually a nice guy." There. She said it. She looked up at him and saw that he looked confused.

"Why wouldn't I like that?" he said.

"Well . . ." Kit hesitated, not sure if she should say more. "Well," she said again, "because I was thinking that you're a nicer person than I would have thought, which says more about me than about you," she added.

Now it was Rusty's turn to grin. "If that's a compliment, I'll take it," he said.

"Take this, too," Kit said, and handed him the box for 1912. Inside, the newspaper clippings were browned at the edges, as if they'd been left too long in the oven, and they were brittle. If he wasn't careful, they'd break like glass between his fingers.

"How's the money quest going?" Kit asked Rusty after he'd been at it for an hour, and she could see his attention starting to fade.

"Good question," he said. "I don't really know. It seems likely that I'm too late. The last thing I heard from the people in the state treasurer's office is that they need my mother's death certificate before they'll even talk to me. Who knows how to get a death certificate?" He gave her an exasperated look, and she shrugged as if she didn't know. "I had to look it up," he went on. "I filled out all the paperwork, and now I wait."

Waiting, though, was something to do. True, if he never took another bite of chicken vindaloo or garam masala curry he would not be sorry, but it wasn't like he had somewhere else to go when this excursion was over; it wasn't as if a job or a house or a family was draw-ing him back or propelling him forward. His grand strategy—if he could even call it that—had been to capture the money and move on. But now that he was here, and now that there were people who had come to expect to see him every day, he found himself sometimes forgetting that getting up, stepping into a pair of khakis and pulling on a blue oxford shirt, and going to the library was not his job—though there was that not so inconsequential difference that real jobs, actual jobs, jobs where you woke up before sunrise, put on a suit, grabbed a coffee and a bagel, and fell in with all the other sleep-deprived, suit-wearing, coffee-drinking bagel eaters, came with a paycheck. "You have to spend money to make money," he told himself most mornings before catapulting out of the sagging double bed at the Tip-Top, but so far it was all spending, no making. He was being frugal, but still.

At times the Four would probe him about the future, asking him what he was going to do next, meaning what job, what profession, once his "little expedition" to Riverton was over. Of all of them, Paddy, the Wednesday gambler, was the most skeptical of Rusty's pursuit, knowing firsthand the perils of the promise of free money. "You need a plan," he'd say, and Rusty would nod and have nothing to say, and in that silence Carl would make a joke, say something like Rusty's plan should be to go down to the Caribbean and become a shoeless beach bum. Then Rich the driver would argue in favor of Rusty going to Hawaii instead, and the other Rich would suggest Maui, and his cousin would counter with Oahu, places neither of them had been to but nonetheless could recite their many virtues. Their banter spared Rusty the embarrassment of admitting he had no particular ambition now that his chosen profession no longer seemed to be an option, and that if he didn't figure this all out soon, he'd be living out of his car.

"Do you know why, when I go to the casino, I don't play poker?" Patrick asked him one day, and then answered his own question: "I don't play poker because I don't have a poker face."

Rusty wondered if the old man was starting to lose it, it was such a strange thing to say.

"In other words," Carl said, translating. "Don't do something you can't countenance."

"Whoa, big word, Carl," business Rich said, high-fiving his friend.

"It happens," Carl said.

But Rusty was thinking, not listening. Was the old doctor talking about the whole bankbook scheme, or was he cautioning against going back to a place like Morris, Maines?

His little, nameless, unremembered, acts /
Of kindness and of love.

—WILLIAM WORDSWORTH

The call came just after three. Sunny was off in the basement, surreptitiously making copies for Rusty on the free employee machine, so she didn't hear the phone ring, and the rest of the staff, gathered in the director's office for an emergency meeting, did, but chose to let it go to voice mail.

"It's that bad, is it?" Evelyn was saying, and Barbara, who had just announced she was taking a leave of absence to spend more time with Larry, hung her head and exhaled loudly.

"I'm afraid it is," she said. "He's stopped speaking. He's lost his words completely."

They sat in silence, taking this in.

"I'd like Kit to take over when I'm gone," Barbara said, and before she could say how long that would be there was a knock on the door and it was Rusty, standing there with his phone held out to them like an offering. They stared at him. He stared back.

Evelyn broke the spell. "We're in a meeting," she said, stating the obvious. She sounded annoyed, which probably had less to do with being interrupted, Kit thought, and more to do with the fact that inadvertently, she—Kit—had jumped the queue to a job she didn't even want. If seniority counted for anything, she—Evelyn—should be put in charge.

"It's Carl," Rusty said, and then immediately corrected himself. "I mean it's about Carl. He's had a stroke."

Smoker. Drinker. Beer gut. Doughnuts. The couch. French fries. Whisky sours. Carl was a marked man. Still, it didn't seem fair, not even to Chuck, who knew a thing or two about how the body could go haywire.

"He's in the hospital," Rusty added. "Riverton Mercy."

"I'd like to go," Kit said, standing up. Whatever this plan of Barbara's was, it could wait. And if Evelyn wanted to run the show, more power to her.

"I'll take her," Rusty volunteered.

"Go, go," Barbara said. "We'll talk when you get back."

But Kit didn't go back. Not that day. She and Rusty joined the long line of Carl's friends rotating in and out of the ICU, two at a time, three hours out, ten minutes in.

"You need to stand on the left side of the bed," they told one another. It was like a game of telephone: "Stand on his left side; his right side is paralyzed." "Make sure you're on the left side because he's paralyzed." "He's paralyzed on his left side, so stand on that side of the bed so he can see you."

When it was their turn, Kit and Rusty stood side by

side on the far side of the bed, holding on to the railing as if they were on the deck of a ship as Carl writhed insensibly, his body electric. His skin was gray, his eyes closed, his hands wound into fists that bounced along the mattress and sometimes landed soft, aimless punches to his chest or thighs. Kit had seen sick people before, and she had seen people who had died, but she had never seen anything like this. It was as if every circuit in Carl's brain had gone berserk and was sending crazy, warring messages to every synapse and axon in it. Carl wasn't talking, but a string of unintelligible sounds were coming out of his mouth.

"We're here, Carl," Rusty said firmly, though he didn't say who was there, because really, what did it matter?

"Where are all the tubes and the IV bags and monitors?" Kit asked the nurse, a lithe, possibly Filipino woman who was shuttling between Carl and the man in the cubicle next to him who, veiled by the thinnest curtain, they couldn't see, only hear. The man was wheezing and his lungs were crackling like popping corn, and someone standing alongside his bed, the way Kit and Rusty were standing alongside Carl's, was praying out loud, reciting the Twenty-Third Psalm over and over like a rosary.

"We don't do that," the nurse said, checking Carl's

pulse and adjusting his johnny, which had inched up his legs and was close to revealing all.

"But it's a hospital," Kit said. "Isn't that what you do do?"

"Not if the patient has a DNR," the nurse said, turning to leave. "A do not resuscitate order as Mr."—she looked at the name on the chart hanging off the side of the bed—"Layton does."

"I only just learned his last name myself," Rusty said, turning to Kit when the nurse was gone. "It's one of the things I really hate about all this."

"All what?"

"Death. Dying. Think about how many times you've read an obituary for someone you thought you knew, only to find that you hardly knew them at all. What they'd done, who they were, what they loved, who they loved. Their last name, for heaven's sakes."

"You've only known Carl for a couple of weeks," Kit said, and didn't know if she meant to console him or criticize him. She appreciated Rusty's sentiment, but it seemed presumptuous. He had known Carl for what—a month at most? In the scheme of things, that was nothing. Even her four years were like seconds in the life of a seventy-seven-year-old.

Their ten minutes were nearly up. The nurse came in to tell them.

"You're sure you can't do anything?" Kit tried again. "Look at him. He's so agitated."

Carl was still thrashing around and one eye was open, staring vacantly, tracking nothing in particular. Was it this side that was paralyzed or the other? Kit couldn't tell.

"We gave him a sedative," the nurse said.

"I think he needs more," Rusty said. "He's going to hurt himself."

The nurse gave Rusty a tight, tired smirk. "We're professionals. This is our job. You have your jobs, we have ours." She turned on the balls of her feet. She was wearing lime-green Crocs that flopped when she walked.

"Carl, this is Kit. I'm here with Rusty, but we have to go," Kit said, directing her words to the man in the bed. "They only gave us ten minutes, and you're a popular guy. The waiting room is like you used to describe Saturdays at the barbershop. Totally packed." She reached under the railing and put her hand on the skin where his neck met his shoulder and fought to hold it there as his body bucked and jerked. Then, for a brief few seconds, Carl's second eye opened and he stopped moving. Kit leaned over until her mouth was an inch from his ear. "You're my favorite," she whispered. "You probably thought it was one of the others, but it was always you."

# Chapter Nine
## 8.2.10 – 8.8.10

Because we live by inches . . .

—ADRIENNE RICH

Dying towns have funeral homes. This was an economic truth Kit had learned in her travels east: even when the last store had been relocated to the mall, even when the elementary school was shut down because there were not enough students to fill its classrooms, the funeral parlor survived. Mill Street Mortuary was around the corner from the library in a compact but strangely grand building; with an arched doorway and ornate Corinthian columns, the place looked like a fraternity house, but a fraternity house on a campus where every other building had been condemned. Carl's service was called for 2:00 P.M., but by 1:30, when Kit turned off the lights of the library, hung a CLOSED FOR THE DAY sign on the front door, and slipped through the back alley to Mill Street, people were converging on the chapel from all directions. Closing the library in the middle of the day was Kit's first decision as director, and it felt good to be able to do that for Carl, who really was her favorite.

Though she had been in Riverton for four years, Kit had never been inside the funeral home, which she'd always supposed was dimly lit and furnished with brocaded velvet pews from which dust would rise when mourners sat on them. But as she followed the flow of people wearing clothes that came out of the closet just once or twice a year, she saw that the sanctuary was a featureless room sheathed with imitation wood paneling, with metal folding chairs for seating. Carl's closed blond oak casket was on a riser at the front, a photo of him as a young man in a Coast Guard uniform perched on top, and next to it a portable lectern. Where to sit? Kit looked for someone she knew, but it seemed that everyone there had already paired up or was huddling with friends. This was when she hated being a single woman the most and missed—actually missed—Cal, missed how she would slide her hand into his when they walked into a room like this and how he would fold his fingers over hers, and how it felt protective and safe.

She caught sight of Chuck, standing in the aisle with his arm around an animated, raven-haired woman with lambent eyes of no particular color, and wondered what such a beauty was doing with Chuck of all people, and immediately felt callous for doubting a woman like that (gorgeous) would choose to be with a man like that (physically impaired). But of course, she told herself, there had been a time before the malignancy had stolen his voice and ravaged his body—but even if there wasn't, so what? As she stood there, berating herself for being so small-minded, a man sitting in the middle of a row in the middle of the room turned, saw her, and called her over. It was Rusty.

"I saved us seats," he said. "If Sunny comes, she can sit there." He pointed to an empty seat on the other side of Kit. "If not, given the fact that Carl oversold the space, I think we should auction it off to the highest bidder."

Kit laughed, loudly enough for the knot of people in front of them to loosen, turn around, and stare.

"It's a funeral. Have some respect," Rusty teased her, and she almost laughed out loud again.

"Isn't Chuck's wife stunning?" Kit said, as much to state a fact as to be on record for saying it.

"So is she," Rusty said, nodding in the direction of the door as Sunny passed through and scanned the room. And he was right. The red tips at the ends of Sunny's bangs were gone, and her hair was washed and held off her face with two silver barrettes that matched the silver choker around her neck. The sleeveless black jersey dress she wore hugged her body, and was so different from Sunny's usual attire of grubby, oversized T-shirts that Kit was even a little surprised Sunny had a body, and for the first time could see the lovely woman Sunny was going to become.

"I have something to tell you," Sunny said quietly as she squeezed past Kit to take her seat as a slow, mournful instrumental version of "You'll Never Walk Alone" was broadcast throughout the room.

"Okay," Kit said. "But not now. After."

The program called for the mayor to speak first, then Patrick, and then the pastor from the Congregational church. Even though Carl had been born Catholic, he had cut Reverend Musgrave's hair from the time it was red and short with a rattail hanging off the back till it was white. Carl had no heirs. His friends were his heirs and his clients were his heirs, and much of the time they were the same people. His wife had died young, before they had children, and despite the best efforts of just about everyone who knew him, and his reputation as a flirt, Carl had never married again.

"I was elected mayor of Riverton," a chubby man with a state trooper buzz cut said, "but Carl Layton was our real mayor. For better than fifty years he held court on Main Street as he cut the hair of anyone who was anybody, and anybody who wasn't."

Kit surveyed the crowd of mostly bald heads, though she imagined Carl knew them when those heads were downy, too, and was moved by how many people had taken time out of their day to pay respects to an old man who appeared to be solitary, but wasn't.

When it was his turn, Patrick walked slowly to the lectern, then called the two Riches up to stand beside him. "At the library, where we've been hanging out every morning for at least the past ten years, we were known as the Four." He looked out in Kit's direction and gave a slight nod. "But now we are three." He talked about Carl and their friendship, and how it went all the way back to the first grade. "Barbers used to be surgeons, Carl would remind me when I was in medical school. He'd also remind me that he was making a lot more money than I was—which wouldn't have been hard. He loved rubbing that in. He loved a good joke. He loved all the guys who came into the shop. Everyone was a friend, and if you were a friend, you were family. Carl didn't have kids. He had all of you. He had all of us. Indulge me for a minute. Reach out and hold the hand of the people on either side of you. Reach out, hold their hand, close your eyes, and think of all the connections Carl made in his life. Go ahead, even if you're uncomfortable. Do it now. Obviously, I don't have all the time in the world."

Kit took hold of Sunny's hand and let Rusty take hers. She gave Sunny's a squeeze and Sunny squeezed back, but kept her hand still inside Rusty's. It was enough to feel his warm skin encircling hers and not reflexively pull back.

"This is how it happens," Patrick said, taking a piece of paper from his jacket pocket, unfolding it and holding it up. "Most of you can't see it from where you're sitting, but this is a copy of our second grade class picture, mine and Carl's. I'm the little guy over here," he said, pointing to the bottom left, "and Carl is two kids over. You might not recognize him because that was about two million doughnuts ago."

As everyone laughed, an unsmiling Patrick reached back into his jacket and pulled out a pen. He leaned on the lectern and appeared to be writing something. The room was so hushed, everyone could hear the scratch of the pen on the paper. Patrick held it up again. Carl's image had been blacked out. So had the girl next to him and four boys in the second row.

"This is how it happens," he said again, quietly and near tears. "They go, one by one, and before you know it, the room is empty."

◆　◆　◆

Again we see the patriarch with his flocks . . .
　　　　　　　　　　　　　　　—EMMA LAZARUS

The reception following the funeral was held in the basement of city hall, which used to be Riverton High School, back when the Four were teenagers. Kit tried to imagine Carl walking down the long, dark corridors, a shy, lanky Carl in his Riverton Bobbins baseball uniform, a Norman Rockwell Carl, but couldn't. The Carl of the past was always going to be the Carl she had known: voluble, chunky, kind, flirtatious.

"This place is so old," Sunny said.

She was walking between Rusty and Kit, their feet carried along by the current of mourners. Sunny spied Evelyn up ahead, surrounded by a gaggle of children and grandchildren, and Kit realized that one of the people Patrick had blacked out of that second grade picture was the boy who grew up to become Evelyn's husband.

"It's funny to think that I'm walking on the same

floor that Carl walked when he was my age," Sunny added.

The basement, when they finally reached it, was jammed. Rusty plowed through the crowd to get them something to eat, and as soon as he was gone, Sunny turned to Kit and began talking, fast.

"I've been doing some more research," she said. Her eyes searched Kit's face, making certain the older woman knew what she was talking about. To be sure she said, "You know what I mean, right?"

Kit nodded. "Are you sure this is a good place?" Kit said. "All these people."

Sunny considered this for a second and then said, "He's not that guy, either."

"What guy?" Rusty said, coming up behind her.

Sunny blanched and looked to Kit for help.

"It's a boy—it's a girl thing," Kit said lightly.

"I like boy-girl things," Rusty said, handing them each a brownie.

"Very funny," Kit said.

"I'm completely serious. Look at me." He made a serious face, then shoved two brownies into his mouth and made chipmunk cheeks.

"Very funny," Kit said again, but like Sunny, she couldn't not laugh at him.

◆ ◆ ◆

### Sunny | imposter

After we went for ice cream and onion rings, Kit and me and Rusty, I spent the night at Kit's house. She had been married once, that's what she said at the drive-in, and I said I knew that. I didn't, really. I knew only that she'd had a different name, and because it was crossed out in the book she gave me, I didn't know what it was. Names turn out to be more important than I thought. I'm Solstice Arkinsky, and Arkinsky is completely made up; as Willow says, it was pulled right out of the air, which is a pun I loved when I was little. Now I wonder if it wasn't pulled out of the air for the same reason Angus Parker was pulled out of the air: because it's made up. And that's what I wanted to tell Kit at the funeral: Steve isn't Angus Parker! He's not Angus Parker, because Angus Parker doesn't exist.

Here's the thing: Angus Parker did exist. There was a boy named Angus Parker who would be around the same age as Steve if he hadn't died when he was two. The FBI—yes, the FBI!—believes that the person it thought was Angus Parker is actually someone impersonating Angus Parker. Someone who was using Parker's Social Security number to obtain a driver's license and a passport and get work, and then stopped being Parker right around the time of the vandalism at that drug company in Pennsylvania. The FBI bulletin, which I found online, says that Angus Parker, whoever he is, is to be considered "armed and dangerous," which is kind of hysterical if you know Steve. True, he knows how to shoot. He was on the pistol team at his high school. His father was military. His friends' fathers were military. Shooting was what they did for fun. Steve says that when it went from knocking cans off a railing to aiming at life-sized pictures of actual people, he couldn't do it anymore. He kept his grandfather's Remington because it had sentimental value, but when he began to think about all the creatures it had killed, and probably people, too, he no longer felt that connection, and he sold it. "Armed and dangerous"—I don't think so.

I didn't know this, that night at Kit's. That night I thought Steve was Angus Parker and Kit Jarvis was Kit S-something, and I wanted to ask her about it, but she didn't give me a chance. She must have known I was going to ask, because as soon as we got inside her house she said she was tired and was going to go upstairs to bed and pointed at the door to the room where I'd slept before and said, "You know the drill." That was it. She climbed the stairs and I was back in the room with the notebooks. Back in the room with "that girl."

I sat at the end of the bed for a while, staring at the boxes that had the notebooks inside. There was nothing stopping me from taking one off the shelf again and digging through it, but I didn't. I was curious, but not curious enough. As long as there are secrets, there are going to be mysteries. That's what I realized, sitting there. As long as someone has something she wants to keep to herself, someone else is going to want to find out what it is. I guess that's human nature. I shut off the light and climbed into bed. The mystery of "that girl" was not mine to solve.

# The Marriage Story

## — PART IV —

D id I blame Cal? I admit it—I did. I blamed him and I blamed his father, and sometimes I blamed myself for listening to them, or for letting myself yield to them, for not saying no, for not standing up for my own body. I wasn't twenty-five yet, and I'd been pregnant once, and I wasn't ever going to be pregnant again. I'd find myself crying over nothing, and crying over everything, and it didn't take long before the words "it's your hormones talking," or, even worse, "it's just your hormones talking," would send me into a rage or into a tailspin and sometimes both. I would have been impossible to live with then, but Cal was in the thick of his training and was rarely at home. He did a rotation in Los Angeles and another in Cleveland, and I stayed behind, ostensibly because of work, but really to wallow. When he'd surface from a long stretch in the hospital, Cal would e-mail me notes, all upbeat, as if he could change my mood by willing me to mirror his. (He was doing neurology and not being sly about it, writing to me about how the same neurons in the brain light up whether someone is actually running or thinking about running or looking at a picture of running, though I think he may have been overstating the picture part.) Every so often, on the phone, he'd say, "We'll find another way," which was supposed to console me, but didn't. Our marriage should have ended there, but Cal was too busy, and I was too scared: Who would want me now?

I went home to my mother for a few weeks and slept in my childhood bed, surrounded by my Trixie Belden books and stuffed animals, the way my mother had gone home after my father died and slept in her old bed, sheltered by old, familiar things. I lay there, under the covers, staring at the wall, as my mother rubbed my back and said nothing. She'd bring me lemon tea and make me sit up and sip it while she sipped a cup, too. No words—not from her, not from me. Then she started putting food on a tray and leaving it on the nightstand, and though she never told me to eat it, she always described what was there in exquisite detail so that after she left the room, my mind would be filled with the

smells and images of lemongrass chicken and Balti-
more crab cakes and popovers and Szechuan noodles in
peanut sauce. It was the popovers that got to me. My
mother left them beside me, left me remembering how,
when I was a kid, I'd tear off a piece with my teeth, let it
melt on my tongue, and without thinking I reached out
and grabbed one and ate it before I could taste it. The
next day there was chicken salad on her angel biscuits,
and the day after that her ridiculously creamy mac and
cheese. She'd bring it up and I wouldn't even wait for
her to leave. I was on my way to regaining the weight
I'd lost since I'd lost the baby and everything that went
with it.

And then, nothing. My mother didn't stop cooking—
not at all. I'd hear her banging around the kitchen, smell
onions sautéing in olive oil, and lie in my bed trying
to discern what would soon be on its way up the stairs
to me. She'd come up every so often, empty-handed,
and when I asked her what she was cooking, she'd say,
"Come down and have a peek," and when I asked her
to bring it up to me, instead, she said, "It will be waiting for you whenever you're ready." It wasn't Lourdes,
exactly, but one day I got out of bed and, in a manner of
speaking, started walking again. The aroma of the apple
pie bubbling in the oven was too much. It was pouring
rain outside, and just as I got to the kitchen the power

went out, so instead of eating pie, I followed my mother down to the basement where the sump pump was again no longer working, to help bail it out. And that's what did it: the image of my mother, illuminated by the kerosene lamp hanging overhead; an older woman with jeans rolled up to her calves standing ankle-deep in water, unwilling to surrender our house to the elements. This was a woman who had not only lost her husband, but lost the life she was living and the life she thought she was going to live, when she was about my age. This was a woman who had the good sense and the patience to never tell me to pull up my socks. She knew I'd have to pull them up myself when I was ready. I was ready.

It is true that Cal did not appreciate it when I referred to myself as "the Barrenness"—he always had trouble with my humor—but he was pleased to find the shades no longer drawn when he came back from Cleveland, and food in the refrigerator, and a wife who did not shy away from his touch. Medical school was ending soon, and Cal was offered a well-regarded internship and residency at Emory, so off we went to our new life in Atlanta, where we expected to be for at least five years or eight years or possibly forever. We found a cute place near Grant Park, in a transitional neighborhood that was on the cusp of gentrification. From the outside we didn't look any different from the other young couples standing in line at the food co-op and the hardware store. (Was everyone pulling up linoleum and refinishing hardwood floors?) We were all fresh, we were all on our way, and there was no question that that way was up. I found a job at the university science library. Cal fell in with an agreeable group of very tired doctors, and when we could, we carpooled with some of them to camp in the Blue Ridge Mountains or swim in Lake Lanier. For a day or two we could pretend, all of us, even me, that we were carefree.

◆   ◆   ◆

It is not to diffuse you that you were born of your mother and father, it is to identify you . . .
                    —WALT WHITMAN

Since Carl died, none of his friends had been back to the library. Rusty, too, was less eager to get up in the morning and head over there. Kit was no longer at her desk, she was in the director's office, and if Rusty wanted to see her he'd have to walk past Evelyn and knock on the office door, and how many times a day could he do that without feeling foolish? He was still working on the archive project, but without Kit nearby, and with Sunny in some kind of funk, it had lost its appeal. So did the whole idea of finding free money, which was beginning to seem as desperate to him as, he was beginning to realize, it must have seemed to others all along. It was time to get serious about finding a real job.

"I'm about to join the ranks of the unemployed," Rusty said, standing in the doorway to Kit's office.

"I thought that happened a while ago," she said.

"Not like this," he said. "I am now one of those people downsized during the recession who's at the public library to post his pathetic résumé online." He pulled a neatly formatted piece of paper from his bag and waved it around.

"Let me see that," Kit said, holding out her hand.

"I've got to edit it," he said.

"Come on," she said.

"No way," he said. "I wouldn't want you to suddenly get intimidated to be in the presence of the former senior executive vice president for client relations oversight."

"I see your point," Kit said as the phone began to ring.

"Power lunch?" he said as she picked it up. "Noon. Outside."

And before Kit could say yes or no, Rusty waved his résumé and shut the door. It was 11:30, just about the time the Four would have been leaving to dine at

Riverton Mercy, where Carl died, a place he hoped never again to go.

**Carl's death** hit Rusty hard—harder than he would have imagined for a man he had only just begun to get to know. When he mentioned this to Kit the first time, she hardly responded, but sitting side by side on the steps of the library as they ate their lunch, she seemed to hear it differently.

"Tell me about your father," she said, doing her best impersonation of Dr. Bondi. She handed him half of the wrap sandwich she'd made that morning, carefully layering slices of tomato, then cheddar, then turkey and lettuce leaves onto a tortilla before rolling the whole thing up and cutting it in half, thinking as she did that she might end up sharing it with him. It was an unsettling revelation—that she was expecting to spend time with him, looking forward to it and looking out for him—and she quickly buried it under other, more benign thoughts about what the day ahead might hold.

"He was a good guy," Rusty said. "Everybody liked him."

"How old were you when he died?"

"You know that. Eleven."

"And then what happened?" Kit asked.

"What do you mean, what happened? He was dead," Rusty said, clearly peeved.

"I get that you were angry," Kit said. Now she was not only impersonating Bondi, she was mimicking him. And it felt weird, like she was in two conversations at once, hers with Dr. Bondi transposed on the one she was having with Rusty. But maybe they were getting somewhere.

"Of course I'm angry," Rusty said. "It was hard. It was confusing. We were just beginning to really get close. We were the guys in the house, you know? We'd watch the Vikings on TV and he'd have a can of Miller in his hand and sometimes give me a sip. I didn't like it, and I told him, and he said I'd get there and that he was looking forward to the day when we'd be watching the game, splitting a six-pack."

Would Dr. Bondi encourage him to keep talking, Kit wondered, or would he have gone silent, waiting like a hunter in a duck blind for Rusty to reveal himself? Rusty was leaning back, eyes closed, arms folded across his chest. Kit knew this pose, knew it from the inside out. Nearby, a driver was struggling to squeeze a black SUV into a tight parking space two doors down from the old barbershop. Kit watched her cut the wheel hard and drive straight back, bumping into the sidewalk, then pull out and try again, adjusting slightly, but not enough. She wondered if Dr. Bondi had as much trouble staying still as she did.

"Tell me about Carl," she said after the driver gave up on the fourth attempt and drove away.

Rusty opened his eyes. From where they were sitting, a sliver of the river was just about visible, and Rusty trained his sights on that. "I really felt that he was looking out for me—cared about me. He and Patrick both, but I think he liked me more than Patrick did. Does," he said.

"Liking people was his business," she said. Was she being mean? She was trying to be provocative. She was beginning to have more sympathy for Dr. Bondi, sitting there on the worn, ungiving library steps, than she ever had perched in the plush brown chair in his office as he patiently tried to save her from herself.

"He wanted to help me," Rusty said.

"Okay," Kit said, "tell me more."

"He was a good guy," Rusty said. "Like my dad."

"That's what I'm saying," Kit said.

"You haven't said anything," he complained. "You've only asked questions."

"It's transference," Kit said. "That's what the shrinks call it."

She flashed, briefly, to an image of Dr. Bondi sitting upright opposite her the very first time they met, explaining the mechanism that would let her substitute him for Cal, or maybe for her father—she no longer remembered—and work out her feelings about them through him. "There's been a lot of disappointment and betrayal in your life, and this will give you the opportunity to express yourself and be heard," he said, and she laughed at him. What bunk! And now she was peddling it herself.

"You saw your father in Carl. Carl wasn't going to bring your father back. He wasn't going to be your surrogate father. But he was letting you feel what your life would be like with an older, caring man in it," she said. As the words came out of her mouth they sounded false and cheesy, but maybe they were true.

"I guess," he said, sounding unconvinced. It was time to go inside.

**That afternoon,** Cyrus Ingram Allen edited his résumé, eliminating anything that could reveal his age, and posted it online and e-mailed it to a headhunter in New York he used to know and to the firms he'd been reading about in the *Wall Street Journal* that were hiring again. His heart wasn't in it, but he no longer had the luxury of heart. Heart did not pay the bills.

◆　◆　◆

### Sunny | fugitive

As soon as I realized that I was probably living with a fugitive, I got scared. Every time Steve got in the car, I reminded him that he could get pulled over for having a faulty exhaust system.

"Enough with the exhaust system, Sunny," he said after maybe the sixth time I said something. "I'm working on it."

How could he be so cool? The police could come and take him away at any moment. Maybe he wasn't guilty after all. That's what I told myself. But then I told myself that was impossible. I was jittery. Willow noticed and made me chamomile tea. That's her go-to cure and it usually works. Not this time.

"What's with you, Sunny?" she said right before bed. "Is it just teenage stuff?"

"Teenage stuff" is what my mother calls anything to do with my changing body.

"No," I said.

"Then what? You can tell me. We tell each other everything."

Well, that was a lie, and it made me so angry I almost told her I knew she was lying to me right then—about that and about pretty much everything else I thought I knew about our family. It was like discovering I'd been adopted and no one would admit it.

"I don't know," I lied back.

"Is it your job at the library? Is somebody bothering you? If somebody is bothering you, you need to let Kit know. Is it Kit? Is she bothering you? I've always hated having a boss . . ." and then she went off on this whole long riff about power dynamics in the workplace, suggesting that that might be something I'd want to do a study unit on, blah blah blah, and I fell asleep.

I didn't wake up any calmer. My parents have always told me that knowledge is power, but the more I knew about them, the less empowered I felt. Angus Parker was dead. He had died twice. But Steve was still alive, and if he'd done what the police said Angus Parker had done, there were people who wanted to find him and put him in jail. Willow, too. And what about me? Wasn't I guilty, too? Guilt by association, guilt by knowing what I know and not telling anyone? No, that wasn't true. I had told someone. I'd told Kit. So she was guilty now, too, and it was my fault.

It was a Saturday, the day I usually helped out Willow at the kiosk. "Helping out" is a euphemism for keeping her company. Saturday is when people like to look at her jewelry, but midweek is when they buy. A mother stops by with her daughter, or a man stops by with his girlfriend or wife, and they look at Willow's stuff and the daughter slips a bracelet over her hand and holds out her wrist and they both admire it. She puts it back and they move on, and then, a few days later, the mother reappears and says, "Remember that bracelet my daughter tried on?" (And Willow always does.) "I want to get that for her birthday." Tuesdays are Willow's best days.

"I think I should stay home today," I said, and Willow did not try to talk me out of it.

As soon as she and Steve left, I went around to the back of the house and got my bike, which I hadn't ridden in a while, and pumped up the tires. It was nine miles to Riverton, not counting our driveway, and I figured I could get there and back before Willow came home from work. It occurred to me that Steve might be dropping her off and coming right back, so I went into the house, wrote a note to tell him I was out for a bike ride, and set off for Kit's house. I needed to talk to her.

# Chapter Ten
## 8.9.10 – 8.15.10

The dark / Encroachment of that old catastrophe . . .
—WALLACE STEVENS

I t was early evening, after work. Kit was walking home when Rusty, whom she hadn't seen for a few days, drove up alongside her, slowed, and asked if she wanted a ride.

"I can walk," Kit said. She'd been looking forward to this slow meander home all afternoon. It was her second full week as director, and Barbara had left her with a pile of bills, a decimated bank account, and a budget that needed to be massaged to make it all work. It made her head hurt. All she wanted was to get home, fill a glass with Chardonnay, and sit on the porch with her feet up, watching the world go by.

"I know that," he said. "That's not what I asked."

"Since when did you become such a stickler for language?" she said, not bothering to hide her displeasure, not only with him for the interruption, but with herself for letting him think it was okay. "This is what happens," she thought. "This is what happens and it happens in an instant: they want more, then they want more than that, and they assume you do, too."

"I can walk, and I will walk," Kit said. She resumed her stroll, pleased to be on her way again, pleased to have recaptured her solitude.

The sidewalk in this part of town was usually empty, so when she heard footsteps behind her, Kit turned around, and there he was again, Rusty, on foot.

"I can walk, too," he said, and fell in beside her. "I'm screwed if it rains, though. I left the top down."

"You could go back," Kit suggested.

"I could go back, and I will not go back," he said. "Not yet. I bought us a bottle of wine, a nice Zinfandel. A big splurge for me, given my reduced circumstances."

He looked so pleased with himself, and so eager, she didn't have the heart to tell him it was white wine she was craving. That, and being alone.

"**Where do** you keep your wineglasses?" Rusty said as they stepped onto Kit's porch.

"In the kitchen. You'll see them. I don't have much stuff," she said, and stopped in her tracks. "I'll wait here." It was easier to be with him outside than in. On the porch, the walls were only waist-high.

When Rusty reappeared, the bottle of wine was under his arm and there were two very full glasses in both of his hands.

"Here, take this," he said, handing her one and putting down the other and the bottle. "I'll be right back."

Kit could hear him opening the refrigerator, closing it, opening a cupboard, closing it. Opening the refrigerator again. Opening drawers.

"What are you doing?" she called out to him, and either he didn't hear or was ignoring her, because no answer came back until, a good ten minutes later, he reappeared.

"I was trying to score us some snacks, but this is all I could find," Rusty said, showing off a plate of crackers, each one dotted with tuna salad and topped with a piece of black olive.

"Where did you find that?" Kit asked, mildly embarrassed to have the near emptiness of her larder exposed.

"I made it," Rusty said proudly. "Years of packing my own school lunch," he added. "Not a lot to work with in there, though. Kind of like my house. The house where I grew up. And my condo in Hoboken. And where I am now, come to think of it."

Down the street, one of her neighbors was blasting reggae through a car speaker.

"That's what they do," she said. "Open the car door and play music."

"I like it," Rusty said. "Do you think they take requests?"

They sat there, slowly draining their glasses, looking out at the robins pecking at the lawn, saying little.

"This is nice," Rusty said.

"Is it?"

"That's what I said."

"I know," Kit said. "But this must be so different from what you're used to. Coming from the city. The big city," she added, unable to contain her scorn. She had seen this before with the summer people who decamped from Boston or New York to some of the lake towns near Riverton, or the leaf peepers who came back every fall, and believed that their time in the country made them better people.

Rusty laughed: "It's definitely different, but I like it." He picked up his glass and motioned to go inside. "It's getting cold," he said, and she was amazed and disconcerted by how easily he moved into her space.

"This is nice, too, after months of living in a motel room," he said, sinking into the living room couch and putting his feet on the coffee table.

As she watched him settle in like a floppy retriever, Kit felt her muscles seize up and her posture straighten. She could hear Dr. Bondi. It was as if he were sitting on her shoulder, whispering in her ear. "It's good to be aware of your feelings, Kit, even if you don't know why you're having them." But she knew. It had been a long time.

"So," Rusty said. "What do you do for fun here?"

Kit didn't know if he meant here in Riverton or here in her house. "Not much," she said. "Read, watch movies, look at cat videos on the Internet." Did that sound lame? Probably, she thought. Did she care? She didn't know.

"What about you?" Kit asked.

"Before I came here, or after?" he said. "You won't like before."

"Try me."

"You're going to think I'm really shallow."

"How do you know I don't think that already?" Kit said. She couldn't help herself.

"It was a lot of clubs, high-stakes poker, that sort of

thing. All work-related, of course," he said, draping his arms over the back of the cushions, a smile on his face, remembering it.

"Of course," Kit said. She tried to imagine him, sleeves rolled above his elbows, sitting in a smoky room—cigars—chips piled high in front of him, but that image kept on getting crowded out by the famous picture of dogs playing poker.

"And now?" she asked.

"Ah," he said, "now. Now I read books you literary types wouldn't approve of, watch TV, and eat Indian food every night. Unless I'm hanging out with you."

"We've only done that one time," Kit said.

"My point exactly," Rusty said. "We've known each other for weeks, and this is just our second date. Third, if you count lunch the other day."

"This is not a date," Kit said. "You . . ." She hesitated. "You invited yourself over." She was back to feeling cornered, and wanted suddenly, and overwhelmingly, to be alone and unaccountable.

"Can I ask you a question?" Rusty said, and then didn't wait for an answer. "Sometimes I get the sense that you like me, and other times I get the sense that you don't."

"I like you," Kit said. "I told you. You're a nice guy."

"Wow," he said.

"Wow what?"

"I haven't heard the 'you're a nice guy' line since—I don't know—college."

"Sorry," Kit said. "I probably haven't said anything like that since college, either. I'm—I'm out of practice."

He looked at her skeptically, squinting his eyes and pursing his lips. "You're out of practice at what, blowing guys off?"

Kit looked stricken. "No. No. Of course not. I'm out of practice at having people here. In the house with me." There, she said it. She knew it sounded pathetic, but it was true. If he really was a good guy, he'd get it. Or at least try to get it.

"You're not playing the spinster card, are you, or the widow card?" Rusty joked, trying to put her at ease and realizing as soon as he said it that it was a mistake. Kit's mouth had gone slack. Her eyes, too, if that was possible.

"Cal's not dead," Kit said when she finally spoke. "Lucky me." Her voice sounded uninhabited.

"Oh, shit, sorry," he said. "Foot-in-mouth disease. Chronic, apparently." He flashed her an embarrassed smile that Kit didn't acknowledge. She just sat there, watching the reflection of the blades of the overhead fan go round and round in her drink.

"Now I get it," Rusty said after a while, and when

she didn't ask what it was he got, said, "That's why you moved here." Said softly, but all in a rush, as if speaking quickly would make the ice he was skating on less thin.

Kit put down her drink. "Actually, no," she said, indulging him. "It's why I left. Not that I had a choice." Was this even true? What was it that Dr. Bondi was always telling her? That even when your back is up against a wall, you are not without options. "You can give up, or you can fight," he'd say, and Kit no longer remembered if leaving was fighting or leaving was giving up. Certainly it was giving up the money, the "substantial gift"—*gift*—the Doctor was holding out to her if she'd stay. "Women do badly after divorce," he explained, reaching for her hand as if she were a small, vulnerable child, and like a small, petulant child, she wouldn't let him take it. "This is for your own good, Katherine. Divorcées"—he actually used that word—"suffer a major reduction in their standard of living." Kit matched his pretend concern with pretend thankfulness, then turned around and divorced his son anyway.

"A pyrrhic victory," she told Bondi.

"But a victory," Dr. Silver Linings said.

"**Where is** he—Cal—now?" Rusty said.

"Cal?" she said, somehow surprised to be reminded

they were talking about him. "Don't ask me. I don't know. Probably with his daddy."

"That's different," Rusty said.

Kit shrugged. "Not really," she said. What was different was talking about it. Here, in her house. Her house. In Riverton. Something she told herself she was never going to do.

"I can't," she said suddenly, and firmly, as much to herself as to him. The tone of her voice had changed. It was brisk and a little boreal.

"You can't what?" Rusty said.

"Do this. With you."

"Do what with me? What are you doing with me?" If he felt the chill coming off her, he wasn't showing it. His tone was jocular. His eyes were playful, cajoling.

"Talking," Kit said simply.

"Talking," Rusty repeated. "Talking with me?"

Kit nodded. "I can't." She had carved out this space for herself, carved it, it sometimes felt, with her bare hands. She had made it small and unaccommodating by design. No one else fit. No room.

"Look," Rusty said. "You have to understand. I like it here. In Riverton. I didn't think I would, but I do. One reason I like it is that I like talking with you. I like you." He paused, let it sink in, but not too deeply. "And I like Paddy. I like the Riches. I liked Carl. I like Sunny. I even like Evelyn. She reminds me of people from when I was growing up in Duluth. But the most important thing I like is me. I like me here." He finished his speech, took a long swallow from the glass he had been clenching, topped it off, sank back into the sofa and looked at her expectantly.

"Let me ask you this," Kit said, choosing her words carefully. "If, tomorrow, you got your old job back, or some job like it, would you be a different person than you were before?"

She looked at him unblinking, with an appraiser's eye, and saw past Rusty's anxious expression to the jeweler with his jeweler's loupe turning first her wedding band—platinum, flecked with diamonds the size of grains of sand—and then her engagement ring—Tiffany setting, round cut, VS1 clarity—round and round, millimeter by millimeter, looking for perfection, imperfection, she wasn't sure which, only that he was judge and jury, until finally he offered her a price so high her first instinct was to talk him down, but she thanked him instead and took the check and called it her buyout.

"I'd like to say yes," he said after a long pause, "but I want to be honest, and I don't really know. That's the truth."

"I can appreciate that," Kit said. So that was that. Even if there had been room for him, even if she had wanted there to be room—not that she did; she didn't—it was folly. Given the chance, he'd go back to a life cantilevered on a stack of dollar bills. He'd look back on his time in Riverton as something sociological or anthropological, talking up their simpler way of life as if he had found himself among pioneers, living on the prairie, milking cows and churning their own butter. In the best case, he'd remember, with a certain amount of affection, the old guys who took him under their wings and, with a certain amount of amusement, the woman with the disorderly hair and catalog clothes, whom he kind of liked, believe it or not, even though no one he knew would understand. And in the worst case, he'd find ways to make fun of them all. Riverton would be the butt of his jokes, and after a while the jokes would get stale, and he wouldn't remember why he thought they (the jokes, the people, the place) were funny.

It was dark now. The wine was mostly gone, and Kit wanted nothing more, right then, than nothing more.

"I can drive you back to your car," she said.

"I can walk."

"I know you can walk," she said. "We established that."

As he rose from the sofa, he caught sight of a picture on the opposite wall and walked over to get a better look.

"I have one of these, too," he said, studying it. "Me and my dad at Lake Superior. I think I was three."

"I wasn't even a year old when that was taken," Kit said. "Lake Erie. He was killed a few months later."

"Brutal," he said.

"I never knew him."

"That's worse," Rusty said.

"You think so? I've always thought it would have been worse if I had."

They stood there for a few awkward seconds, studying the photograph, and then Kit pointed to the door and said, "The doorknob is a little jiggly, let me get it for you," and nearly pushed him through it.

# The Marriage Story

## — PART V —

A tlanta was good at first. It brought me out of the unlit tunnel I'd been stuck in since I lost my first and all babies, and now that I was on the other side, Cal and I treated each other with acute consideration. Our life together was like that slapstick routine where two people get to a door and one of them says, "You first," and the other says, "No, you first," and the first one says, "You first," and on and on and on and no one goes through. We'd say "please" and "thank you" for the smallest things and tiptoe around each other, afraid to offend or appear anything but healed and content. People who didn't know us, new friends, would tell us how cute we were with each other and how in love we seemed; women would confide that they wished their husbands would treat them with such tenderness. If only they knew.

I tried. I tried for years because what else was I going to do there? Cal was in the most intense part of his training, exhausted, distracted, and often absent from home so he could be exhausted, focused, and present at the hospital. His priorities were my priorities; they had to be. By default, it seemed, I had become the abiding, pliant wife the Doctor wanted me to be.

At work, where the head librarian tried to keep us up to date on cutting-edge scientific research, we'd look at images from the Hubble Space Telescope projected onto an enormous screen, and I'd find my mind drifting, and then my body, as if I were out there in that vast, cold darkness, blessedly unencumbered by mind or by body. I'd listen to geologists talking about drilling into the earth's core and wonder why they cared so much about what was on the inside when there was so much to be concerned about on the outside. Epidemiologists from the Centers for Disease Control came in to talk about population studies and mortality versus morbidity and my ears perked up: I was intimately acquainted with both. Then they would leave and I'd be back to sitting on a high stool in the middle of the reading room, answering the stray question when it arose, but mainly making sure no one was cutting out pages from the biochemistry textbook—it was a thing some enterprising premed students started doing to ensure their fellow premeds wouldn't be able to do the assigned reading—or pocketing one of our overpriced academic journals. Think of a corrections officer in a prison guardhouse and you'll have a good idea what I looked like and what I did.

I didn't have the energy to admit to myself at first, let alone my weary husband, whose work was relentless, that my job was tedious. What was the point? We were where we were because of him. And what was my tedium compared with his? He was going to be a physician and I was just the physician's wife; my work was simply a placeholder. Still, just as he was born to be a doctor, or raised to be one—because in Cal's case, nature and nurture were indistinguishable—I had to believe it was the same with me: I was born to spend my days among books. It wasn't noble or heroic like neurosurgery—I got that. But I also got that I loved Wallace Stevens and William Carlos Williams. I loved Charles Dickens and George Elliot. I loved Mary Oliver, Langston Hughes, Emily Dickinson, and Toni Morrison. And I loved libraries, because that is where I found all of them, and that was where I could hand them off to others. When I took the job at the science library, I told myself I was the kind of person who could find poetry in the periodic table, or see plotlines in the progression of cancer from one cell to the next. I tried to be that person. I wasn't that person.

Meanwhile, one by one, the wives of Cal's male study partners got pregnant, as if pregnancy were on the rotation between nephrology and otolaryngology. I went to the baby showers, patted the bellies, cooed at the pictures, and learned to stop telling the truth about my own situation because people, even smart, educated people, seemed to think that my infertility might rub off on them. Then the babies started coming and there were playdates and clothing swaps and birthday parties, and my most generous interpretation was that those women simply forgot to include me. It was hurtful and isolating, especially because I couldn't say anything about it. Compared with the challenges Cal was facing every day, my concerns seemed trivial. Try mentioning you felt left out when Lindsay didn't invite you to Emma's birthday party at Chuck E. Cheese to someone who just came off a fifteen-hour double lung transplant of a patient with cystic fibrosis who didn't make it out of the operating room. You wouldn't.

Exhausted as he was, Cal was thriving at the medical center. Older doctors were asking to have him on their service; he became chief resident a year earlier than anyone had become chief resident before. At departmental get-togethers, his supervisors made it a point to pull me aside and let me know I was doing God's work, not complaining when Cal missed holidays, not complaining when he was gone for days and nights at a time, not complaining when he got all the glory because, though all the glory was deserved, having a fixed address, clean clothes, bills paid, food on the table, and all the other things that passed in their world for domestic life were essential to the whole enterprise, not that anyone usually noticed. "Things seen and unseen," one of them said, as if to console me by bastardizing Corinthians.

It was the same with the Doctor, who wrapped strange thank-you notes written on pads of paper left behind by pharmaceutical reps hawking Viagra and Paxil around the checks he would send at Christmastime. In one, he said that he thought physicians' wives should be beatified, which I took to mean that we were not. "There already is a Saint Katherine (more commonly known as Saint Catherine)," I was tempted to write back, but didn't when I found out that her feast day had been removed from the Holy Roman calendar because none of her deeds and virtues could be verified.

Cal was offered a neurology fellowship at Columbia and the joint neurology-neurosurgery position at UCLA, but when Emory matched their offers and threw in more support for his lab, Cal turned the others down, said he didn't want to pack up and move his research, and that he was happy where he was, and as far as he could tell (not far, not his fault), I was, too.

We stuck it out in Atlanta for five years, and I convinced myself it wasn't bad. There were perks. When the dean of the medical school, where Cal was now an assistant professor (and the rumor factory had him pegged to be dean himself one day), heard that "Cal's wife" had left her job at the science library, he greased the skids for me (well, more accurately for "Cal's wife") to become the head research assistant for a multiyear project correlating demographic information with that morbidity and mortality data I was drawn to in my other job. We'd look at the census and phone books and birth and death records and map the progression of the flu through the country, identify where sexually transmitted diseases were most prevalent and try to predict where they'd travel next. It wasn't Dickens, but in those numbers you could see the outline of human stories and even begin to color them in. I made friends with the people in my group, and would go out now and then with the ones, like me, who were not especially tied down by children or spouses. Cal and I were living largely parallel lives, though when we'd intersect, we were friendly and companionable. If you had seen us together, you would have said we were happily enough married. If you'd asked me, I would have said that we never argued.

Cal's mom died when we were in Atlanta. After the burial, the Doctor pulled Cal aside and talked to him privately in his office while I served crudités and lemon pound cake to the people who came back to the house, which had fallen into mild disrepair over the months Lydia was ill. (We didn't know; the Doctor didn't want to distract Cal.)

"Thank you for coming," I said over and over again, only to hear "She was a great woman," and "You must be devastated," to which I could only think to say "thank you for coming" again.

When Cal emerged from his father's office, his expression, which looked sad and tired going in, had flatlined. His mouth was fixed and rigid; his eyes were senescent, as if they had finally seen too much. His hands—his very talented hands—were squeezed into fists. The Doctor was close behind, and even though he had just put his wife in the ground, he looked jolly. One of his golfing buddies sidelined him, and I watched the Doctor's face reassemble and become grief-stricken again. If this were *Hamlet*, he'd be Polonius.

"What's going on?" I asked Cal when I caught up to him walking angry laps around his parents' pool. His fists were still clenched, and the rain, though only a drizzle, had flattened his thinning hair and was streaking his glasses. Though we had flown in on separate planes, we'd been together for an uninterrupted thirty-two hours, which was a record in those days. I pried his fingers back and held both his hands. Anyone looking out at us from the dining room window would have assumed I was consoling him; they would have thought Cal was overcome with sorrow. But it wasn't that at all. He wasn't sad; he was furious.

"He just got me to agree to give up Atlanta and move back here," Cal hissed. He sounded like a cat. An angry, cornered cat.

"What do you mean?" I said, genuinely confused. This was Dr. Calvin Sweeney, associate professor of neurology and neurosurgery, boy wonder. This was Dr. Calvin Fortune Sweeney—or, as his students called him behind his back, "Dr. Calvin 'Always Good Fortune' Sweeney"—who was expected to unravel the genetics of Parkinson's disease and find the cure for Alzheimer's and perform the world's first brain transplant. (Well, maybe not the brain transplant, but the expectations for what Cal would accomplish were enormous.)

"Just what I said." This time his voice was uninflected, hollow.

"Here? To this house?"

"No, but close enough. It doesn't matter where. He says it's time to come back."

"But why? That doesn't make any sense. You're doing great things. You're going to do great things." How many times had I heard people say this to me about Cal? How many times did he hear it? No doubt the Doctor heard it, too.

"He's jealous," I said. "That's what this is, Cal. He can't live with the fact that you are a star." By now we were both soaking wet, and someone on the other side of the glass was knocking on the dining room window to get our attention.

"He may be jealous," Cal said, "but he's proud, too. He wants more credit. He wants people to see that his hand is behind everything I accomplish."

"Well, it's not. He doesn't own you," I said indignantly. "You're thirty years old. You don't have to do what your daddy says." I didn't bother to hide my scorn.

"You don't have a daddy," Cal said. "You can't understand."

I dropped his hands and backed away. "Nice, Cal," I said.

He could be cutting. Usually it was so subtle I could convince myself it wasn't happening. Cal had cultivated this midwestern, gee-shucks, humble Mr. Nice

Guy persona, maybe in contrast to his blustering father, maybe because it worked for him, so when he said things I found hurtful, it was confusing. It was like dissonant music: I didn't know what I was listening to. But there was no mistaking this; this stung.

"I'm upset," he said, as if that made it all right. And then he told me that back when he was applying to college, the Doctor and he made a deal: Cal's parents would pay for his education, college and medical school (because of course Cal was going to be a doctor), so he could start his career without debt. In return, Cal promised if he took the money, he'd come back to practice if the Doctor ever asked him.

"It seemed so theoretical at the time," Cal said.

"But you were so young!" I said indignantly. "You shouldn't have to keep a promise you made back then."

"I was young when I made a promise to you," he said bitterly. "So should I break that, too?"

◆　◆　◆

I do not on gray ashes count my sorrow . . .
—ANNA AKHMATOVA

As soon as Rusty left, Kit took the Lake Erie photograph off the wall and studied it carefully. It was a picture that had followed her from place to place to place. It was never not on a wall or mantel or bookshelf, no matter where she lived, and as a result had become part of the backdrop of her life, ambient as air. Looking at it now, what she couldn't believe she'd never noticed before was the resemblance between her father and the man she married. It wasn't anything specific—not their eye color or the way they combed their hair or the slant of their noses. Rather, it was their unmistakable self-possession, the way they held their bodies, the certainty that appeared to emanate from the square of their shoulders. Kit was remembering, again, how she'd slide her hand into Cal's and he'd lock his fingers around hers, and wondered if the safety she felt then was vestigial, left over from those early months with her dad.

**She heard** footsteps on her porch, and then knocking at the same time as Rusty's voice.

"Hey, Kit," he called, and her heart sank. Why couldn't people leave well enough alone?

"Yo, Kit," Rusty called again, knocking harder. "I'm really sorry to disturb you. If you can hear me, please open up."

Kit could hear him—she could hear him just fine—but the last thing she was going to do was to let him think that she'd come running at the sound of his voice. It was dumb, she knew, childish, or girlish, and then her phone started ringing and she reluctantly got out of the chair and went to the door. Rusty was standing under the yellow bug light, his face a garish citron, still staring at his phone.

"Sorry," Rusty said, looking up. "I guess the place where I left the car wasn't a parking spot. There's a boot on it."

"Did you call the number on the ticket?"

"That's the odd thing," Rusty said. "It went to voice mail. So I called the Riverton police directly, and that went to voice mail, so I called 911, and the dispatcher said to call back later, everyone is out on a call. Good thing it's not a real emergency. I'm sorry to ask, but would you mind running me up to the Tip-Top?" And when she didn't answer right away he said, "Or I could call a cab."

"I'll get my keys," Kit said. "Wait here."

**"I don't** think I've ever seen you drive," Rusty said as she unlocked the doors of the Volvo sedan in the driveway.

"I like to walk," Kit said.

"So you've said." He paused. "I'm sorry if—"

"No," she said, and after that they drove without speaking, Kit looking straight ahead, Rusty training his eyes to the right, to the river. A police car came up fast behind them, and Kit pulled over till it passed, and Rusty joked they were coming after him, and then another cruiser went by in the opposite direction and made a screeching U-turn not far behind the Volvo. Kit pulled over again, and waited until there were no flashing lights in the rearview mirror and none coming at them.

"Weird," she said. "There must have been a bad accident on the highway."

But when they got on the highway it was clear, a few cars going north, a few going south, almost all of them with kayaks and canoes and paddleboards and bicycles hanging off them like giant Christmas tree ornaments. Just before the exit for the Tip-Top, three fire trucks, sirens blaring, cut them off, forcing the Volvo over the rumble strip and onto the shoulder before Kit had time to slow down.

"Oh no, oh no, oh no," Rusty repeated as the car bumped along, and Kit, heart pounding, fighting to keep the wheels from running up on the grass, said, "It's okay, it's okay, it's okay," until her foot was firmly on the brake, and it was.

"It's okay, Rusty," she said sternly, when he didn't stop keening. And then, more softly, "It's okay," and Rusty shook his head and pointed west, over her left shoulder, to a curious spectral glow illuminating the scrim of trees on the rise above the road and a black funnel cloud reaching skyward.

"It's got to be the Tip-Top," he said. "It's got to be the Tip-Top. Oh fuck, oh fuck, oh fuck."

**The roadblock** started at the bottom of the motel access road. People in yellow turnout gear patrolled the entrance, waving everyone away except first responders, firefighters, and the police.

"But he lives there," Kit said, pleading with a small woman who was lost inside her oversized jacket and overalls. Even her helmet was too big and had slipped forward, its brim covering the tops of her eyes.

"We have to keep the road clear," she said.

A radio, clipped to her belt, was broadcasting static, and then a raspy, mechanical voice said, "Winchester One, five minutes out," and Kit said, "That's Chuck," and the woman pushed back the helmet and leaned her face into the car, and Kit realized she was looking at Chuck Odum's beautiful wife.

"I know you," the woman said. "You're Chuck's boss now."

"I don't think anyone is Chuck's boss," Kit said, laughing.

"True enough," the woman said.

"I'm Kit," Kit said.

"Linda," Chuck's wife said.

"This is nice, but I need to get up there," Rusty said, and jumped out of the car and started running up the hill.

"You're not authorized," Linda Odum yelled after him, but it was too late. He was sprinting and soon out of sight.

"Look," Linda said. "Find a place to ditch the car, and you can head up there and find your friend. Everyone is busy. They probably won't notice."

"Thanks," Kit said, as the woman backed away from the car.

**Ditching the** car was easier said than done. Cars and trucks were parked on both sides of the road, almost all with first responder or EMT license plates, or volunteer fire company stickers displayed in the back window. Kit followed them around a bend, noticed a spot on the other side of the road, and did a messy three-point turn and pulled in behind a Silverado jacked up on massive off-road wheels. She checked her watch. It was after ten. She could just make out the insistent wail of a siren, getting louder as it charged up the highway. She started to walk and then to jog. It was dark on the road, and it was narrow and twisty, and she wasn't wearing anything reflective. She picked up the pace.

"There you are," Linda said when Kit approached the roadblock. "Just stay out of the way. If anyone asks, you snuck in," and waved her through.

The access road was steep, and as she walked, Kit had to avoid rivulets of water coursing down from the top, carrying sand from last winter's snows and detritus loosened by the pressurized hoses. She was winded, and as she began to breathe through her open mouth, bitter flakes of soot landed on her tongue and she had to stop and spit, and as she did, she noticed the sky—what she could see of it—was flecked with what looked like black snow tacking lazily toward the ground. A tanker truck went by, heading downhill to the river for more water, and pretty soon she started to pass fire trucks and rescue vehicles, idling by the side of the road, waiting their turn to head up to what was left of the Tip-Top. No one tried to stop her or question what she was doing, so Kit made her way around them, climbing higher, smoke filling her nose, until she could see flames taunting the long arcs of water trained on them from a phalanx of fire engines lined up side by side. Someone had set up klieg lights around the perimeter, which made the whole scene look like a movie set, but there was nothing pretend about the heat coming off the building, which was fully engulfed.

"You can't be here," a sweat-stained man said to her,

and pointed to an area at the far end of the parking lot where someone had set up cots and a water station, and where she could just make out Rusty, kneeling, talking to someone sitting on one of the cots who, as Kit approached, put her arms around him.

When she got closer, Kit could see tears had streaked the soot on his face.

"I told him," the woman was saying. "I told him." She was older and spoke with an Indian accent.

"I know, I know," Rusty said, soothing her. "It was an accident."

"It was not an accident," the woman said. "I told him."

"I know," Rusty said again. "He's going to be fine."

"Rusty," Kit said. "I'm glad I found you."

"This is Mrs. Patel," Rusty said. "My landlady, I guess you could say."

"Grandmother," she corrected him. "Your Indian grandmother." She was smiling now, and then, just as suddenly, tears began to flow down her face.

"I was so worried, so worried," she said to Kit. "I thought he was still inside. I knocked on his door and no one answered, and the door was locked and the key was in reception where the fire started." She was sobbing now, rocking back and forth, and Rusty was holding her. "I was so worried about you."

"Everyone is okay," Rusty said. "That's what matters." And then, looking up at Kit, "Her husband is in one of the ambulances. Smoke inhalation. They're giving him oxygen." And then, to Mrs. Patel, "Do you want to go see him?" And when she said she did, Rusty helped her up off the cot and took her arm in his and told Kit they'd be back.

While she was standing there, a firefighter came up and asked her to fill a couple of water bottles, and then another came by asking to lie down for a minute, and before Rusty came back, Kit was running the rest station, even though no one knew who she was or what she was doing there. The fire was relentless. As soon as the firefighters vanquished it in one spot and turned to another, it would reignite, first as a small flame and then, when it found a stray piece of curtain that had somehow escaped being soaked or a splinter off a joist, flare up again. "Like Wile E. Coyote," she heard a firefighter say.

It was over just before sunrise. As the sky brightened, the klieg lights were turned off, and before long the curtain of daylight was raised on a scene no one would have predicted. There was nothing left. Not a single beam or wall or bed or television or towel rack. The footprint of the Tip-Top was a slurry of ash and melted plastic, smoke hovering above it like an incubus. Every so often a small flame would suddenly appear and just as suddenly subside, like a trick candle on a birthday cake, Kit thought, standing next to Rusty, watching it.

The elder Patels were going with their son and daughter-in-law to a relative's motel somewhere else in the state, and when they asked Rusty if he'd like to come with them, as their guest, Kit said, "No, he's coming with me." The words just flew out of her mouth, surprising Kit most of all.

"You couldn't go with them," Kit explained, as she and Rusty reached her car and she was telling him why she jumped in before he could answer the Patels. "You don't have a vehicle, remember?"

"Thank you," he said, distracted. "They are very good people. Very generous. They cook for me. Every night. I don't think they've charged me in a month. I tried to pay, but they said anyone who liked their rogan josh and lime pickle as much as I did was family."

They were back on the highway. The sun was up. The only other vehicles were fire trucks and ambulances, their sirens off, lumbering back to base with no sense of urgency. Rusty turned away and rubbed his eyes.

"The truth is," he said, and stopped. "The truth is after a while I got tired of it. I was just hungry. It was just free food. I am such an asshole.

"At least I come by it honestly," he mumbled.

"What are you talking about? You've been through a lot tonight, but stop being an idiot."

Rusty cleared his throat. He was about to speak, then stopped, sighed, closed his eyes, and absently pinched and kneaded the skin on his forehead.

Kit looked over, thinking he might have fallen asleep. She'd read about soldiers, during World War I, being so exhausted that they would fall asleep in the thick of battle, standing up, firing their weapons. She knew Rusty was bone-tired. She was, too, and she hadn't watched all her belongings go up in smoke.

"Remember that lunch?" Rusty began. "The one with Carl and the other guys? At the hospital?"

"Green Jell-O parfait," Kit said.

"Exactly," Rusty said. "There was a reason they took me out. They wanted to tell me something."

"Okay."

"You know about my mother, right?" Rusty said.

"You mean the bankbook from 1950?"

"That," he said, "and that she was adopted."

"Right," Kit said, beginning to connect the dots in her head.

"Well, here's the thing: both Carl and Patrick remembered that there was this kid a couple of years older than they were, the great-grandson of one of the original mill owners, so an heir to one of the first families of Riverton. Wealthy, and a real jerk, apparently. And what they remember is that around the same time that my mother was born, this guy got one of his family's housekeepers pregnant and was bragging about it, bragging about what he did and how he did it and saying disgusting things about the girl. So, therefore, an asshole. Actually, much worse than an asshole."

Rusty paused, and a dozen questions came into Kit's head, and she tried to work out how to ask them without sounding like she found the whole story far-fetched. Plausible, but far-fetched.

"It's speculation. You don't know if it's true," Kit said. "Wasn't your mother from Minnesota?"

"My mother was adopted by people from Minnesota, but that doesn't mean she was born in Minnesota. She was actually born in upstate New York."

"So what's the connection to Riverton?" Kit asked, and knew the answer as soon as she'd said it.

"The bankbook," she and Rusty said at the same time.

"Carl said it was probably some kind of payoff or hush money, or even the family trying to do right by this girl."

"What happened to her?"

"They didn't know. Carl said he was pretty sure she

never came back to Riverton. But why would she? But where do girls like that go?" His voice trailed off. "I like the story my mother told me, that she was adopted at birth and those people are her true mother and father. It's vague, but a lot better than 'I was the product of'—I don't know what you'd call it, I don't even want to go there—'by an entitled bastard.'"

"Fair enough," Kit said, "but your mother probably didn't know, right?" And then, because she couldn't help herself, "Is he—that guy—still alive? He'd be, what? In his eighties?"

"Nope," Rusty said. "And that's the only good part of the story. Patrick said that he was one of those guys who thought he was invincible, and took a dare to jump his motorcycle over the narrowest part of the river and clipped a stanchion and got tangled in his bike and went under. As I said, a real asshole. My grandfather. Me. It must be genetic."

"The Patels love you," Kit said. "They don't think you're an asshole."

"Well, they should. When they wouldn't let me pay, I told Mr. Patel that I was going to buy him a microwave to replace the crappy old hot plate with frayed wires he used to heat up his food, but I never did."

"So you think this is your fault. Is that what you're saying?"

"Isn't it?" he said. "They lost everything."

They were pulling up to her house, and as tired as Kit was, she found herself angry, too.

"They have insurance," Kit said. "They will be fine. It wasn't up to you to upgrade their appliances. It would have been nice, sure, but they knew the thing was a fire hazard. They could have, and should have, replaced it long before you showed up. The only person who lost everything is you. If you were really an asshole, you'd be angry at them."

"Come on," she said, leading him into the house, past the bottle of wine they'd emptied so many hours before, past the photograph she'd left askew on the coffee table. Kit climbed the stairs and Rusty followed, and when she sat down on the bed and pointed to the other side, he sat down, and when she took off her shoes, he took off his, and when she lay down, unwashed and fully clothed, he lay down, too, and under a cover of sunlight, both fell fast asleep.

# Chapter Eleven
## 8.16.10 – 8.22.10

**Sunny | truth**

The mall opens at ten, but Willow tries to get there early to set up her kiosk, which means my parents usually leave the house around nine. I was on my bike at nine fifteen–ish, and rode the back way into Riverton and got to Coolidge Street around ten after ten. If Steve went home right after helping Willow, he'd already know I was gone, though he'd have no idea where I was. Two can play the secrets game.

Kit's car was in the driveway, but when I knocked on the door, she didn't answer. I knew she liked to bring her coffee and a book up to the top of the house where we'd watched the fireworks, and figured that if she was up there she'd never hear me knocking, so I tried the door and it was open, so I stepped inside and called her name again, and again she didn't answer.

I didn't try to hide the fact that I was in her house. I coughed. I dragged my feet so my sneakers would skid on the floor. Nothing. When I got to the bottom of the staircase I called out her name again, hoping my voice would carry up to the cupola.

"Kit!" I shouted. "It's Sunny. Are you home?" I was just about to say it again when I heard voices, Kit's and someone else's, and I was so mortified I would have run out of there if Kit hadn't come to the top of the stairs and was looking down at me.

"Sunny?" Kit said, as if she wasn't sure that was my name. She was wearing the same clothes she'd been wearing at work the day before, only now they were filthy and so was she. Seriously, she looked like she'd come down the chimney. "Sunny," she said again. "What are you doing here?" She didn't sound angry that I was in her house, only confused, and before I could answer she said, "Are you worried about Rusty? He's fine. He's here. He came back with me."

And then, from the bedroom, I heard Rusty say, "Hi, Sunny," and I was mortified all over again. "Thank you for worrying about me," he said, and let out a loud yawn. "That's really sweet."

Now I was beyond embarrassed. Not only had I

walked in on Kit and Rusty, I had no idea what I was being thanked about. "No problem," I said.

"Wait down there," Kit said. "I have to take a shower."

Rusty must have fallen back to sleep, because he said nothing and wasn't with Kit when she came down the stairs in clean clothes, with a clean face.

"I'm going to the store to get food for breakfast," she said, grabbing up her wallet as she walked toward the door. "Are you coming?" she called over her shoulder when I continued to stand there. (I think I was in shock.)

"Let's see what they're saying about the fire on the radio," Kit said, pressing the presets when we got in the car. Apparently, nothing. It was all music.

"We'll have to wait till the top of the hour," she said, and sure enough, when the news came on at eleven, the first story was about the eighteen-alarm fire at the Tip-Top Motor Inn outside of Riverton.

"Eighteen-alarm fire!" I said loudly, because this was the first I was hearing about it.

"I know, I know," Kit said. "I'm pretty sure I counted twenty different fire departments. There were still at least two up there when we left this morning, just in case there was a flareup. Not that there is anything left to burn."

We listened to the report. One minor injury, three firefighters sidelined when their truck rear-ended a parked car, and the Tip-Top gone. Burned to the ground.

"We stayed there, you know," I said.

"I remember," Kit said. And then, more to herself than to me: "At least he didn't lose his car."

**The big** supermarket, the one with the bakery, is next to the mall where Willow works, and I was worried I'd run into her, but Kit pointed out that she'd be working, not shopping for bagels. We got lots of stuff, and then, when we were walking down the toothpaste aisle, she said, "Rusty's going to need one of these," and put a toothbrush into our basket, and then a razor, though it took her ten minutes to decide if it should be the kind with four blades or five, a battery or no battery, a rotating handle and on and on. You'd have thought she was buying a car.

After we'd checked out, she said she had an errand to run in the mall, so I waited for her in the car, which was already getting pretty hot. When she came back she had bags from Banana Republic and J.Crew and Jockey, which she tossed in the backseat.

"Clothes," she said. "For Rusty. He lost everything." As if, by then, I didn't know.

◆ ◆ ◆

When the winter came, / I'd not a pair of breeches / Nor a shirt to my name.
                            —EDNA ST. VINCENT MILLAY

Kit held up a pair of men's khaki shorts and wondered what "medium" really meant. It had been years since she shopped for men's clothes—for Cal's clothes—and didn't know if sizes had changed, now that people were "bigger" than they used to be. "All women want to be a size 8, so we call everything a size 8. It makes them feel good about themselves. If our clothes were true to size we wouldn't sell anything," she'd read in the style section of the *New York Times*, in an interview with a famous designer. Were men less deluded? she wondered, measuring the medium against the large and seeing that they were nearly identical. If she bought the large, would Rusty think she thought he was fat? Maybe men liked to be thought of as large. Maybe medium sounded wimpy.

A young man with gelled hair and crisply pressed pants, whose name tag said KENNETH C., SENIOR SALES ASSOCIATE, interrupted her musing. "Can I help you?" he said.

"I don't know," Kit said. "I'm looking for some

clothes for a friend, but I'm not really sure what size he is."

"I see," Kenneth said, "so he's a friend, but you don't really know what size he is."

"Yes," Kit said. "He lost all his stuff in that fire."

"Oh," Kenneth said. "Let me check with my manager," and was gone. Kit draped the medium shorts over her arm and moved on to the shirts, choosing a cornflower-blue polo, like the one she'd seen Rusty wear at the library, and a dark green T-shirt made of organic cotton.

Kenneth caught up with her in accessories, as she was shopping for a belt.

"Here," he said, handing her a piece of plastic. "It's a twenty-five-dollar gift card. Our compliments. We try to help out when we can. Just scratch off the silver strip." He took the card back and scratched it off with his fingernail. "You're supposed to use a coin," he explained, handing the card back to her.

"Thanks," Kit said. The belt in her hand cost sixty-five dollars. When did belts get so expensive? Cal had two belts, a black and a brown, and now she knew why. It was impossible to choose. She pulled a brown one off the rack and held them up side by side.

"Nice. You never know," Kenneth said.

"I guess not," Kit said, taking them both.

At the underwear store, Kit caught sight of her reflection in the window as she compared boxers with boxer briefs and was suddenly self-conscious. She was buying underwear for a man she didn't know well—not just buying them, but trying to decide which he'd like better. Cal was a boxers guy, though not in the beginning. In the beginning, he wore the same dingy white cotton BVDs he'd had in high school, until Kit threw every one of them in the trash one day and replaced them with something she said was more manly. He didn't care. Underpants were underpants. Rusty, Kit thought, might care. She could call him to ask, but that would be weird. So she got one of each, and a three-pack of socks, and when she got home put all the bags on the bed—he was just waking up again—and said, "I don't think the clothes you were wearing last night survived the fire," even though they were still on his body.

Kit and Sunny laid out breakfast—by now brunch—on the coffee table, and when Rusty finally came down the stairs, he was wearing his new shorts and the green T-shirt and maybe the boxers or maybe the boxer briefs.

"You're good at this," he told Kit, twirling around for her and Sunny, modeling his new clothes, and Kit felt— She didn't know how she felt.

◆ ◆ ◆

### Sunny | lockup

After brunch, Kit and Rusty started talking about his car, and Rusty made a phone call to the police and got Evelyn's son Jeffrey on the line, and he said that if Rusty came in to pay the fine, Jeffrey would get the towing company to remove the boot, so that's what he decided to do. Rusty needed Kit to drive him, and because I was sitting there, they seemed to assume that I was going, too. It did occur to me that Steve might be wondering where I was, but my attitude was "let him worry." He had me worried, which is why I was at Kit's in the first place, but because of the fire, I hadn't had a chance to tell her about it. I should have brought it up when we were in the car, but Kit was going on about the fire, and about Rusty and the motel owners, and there never seemed to be the right moment.

We got to the police station around 2:30. The jail cells were both empty. I know this because while Jeffrey was helping Rusty, Evelyn's other son, Jack, asked if I wanted a tour of the building, and the tour consisted of showing me the two jail cells in the basement. They were mirror images of each other, each with four bunk beds and a metal sink-toilet contraption, and that was it. It was humid down there; there were no windows.

"You want me to lock you up so you can see what it feels like?" Jack asked.

I said, "Sure," and he opened the door, told me to go inside, and, once I was in, pulled it hard, so it closed with an ominous, thunderous bang.

"I'll be back," he said, leaving me there and going back upstairs.

"Hey!" I called as his footsteps receded. "Let me out!"

"That's what they all say," he said, laughing.

**"That's not** funny!" I heard Kit say as she came down the stairs with Jack. I was in the cell for about five minutes, just long enough for Kit to notice that Jack had returned without me, though it felt longer than that.

"We do this all the time, Kit," he said. "You know, scare the kids straight and all that." He jangled his keys, pretended the lock was stuck, pulled on the door, tried the key again, and again it didn't open.

"Oh, come on!" Kit said. "Are you kidding me?"

And then Jack broke out in a big smile and said, "Yes!" and the door opened, and I walked out.

"Well, he's right," I said to Kit. "I would not want to spend time in there."

As we came up the stairs into the main part of the station house, we passed a small office, messy, with one glass wall, and when I looked through it to the other side, I saw a familiar photo, but enlarged to poster-sized, tacked on to the bulletin board. I nudged Kit so she would see it, too.

"What's that?" I asked Jack, sounding as innocent as I didn't feel. I knew all too well what that was. It was that grainy old security shot of Angus Parker from back in Pennsylvania—which is to say, that old picture of probably Steve.

"That's the room where we do our detective work," Jack said proudly. "No one's in there now because the boys are helping at that fire investigation."

"Do they think it was anything but a faulty wire?" Kit said.

"Can't say," Jack said. "I guess we'll find out."

"Who's that?" I asked, when it looked like we were going to move on.

"Oh, him," Jack said. "He's the guy we think pulled that stunt at Culvert Medical and maybe some other stuff. He's wanted in Pennsylvania, too, but we've got him in our sights."

"Wow," I said.

"Yeah," he said proudly. "We may be a small department, but we do good work."

"So you really think you've got him," Kit said, catching on that she was supposed to egg him on so that he'd tell us what he knew without knowing why it mattered.

"Like I said, we've got him in our sights. We're closing in. Got his fingerprints. Not sure what he's been doing for the past ten years. Sly fox. Probably nothing good. If people knew he was around here, they'd be scared and upset, so we're not going public until we've caught him."

"Smart," Kit said.

So now she knew what I'd ridden my bike over to tell her: Steve was probably the guy who set the animals free at Culvert Medical on July 4th. July 4th, Independence Day. Steve likes a good joke.

◆　◆　◆

We thought we were beggars, we thought we had nothing at all . . .

—ANNA AKHMATOVA

Once he had paid the fine and the boot was removed, Rusty drove up to the Tip-Top, or what was left of it. The motel sign was still there, high above the highway, and when Rusty got to the access road it was no longer blocked. Water continued to trickle down from the ruins, and as he drove he noticed empty soda bottles and coffee cups strewn along the side of the road. The parking lot, so crowded not that long ago and so full of activity, was nearly empty.

An officer from a private security firm, dressed like a policeman and holstering a Maglite, stepped out of his car and walked over to Rusty's, which was idling opposite what used to be room 7.

"You can't be here," he said, drumming on the shaft of his flashlight with his index finger.

"That was my room," Rusty said, pointing to nothing.

"That's tough," the officer said, softening. "I heard that not a thing was left. Not even a paper clip."

"Yeah," Rusty said. "You should have been here last night. It was crazy."

"Something about the old man's hot plate, right?"

"That's what they were saying," Rusty said. "But who knows."

"Well, they'll never figure it out now, will they?" he said. "Take a good look—they're bringing in the dozers tomorrow. In a week, you'll never know what was up here."

"They'll rebuild," Rusty said, as if he knew.

"Nobody's told me anything about that," the guard said.

---

**Before he** lost his job, Rusty didn't give much thought to people who lost their jobs. People got fired, sure, but the job market was lush and they always seemed to land on their feet, so the whole thing seemed like floor exercises: you started at one end of the mat and, after a couple of twists and turns, you stuck your landing at the other, took a bow, and went on. Then he lost his job and was surprised to find that there was nothing cushy underfoot. Not that it mattered. His whole life was up in the air. He could have been a bird—no, an insect.

Losing the apartment in Hoboken was different. It felt like molting. It wasn't that his skin had become too small to contain his body; it was that he had shrunk and his skin was too big and slipping off his frame. All the accoutrements—the steam shower, the five-figure Swedish mattress, even the double Gaggenau ovens—things he never had any use for, really, and then not at all—mocked him. They were mirrors, reflecting who he had been and who he wasn't any longer. He hoped that whoever was sleeping in his bed now had better dreams than he ever did.

To go from all that to his room at the Tip-Top should have been hard, but wasn't. "This is who I am now," Rusty told himself, drinking bitter coffee he'd made in the ancient two-cup drip machine that sat next to a squat television of the same vintage. If anyone came looking for him, Rusty reasoned, they'd never find him here—and when no one did, he told himself, that was why. But the place grew on him. It was a little run-down, yes, but it was clean. It was a little remote, but it was quiet. But most of all, it was uncomplicated. He liked hearing old Mrs. Patel, in her lilting voice, on the wake-up call every morning. He liked being able to slide down the bed a few inches and turn on the TV with his foot. He liked the way Mr. Patel would tell him on Monday what they would be having for dinner every day that week, and how the aroma would greet him every evening, and how that was a happy thing, even as he grew tired of it. And it was that happy thing that brought every other thing crashing down. Talk about downsizing. He was fully downsized. Everything he owned was in his car. In New York, homeless people hauled their stuff around in shopping carts. "That's what this is," Rusty thought, patting the side of the Mercedes with his hand. "A very expensive shopping cart."

"I must be in shock." That's what he wanted to say to Kit and Sunny when he got back to the house. "I must be in shock because I am not panicking even though everything is gone."

And soon, he'd tell them, he'd be gone, too. He'd

thank them for their kindness, Kit especially. He'd thank her for sticking it out during the fire, for taking him in, for feeding him, for buying him new clothes. She knew he had no way to repay her, and she did it anyway. Rusty tried to remember the hours before the fire, when they were sitting at her house, drinking the wine he'd brought. He had been good at angling—angling was what he did for a living (catch and release with women, catch and reel in with clients)—but he no longer had the feel for it. When she asked, he told Kit that he thought yes, maybe, if someone dangled the right lure, he'd go back to his old life, but he wasn't sure when he said it, and he was less sure now. Income was good, and status was good, and having a business card he could hand out that declared who he was in the world was good. That's what he was thinking when he answered Kit's question.

It wasn't true that you could do whatever you set your mind to do. That was just something people said. But if your mind was not set on doing something, and you had no idea what you wanted to do, you could do anything—anything at all, Rusty told himself—so why panic?

# The Marriage Story

## — PART VI —
### (THE END)

Cal strung the Doctor along as much as he could, but eventually the string ran out and we had to move. Cal was upset, I was upset, his supervisors were angry, and our friends in Atlanta were sorry enough, but in that world people came and went all the time. Cal dismantled his lab. (Mice were killed.) I packed up our house and watched the movers load years of our life onto a truck. We had two cars by then, so Cal and I caravanned, he in front, me behind. When he'd signal, I'd signal. When he'd speed up or slow down, I'd speed up or slow down. I know there is a metaphor there, and I knew it then, but the only one I could come up with was synchronized swimmers, which was only partially apt, since it felt like we were drowning.

Cal's father was an investor in the hospital where

Cal would be working, and he did not hide the fact that Cal, with his long list of publications and his reputation at Emory as the up-and-coming neurosurgeon, was the trophy mount the place needed to be competitive. When he made the announcement, he called it a coup for the hospital. It felt like a coup, too—like Cal and I were being held hostage by rogue forces that would determine our fate. The hospital corporation bought a house and handed us the keys, and made a big deal of the signing bonus Cal was getting, as if he were a free agent being courted by a big-time sports franchise. In private Cal was in a rage about having to play in the minors, but in public he was all about how much more autonomy he'd have now that he was freed of the Emory bureaucracy, and how much more free time he'd have without his lab obligations. It was difficult to tell which was the real Cal—the thwarted, derisive one or the humble, solicitous one—and as disconcerting as this was to me, it must have been more so to Cal, who turned out to be very good at telling people what they wanted to hear. The Doctor also put on a good show, trotting out his brilliant son at grand rounds, where Cal gave a talk on the innovative research he was no longer going to be able to do. That was the irony of it, the dead elephant in the room. Everyone clapped. Even me.

To compensate, I guess, Cal bought a sailboat. It was

a sleek beauty, twenty-two feet long, porcelain white with yellow-and-blue-striped sails, and enough room to sleep two on benches that lined that cockpit, port and starboard. "Port" and "starboard" were about the only sailing terms Cal knew, but he threw himself into his new hobby as if it were a brain that needed to be mapped before it could go under the knife. There was another doctor who sailed, Jens Jahron, an anesthesiologist Cal worked with, whose idea this was. He sold Cal the twenty-two-footer that had gotten too small for his growing family, then turned around and bought the forty-foot double-hull catamaran he'd had his eye on for a long time but couldn't buy until he unloaded the smaller boat. The deal was that he'd teach Cal to sail, which turned out to mean that when Cal wasn't at the hospital he was, more often than not, down at the marina.

You don't have to go far out from shore before Lake Huron looks like the ocean. When the air pressure drops and the wind picks up, fifteen- and twenty-foot waves rake the water and crash hard against the pilings at the pier, sometimes taking them out. Cal, at the helm, was a risk-taker, only he didn't see it that way. To him, the gusts and gales of the natural world were another force to be bested, like mitosis and neuronal atrophy. The few times we went out alone together, I had to beg

Cal to keep the boat close to land so we never lost sight of buildings and promontories. Terrestrial life seems so steadfast and solid when you are seesawing side to side on liquid rollers, and it was reassuring to see trees, rooted to the ground, and houses secure on their foundations. When the boat started to heel, all I could do was close my eyes and hold on to the lifeline with both hands and listen to Cal trash-talk the elements.

Jens couldn't sail his cat boat by himself, and his wife had her hands full with their three kids, so he often asked Cal to crew for him, usually on Sundays if neither of them was on call. Cal had started going to church again, a large Pentecostal congregation that I found cloying and in-your-face, but Cal said it was "centering" for him. That was his word. He said that when he was back in Atlanta, researching genes and drug therapies in the lab gave him the energy and hope he needed to go into the clinic and tell people they had glioblastomas or Parkinson's or any number of lacerating diagnoses that cut them to the quick. He said that without that, his clinical work would have been excruciating. But now, with no research to balance out the harrowing diagnoses or feed his hope and that of his patients, he was at least able to find comfort in those bleak hours knowing that the resurrected Jesus had a personal relationship with him. It struck me that Cal's ego, having been fed a nonstop diet of exaltations over the years, had become so expansive that he imagined Jesus having a relationship with him, not the other way around. I could have said something snarky, but who was I to try to take church away from him when the reason he started going in the first place was that he had been deprived of something he found so crucial.

In the very beginning Cal urged me to join the congregation, too, which I think had more to do with the pressure he was feeling to conform to church norms (husbands had wives) than anything to do with my salvation, though the way he seemed to think he'd convince me was to make an oblique reference to my infertility. "You've lost something central to your self, you know," is how he put it. I told him that yes, that was true, but I didn't believe for a minute that even the most loving God could fill that hole. "Love is love," Cal said, which struck me at the time as obvious, true, and inscrutable.

Sunday mornings, Cal would go to church and I'd sleep in, and then we'd take different cars to the marina because he didn't want to waste time driving back to get me. We'd meet up with the Jahrons, and the guys would get ready to sail, and Sally Jahron and I would lay out food for a picnic in the galley, and the kids would play hide-and-seek while Sally tried to make sure none of them fell overboard or got caught up in the ropes and lines. Then we'd set out, motoring away from the dock until we were past the last set of buoys, and the sails would go up like flags of a proud nation, and we'd all cheer as the wind carried us forward. The kids would sit, legs dangling, at the bow. Sally and I would lie on the deck, me with a book, she with her eyes on her children, ever ready to haul any one of them back from the brink, while the men stood downwind in the back, talking shop and occasionally interrupting themselves to let us all know that we were going to come about.

If you had asked me then, I would have said that my marriage was neither bad nor good, neither hot nor cold. Without the ballast of children, we bobbed around each other, frictionless. Cal had his work, his church, his boat, and he had me. I was the constant. I was the one who was always there and always had been. I thought that that was what mattered. In math, the constant variable stays the same, while the other variables have no fixed value. But in life, as those variables take on more precedence, the value of the constant diminishes. I didn't understand that. I was the constant—loyal and accommodating, fitting my schedule and my aspirations and my needs to his, year after year—and as I say, I was certain that that, above all else, is what counted.

---

**When Sally** found out she was pregnant again, she signed up for a mother's helper for the summer from one of the countries that used to be in the Soviet Union. Slovenia or Slovakia—we were all getting them mixed up. The agency placed girls who had grown up in orphanages with American families that could use help, which was supposed to be a win-win all around: the girls would get to be part of a family, and the family would get an au pair. But as the Jahrons found out as she came off the plane, calling Beata an au pair was stretching it, since she appeared to be not much older than the oldest Jahron boy, who was twelve. When Sally called the agency in a panic, because that boy was already precocious when it came to girls, and because she was angry that instead of a mother's helper she'd gotten another child to mother, they explained that the date of birth on Beata's passport was a best guess. "She's an orphan," Sally was reminded more than once.

"You like fiction. Her age is a fiction," Sally complained to me, but the girl had already moved in. What was she going to do?

Beata, small as she was, spoke accented English sternly, with a gravelly tone that gave her an air of authority that brought even the rambunctious eight-year-old Jahron twins into line. They brushed their teeth when she told them to brush their teeth, went to bed when she told them to go to bed, picked up their toys before she asked, didn't ride their bikes in the street. "It's like they are on drugs," Sally told me. "I love it. I love her!"

As a bonus, Beata was a homely girl, of no interest to the twins' older brother, whose idea of feminine beauty was in the process of being formed by certain sites on the Internet. In contrast, Beata, at fifteen—the stated age on her passport—was skinny and pale with a band of pimples straight across her forehead like points on the X axis of a geometry problem. She had limp brown hair, ragged at the shoulders, that might have been chopped to that length with a butcher's knife. Sally took her to Supercuts, and when Beata came out of the shop, her hair was still limp but the ends had been evened out and curled naturally under her chin. Did she like it? Hard to say. Beata wasn't quick to smile, though when she did, you could catch a glimpse of the little girl she could have been. Sally bought her a stuffed bear, and at night, Beata clung to it like a life preserver.

When Beata came back the next summer to help with the three Jahron boys and their new baby sister, she was still the authoritarian she had been the year before, but instead of looking twelve, she looked twenty. She had grown a few inches in height, styled her hair with bangs that ensconced her pocked forehead, and filled out in her hips and chest. Beata was now the heritor of breasts that rivaled Sally's, and Sally was nursing. The girl still had tiny ears, close-set brown eyes, and a narrow, rodent-like face, more mole than dormouse, but when you looked at her, your eyes were instantly drawn downward to her breasts, as if the magnetic poles had been reoriented east and west. Jens and Cal claimed not to notice, which incited Sally to spring into action, hauling Beata to the mall to refresh the girl's wardrobe with loose tops and a one-piece bathing suit that appeared to shove all that flesh back where it came from.

"Men are pigs," she said to me when we were out on the water and she was nursing her infant. "Men are babies."

"So you're saying men are piglets," I said lightly, trying to divert this conversation. The kids were around, and Cal and Jens were nearby, too.

"Come on," Sally said. "Think about it for a minute. Why are men obsessed with women's breasts?" She pointed to her own, which were leaking milk. "That's why," she said. "It's a mommy thing, plain and simple."

**Beata had** not only gotten breasts in the months she'd been gone, she'd gotten God. This was somewhat disturbing to Sally and Jens, who were, they said, "practicing atheists," so it fell to Cal to pick up Beata on Sunday mornings and take her with him to church. He put on a tie and shined his good shoes and made sure that his car, which the rest of the week was filled with empty soda cans, moldering coffee cups, and muffin liners with scraps of blueberry or corn bread still attached to them, was tidy. When I asked him what they talked about on their rides together, he said, "Not much, just humdrum stuff," or stuff about her school, or their work, or about life in the United States, which she, apparently, aspired to. Sometimes, he said, she'd be quiet and sullen, and he'd catch a glimpse of what it would have been like to be a parent to a teenager, which made my heart beat fast for a second and reminded me that Cal, too, was hurt by what had happened to me. So it made me happy for him that he could play that role, if intermittently, in Beata's life. They joined the choir, the two of them, and I'd hear him humming hymns in the shower. She had a good voice, he said. Robust. A second soprano, not the alto I would have pegged her for. Choir practice was Thursday nights, and Thursday was when the library where I worked was open late. So I'd stay there, and Cal would have dinner with Beata and then take her to choir practice. It was sweet. It was wholesome. It was church, for God's sakes.

# Chapter Twelve

# 8.23.10—

**Sunny | home**

As soon as we left the police station and were back in Kit's car, I burst out crying. "Why would he do those things?" I must have said a million times, but I knew, or at least I knew what Steve would say, which was "How could I not?" I could see that Kit was trying to figure out what to do, but I told her I was fine, not to worry, I was just scared, and she said of course I was scared, and that maybe she shouldn't tell me, but that she was scared, too, for Steve and me and Willow.

"I don't want to live in the wilderness again," I howled, and that's when Kit started up the car because she was worried that one of the policemen—they are all men in

Riverton and the dispatchers are all women—would see me and want to know what was going on. As we drove, I told Kit about the time we lived at #3, focusing on the hard parts, since I didn't want her to get the idea that it was even a little bit fun, even though it was a lot of the time.

"Where are we going?" I asked when I realized we weren't going back to Kit's house. That's when she told me we were going to my house, to talk to Steve and Willow.

"Willow probably won't be there," I said. "It depends on how well she did at the mall. When she gets to five hundred dollars, she stops and comes home. But that doesn't happen very often, so she's probably not there."

The Subaru was in the driveway when we pulled up, and Steve was bent over the engine. He waved and came over, and Kit rolled down her window, but he came to mine and asked if I'd had an accident or something since I'd left on my bike and came home in a car. As soon as he said it I realized I'd totally forgotten about the bike. Riding the nine miles to Riverton that morning seemed like it had happened in a different century.

"I'm going to go now," Kit said to no one in particular. "Unless you want me to stay," she said to me.

"Why would she want you to stay?" Steve asked. It was a question neither of us bothered to answer.

Instead, in my most mature voice, I said, "We need to talk," to Steve. And to Kit I said, "I think it would be better if I did this alone, but maybe you could just stay in the car?"

So Kit stayed in her car, and Steve and I went into the house, the whole time with him saying, "What is this about Sunny? What is this about?" Rather than answering him directly, I went into my room, found the HIST binder, and pulled out the Angus Parker passport and held it up to him.

"Where did you get that?" he asked, even though he'd just seen me take it out of the binder.

"No," I said to him, "where did you get it? It's your picture." And then I rooted around in my backpack and finally found the photocopy of the newspaper article about Parker and what he'd done in Pennsylvania. "You need to tell me what's going on," I said.

"I can't," Steve said. "I just can't, Sunny."

"Why? I'm not a little kid anymore!" If I wasn't yelling, I was definitely close to it. Steve, though, was pacing around, tugging on his chin, getting engine grease all over his face, and talking very softly.

"I'm not a little kid and you can't just cart me off into the woods to live in a tent for months and months," I said.

"No one is going off to live in the woods," Steve said,

his voice still calm and gentle, as if he were channeling Willow.

That's when I told him about what they'd been saying at the Riverton police station, and when I said that they said they were closing in on Angus Parker, Steve's grease-stained face became ghost white and he started pacing more quickly, back and forth from my room to the kitchen and back, still unwilling to tell me about Angus Parker.

"What have you done?" I yelled at him, even though it was pretty clear what he had done.

He didn't answer.

"And just so you know, I want to go to school!" I shouted at his back. "Real school, with real teachers, and desks, and lunch in the cafeteria."

"No, you don't!" Steve said as he made the turn, walking back toward me. The vein on his forehead that pops out when he is angry was more prominent than I'd ever seen it. "No, you don't."

"Yes, I do!"

"You wouldn't last a day in one of those—one of those government schools."

"First of all," I said, "they are public schools, not government schools. Public, as in 'we the people.' Second of all, even if I only last a day, I want to have that day."

"And then you'll turn out just like everyone else,"

Steve said, walking away from me again. "Why is she still here?" He was pointing to Kit's car through the window.

"She's here because I am going to go live with her!" I said. "If you are Angus Parker, then you are not my father! And even if you aren't, you've been lying to me all my life!"

I was pretty worked up. Before he could stop me, I walked out the front door and started trotting toward Kit's car.

"Let's get out of here!" I said, panting.

"Are you sure?" Kit asked. She looked confused.

"Can we just leave, please?" I said.

I could see Steve, still walking in circles around the house. He wasn't even coming after me.

"He's not even trying to stop me!" I said to Kit as she turned the car around and headed down the driveway.

"Stop you from doing what?" she asked.

"Coming to live with you," I said.

◆　◆　◆

Lose something every day.

—ELIZABETH BISHOP

When Sunny went inside the house to talk with Steve, Kit turned off the car, slid the seat back, closed her eyes, and tried to sleep. She was bone-tired but couldn't turn off her brain, couldn't block the stampeding memories of the fire, the police station, the funeral, the library, couldn't shutter the mind's-eye view of her house, this morning, waking up next to Rusty, couldn't pull back from the swirl of events—the vortex—she'd been drawn into. The images were not orderly, nor were her thoughts. She felt like she was falling, jerked herself up, and realized that she'd been asleep for an instant, in spite of herself. So much drama, and so much to come. There was drama unfolding a few yards away, as Sunny talked with Steve or Angus—or whoever he was. There was drama adhering to Rusty like neon-yellow Post-it notes: unemployment; homelessness; an unsettling family history. She had organized her life to be as uneventful as possible, and now this.

"Someone should write a poem that rhymes 'drama' with 'trauma,' something with a repeating rhyme scheme, so we can hear it over and over," she remembered saying to Dr. Bondi. She said it for laughs, but he didn't hear the humor—or if he did, chose to ignore it. Everything was fair game for analysis in that room, even her jokes. Maybe especially her "jokes" she imagined him saying, curling the first two fingers on both hands into quote marks. She also remembered telling him that she liked her life better when it was routine and predictable, before the dramatic events she hadn't even been aware of rose up from the deep like an underwater volcano and spewed it to bits. And she remembered him lifting an eyebrow and looking at her skeptically and saying, "Really?" and "Why?" and then listening to her explanation, which sounded pitiful, even to herself. "Because that life was easier," she said, and he said, "But was it better? Was it a good life?" and she said, "That's not the point," and he let that sit with her for a long, uncomfortable minute.

"Look," he said, leaning back in his chair and folding his hands together. "You use the word 'drama' like it's a bad word. But here's what you need to understand: stories are not just in books or movies. Everyone's life is an unfolding story, and all stories have good guys and bad guys, and all stories have conflicts and resolutions, and all stories—if they are interesting—have drama."

"And what I'm saying," Kit said, "is that I would have liked my story to be less interesting. Way less interesting."

"And what I'm saying," Dr. Bondi said, "is that there is no such thing as less interesting for anybody. Somewhere in the unfolding story, something is going to happen that will change everything that happens after it. In a sense it's happening all the time, but it's visible only at those dramatic times—someone gets sick, or twins are born, or your job moves to Mexico, or you get mugged on the bus, or you meet your future spouse on the bus. What you're thinking of as the end of the story now, Kit, is only the end of a chapter. And there are many more to come."

"Unless I get mugged on a bus," Kit said.

**"So Bondi** was right," Kit thought. "And this is the chapter in which I assist an eccentric, nearly feral child in alerting her fugitive father to his imminent arrest, while at the same time lending a helping hand to a man who, through no fault of his own, has hit rock bottom, while also running a public library on a frayed budgetary shoestring that threatens to snap at any moment. So much action." But the real story, she knew, was more sensational and more uncertain: she had let—no, invited—Rusty into her bed to sleep next to her. True, it was chaste and expedient, but it was real. The die that had been cast once she understood her husband had betrayed her (and with a girl—a repulsive, unattractive girl), causing her mind to separate from her body, had been rolled back.

◆ ◆ ◆

### Sunny | home

I thought that Kit might slam on the brakes when I told her I was coming to live with her, but she kept on driving, and when I turned around to see if Steve was running after us, or at least waving from the porch, all I saw was the house where I'd lived for most of my life getting smaller and smaller and disappearing.

"Stop!" I said, and then she did hit the brakes, hard, and we both lurched forward and back, and our heads hit the headrests at the same time and made a thunking sound as dirt from the car's tires rose up from the ground and pieces of gravel rained down on the hood.

"Sunny," Kit said sharply, and at the sound of my name I started crying again.

"He doesn't even care about me," I wailed, and she said, "Of course he does, he's just worried and confused." I said I was scared, and she said, "Of course," and I said, "I don't know what to do," and she said, "Of course you don't," and I said, "I don't want to go into hiding," and she said, "Of course you don't," and I said, "But I don't want to lose my family," and she said, "No one wants to lose their family," and she began to wipe away tears, too, which made me feel better.

We sat together like that for three or seven or ten minutes, and got so hot we had to roll up the windows and turn on the air-conditioning even though, as I told Kit, we don't believe in air-conditioning.

"Well, you know what they say," she said. "The only completely consistent people are dead," and at that very moment we heard the Subaru coming up fast behind us, and though I was pretty sure Steve could see us, sometimes when he's going down the driveway he's looking through his CDs and not paying attention to what's ahead of him, so I braced myself for impact.

He didn't hit us. He pulled up next to us, and I rolled down my window and wondered if he'd feel the cool air exiting Kit's car and if he'd say something critical.

"Sunny," he said, obviously confused. "I didn't expect to see you. I'm sorry."

I don't know what hackles are exactly, but whatever they are, mine stood straight up when he said this. "You're sorry to see me?" I said, and not nicely, but like I was accusing him of something.

"No. No," he said, looking flustered. "I'm sorry for what happened back there. You caught me by surprise and I didn't know what to say and I—" He looked at his watch and said, sounding desperate, "I've got to go get Willow."

He looked scared. I'd almost never seen him look

scared. Not Steve. Steve was strong. Steve was tough. I think it's because he grew up military. "Army of one." "Deeds, not words." "With courage and knowledge." Like it or not, he knows all the mottos.

"I need to get your mother," he said. His voice was shivery. His eyes were distant, but intense, like he could almost see what was ahead.

"Wait! I'm coming with you!" I said, and leaned over and put my arms around Kit and gave her a big hug, because who knew when I might see her again, and practically jumped out of her car and into ours. "Your mother," he said, and that's what did it. It reminded me—trifecta, troika, triplicate, trio—whatever happens, that's what we are, Steve and Willow, and me: a totality.

◆　◆　◆

"Faith" is a fine invention . . .

—EMILY DICKINSON

Kit drove home in a daze. It was shocking to hear Sunny say that she was coming to live with her, and Kit hadn't even begun to process that idea when Sunny changed her mind and went with—went back to?—her father. She knew Sunny had said the words; she remembered hearing her saying them, but they were a wisp of smoke now, lost to the air. And it was flat-out a crazy idea. She was in no position to take in a teenage girl. She lived alone. Her house was her refuge, the place where no one could unsettle her, a place apart. And there were rules, rules she'd mastered in the days and months after the fault line she hadn't known was under her split her life into before and after. Rule number one: The only person you can count on is yourself. Rule number two: Given the chance, other people will always disappoint you—or worse. Rule number three: If you share, they will take. Rule number four: Don't open the door when someone knocks.

"The only completely consistent people are dead," Kit said again, out loud to herself, remembering how she opened the door for Rusty, not once, but three times in less than a day, and nothing bad happened. Yet. In her imagined conversation with Dr. Bondi, she would tell him this, and he would tell her, once again, how much stronger she was than she knew, and she'd question what that had to do with anything.

"Here's the challenge, Kit," she knew he'd said, "when you go to the door, don't stand there staring at it, and don't pretend that whatever is on the other side of it isn't real until you open it. It's real. It's there. Would Cal be a different person, making different choices, if you hadn't opened the door to the police? The door is an illusion. You can try to hide behind it, but sooner or later it's going to blow open, if only in your mind."

He'd give this speech and she'd argue with him, and bring up counter-examples, and talk about moats and barbicans.

"Fine," he'd say, "if you want to live in a fortress," and she'd say, "That's a good question," and he'd say, "It's not a question. It's a fact, Kit, and here's another: it's not a coincidence that a lot of ancient fortresses were also prisons."

◆　◆　◆

One wants a teller in a time like this . . .
—GWENDOLYN BROOKS

Kit wasn't home when Rusty got back to her house, so he sat on the porch swing, dozing, waiting. If nothing else, the fire was clarifying. He had watched almost everything he owned disappear. He had watched the Patels pull together as a family, then feel them pull him in, too. He saw people, strangers, put themselves in harm's way. And he saw in all that activity that Patrick was right—the promise of free money was a trap. In his case, it was a trap that kept him at arm's length from making decisions about his own life.

There was no reason to stay in Riverton any longer, and he wanted to say good-bye to Kit and thank her before heading out, maybe to Duluth, maybe to New York, maybe to India to track down his sister, maybe into the mountains. He thought he'd been free when he'd left Hoboken in June, but freedom, he was learning, was not a set point, like the temperature at which water freezes, but something mutable, a moving target. He was freer now than he had been then, and why not embrace that? Go somewhere. Do something. Get a life.

He must have been sleeping, because when Kit arrived the air had grown cooler and the sun was no longer overhead.

"Hey," he called as he heard her come up the path so she wouldn't be startled to find him there.

"You could have let yourself in," she said.

"I didn't think you'd like that."

"Yeah, you're probably right," she said, sitting down next to him. "What a day."

"What a night," he said, and for a second she thought he meant sleeping in the bed with her, but before she could embarrass herself by acknowledging that, she realized no, he meant the fire.

"Yeah," she said.

"I came to say good-bye," he said after a while. "I'm leaving."

"You can't!" Kit said with an intensity that surprised even her. "You have no place to go."

"That's the great thing," Rusty said. "I can go anywhere. I'm free."

"Very funny," Kit said.

"Very funny what? What do you mean?"

"I mean that's a very funny way to describe being homeless and out of work. It's very . . . creative."

"Are you trying to burst my very fragile bubble of self-confidence and resolve?" Rusty said, pretending to frown.

"That's me," Kit said, "burster of bubbles." She was sorry he was going, yes, but relieved, too. Whatever might have happened between the two of them, and whatever might not have happened, was off the table. Whatever conflicting feelings she had would be rendered moot. Should she stand up, put out her arms for a good-bye hug? Should she stick out her hand for him to shake? Kit was unsure of the protocol, so she sat there, waiting for Rusty to make his exit. Yet having declared he was leaving, Rusty didn't budge. The balls of his feet stayed planted on the porch floor, gently pushing the swing back and forth, and him in it, like a cradle.

"So if you are really leaving, you'll want to go up to the top of the house so you can get a final, panoramic view of our fair city," Kit said finally, when the rhythmic creak of the swing had slowed, and she was no longer sure if he was still awake.

"What?" he said, rousing himself.

"Follow me," Kit said, and stood up and pushed on the front door, and held it open as he stepped in.

**"This is** amazing," Rusty said, when they were standing in the belvedere. Rusty moved in a slow circle, taking in the view. "You know," he said, facing the park behind Kit's house, "if my grandfather is who the guys think he was, he could have lived over there. Before they tore the house down, of course. He could have walked on that lawn."

"If he did, he probably came over here," Kit said, "since this is where the servants lived."

"Where my grandmother lived, you mean," Rusty said quietly.

Kit nodded. "Yeah."

"Like she could have stood up here and looked out over the town, too," he said. "Though it would have looked different."

"Possibly," Kit said. "You never know."

"Nope," Rusty said. "I guess I won't."

Rusty leaned over and ran his fingers over the grain

of the wood floor. "Her DNA might still be here, in the cracks," he said.

"Her DNA is in you," Kit said. "It is you."

**Kit closed** her eyes. She was so, so tired.

Kit jerked awake. The sky was darkening. Bats were beginning to stir.

"You looked very peaceful," Rusty said. "It was nice. I almost left, but then I decided that that was the coward's way out."

"Meaning?"

"Meaning that when I told you yesterday—just about twenty-four hours ago, to be exact—that I liked you, and you blew me off—"

"I did not blow you off—" she interrupted.

"—and you blew me off," Rusty continued, "before I left I wanted to ask you why, because otherwise I'm always going to wonder. I'm not saying that I'm the best person in the world, but I wondered if it had something to do with the fact that right now I'm kind of a loser. Like you said. I don't have a job. I don't live anywhere."

"I did not say you were a loser!" Kit was indignant. "You are putting words in my mouth."

"Quote, 'That's a very creative way to describe being

homeless and out of work,' unquote, she said after he described his own situation as being, quote, 'free,' unquote."

"I did say that," Kit admitted. "But I didn't mean to suggest you were a loser. And if you remember, last night when you were here you did live somewhere. We didn't know about the fire."

"Right. I was living in a mom-and-pop motel on top of a hill overlooking the highway. Please be serious."

Kit felt herself color. She was toying with him. She didn't mean to, but she was.

"If you are going to give me the 'it's not you, it's me' speech," Rusty said, "don't bother." And when she didn't say she wasn't, when she didn't say anything at all, he stood up. "I'm going to get on the road now," he said, and started down the stairs.

"Wait a minute," Kit called out as he approached the second-floor landing. "If you wouldn't mind, I'd like to show you something. So you'll understand that it really is me, not you. I wouldn't want you thinking otherwise. It's—it's in my room."

Kit came down the stairs, and he let her pass and stood in the doorway to her bedroom as she retrieved a sheaf of unbound papers in a file folder from the back of her closet.

"Here," she said, handing it to him. "Read this."

He looked at the first page of what she'd handed him. "The Marriage Story, Part 1" it said.

"Don't ask, please—just read. But do me a favor, do it downstairs. I've got to lie down. You can leave it on the table when you go out."

◆　◆　◆

men have power / and sometimes one is made to feel it . . .

—MARIANNE MOORE

She had opened the door. She had opened it for Rusty, and he walked in, and soon he would walk out, but she had opened it. "Small steps, baby steps, that's what you'll be taking for a while," Dr. Bondi said in the aftermath, when every step was an effort, and all she wanted to do was curl up in her bed, but she couldn't, since it had been Cal's bed, too, and as many times as she washed the sheets and aired out the blankets, she could still pick up his scent and it infuriated her.

"Listen, Kit," Dr. Bondi said to her, "what you've got to understand is that you didn't lose your life. You lost the life you thought you were living. And those are two different things. You are alive. It may not feel like it, but you are. And part of being alive means experiencing loss. We lose things every day—I'm not talking about eyeglasses—yes, we lose those, too—I mean things like eyesight. Our eyesight diminishes over time, our hair falls out. That's natural. It's so natural that we chalk it up to inevitability. But that's loss. Loss is inevitable. It comes in many sizes. Yours is huge—don't think I'm discounting it. But the small, everyday losses help us deal with the big ones. It's muscle memory. And the fact that you are in so much pain is actually a good sign. I'd be worried if you were numb. It tells me that you are alive."

"So I should be grateful for the pain?"

"I'm not saying that, Kit. I think you know that."

"I don't know anything," she said, expecting him to contradict her. But he didn't. "And the pain? The loss? Does it go away?" she asked.

"No," he said carefully, "but it will get less bad."

"So that's what I have to look forward to—that my life will be less bad," she said, making it clear how inadequate she found this.

"Yes," he said. "It will get less bad."

**But he** was wrong. It got worse. She had been the wife of someone everyone, it seemed, considered to be a great man. A hero. A saint. Brilliant. A risen star. They said so, over and over, on the TV and radio the morning that Cal's boat was found, drifting and unoccupied, its captain missing and presumed dead.

**"You've made** a mistake," Kit told the police officers when they knocked on her door in the early morning. "He's at a conference, in Chicago. He left yesterday."

But they insisted. The boat was sighted by the crew of a lake freighter before sunrise, jerking drunkenly this way and that, its sails luffing like laundry hung out to dry. The Coast Guard boarded it, checked the registration, and hauled it back to the marina, where the harbormaster said yes, he remembered seeing Cal take the boat out the day before.

"I don't understand," Kit said more than once. "He was a good sailor."

And each time the police officers would remind her that anything is possible out on the water.

"This is crazy," Kit said. "Cal went to Chicago. He's in Chicago. He's a doctor. He's at a doctors' conference."

"Well, if he went there, Mrs. Sweeney," one of the officers said, "he must've went in a sailboat."

"We're sorry," his partner said.

Cal, dead. Those words cycled through her head; that's where the storm was, in her head. The phone was ringing, and Kit rushed to answer it, sure it was Cal, hung up when it wasn't, and then it rang again and she rushed over, and again and again, and each time it was a reporter wanting a statement. And then she picked up the phone and it wasn't a reporter, it was Sally Jahron, calling to report that all four of her kids came down with a stomach bug during the night and did Kit know when Beata would be back from that choir retreat with Cal.

"Choir retreat?" Kit said, dumbfounded. "I thought . . ." she began, then stopped. Sally must not have listened to the news and didn't know about the boat yet, and the reporters didn't know about the girl yet, and once they did, the story was going to change. Kit, operating on instinct and adrenaline, wanted to give herself as much time as possible between story number one—hero husband—and story number two—what? Pedophile?

"He didn't say," Kit told her, which was the truth.

"No good deed goes unpunished," Sally said. "Gotta go."

**The Doctor** arrived within the hour, pushing through the scrum of cameramen assembling on the front lawn, bringing with him the hospital PR flack, a pencil-thin, fidgety man with a slight lisp named Booth who seemed to Kit to be in precisely the wrong profession—but what did she know about men and their character? Nothing, obviously. The two of them set up camp in the kitchen, talking about Cal as if he were a Thoroughbred race-horse who had met an untimely death on the verge of the Triple Crown. Back and forth they went, working on the press release, lobbing laudatory adjectives into the air then swatting them away: none was good enough. Kit listened—Booth and the Doctor sounded far away, they sounded insane, she felt insane—finally interrupting them with the words "he was with a girl," words so incongruous they didn't hear them and didn't stop, just stayed on task, hunched over the PR man's laptop, crafting the perfect tribute.

"He was with a girl," Kit said again, hollering from the living room, where she had flung herself down on the futon she'd had since junior year. Her transitional object, she called it. "He, Cal, your son, boy genius. Was with a girl. The Jahrons' au pair. She's missing, too." Her voice kept getting louder and louder, till she was shouting and shaking with rage.

"Katherine!" the Doctor thundered, as if shutting her up would make it untrue.

The PR man stopped typing, his hands stilled on the keyboard. "If that's correct, we have to reposition," he said in a strangely singsongy voice, like this was just a little wrinkle that could be straightened out with some clever word massage.

"It is correct," Kit said, deflated. She'd had her little

revenge, watching the mask slip as the Doctor lost his cool, and it was short-lived and unsatisfying.

"How old would the girl have been?" Booth asked.

"Maybe sixteen," Kit said. She didn't have the energy to go into the whole orphan passport business.

"Oh, Lord, thank the Lord!" the flack said, breaking into a broad smile that revealed a set of Invisi-braces fencing his upper teeth.

Kit was livid. "We are thanking the Lord that my husband was with a sixteen-year-old girl? Jesus."

"Age of consent, age of consent, age of consent," the PR man chanted. "The age of consent here is sixteen. Thank goodness."

"Really?" Kit sneered. "What a relief!" and pitched herself off the futon, grabbing her keys and purse in a single motion as she headed to the garage and into her car and through the gauntlet of reporters who would have to step aside if they didn't want to get hurt. If it looked like she was on a mission, she wasn't. She just needed to get out of the house and away from those men, and away from Cal, as if that were possible, and so she drove fast, her arms perfectly rigid in front of her, until the tears made it hard to see and she pulled over and beat the steering wheel with her fists, over and over, bellowing and crying and crying until her chest was heaving and she couldn't catch a breath.

She collapsed there, head in her hands, hearing her body fight the air for air as if it were someone else's body, wishing it was someone else's body, until, spent, the words "let us advance on Chaos and the Dark" floated into her mind. Kit couldn't remember where they came from or who had said them, and this infuriated her even more, like it was one more thing Cal had taken away from her: not only her marriage, not only their life together, not only her memory—because as far as she could remember, they had made a promise to be faithful to each other—but her mind, too. She couldn't think. Her brain was dark. It was chaotic. But eventually, as her breathing slowed to a steady pant, she remembered that it was Emerson who said it, in the essay "Self-Reliance," a piece of writing she thought was obvious and redundant when she'd read it as a knowing, untested seventeen-year-old. Yet here it was again, decades later, its central message retained and undeniable, and as Kit turned the key in the ignition and brought the car back to life, she realized that her memory was sending her mind a scrap of advice: Get going. She wasn't sure that driving to the marina would advance anything, but it was a start.

**The rumors** began as soon as the Jahrons called the church. Questions about the girl and what the two of them were doing on Cal's boat that evening, and gossip about seeing the married doctor out on the town with Beata for months and how the wife didn't do anything to stop it. "But she was unattractive!" Kit wanted to yell. "Ugly."

"I've heard of men sleeping with the nanny, but I've never heard of men sleeping with someone else's nanny," Sally Jahron said before the girl's body surfaced, a gaseous balloon of decomposition. So yes, Kit told Dr. Bondi, it got worse.

◆ ◆ ◆

The heavy bear who goes with me, /
A manifold honey to smear his face . . .
—DELMORE SCHWARTZ

Rusty stood at the top of the stairs, quietly calling her name. He'd left a light on downstairs, and he was standing in its faint glow, but the path ahead to Kit's room was completely dark. He needed to wake her, needed to talk to her, so he called her name until he heard her stir, and felt his way down the hall, closer to the closed door, and said, "Kit, it's Rusty," and the bed creaked and she said, sleepily, "It's after midnight," and then, with more presence of mind, "Why are you still here?"

"Can I come in?" he asked, and she said, "I guess so," and he said, "Don't turn on the light," and she said, "I wasn't going to."

Rusty could just make out Kit's form under the covers, saw there was room, and sat down next to her. Kit could hear him breathing, in and out, in and out, and it was so regular she found herself drifting back to sleep. To the extent that she was conscious, she was surprised she didn't mind him sitting there. It was a fleeting recognition, a whiff of a thought, and then it was gone.

"I'm so, so sorry," he said at last.

Kit woke with a start.

"Oh," he said. "I didn't realize you had gone back to sleep."

"It's okay." Her eyes were still closed, but even so, she covered them with her hands.

"I'm so sorry," Rusty said again.

"Welcome to the club," she said, and let out a long, rancorous breath.

He was quiet then, his shoulders hunched, his hands resting on his thighs.

"I used to be a good person," Rusty said after a while.

"From what I've seen of you, you are a good person now," Kit said, confused. She wasn't sure why they were talking about him. "You were great with the Patels the other night. With Mrs. Patel. I saw you. You were great with Carl in the hospital. Gentle. Patient. Don't sell yourself short."

"Selling things short—that's what I did," Rusty said. "Betting on failure. That was me. You do it enough, you don't even notice that your success is built on someone else's misery. You go to work and you want to do better than the guy sitting next to you, you want to be recognized, so you do what's necessary, whatever it is, and it's not just appreciated, it's rewarded. You start worshipping the wrong things, only you believe they are the right things. You're convinced of it. And you start believing what people say about you. It's an easy slide. Suddenly you've got more money than you can count. Numbers don't go high enough. And you think you don't need anyone, because you can have anything. At least that's the way it was for me."

"Why are you telling me this?" Kit said, eyes wide open, suddenly alert to the possibility that he was, somehow, trying to defend Cal.

"I'm not sure," he said. "It's just something I want you to know."

They sat in silence, their eyes gradually adjusting to the dark, so that she could see his head was leaning into his palms, and he could see her staring him down—at least that's what it felt like.

"I'm talking about me, not him," Rusty said. "To be clear."

"That's good," she said.

A garbage truck was making its way down Coolidge Street, the sigh of its brakes and the scrape of trash barrels getting closer and closer, and they both listened as if they were listening to something that mattered, and Rusty said, "They're up early," and Kit said, "Or late," and he said, "Or late," and they continued listening as the sounds faded and disappeared.

"Would it be okay if I lay down?" Rusty said, and instead of answering, Kit moved over and he stretched out, and for the second night in a row they were in her bed together, and this time he reached over and snaked his arm under her head and grabbed on to her shoulder and she let him.

"I didn't used to be like this," Kit said.

"Like what?"

"Tense. Scared. Whatever the opposite of 'tactile' is."

"For the record," Rusty said, "I didn't used to be like this, either. I was not the sort of guy who lay in bed with a beautiful woman with my clothes on, just talking."

"I'm not beautiful," Kit said.

"Who said I was talking about you?" Rusty said, and gave her shoulder a squeeze. "Talking is scarier."

"Talking is scarier than what?" Kit said.

"Sex," he said. "Way scarier. But why?"

"Intimacy," she said.

"That's not what I meant," he said. "Why are you scared?"

"You read all about it," she said.

"But what happened to you? I'm not being stupid. I'm trying to understand."

"I guess what happened to me is that I became some-one's wife. That's what the shrink said. He said that in some fundamental way, I ceased to be real."

"Was he blaming you?" Rusty asked.

"I don't think so," she said. "But it's a little like that children's book, *The Velveteen Rabbit*, but in reverse: if you're not loved for who you are, you cease to be real. Definitely for the other person, and maybe for yourself, too."

"Okay," Rusty said. "I guess that makes sense."

They were quiet again, listening to the chatter of shutters, opening and closing in the wind; listening to the wind.

"Can I ask you another question?" Rusty said after a while. "Why Riverton?"

Kit inhaled slowly, registered the smell of creosote on Rusty's hair, and breathed out audibly. "Mainly because no one would know me or know anything about me. You know, hiding in plain sight. And I couldn't stay where I was. It was too awful. Humiliating. Trust me, you don't want to be the wife of the doctor who ran off with the dead nanny. You can't go anywhere. You can't work, especially not the kind of work I do. People are always pointing, saying things, and even if they aren't, you think they are, especially because of the trial." She rolled over on her side, facing the wall, so her back was to him.

"What trial?" Kit felt his breath on her neck. Each word a warm puff, like smoke signals, but close.

"Cal's. Cal's show trial. Which is what happens when your father sits on the board of the same country club as the prosecutor, the DA, the judge, and the defense attorney," she said, talking into her pillow. "You get charged with negligent homicide, not murder, and you get weekend house arrest for six months and a couple of years' probation and life goes on. His life. Beata is dead and for all intents and purposes so am I."

"I don't think—" he began.

"You don't know," she said sharply. And then, more gently, "So much irrelevant crap came out at the trial, like the fact that we couldn't have kids, as if that gave him license to screw around with a teenager. And how I never went to church with him. Stuff about sex. Stuff about my work schedule. Anything to make him look like the victim . . ." Kit's voice trailed off. She was wide-awake again, heart racing. Other people knew these things about her because other people were there in the courtroom or read about them in the papers, but aside from her conversations with Dr. Bondi, she had never named her humiliations out loud.

Kit turned onto her back and she and Rusty lay side by side, shoulders barely touching. A mouse skittered overhead, and then another, chasing after it.

"It could be worse," Kit said, when neither had spoken for quite a while. "They could be flying squirrels."

"The therapist I used to see would be so proud," she added. "He was all about looking on the bright side. Though the mice are probably up there gnawing on the electrical wires."

"Well, looking on the bright side," Rusty said, "that means they will electrocute themselves soon and die. Very convenient."

"Until they start to smell."

"Wait a minute," Rusty said. "I thought we were looking on the bright side."

"Not my strong suit," Kit said.

They lay there peaceably then, street sounds intermittently lapping up against the sides of the house like a gentle inland surf, and talked in spurts about nothing in particular, just random associations—his lost sister, their fathers, the Four and what would happen to them now that Carl was gone, lines from poems that carried her through, Sunny, onion rings, his mother, her mother.

"This is like a slumber party," Rusty said, not bothering to suppress a loud yawn. "Or what I imagine a slumber party is like."

Kit laughed. "The only way this resembles a slumber party is that we are not slumbering," she said.

"So tell me, what goes on at slumber parties?" Rusty asked in a conspiratorial whisper.

"Oh, you know, gossiping about crushes and who likes who and dancing to 'Girls Just Want to Have Fun' and—"

"Before my time," he interrupted.

"Thank you for that," she said. "And doing a crafts project like making fortune tellers."

"Fortune tellers?"

"Yeah. You fold the paper in quarters and then in quarters again, and you write answers on four of the squares, which no one can see, and numbers on the other squares, and you ask someone to ask a question, like 'Will Rusty ask Melissa to the sixth grade dance?'

and tell them to pick a number, then whatever is under the flap for that number is their fortune."

"So who is Melissa?"

"You'll have to ask the fortune teller," she said. Though the room was dark, he could hear her grinning.

"Touché. But did he ask her to the dance?"

"Ditto."

"I'm sensing a pattern here," Rusty said. "So what else happens?"

"We definitely watch a movie. Anything with Rob Lowe." She laughed again. "And then, when we are in our sleeping bags and the lights are out, we tell ghost stories. Very scary ghost stories."

Listening to her, Rusty detected a lightness in Kit's voice he hadn't heard before, as if it were shed of all burdens or ignorant of them: it was what he imagined to be Kit's "before" voice.

"Pull up the covers," he commanded her playfully. "Up over your head. Now."

"What?"

"No questions, just do as I say."

"Rusty—"

"That's a question. Just do it, or if you'd like, I can do it for you."

"Rusty—"

"Nope."

"Rusty, if you want me to pull up the covers, you need to get off the bed. You're pinning them down."

"Oh," he said, embarrassed, and stood up for a second while Kit slid down till she was no longer visible. "Okay," he said. "Are your eyes open or shut?"

"What does it matter? I can't see a thing," she said, her words muffled by the batting.

"Good point. Just checking," he said. "Now, tell me a ghost story."

There was silence, then a prolonged sigh, like air escaping a tire.

"I already told you a ghost story," she said at last. "The one where the wife was invisible to the husband and the truth of the marriage was invisible to her."

"Not what I had in mind," he said, trying to make light of it.

"Sorry," she said. "It's the only story I know."

Her tone had gotten heavy again. It was impendent, like weather. She heard it herself and knew he did, too. What else did she know? That people want sunshine 24/7. Why should Rusty be any different?

"All right," he said, filling his lungs as if he were about to free dive into deep, inky water, "then tell me that story again. But this time tell me the whole story."

He asked for it, so she obliged. He was almost gone anyway.

She told him about driving to the marina that morning and boarding the boat before the police had gotten there, and seeing the quilted overnight bag she'd given Beata as a going-away present the summer before stuffed in the hold, and Cal's dopp kit tethered with a carabineer to a hook in the head just like it always was when he spent the night on the boat, and opening it up and seeing the condoms—"His father would be proud," she said ruefully, though of course he was married to a woman who was in no danger of getting pregnant—and then searching for and not finding that amber vial she'd handed over to him years before that she knew he'd never bothered to remove—maybe he forgot it was there, maybe it was a talisman, but now it was gone.

So the girl had been pregnant. That's what this was all about. It wasn't like Kit could go to the police and explain that the crucial piece of evidence was something that wasn't among her husband's razor blades and dental floss. What did Cal used to say about his research? You can't prove a negative? She had proved it only to herself. She told Rusty about walking back to her car in a stupor. The girl had been pregnant. The girl was carrying Cal's child, just as she had once. She told him how she sat there in her car long enough to see the police finally show up and wrap yellow caution tape around the boat, and long enough to realize they had it all wrong. The orphan girl was dead and the brilliant, righteous doctor was probably alive. Maybe you can prove a negative, she said to herself, because if Cal had picked up Beata at the Jahrons' and driven to the marina, his car would have to be there, but it wasn't.

Kit told Rusty how she got out of her car and walked up to the policemen stringing the caution tape and explained that this was her husband's boat and she needed to see something, and how they said it was now off-limits to everyone, and they argued, and how she finally got them to open the hatch at the stern and tell her what they saw, and how one of them said, "Nothing," and the other gave a patronizing shrug. What they didn't know, and what she didn't tell them yet, was that this was where Cal stored the inflatable dinghy he carried in case of emergencies. And dropping your pregnant girlfriend into the lake, maybe because she balked at swallowing those pills, maybe because those pills were not working, maybe because she had threatened to expose you, or maybe—to give him the benefit of the doubt—because she accidentally slipped and fell, definitely qualified as emergencies. Kit mentioned none of this to the police.

She told Rusty that somehow she had the wherewithal to drive home and make the call to the investigators so the Doctor and the PR man could hear her speak the words: "You will find Dr. Sweeney at the Palmer

House in Chicago at the American Neurological Society annual meeting." She said this with authority, though she didn't know for sure, but there had to be some benefit from all those years of marriage, like knowing the other person's habits of mind. And that's where they found him, nodding off in the second-to-last row of the Wabash conference room while a woman from Duke gave a paper during one of the evening sessions about gamma knife surgery techniques. The dinghy was in the trunk of Cal's car. Still, he claimed innocence, even when the evidence was right there incriminating him. People who don't think the rules apply to them, Kit was beginning to learn, are surprised and offended when others don't recognize and honor their exemption.

And she told Rusty how, when the girl's body was finally retrieved, it had deteriorated so much that an autopsy would have proven nothing, and how the au pair agency didn't want to pursue it anyway because it was bad for business.

"So," Kit said, emerging at long last into the bedroom's fresh air from the tent she had made from the blanket and her knees, "enough gory details?"

"I guess," Rusty said. "But he never went to jail?"

"Not after that first night. He made bail and wanted to come home, but I told the Doctor that if he did, if he ever came anywhere near me, I'd tell the police what I knew. This was before they found the body, so there was a real chance there would be solid evidence."

"So you never saw Cal again?"

"No, I did. I saw him in court during the trial. He tried to pass me notes. I made sure he saw me tear them up and throw them away. What was there to say? That he was sorry? And remember, his lawyers were doing their best to throw me under the bus.

"They trotted out Cal's pastor, who gave this long, meandering sermon about original sin that seemed to implicate me and the girl and exonerate Cal as a stand-in for all men. They called on the hospital president, who told this story about Cal taking care of a six-year-old with cancer that had everyone in the courtroom in tears, me included.

"Cal testified last. Instead of dressing him in a suit, they had him wear his scrubs, as if he'd just come from saving lives. It was a brilliant tactical move. Yes, a girl was dead, but think of all the people who weren't.

"'Did I stray?' Cal asked rhetorically. You could tell—well, I could tell—that he'd rehearsed his lines. 'I admit it,' he said. 'I did. I love my wife, but we have grown apart. I had my career, she had her job—'"

"Wait," Rusty interrupted. "He said that?"

"Oh yes," Kit said. "And no one seemed to think anything of it, except for me. It was like hearing for the first time what he really thought of me and what I'd chosen to do with my life. I realize no one thinks being a librarian is as awesome as being a neurosurgeon, but I always thought I was doing something valuable, putting books in the hands of readers. Books can save lives, too. I really believe that." And then, more to herself than to Rusty: "Like mine.

"Anyway, it made me feel really sad. And embarrassed. He might as well have called me 'little lady.' And then he mentioned our childlessness—didn't say why, just that we didn't have children—which sounded like it was both my fault and the great disappointment of his life, which segued into his paternal relationship with Beata, which is when I got up and walked out. So I wasn't there for the part where he said that he only wanted to do right by the girl—nothing about doing right by me—and give her the love she'd never had, and I wasn't there when he said the boat trip was when Beata thought he was going to tell her that he was leaving me so they could be together. As if a thirty-eight-year-old physician with standing in the community was publicly going to take up with a sixteen-year-old. Instead, he told her he had prayed on it, and while he wanted her to have the love she deserved, it couldn't be with him. What was she supposed to do when it was God himself who was saying no? Have a fit, apparently. Cal testified that she started hitting him and wailing, that she was out of control, so he went into the cockpit to get a sedative and when he came back she was gone. Just gone. He called her name, called her name, called her name. He shut off autopilot and reversed course. He pulled out the safety torch and scanned the water. Nothing. Beata had disappeared without a trace. She wasn't a very strong swimmer, Cal told the court, and she wasn't wearing a life vest. He got out the rescue dinghy, anchored the boat, and paddled around, looking for her. He figured that by that time she would have been unconscious, but he kept looking. He was frantic, he said, and exhausted, and found himself being carried farther and farther from the sailboat and from Beata, wherever she was. 'I was in shock,' he told the court, and showed them a poster of the brain that was meant to illustrate how, when the body is in shock, the mind reverts to well-worn patterns. This was his explanation for why he didn't call the police or the Jahrons or even me when he got back to shore, but why, instead, he got into his car and drove to the place he was supposed to be. He called it the 'autonomic stress response' and said it was well documented in the literature."

Kit tossed off the covers, jumped out of bed, and catapulted from the room.

"I'm so dry," she called over her shoulder, and rushed

into the bathroom and stuck her head under the tap. She drank sloppily, letting the water run across her cheek and down her chin and neck. It was bracing, a cold slap. "What am I doing?" she wondered, and made it a point not to look in the mirror.

"Nice PJs," Rusty said when she shuffled back into the bedroom.

Kit glanced down. She'd forgotten what she was wearing—gym shorts and a T-shirt that said CREATIVE PESTS.

**Later, as** the day was quickening and they were still lying on her bed, awake, listening to each other breathe, he said, "People can be so selfish. I certainly have been."

"We've all been," Kit said.

"I think you get a pass on this one," he said.

"That's the thing," she said. "I shouldn't. I could have testified against Cal, but I didn't. I didn't want to expose myself that way. So I took spousal immunity since we were still technically married."

"But that's not selfish—it's completely understandable," Rusty said. He started to reach for her hand, then pulled back.

"That girl had no one," Kit said. "No one. The Jahrons weren't about to do anything that would jeopardize

Jens's career—he worked for the hospital that Cal's father owned. The prosecutor wanted the whole thing to go away; he was a family friend, and there was no evidence of a motive. There was no one to speak on behalf of the girl except me, and I didn't do it because I just didn't want to, and why should I? She had ruined my life enough as it was."

"And you feel guilty for that?" Rusty said, incredulous.

"I guess I do," she said. "But then I tell myself that it wasn't as if justice was going to be served no matter what I did. Justice didn't stand a chance. And I hate that. I hate that I stopped believing in things I didn't even know were matters of belief, like justice and fairness. Or honesty. Or the promises people make to each other. Of all the things Cal took from me, that's what I think I miss the most: the apparently naive belief that you keep your promises. You know what the prosecutor told me? The prosecutor, who was supposed to be on my side? He said, 'Everyone cheats,' as if that was supposed to make it all right."

They fell forward into silence, as Kit entered that courtroom yet again, so much bigger in her imagination, and the slimy, insinuating voices of Cal's lawyers, of his father, of the prosecutor, of people she didn't know she knew, saying Mrs. Sweeney this and Mrs. Sweeney that, twisting a simple thing like working late on Thursdays into a gyre slipped tight around her neck, then parading the intimacies of her body for all to see as if she were an exhibitionist, as if she'd asked for it.

"Somehow, I was the one who ended up on trial," she said.

"Um," Rusty said, and stopped. "I'm not sure this is even an okay question." He stopped again. "This is hard. I really don't want to say the wrong thing." He looked at her for affirmation, but she had put her hands over her eyes as if they could stop her from seeing that courtroom, those lawyers, her husband, that girl.

"What?" she said. They had come this far, what more was there?

"Did you love him? I mean until all this happened?" Rusty said.

Kit exhaled loudly. "Oh God, if you only knew how many times I asked myself that. I thought I did, if love is caring deeply about someone else. I cared about Cal. I wanted the best for him. I had known him so long. I arranged my life to fit his life, so he could get what he wanted. Is that love? I thought it was. I didn't see—or I chose not to see—that for the most part, for him, I was just the box on the form where they ask if you're married. Wife, check. I should have trusted my instincts

back in college. But who does? You're twenty years old."
She shook her head. "Ugh," she said.

"Is Cal—do you think Cal—"

"Is a murderer?" she finished the sentence for him.
"Yeah."

"Like I said, I feel like he took my life and shredded
it. But do I think he's some kind of sociopath? No, not
really. Something bad happened on that boat and only
Cal knows what it was, and he has to live with it. And I
have to live with the fact that the man I married was not
the person I thought he was. No, that's not true. Success changed him. His talent changed him. The more
important he became, the more self-important he became. They are not the same thing, though they probably both come from believing you are the one person
in the world who can bring some deathly ill person back
from the brink. And you do bring them back, again and
again, the ones with the tumors that no one else will
touch, the ones who have run through every course of
chemotherapy, so who cares if you are rude to the server
at the restaurant? Who cares if you can't be bothered to
buy your wife a birthday present? Who cares if you run
a red light? Who cares if you hold hands in church with
the girl you have gotten pregnant? What's the big deal?
The big deal is you.

"I'll stop now," Kit said, sighing. And then, after a

long pause: "'People change, and smile: but the agony abides.' It's a line from a poem. T. S. Eliot. 'The Dry Salvages,'" she explained when Rusty didn't react.

"Hmm," he said.

"Hmm what?" she asked, feeling suddenly exposed and a little embarrassed, spouting lines of poetry in bed with this man, telling him her secrets.

"Isn't that what we are?" Rusty said.

"Are you making fun of me?"

"Why would I do that?" he said, surprised.

"Okay," Kit said. "Sorry. Isn't what what we are?"

"Salvages." He sounded very proud of himself, as if the teacher had asked a question and he was the only one in the class who knew the answer. "We're salvages. Well, you are. I'm working on it."

"Eliot pronounced 'salvage' as if it rhymed with 'assuage,'" she said. She couldn't help herself. It was something she knew.

"Well, Rusty pronounces it to rhyme with 'savage,'" he told her. "'Salvage.' Look it up, Miss Poetry Mouth. It's a good thing. Now I am making fun of you," he added.

"Miss Poetry Mouth. You've got a way with words," she said.

"Just so you understand you're not the only one," Rusty said, pulling her close.

"My therapist in Michigan told me he couldn't promise things would get better, only that they would get less bad," she said, holding on to the last shred of wakefulness as she felt it slipping away.

"And?" Rusty said. But she was asleep.

◆  ◆  ◆

In which the heavy and the weary weight /
Of all this unintelligible world, / Is lighten'd . . .
—WILLIAM WORDSWORTH

The call came at seven sharp, waking both Kit and Rusty. Kit fumbled around until she found the phone and greeted the caller with a less than enthusiatic hello.

"Kit, it's Patrick. I know it's early, but we're reading Carl's will Monday, and I think you're going to want to be there. Rusty, too, if he's around," and before she could say more than "okay," he had disconnected.

"What is it with old guys and phones?" she said, staring at the one in her hand.

**After opening** up the library, Kit headed back over to Mill Street.

"I'm probably not dressed for the occasion," Rusty said when she met up with him, "but I think Carl would forgive me." He was wearing the clothes Kit had bought for him, the polo shirt and shorts, and looked like he was going out to play a round of golf.

The lawyer's office was up a back flight of stairs, one floor above the mortuary.

"Very convenient," Rusty said as they went by. "One-stop dying."

**"You're looking** very dandy," Kit said to Patrick, who was wearing a three-piece suit, even though the day would soon grow hot.

"And you look exhausted," Patrick said. "Are you getting enough sleep? Oh, I forgot," he said, nodding in Rusty's direction. "The fire."

There were five chairs arrayed in front of the lawyer's desk, and now that they were all assembled—Kit, Rusty, Rich, Rich, and Patrick—Patrick took one of them and turned it around so it was facing the rest.

"You're probably all wondering why I called you here this morning," Patrick began.

"No," Rich the driver said. "We're wondering why you called us so goddamned early on the day of rest."

"I was up," Patrick said simply. "Anyway, as I was saying, I called you here because, as some of you know, I am the executor of Carl's will, and today is the day it is going to be executed." He cleared his throat and pulled on a string hanging off his jacket cuff until it broke, and then took an official-looking document from the lawyer's outstretched hand.

"'I, Carl Layton, being of sound mind and body—'" he began in a formal, stentorian voice.

"That's a joke!" one of the Riches said.

"No comments from the peanut gallery," Paddy growled. He began again: "'I, Carl Layton, being of sound mind and body, do hereby swear, on this tenth day of July, 2009—'"

"A year ago," Kit mumbled. Patrick glared at her but continued on without comment.

"'As you may know, I am a parsimonious man,'" he read. "'And if any of you don't know what that means, it means I was a cheapskate.'"

"You can say that again," Rich (driver) said. "He was always 'forgetting' his wallet when we went to lunch."

As Patrick read on, Kit had to keep pinching herself to stay awake. Rusty, she noticed, was pushing a pen cap into his cheek—same thing. Carl's will directed the estate to donate some money to the Humane Society, some to the United Way, and a large gift—$10,000—to the hospital, "so there might be many more delicious meals there." At the mention of the hospital and food, both Riches and even Patrick started to tell funny Carl-at-lunch stories, and after a while, Kit nudged Rusty, and they got up to leave.

"Thanks, Patrick, for including me," Kit said. She was weary. It was time to get back to work.

"Yeah, thanks," Rusty said. "I'm really glad to know the lunches will continue."

"Where do you two think you're going?" Patrick growled. "We're not done. You don't leave in the middle of a will being read."

Schooled, Kit and Rusty sat down, and Patrick gave a few theatrical coughs and then continued. There were more donations: to the food pantry, and to the high school marching band, and to the Boy Scouts, the Cub Scouts, the Girl Scouts, and the Brownies. Kit was impressed by Carl's generosity and bored with the whole thing. Work—her office, her office door—was so close—so close—but there was no getting to it.

"Okay, listen up," Patrick said after getting through the part about the Scouts. "You are going to want to pay attention. Can everyone hear me?" They all nodded like obedient children. "Okay, here goes:

"'All other assets of mine, including physical property, are to be put into a trust for the purposes of supporting the Riverton Public Library, where I spent many wonderful hours, to be overseen and administered by my four dear friends Richard Everett, Dr. Patrick Randall, Elliot "Rich" Hazelton, and Katherine

Jarvis, also known hereafter as the New Four, or by a trustee appointed by them.'"

"Wow," Kit said as she wiped an unexpected tear from her eye. She was the one who started calling them the Four. Now she was one of them—"my dear friend," he had called her—and it moved her more than she could say.

"I'm very happy to be able to bring down the average age of the Four," she teased, trying to deflect her emotion, "but which one of you is Elliot?" she said, looking from Rich to Rich. "And why?"

"It started out as joke, when we were kids," Rich the executive said. "We were cousins, just a few months apart, and everyone used to say it was like we were twins."

"People would say, 'Which one are you?' and we'd always say Rich, just to trick them, even though when I look at the pictures, we don't really look that much alike," Rich the driver (Elliot) said.

"So maybe the joke was on us," his cousin said. "Anyway, it stuck. And Rich is a better name for a taxi driver than Elliot."

**So what** do you think?" Patrick asked Kit as they all milled about, eating the doughnuts he had brought in honor of Carl.

"I think it's great," she said. "It means that you guys will start coming back to the library, and it means we'll be able to afford coffee in the break room again."

"You'll be able to afford a lot more than that," Patrick said, smiling widely. "As of last Friday, Carl's account at Schwab was worth six million dollars. To be precise"—he consulted a computer printout—"$6,458,593.19. Carl was a damned good barber, but it turns out that he was an even better investor."

"What?" Kit asked, stunned. "What? How did that happen?"

"I don't completely know," Patrick said, "but here's where I think Rusty comes in. Carl's great-uncle used to work for one of the original mill owners as his personal secretary and bookkeeper, and apparently he was rewarded handsomely in the man's will."

"What does that have to do with me?" Rusty said.

"Maybe nothing," Patrick said. "But if your grandfather is who we think he is, then your great-grandfather was one of the original mill owners, so it could have been him."

"Seems kind of weak to me," Rusty said, but no one was listening.

"Carl's uncle didn't have any kids," Patrick went on, "so I'm guessing that when he died, Carl inherited his money and then did very well in the market. What do you think he was doing in the library every morning? He was reading the *Journal* and the *Financial Times* like they were the *Daily Racing Form*. He knew about Microsoft and Apple and Intel before anyone else did. He bought gold before the crash. Of course, it's an endowment—it's not like you're leaving here with your pockets full of cash. You're leaving here with all of us being responsible for stewarding that money or finding someone who can."

◆ ◆ ◆

### Sunny | the plan

As soon as we picked up Willow from the mall, we had a family meeting, on the side of the road, in the car. Steve asked me to tell Willow what I'd told him, and as I did, her face got paler and paler, and when I was finished she said "What are we going to do?" at least three times.

"Sunny doesn't want to go into hiding," Steve announced.

"Oh, honey," Willow began, but Steve cut her off and said, "And I think she's right. This is my crusade, not hers. I'm not even sure it's yours," he said to Willow, who tried to protest, but when Steve gets going it's hard to talk over him.

"What can we do?" Willow asked, and that's when Steve came up with the plan, one part of which entailed Kit letting me stay with her while they went on a meditation retreat. That was the second part.

"That's crazy," I told them. "Going on a meditation retreat sounds exactly like going into hiding. You don't get it. You need to do something now. This is a"—and then I swore—"emergency!" And for once I think my parents were listening to me. (Maybe I should swear more often.) "You need to find a lawyer. You need to turn yourself in before the police arrest you. Do you want to spend the rest of your lives in jail?" I was pretty worked up.

"What I'd like," Steve said, as if I were that lawyer, "is a deal to keep Willow out of jail because she was only the driver. She didn't do anything."

"And what I want," Willow said, as tears poured down her cheeks, "is for Steve to get sent to one of those prisons that aren't so bad."

"Do they have those?" I asked, and told them about the Riverton jail, which broke the spell, and I was back to being me again, not some lawyer who could cut them a deal.

"You're right, Sunny," Steve said, which may have been a first for Steve. "We need to find a lawyer. It's time for me to stand up for what I believe and stop being anonymous." He also said that maybe it was time to get a new car.

So we went home to pack—not the whole house, because Steve was hopeful that Willow and I would be back there before too long.

"No camping gear," I said.

"No camping gear," they agreed.

For this plan to work, we'd need Kit to agree to it, which wasn't a sure thing, so on Monday morning we drove over to the library, and Willow came in with me to ask her. Evelyn said Kit wasn't there, that she was at a meeting with a lawyer, which freaked Willow out—was she turning in Steve herself?—before Evelyn explained that it had to do with Carl's will. Evelyn also told Willow that the earrings she was wearing, which Willow made, of course, were more beautiful than anything she'd ever owned, and without missing a beat, Willow slid them out from her ears and put them in Evelyn's hands and said, "That is no longer true." I think it's possible that when you think that the future might bring great sadness, you become more generous than you ever had been before, so you can carry other people's happiness with you.

Evelyn said Kit would be back soon, so I showed Willow all the nooks and crannies of the library, and introduced her to some of the little kids I'd gotten to know from story hour. When Kit and Rusty finally showed up, they looked even worse than when I'd seen them on Saturday, but they were giddy like they had just pulled off a hilarious prank, and they called everyone in the entire library over to the circulation desk. Rusty took a couple of bottles of ginger ale out of a Dollar Tree bag and opened them, one by one, as if they were champagne, and Kit dumped out bags of Dollar Tree cookies, and that's when she told us about Carl's gift, and everyone clapped and whooped and stomped their feet.

When the party finally broke up, Willow went with Kit into her office, and I helped Chuck clean up, and he said, "I hear it's your last week," which made me wonder where he'd heard that from—were they planning a party? Would they miss me? But then I remembered it was in big letters on the calendar in the staff room because I had written it there. Just one week more and then the court would throw away my record and at least one member of our family would no longer be a criminal.

Willow was in Kit's office forever, and when she came out she was smiling and crying at the same time, and Kit was telling her it would be all right, and Willow was telling Kit that it was only for a few days, and then she said the same thing to me and pulled me into a big,

Willowy hug that lasted way too long, but I was glad because I was crying, too, and by the time she let go I'd stopped. I walked her back to the car and we told Steve the news, and he got teary himself and made me promise that wherever he ended up, that I'd come visit him and write to him and all that.

"I used to think—" he said, and then stopped because there was a catch in his voice. He tried again. "For a long time, Sunny, I thought that loving the whole world—do you know what I mean?—doing the right thing, or what I believe is the right thing, to make the world a better place, was the highest form of love there was, no matter the consequences. I should have stopped thinking that the moment I saw your beautiful mother push you out into the world. But I didn't. I'm not apologizing for what I did," he said. "I believe it's our obligation to protect creation, especially those creatures that can't defend themselves, but I am apologizing for how I did it, and I hope you know that I am sorry."

"As long as you're apologizing," I said, "could you apologize for not letting me go to the doctor when I broke my foot that time when we were living at #3?"

Steve looked stricken.

"Dad," I said, which got his attention. I never call him Dad. "Dad," I said again, "I'm joking."

◆    ◆    ◆

And tell me truly, men of earth, / If all the soul-and-body scars / Were not too much to pay for birth.

—ROBERT FROST

After the celebration, and after Willow had left and Sunny came up the library steps bouncing a beat-up roller bag behind her, Kit sat down in the director's office to catch her breath. Rusty came to the door and she filled him in about Sunny, and asked if he'd like to stay for dinner with them, but if he did, would he go to the store and pick up some groceries.

"I will do you one better," he said. "I will even pick up more chairs."

**There were** four matching ladder-back chairs around the kitchen table when Kit and Sunny got home, and a pot of pasta boiling on the stove.

"Can we have candles?" Sunny asked, and when Kit told her she didn't have any, Sunny went into the living room, opened her suitcase, and pulled out two beeswax tapers and a pair of hammered silver candlesticks.

"Willow made these," Sunny said proudly, and Kit realized that she had brought them to remind her of home.

When dinner was on the table, and the candles were lit, and the three of them were sitting on the new chairs, Sunny put her hands out, palms up, and it took her a second, but then Kit understood what she was doing and put one hand in Sunny's and the other in Rusty's, and then without words, Rusty reached over and took Sunny's other hand just like they had done at Carl's funeral.

"This is what we do at my house," she said. "We hold hands and say what we are grateful for. I'll go first.

"I am grateful for this food and for everyone who helped to get it to me—we always say that," she explained. "And I'm grateful that I didn't have enough money to buy the dictionary, because if I did, I wouldn't have gotten to work at the library."

"Turns out it wasn't called the Robbers Library for nothing," Rusty said, and winked at her.

"Very funny," Sunny said. "I'm being serious."

"Sorry," Rusty said, but he was still smiling.

"It's your turn," she said, turning to Kit, who was thinking about the notebooks in the other room, filled with all the things she was grateful she was not. It wasn't what Dr. Bondi intended when he gave her that assignment, but maybe it had been enough, an opening she could peer into and see that however bad it was for her, she was really, actually okay.

"I am grateful for friends," she said simply, "and especially, today, for Carl."

"It's your turn," Sunny said to Rusty.

"I know it's my turn," Rusty said, "unless there are some invisible people here with us tonight," and then looked at Kit, worried he'd said the wrong thing, but she seemed serene sitting there, her eyes iridescent in the candlelight.

"Let's see," he began. "I am grateful that I lost my job. I am grateful that all my stuff burned up."

"Wait, stop!" Sunny interrupted. "I forgot to tell you. Remember when you asked me to make copies of all that stuff. Your mother's bankbook. Her birth certificate. All those forms?"

Rusty nodded.

"I gave them to you, right?" Sunny said eagerly.

He nodded again.

"And they were in the fire, right?"

He nodded again.

"I forgot to tell you that when I made those copies I didn't realize the machine was set to two, so there were two copies of everything, and when I realized it, I put the second copies in the recycling, and you know how Chuck only puts out the recycling like once a month? I checked this morning when I went down there with Willow and they are still there!" Sunny caught her breath and looked at him expectantly.

"Let's leave them," Rusty said.

"Leave them?" Sunny said, disbelieving. "What? Why?"

"Because I don't want them right now. I'm done with that."

"Why?"

"Sunny, will you please let me finish saying what I'm thankful for before this beautiful pile of spaghetti gets cold?"

"Sorry," Sunny said sheepishly.

"Where was I . . . ?" Rusty teased her. "Oh yes. I am grateful that all my stuff burned up. I am grateful to Kit for many things, including my underwear." He hoped she would smile, and she did. "And I am grateful to my mother, because without that bankbook I never would have spent the summer in Riverton."

When they dropped hands, Sunny reached over and slid some spaghetti onto her plate. "Watch this," she said, and twirled it expertly up her fork.

"You could stay," Kit said.

# Acknowledgments

Like Kit, I am grateful for friends, Sara Rimer, Lisa Verhovek, Shawn Leary, Sam Verhovek, Barry King, Warren King, Missy Foote, Dick Foote, Andrew Gardner, Caroline Damon, Kathy Wilson, Sally Carver, and Jacob Epstein, this time especially. Thanks, too, to my old friend Andrew Rosenheim, for the introduction to the talented Sara Nelson, whose editorial guidance has been inestimable. And thanks to Sara's team at Harper-Collins, Amy Baker, Mary Sasso, James Iacobelli, and Daniel Vazquez. Kim Witherspoon, at Inkwell Management, is not only a phenomenal agent, she is a phenomenal reader, and I have been the lucky beneficiary of her insightful counsel yet again. Also at Inkwell, thank you to the tag team of Emma Schlee and Maria Whelan. In Hanover, Dr. Dominic Candida's graduate seminar was an essential introduction to cognitive behavioral therapy. In Middlebury, my colleagues and students (and former students) were a balm, as always. At the *New York Review of Books*, Robert Silvers (of blessed memory), was a constant source of encouragement and perspicacity. Above all, I have been sustained and inspired by my two McKibbens, Sophie and Bill, who do such good work in the world.

# About the Author

**Sue Halpern** is the author of seven books of fiction and nonfiction, most recently *A Dog Walks into a Nursing Home*. Her writing has appeared in *The New Yorker*, *New York Times Magazine*, *New York Review of Books*, *Rolling Stone*, and *Conde Nast Traveller*. She lives in Vermont with her husband, the writer and environmental activist Bill McKibben, and is a scholar-in-residence at Middlebury College.